Y0-BDI-614

Praise for Lenora Worth and her novels

"Worth's charming characters and descriptive details sparkle in this second installment of the Cajun series, which will have readers eager to read book three in hopes of discovering the identity of the mysterious owner."
—*RT Book Reviews* on *Sweetheart Bride*

"This heartwarming romance will draw readers in."
—*RT Book Reviews* on *A Certain Hope*

"Her best story yet, it is filled with spiritual depth and hidden meaning."
—*RT Book Reviews* on *Heart of Stone*

Praise for Renee Andrews and her novels

"There are a number of tender moments, and the characters, especially the Secret Santa, prove that it is more of a blessing to give than to receive. Andrews' book contains plenty of holiday spirit."
—*RT Book Reviews* on *Yuletide Twins*

"There are many emotional scenes that will have the reader quickly falling in love with the characters, particularly Cody.... [N]umerous situations...will tug at the reader's heartstrings."
—*RT Book Reviews* on *Second Chance Father*

"The characters in this sweet love story possess a depth that make this romance a standout."
—*RT Book Reviews* on *Bride Wanted*

With over seventy books published and millions in print, **Lenora Worth** writes award-winning romance and romantic suspense. Three of her books finaled in the ACFW Carol Awards, and her Love Inspired Suspense novel *Body of Evidence* became a *New York Times* bestseller. Her novella in *Mistletoe Kisses* made her a *USA TODAY* bestselling author. Lenora goes on adventures with her retired husband, Don, and enjoys reading, baking and shopping…especially shoe shopping.

Renee Andrews spends a lot of time in the gym. No, she isn't working out. Her husband, a former All-American gymnast, owns a gym and coaches gymnastics. Renee is a kidney donor and actively supports organ donation. When she isn't writing, she enjoys traveling with her husband and bragging about their sons, daughters-in-law and grandchildren. For more info on her books or on living donors, visit her website at www.reneeandrews.com.

Sweetheart Bride

Lenora Worth

&

Yuletide Twins

Renee Andrews

◈HARLEQUIN®LOVE INSPIRED®

LOVE INSPIRED BOOKS

Recycling programs for this product may not exist in your area.

ISBN-13: 978-1-335-44817-0

Sweetheart Bride and Yuletide Twins

Copyright © 2018 by Harlequin Books S.A.

The publisher acknowledges the copyright holders of the individual works as follows:

Sweetheart Bride
Copyright © 2013 by Lenora H. Nazworth

Yuletide Twins
Copyright © 2013 by Renee Andrews

www.Harlequin.com

Printed in U.S.A.

CONTENTS

SWEETHEART BRIDE

Lenora Worth

To Linda White. Thanks for reading my books!

And the God of all grace,
who called you to his eternal glory in Christ, after
you have suffered a little while, will himself restore
you and make you strong, firm and steadfast.
—*1 Peter* 5:10

Chapter One

The soft sound of wedding music flowed through the quiet church. A hush fell over the crowd of people gathered to celebrate the wedding of Alma Blanchard and Julien LeBlanc. Candlelight gave the tiny sanctuary a muted, dreamy glow. The groom beamed a bright, loving smile as his bride seemed to glide up the aisle, escorted by her misty-eyed father.

Alma's older sister Callie, the maid of honor, looked radiant in a light golden silk dress with a flowing skirt. She smiled at her sister, her expression full of love and hope.

The other bridesmaid, wearing a similar dress with a fitted skirt, tried hard not to squirm and fidget. Brenna Blanchard sent up a little prayer for courage and self-control.

Dear Lord, please don't let me bolt out of this church.

She couldn't, wouldn't do that to Alma. Alma and Julien were so in love. They'd been in love since high school, but circumstances and stubbornness had torn them apart for ten long years. It was their time to shine.

Brenna could hang on for a few minutes. As long as she didn't think about her own broken heart and the fact that technically, she should have been the one getting married, she'd be okay. Concentrating on the beautiful arrangement at the center of the aisle, she marveled at how her sister Callie could take sunflowers, mums and yellow roses and turn them into something exquisite. And what was the deal with all the Louisiana irises, anyway? Maybe Alma had a thing for irises?

Brenna forced herself into a serene pose as she smiled at her sister. Alma did look lovely in their mother's reworked wedding dress. Hadn't Callie worn that same dress on her wedding day? Wouldn't that sort of jinx the dress because she'd gotten a divorce?

No, this was their *maman*'s dress. Lacy and flowing and full-skirted, with a portrait collar. Beautiful.

Brenna's eyes misted over, the ache in her heart still an open wound. She wished their deceased mother, Lila, could see Alma now. She'd be so happy.

I'll be happy for you, Mama, Brenna thought now, her gaze scanning the crowded church. I won't be sad no matter how much I miss you, no matter how much I wish I could be the one walking up that aisle.

Brenna had a brief flash of pain, like a thorn from one of Callie's beautiful roses, as she thought of her ex-fiancé and wondered why she'd had love and lost it. Oh, wait, according to Jeffrey, her former fiancé, she wasn't good enough for him. He'd never said that out loud, but he'd shown it, loud and clear. Jeffrey *hadn't* said a lot of things, but she'd found out so much about him too late. Never again would she be interested in a man who held everything inside or kept things from her.

Never.

But in her heart she knew she really hadn't loved Jeffrey the way her mama and daddy had loved each other. She'd never loved him the way Alma loved Julien. She'd kind of stumbled upon Jeffrey and decided he'd make a perfect groom and a good husband.

Not. Maybe the brooding type wasn't her type, after all.

Brenna saw Alma's smile light up when her gaze settled on Julien, saw the way his grin went from happy to awestruck to humble with each step her beautiful sister took toward him.

I want that kind of love, she thought as she stood tall and held her head high. I want someone who will look at me the way Julien is looking at Alma right now.

Brenna glanced out into the crowd and locked eyes with a man sitting toward the back on the outside aisle, a man with dark hair and dark eyes, dressed in what else—a dark suit.

Who's the good-looking stranger? she wondered.

And why did he keep staring at her?

Who's the looker? Nicholas Santiago wondered, his gaze lingering on the second bridesmaid on the left. The bridesmaid who looked as if she'd rather be anywhere else but here.

She had hair the color of the tallow tree leaves falling outside, a rich golden-hued auburn that only burned brighter against the creamy gold of her dress. He couldn't see her eyes, but he'd guess they were a vivid green or maybe a vivid hazel. She shouted fire and heat, which probably meant she also liked a bit of drama.

Well, so did he.

But lately, he'd had too much drama. And coming to a sweet wedding simply because his new friend Callie Blanchard Moreau had invited him had seemed like a good idea when he rolled into town a few weeks ago. Now, Nick wasn't so sure. Too many bad memories.

"Please come, Nicholas," Callie had said. "Weddings are a good way to meet people. If you're going to be here for a while, you need to meet everyone. And we'll feed you. Alma insisted on cooking most of the food for her own wedding. You might even get a mention in Mr. Sonnier's 'Ain't that Good' column because he'll be here covering the wedding to help promote Alma's gumbo. You know, he's helping her to mass-produce it and sell it all over Louisiana. She hopes to expand in the next couple of years."

Callie was a talker, but the woman knew her flowers. And he'd need her help once he got the old Dubois estate, known around here as Fleur House, renovated for his picky client. They'd been good friends since he'd first come to Fleur a few months ago to check out the old antebellum mansion and purchase it for his secretive boss. Nicholas had remembered his mother's birthday, and Callie had helped him wire some flowers to her back in Texas. After they'd talked about the renovations at Fleur House and how he needed help decorating it, Callie had mentioned one of her sisters was an art expert. And that the sister would be at the wedding, of course.

So here he was, being courteous, being neighborly, by attending a quaint little wedding in a simple little church on a crisp fall Friday night.

And a good thing, too. He really wanted Callie to

introduce him to that fidgety, adorable redhead and he sure hoped she was the sister who knew her art.

Brenna checked her lipstick and turned to head back in to the reception. The church fellowship hall was beautiful. Callie had outdone herself with the fall theme. And irises everywhere. She must have forced those to bloom this time of year, or found some that rebloomed in the fall. Callie could do anything with flowers. She'd managed to make this big, plain white room turn into what looked like a fall garden.

Shaking her head, Brenna rounded a corner and ran smack into *him*. The one she'd named Tall, Dark and Dark.

"Oh, I'm so sorry." He grabbed her by both arms, holding her steady while she stared up into those well… yes…dark eyes. "I should watch where I'm going."

"I'm okay," Brenna said, touching a hand to her up-swept hairdo. "Nice reception, isn't it?"

How dumb could she be? Did he actually care about the reception?

He gave her a once-over. "Very nice."

Brenna hoped he didn't notice the blush popping out over her freckles. She did not blush prettily.

"See you later maybe?" He waved a hand in the air and Brenna immediately noticed his expensive gold watch. So like Jeffrey's.

That turned her off enough to start walking away. "I should get back."

"Hey, don't leave in such a hurry."

He had a bit of an accent. Hispanic maybe. That would explain the hunky dark good looks.

She turned, smiled at him. What would it hurt to

flirt with a nice-looking man? He wasn't wearing a wedding ring and…neither was she. She needed to stay in practice, didn't she? But she couldn't find the courage to have her heart stomped again.

"I have bridesmaid duties." She thought hard, but couldn't remember exactly what those duties might be.

"Very important job," he said, coming to stand with her while they gazed out on the crowded room. "The first being, of course, to stand around and look gorgeous?"

Brenna giggled. "You're not serious, right? I mean that's a line, isn't it?"

He grinned and the brilliance of it sizzled the paint on the walls. "Did it work?"

Well, she was laughing. That was something new. But Brenna didn't want to laugh. So no flirting, no laughing. And nothing left to say. Awkward.

"Oh, good, you two have finally met each other." Callie twirled and pranced toward them. "Brenna, this is my friend Nicholas Santiago." She smiled at him, then touched a hand on Brenna's arm. "And this is my baby sister. I think I mentioned her to you. She's home for a while from Baton Rouge."

The man gave Brenna another one of those smoldering looks. "So you're the little sister. Wow."

"That's me," Brenna said, smelling a setup. "Wow. Nice to meet you, Nicholas."

"Nick," he said, taking Brenna's hand. "I was about to introduce myself. Once we got out on the dance floor."

Brenna bristled. "I didn't say I'd dance with you."

"But you will," her bossy sister said, pushing her toward Nicholas. "Don't be rude to my friend."

I…uh…"

But it was too late. They were suddenly moving across the dance floor to the tune of a Cajun-inspired waltz. Brenna glanced around and saw her sisters smiling and waving. She'd deal with them later. Her daddy, Ramon, waved to her from where he sat with Julien's friend Tebow and Tebow's mother. He'd been hanging out with that woman way too much lately.

"You have such an interesting family," Nicholas said. He wasn't looking at her family, though. He was looking down at her.

"Yes, they're very colorful and ever so helpful."

"You have a cute Southern accent."

Still looking at her.

So she stared back. "You have a different kind of accent."

"I was born in Mexico but moved to Texas when I was a teenager."

He said it with a thickening of his accent. *Me-he-co.* She almost missed a step.

"How did you wind up here?"

He laughed at her deliberate smile. "Good question." Then he whirled her around again. The man smelled like a fresh rain out on the sea. So good. No, not good. Not good at all.

Brenna pulled in her flaring nostrils. "Well, *what* are you doing here?"

"I'm an architect. I'm here to oversee the renovations on the Dubois house. We've been working on it for a month or so now. Just about finished with the inside."

"Fleur House." That got Brenna's attention. "Oh, I love that house. I used to go past there and wonder what kind of art was inside those old walls. I'd decorate it inside my head. I always heard Mr. and Mrs. Dubois had quite a collection at one time. Of course, I never actually got to go inside the house."

He gave her what looked like a teasing glance. "Callie tells me you have a deep appreciation for art."

"Appreciate. Yes, more like a passion. I make my living from selling it," she replied. "I work in a gallery in Baton Rouge." Or at least, she had. "Budget cuts have forced me on an indefinite layoff, however."

He nodded, inclined his head toward her. "Brenna mentioned that to me. It's good to know. I might need some help with the renovations. My employer will expect some world-class pieces and I could use a hand picking them out. I know what I like, but he has very refined taste and a big wallet to back it. And although he told me to surprise him, I need an expert." He winked. "I think you'd be perfect."

Brenna scanned the room for Callie. So she could murder her. "What a coincidence. Because I know my nosy sister wouldn't dare put you up to dancing with me just so we could discuss art, now would she?"

He actually looked confused and then he grinned. "No. I wanted to dance with you *before* I knew you were Callie's sister." Leaning close, he said, "I have to admit, I was hoping you were the art expert, however. I saw you fidgeting up there by the bride. You obviously don't enjoy weddings."

Brenna wanted to explain exactly why she didn't enjoy weddings, but that would be rude. "I'm very happy for my sister, but weddings give me the hives."

"Oh, I see. You're not ready to settle down."

"I'm just not ready to settle," she said on a snap.

"Hmm, someone is bitter."

"Very."

"I'm sorry." He whirled her around the floor, bringing admiring stares from the onlookers. "If it makes you feel any better, I've been burned a few times myself."

"It should, but it doesn't." She didn't want to be mean, but this man was annoying. But easy on the eyes while he was being annoying. His suit looked expensive. His hair glistened like wet ink. And those eyes—part pirate and part heartbreaker.

Brenna was pretty sure she heard sirens and warning bells going off inside her head.

"I won't tease you anymore," he said, turning serious.

She changed the subject. "And as far as getting my advice on art?"

"I'm a businessman, Brenna. I need an art expert. Your sister was thrilled to tell me about you and how talented you are, but if you're not interested—"

"I am," Brenna said, wishing she could climb into the wedding cake and never come out. "I mean, I'm always interested in acquiring good art. But my expert opinions don't come cheap."

"I'm willing to pay you a fair salary," he said, giving her one last glance. "I enjoyed our dance. But if you'll excuse me, I have to get back to work."

"On a Friday night?" Brenna said, more to herself than him. She had actually begun to enjoy talking to him.

"Every night," he replied. With a wave and what seemed like a dismissal, he turned and left.

And Brenna realized the music had stopped.

Chapter Two

"Order up!"

Brenna skidded on her sneakers, then stopped an inch from Winnie. "Did y'all get that order for the Western omelet, heavy on the sausage and salsa?"

"Got it," the cook called through the pass-through. "Told you that five minutes ago."

"And my customer's been waiting ten minutes."

Brenna pushed at strands of damp hair. Filling in for her sister had seemed like a good idea a week before the wedding, but now her feet hurt, her back hurt and she needed a long hot shower. And it was only eight-fifteen on Monday morning.

How did Alma do this day in and day out?

"Got a new customer in your section," Winnie said with a smile. "You'll get the hang of it. It's like riding a bike."

"Yes, but bike riding is much more fun than this," Brenna replied with an impish sticking-out of her tongue.

Then she glanced down the aisle and saw a gleaming dark head and a crisp white button-up shirt. "No, not him."

"What is it?" Winnie stared toward the table by the window. "Just a handsome man needing food."

Brenna lowered her voice. "Not just any man. Nicholas Santiago. I met him at the wedding. He made me... nervous."

"Oh, I see. I do believe you not only met him, but didn't you dance with him, too?"

"Uh...sorta. Only because Callie made me."

"Yeah, right." Winnie handed her a menu. "Well, we're busy, so you need to let go of being nervous and go make nice."

"You are no help," Brenna replied. "Look at me."

"I see you," Winnie said on a chuckle. "But I don't see those overpriced walking shoes walking toward that waiting customer."

"You're mean, too," Brenna said, but she couldn't hide her smile. Winnie wouldn't hurt a fly. Or at least Brenna thought she wouldn't. But Winnie would defend to the death anyone she loved. And Brenna knew Winnie loved her.

So she had to do her job and do it with a smile.

And pray he wouldn't recognize her.

"What'll it be," she said, staying off to the side. Hoping he wouldn't glance up.

He did. Then he grinned, the effort splitting that interesting face while she was pretty sure the sun split through the clouds outside.

"Hello. Bridesmaid number two, right?"

"Always the bridesmaid," she quipped, then instantly regretted it.

"And a woman of many talents."

She shook her head. "This isn't one of them. I'm helping out so my sister can enjoy her honeymoon."

"I see." He took his time glancing over her Fleur Bakery T-shirt and jeans. "Cute. Especially the 'slap-your-mama' part."

"Cute?" Brenna wanted to die. "I'm hot and tired and so not a morning person. I really do want to slap someone. But not because of good cooking, even though we do offer that." She hissed a sigh. "What do you want for breakfast?"

"Hmm." He kept his eyes on her. "How about one egg, scrambled, dry toast and fruit."

"You call that breakfast?"

He laughed, his eyes twinkling. "What would you suggest, then?"

"Eggs, country cured ham, biscuits that will make you weep for butter and some of Alma's mayhaw jelly with a big cup of our famous strong coffee."

"I'll take it."

She gave him a long stare, then grinned. "I thought so." Putting her pen over her ear, she shot him a mock-sweet smile. "I'll be right back."

Nick enjoyed watching her work the room. She seemed to know enough to make a passable waitress, but he could tell this definitely wasn't her thing. He imagined her in a conservative suit with sensible but attractive high heels, her briefcase and designer purse on her arm. He imagined her dancing with him again and wondered why he couldn't forget the scent of her floral perfume.

Dangerous territory, this. He'd come here to do a job. And it was a big job. Probably one of the biggest renovations of his career. His client paid top dollar for discretion and design.

Nick intended to provide both.

But he did need someone to help with the art and decor.

Could he help it if the only woman in town he was actually attracted to also happened to be an art expert who was out of a job and waiting tables?

Coincidence? Or divine intervention?

His mother had been praying for him to settle down with a pretty woman so she could have grandchildren.

But wait, he'd come close only once or twice to having that perfect domestic life his family expected. Hadn't worked out so great. Maybe he should just focus on business. And try to forget the past, as his mother and aunt suggested every time he went home.

Brenna brought his breakfast and yes, the biscuits did look good. But so did the bearer of the biscuits. Although she looked completely different today from the way she'd looked at the wedding a few days ago, Brenna Blanchard was still a pretty woman. Her hair, caught in a big clamp, was falling in damp wisps around her face. He couldn't decide if she wore makeup or not, but that didn't matter. Her skin shimmered with a glowing sheen that made her appear young and care-free.

He quite preferred this look, actually.

Okay, strike that.

He liked her both ways.

Still dangerous. So he told himself to stop obsessing about Brenna and get on with his meal. The food was great, the service wonderful. He'd eaten here several times and he was sure he'd be back a lot before he was done with this job.

And he'd have plenty of opportunities to get to know Brenna Blanchard. He'd just need to remember it was all about the art for the house, all about pleasing his wealthy boss.

And not at all about remembering Brenna's silky hair and shimmering skin.

Brenna checked on her tables one last time.

Saving Nicholas Santiago for last, of course.

"How was your breakfast?" she asked, noting he sat reading over some papers.

"Very good." His smile told the tale.

"Most people leave here with a smile," she said, glad she hadn't spilled anything in the man's lap. "Want some more coffee?"

"Only if you sit and have a cup with me?"

"I'm working here," she said, exaggerating the term.

"Don't you get breaks? I'd like to discuss what we talked about at the wedding. I really do need some advice on how to decorate this house."

She glanced around. "We're not too busy. Let me get a cup and I'll talk to you for a few minutes."

She hurried to the back of the counter and found Winnie. "Can I take a short break? I need to talk to Nick. He might have a job for me."

"Oh, it's Nick now?" Winnie giggled. "What? Tired of this cushy job already?"

"Never," Brenna said with a mock-smile. "But I need cold, hard cash. And he needs an art expert."

"A match made in heaven," Winnie replied. "Go. Who wouldn't want to take a break with that hunk?"

Brenna swallowed her trepidations and told herself she could be professional and businesslike. She would not mix any pleasure with this business. She needed work to keep her mind off her many failures.

"Okay," she said as she slid into the seat and poured herself some coffee from the pot she'd left on the table. "Fifteen minutes."

"I can handle that," he said. "Let's pretend this is a real job interview. Tell me about yourself."

Okay, now she was nervous. Sitting here in a T-shirt and jeans didn't feel professional. And she didn't have her résumé in front of her. "Well, I went to LSU in Baton Rouge, majored in Art History and minored in Business. For the past three years, I've worked in the Hutton Gallery as a curator and director of operations. But budget cuts caused me to be laid off indefinitely." She sat back against the booth. "As you've probably noticed, there isn't much in the way of art here in Fleur."

He nodded. "You don't appreciate the Fleur Bayou Museum?"

"Of course." She grinned. "I helped create that museum when I was still in high school. But I never could find anyone willing to keep it open on a daily basis. It's only open when Mrs. LaBorde's gout isn't acting up—which is a whole lot these days. So the museum is more neglected than noticed."

He burst out laughing, his dark eyes sparkling. "I think I met Mrs. LaBorde at the wedding. Charming woman."

"You're just being polite," she said, touched that he'd enjoyed her joke. "She loves working at the museum, but she does have a life, after all."

"And it is a small place," he added. "I checked it

out the first day I arrived. I wanted to get a sense of the place. And now that I know you had a hand in the content of that one-room history trove, I'm doubly impressed."

"So did it help you to understand the history of this area?"

"It did."

He started asking her questions about the Cajun and Creole history of Fleur and the Spanish influence of the area. Before Brenna knew it, thirty minutes had passed.

"Oh, I have to get back to work! Sorry we didn't get to discuss Fleur House and what you might need from me."

He stood when she did, then reached out for her hand. "You're hired."

Surprised, Brenna took his hand and shook it. Or rather let him shake her hand. "But you don't even know if I'm right for this job."

"Oh, you're perfect."

Relieved and pleased but a bit wary, Brenna pulled her hand away. "And how do you know that?"

He gave her one of those simmering looks again. "By the way your eyes lit up when you were talking about that little shanty museum you created. You love this area and you love art. That's all I need to know."

Her heart did a little flip of gratefulness. Jeffrey had never understood her deep love of history and art. He'd teased her about finding a real job with a real salary. He'd never appreciated the town of Fleur, either. Called it a hick-boonie town.

"So what do you say? Do you want the job?"

"Well, yes." Her heart raced with excitement. "That was easy."

"I think so, too. Because you're the first art expert I've interviewed today and probably the last, I'd say breakfast was a success."

"Thank you," she said to Nick. "When do you want me to start?"

"Immediately," he replied. "But you can wait until your sister is back. I know you're needed here."

"Good. I appreciate that. But I can put in a few hours at the house between the lunch and dinner shifts. Besides, Alma will be back next Monday."

"That should work out great." He dropped a twenty on the table. "I enjoyed the meal and the conversation."

Brenna didn't know what to say. "I'm glad you did. I guess I'll see you Monday. Where should I meet you?"

"At the house," he said. "We'll do a walk-through." Then he touched her arm. "But aren't you forgetting something?"

"I can't think of anything," she said, alarmed. "Have I messed up already?"

He laughed. "Relax. You've done everything right. Except ask about the salary? Don't you want to know about the pay?"

Brenna breathed a sigh of relief. "I'd probably do it for free, but pretend you didn't hear me say that."

"I didn't." He smiled and named an amount. "Does that sound fair?"

Brenna tried to hide her surprise. He'd just offered her more than she'd made in a year for what should be a short amount of work. "More than fair," she replied. "And Nick, thank you."

"It will be my pleasure," he said, his gaze dropping to her face. Then he handed her a card. "Here's my number. I'll be in touch."

Brenna hurriedly scribbled her cell number on the back of a napkin. "And mine, in case you change your mind."

"I won't," he said. He gave her another devastating smile and strolled out of the café.

When Brenna heard a whoop and some giggles coming from the back of the restaurant, she hurried to do some damage control. Rumors would be flying, no doubt about that. She was in way over her head with this man. No doubt about that, either.

Chapter Three

Callie came waltzing into the café and strolled around the counter to pour herself a cup of coffee. "I hear Nick came by to see you this morning," she called to Brenna.

Cringing for the second time that day, Brenna shut the door to the supply closet and grabbed her smirking sister by the arm. "Do you have to announce that so loud they heard it in New Orleans?"

"Well, did he or didn't he come by?" Callie asked, her loosely knotted bun bouncing against her head. Why did she always have to be so perky?

"Yes, he came to eat breakfast," Brenna replied. "And how do you know this already?"

"I have my sources," Callie said, spinning on her short suede boots. She slid onto a barstool and did a matching twirl. "I knew you two would hit it off right away."

"We didn't hit it off," Brenna replied while she stacked napkins into the nearby holder. "But he did offer me a good job."

Callie actually clapped. "Sounds like you did more than just *hit* it off. This is better than I expected."

Brenna held up her hand. "Whoa! Don't get the wrong idea. We clicked enough that I think I can enjoy working for him. The man offered me a huge amount of money, so yes, we got to know each other rather quickly."

Callie beamed with pride. "I told you he'd hire you on the spot, didn't I?"

"You did and he did," Brenna confessed. "It seems a bit too easy to me. I'm afraid there's a catch."

"What catch? No catch other than you'll be doing the work you love with a handsome man who also appreciates art and beautiful homes." Callie grabbed a piece of sweet potato pie and began to dig in with relish. "Oh, this is so good. I love Winnie's sweet potato pie."

Brenna giggled. "I can tell." She took a fork and had a bite, then dropped the fork onto a napkin. "I miss Alma."

"Me, too. She'll want to hear all about this. You and Nick, I mean."

"Hey, there is no 'me and Nick,' got it?"

"Got it," Callie said between chews. "I wonder if he'll want children. Does he know you're kind of gunshy in that area?"

Brenna slapped her sister on the arm. "Will you stop talking like that, please? I don't intend to marry the man. I just want a good job for a good day's work."

"And I just want nieces and nephews and another wedding to plan. And I wouldn't mind living at Fleur House, while we're wishing."

Brenna pretended to not notice the sadness in her sister's eyes. Callie deserved to be happy and she'd make such a wonderful mother. She said a prayer for her sister, then teased, "Get your own man. Preferably, the one who actually owns the house. I hear he's filthy rich and quite mysterious. He'll have to show up to claim his property sooner or later. You'd better be ready."

Callie shook her head. "No, I had my turn. One divorce is quite enough for me, thank you." She gave a dainty shrug. "But this mysterious owner is intriguing."

"So you'll just mess in my life to occupy yourself until the owner shows up?"

"Yep. Seems to be working. Wait until I tell Elvis. He'll be thrilled, too. He loves Nick."

Brenna finished filling napkin holders. "That big mutt loves anybody who breathes. But I can agree with your dog on one thing. Nick is nice-looking."

"Of course he is. Would I set you up with just any ol' body?"

"We are not set up, remember? We're working together."

"Got it." Callie finished her coffee and pie, then waved her hand in the air. "Just working together. Right."

Brenna shook her head, then finished her busywork, her mind in turmoil at the thought of working so closely with Nicholas Santiago. She didn't even know the man and already, he was messing with her head. Telling herself to stick to the plan—business, business, business—she decided it wouldn't hurt to research her new boss just so she'd be familiar with his style and the demands of her job. She'd do that first thing when she got home tonight.

He'd research her, see what kind of credentials she had. Nick rarely hired anyone without doing a thorough vetting, but he had no doubt Brenna Blanchard would be an asset to his renovation team. She knew the area, knew the history and she seemed to have a passion for art and literature—two things his boss demanded in all of his employees.

Nick remembered the pride she'd displayed when discussing Fleur and the surrounding areas. Brenna might not want to spend the rest of her life in her quaint little hometown, but she sure did care about the place. That was the kind of intimate passion he needed to renovate and decorate Fleur House. While he had a great interior designer ready to re-create and decorate the house, he also wanted a curator to oversee hanging the art pieces his employer already owned and to buy other pieces to complement the entire house and collection.

Brenna would do the job and he'd enjoy the fringe benefits of her delightful company. A win-win situation. Or one he'd regret when it came time to pull up stakes and leave. Which he'd have to do sooner or later.

Nick got up and looked out the window of his temporary home—a construction trailer parked behind Fleur House. The nondescript trailer served as an office and a place to stay. He'd designed it that way so he didn't have to rent out a room or stay in run-down hotels. And while Fleur had some quaint little cabins along the bayou, he much preferred to be alone in his own traveling home. He liked the privacy and the ease of transporting himself.

A quick, clean getaway.

That was how the last woman he'd left had described his mode of operation. Or rather, she had called his trailer a means of a quick and easy escape.

And she'd been so right.

He liked to get in, do the job and get out.

No ties to bind him. No hassles to hold him.

So why was he sitting here now doing an online search for any information he could find on Brenna Blanchard?

Because he needed to know her so he could work with her. Of course.

When he pulled up a society picture from the Baton Rouge *Advocate* newspaper, Nick pored over the words with a hungry intent. Dated a few months ago, the caption stated that Brenna Blanchard and her fiancé, Jeffrey Patterson, had attended a dinner to raise funds for a Baton Rouge art event. The note went on to talk about Brenna's position at the art gallery and Mr. Patterson's work at a Baton Rouge law firm. Nick quit reading after that, but he couldn't take his eyes off the woman in the picture.

Brenna, dressed in a shimmering dark blue cocktail dress, smiled up at the man next to her, her gaze bright with love and admiration. And happiness.

Fiancé?

Had she been engaged to this man?

If so, they must have broken up. Maybe that was why she was unemployed and back in Fleur. Her attitude regarding marriage indicated she wasn't the marrying kind.

And she wasn't wearing an engagement ring now.

So much for vetting.

Nick had more than enough information on Brenna Blanchard. She wouldn't stick around too long, either.

So he had nothing to worry about really.

* * *

She worried with the collar of her blouse.

Not sure how to dress for her first official meeting with Nicholas, Brenna waffled between jeans and a T-shirt to a blue button-up cotton shirt and dress pants.

She finally settled on putting the button-up shirt over some nice trouser jeans. Sensible cushioned loafers would be better than heels while walking throughout the house. She didn't want to listen to the tap-tap of her shoes while she was trying to envision art on the walls.

Or maybe she didn't want to distract her new boss with a pair of high heels because she planned on keeping this relationship strictly professional. But she did mist herself with perfume, just for good measure.

After researching him online, she'd found him only in a few professional pages, but his work reviews were all five-star. Clients raved about his work ethics and his professionalism. Apparently, he was that good. His client list read like a who's-who of prominent Texas tycoons. Only she couldn't find any reference to Fleur House or his current client. That was interesting.

She'd found something else interesting, too.

Nicholas Santiago was also an artist. Some paintings had shown up under the name Nick Santiago, paintings he'd done as a teenager. Or at least she figured it had to be the same Nick—her Nick? Well, not her Nick, but the man she'd agreed to work with. One of the paintings was of a beautiful dark-haired girl on a horse. She looked young and carefree. He'd won an award for it in high school.

"Jessica." That had been the name of the painting.

Of course, now she wondered who Jessica was and what did she mean to Nick.

She'd seen another article, but Callie had called her and they'd chatted too long for her to go back and read that one. It had something to do with that painting, though. She'd have to remember to read that later. Right now, she had to get to Fleur House.

A few minutes later, she was in her car about to leave when her daddy, Ramon, came strolling out of the house. She loved being back here with her father. She tried to pamper him as much as she could, but her overly protective father seemed to think she was fifteen again. So he lectured her. And worried about her.

Brenna cranked the car and tried to make a quick exit.

In spite of his bad knees, he shot down the brick steps of the white clapboard house. "Where are you off to in such a hurry, missy?"

Brenna stuck her head out the open car window. "Papa, remember I told you I got a part-time job? Today's the day for the first meeting with Nicholas."

Ramon adjusted his suspenders and eyed her with a sharp intent. "You mean that fancy fellow over from San Antonio? Are you sure about working for some stranger?"

"Very sure." She cranked the car and waved at her perpetually perplexed father. "The pay is good, so I'll be able to help you with some rent money."

"Don't need no rent from my own daughter," Ramon said on a disgruntled huff, his south Louisiana accent thickening like a steaming roux.

They'd already had this argument. "I know that, but your daughter wants to contribute."

She blew him a kiss and took off before he insisted on escorting her. Papa was such a sweetheart. It was rather endearing how he watched over his three girls. But they all put up with it because they loved him and they all missed their mother, Lila. Especially Papa.

That strong thread of love kept Brenna going each day when she woke up in her old bed and stared at the aged pictures of her cheerleading days and the pictures of now-old rock stars she often dreamed about. Those still hung curled next to her prints of Van Gogh and Monet. She'd always loved sunflowers. She'd dreamed of going to Europe to explore all the places she'd only read about in art books. Maybe even get back into painting pictures herself.

So many dreams, and all for naught. She'd had to admit defeat and come back home. Who could paint that picture?

But at least she had a welcoming home and a solid foundation of faith to guide her. Jeffrey Patterson, her ex-fiancé, had frowned on such things. He didn't need anyone to "guide" him, as he'd often told her.

Now she had to wonder what she'd ever seen in the man. Maybe a bit of prestige and a way to penetrate the high-brow society of Baton Rouge? Now she realized she didn't need those things as much as she needed someone to love with authentic intent. And someone to love her back completely.

So when she pulled her car up the winding drive of Fleur House and saw Nicholas standing there in jeans and his own button-up shirt, she ignored the little dips and sways of her battered heart. The man cut a fine figure, there on the porch of the looming mansion.

Too fine.

Maybe she should turn around and go back to waiting tables.

Nick heard the car roaring up the drive. So she drove a late-model economy car that looked like a go-cart. Interesting. The car was cute in a strange kind of way and seemed to suit her. He watched as she climbed out and adjusted her briefcase strap over her shoulder. Even though she was dressed in casual clothes, she looked ready to be professional. He needed to be professional, too.

"Hello," he called as he moved down the rounded stone steps to meet her. "You're right on time."

She smiled and shook his hand. "I didn't want to be late."

Nick discreetly checked her fingers for an engagement ring. Her fingers were bare, but she wore a nice watch on one arm and a dainty flower-encrusted bracelet on the other. Sunflowers. Quaint and totally unexpected.

He let go of her hand, the memory of her slender fingers now burned into his mind. "I think you're already familiar with the layout of the house, but we can do a walk-through and I'll explain what I'd like to do. We've cleared away the debris and cobwebs and done most of the heavy renovations, but we kept some of the furniture the previous owner sold with the house."

She took a sweeping look at the brick-and-stone house. "Are you the decorator, too?"

"No, I have a designer coming from San Antonio to oversee that area. I'll mostly work on the structure and design of the house, preserving its history but improving it and bringing it up to speed, code-wise. The owner understands the historical significance of this place, but he requires the modern amenities, too."

Her gaze landed back on him. "And who is this mysterious owner?"

He held up his index finger and wagged it. "I'm not at liberty to say right now."

She gave him a questioning glance but didn't press. "All right, then. As long as his money is green, I'm good with that. Let's get on with the job."

Nick smiled and guided her up into an enclosed porch surrounded by an intricate stone facing that consisted of wide arches and then opened to the double front doors. "We've kept all of the fan transoms over the doors. Brings in a lot of light all over the house. Most of the windows have been replaced with more weatherproof glass, but we'll make sure we keep the hooded design."

"Wow." Brenna stood in the big open hallway and stared at the curving staircase. "This sure looks different. Last time Callie and I sneaked in here, it looked like cattle had run through the house."

"I wouldn't doubt that cows might have found shelter here along with a lot of other things," he said. "It was a mess."

"But it's gold underneath all that grim."

Nick knew this project would be his biggest challenge. "It is a work of art," he said. "But a true representation of a time gone by."

Even though the wallpaper had been aged and crumbling and the floors were scratched and rotted out in places, the house was striking.

Brenna seemed to see that, too. "It's just as beautiful

as I remember—from peeking in the windows, even as run-down as it looked back then. I can't believe I get to help with the renovations. Callie loves this place more than I do. She's always dreamed of living here."

"Yes, she's mentioned that to me several times."

Nick enjoyed the blissful expression on Brenna's face. It took his breath away, but he held that breath so she wouldn't notice. But this attitude was new and refreshing. Most of the women he knew only wanted the house, not all the pain and work that would need to go into the house. They'd be bored with the details but more than willing to find someone to help them gut this house and make it what they thought it should be.

Brenna wanted it to be the same, only better.

That made her the perfect choice for helping him to find just the right pieces to complement the enormous walls and high ceilings throughout the place.

"Italianate Second Empire," she said on a sigh of appreciation. "Built in 1869 by a rich man from Paris who married a Creole woman from New Orleans. She named the town and the house. It's called Dubois House, after their last name, but the locals call it Fleur House. She did, too. I think because the gardens used to be full of all sorts of exotic plants and flowers."

"I'm impressed," Nick said. "And to think I had my doubts about hiring you."

She clutched her briefcase strap. "You did? But you said I'd be perfect."

Why did that little bit of uncertainty in her voice shake him to his core?

"I think you are." He tested her a bit more. "But we didn't exactly go through a formal interview."

"No, we met at a wedding. And didn't hit it off too

well. And you hired me in a diner, after I'd waited on you with an attitude. I had my doubts, too."

He accepted that and bowed his head in agreement. "*Sí*. That makes us even."

"And…cautious."

He'd have to remember that.

"The parlor is to the right," he said, trying to stay on track. "And the dining room to the left."

She rushed into the huge square parlor, her flats making a nice cadence against the aged wooden floors. "Look at these windows—love those high arches. And that fireplace. I can just see some sort of outdoor scene surrounded by a gilded frame. Or better yet, a blue dog painting."

"Blue dog?" Nick chuckled. "You mean by George Rodrigue?"

"Yes, maybe something that bold and different would offset these amazing floor-to-ceiling windows."

She had that dreamy look on her face again. That look that made him want to sweep her into his arms and dance her around this big, empty room.

"I'll make a note—blue dog."

"Is he married?"

"Who?"

"Your boss?"

Nick snapped back to reality. "Uh, no. He was once, but his wife died."

She stopped smiling. "How awful. Our mother died several years ago. Breast cancer."

"I'm sorry. Callie did mention that. I can't imagine going through that. I still have both my parents and I'd be lost without them." He didn't tell her that he *had* lost a loved one, too. He knew the pain of grief, but he refused to open up that wound to someone he'd just met. "Your mother sounds like a special person."

She turned, her forest-colored eyes full of a richness that looked every bit as pretty as any picture he could imagine. "She was. You're blessed to have both of your parents. Enjoy them and love them."

"Good advice." He did love his family, but they'd grown apart over the years. Did he dare tell her that grief had stricken his family to the point of denial?

Better to focus on work.

He motioned toward the dining area. "Let's go to the other side."

Brenna let out a little squeal of delight, her smile lighting the room with an ethereal glow. "Look at that mural. Can we keep that?"

"Yes," he said, thinking he'd meant to do away with it. He'd have to tell the interior decorator that the elaborate rendition of a garden party with a steamboat in the background was off-limits.

Because he'd decided he didn't want to do anything that would take that beautiful smile off Brenna Blanchard's face.

And he'd also decided that he was in serious trouble.

Chapter Four

"Really?" Brenna smiled big at her new boss. "Just like that, you'll keep the mural?"

"I'm not always so agreeable," Nicholas said, giving her an exaggerated frown. "Your enthusiasm is obviously wearing off on me."

Brenna couldn't believe it was that easy. She'd prepared herself for a difficult task at every turn. "You seem like the type who bosses everyone around with a growl, waving your hand at this one and that one while you're on your phone with someone mysterious and even more demanding than you."

He actually laughed out loud.

And took her breath away.

"You've got me pegged, I see."

"I've worked with many highly demanding artists and supervisors," she said, her smile dying. "I miss that."

He motioned toward the stairs. "So you think you'll get bored with just me to growl at you?"

The thought of him actually doing that only added

to the tremendous attraction she felt toward him. Bad, bad idea.

"No, I'm never bored. I always find something to do. But please, growl and be mean. Keeps me on my toes."

"I gave you the mural," he said after they reached the bottom of the stairs. "Make it beautiful for me."

Brenna did a slow swallow to get her breath under control. She got the distinct feeling this man didn't give anything easily. "I will," she said on a meek but firm tone. "And if I make everything else I choose beautiful for you, will that be a good thing?"

He put his hand on her back and urged her up the stairs. "That will be a very good thing. This house is the biggest renovation of my career. It's a make-or-break deal."

She whirled, one step above him, and stared down into his dark, rich-chocolate eyes. "And you picked me to help out. Are you loony?"

His eyes went even darker. "I've been called loco, *sí.*"

Brenna didn't think the man was crazy. No, rather she decided she was the loony one. Her impulsive nature always got her into trouble, but her sensible side usually tugged her back to earth. And even though she was standing on a centuries-old staircase looking down at a man who most certainly would make any woman swoon, no matter the time or place, she held herself aloof and told herself to snap out of it. She was here for a job not a new boyfriend.

"I've been called that, too," she said before turning away again. "We should get along just fine."

He did that growling thing. "Take a right on the landing."

"What are we looking at now?" she asked, afraid to glance back at him because she could feel the heat of his gaze following her. No, stalking her like a big cat out in the swamp.

He made it to the landing and looked around the wide, empty hallway. "This floor contains four bedrooms and baths for each. The baths were installed much later after the house was built, of course. We've finished the basic renovations, but we still have a lot of work to do up here. We enlarged the baths and the closets and made sure the structure is sound as far as wiring and knocking down walls. But your job is to pick one piece of interesting art for each room, especially the master bedroom."

"I'm on it," Brenna said, scribbling notes while she tried to ignore his sultry accent and his growling explanations. "Does your…mysterious owner have any preferences?"

"He has a few, but in this case, he told me to surprise him."

"Surprise. That's a new one. I like a good challenge." Brenna thought about that, then whirled. "Are you the owner, Nicholas?"

He backed away, hands out and pushing toward her. "I am not and that is the truth." He tugged her into a gigantic room with two sets of exquisite bay windows—obviously this was the master suite. "You see that trailer down there?"

Brenna nodded, ignoring the panoramic view of the Big Fleur Bayou and the bay out beyond for now. "Nice, but not quite as big as the house."

"That is my home," he said. "I renovate and design houses. But I prefer spending most of my time in my trailer or in a small hacienda on my parents' property in San Antonio. So I need you to understand—this is not my house. I have no desire to live here. I'm only here to prepare this estate for the new owner and then I'll move on to my next project."

She believed him. Nicholas didn't want to settle down. She got the message loud and clear. So she put aside her shock and awe and disappointment, then tried to throw him off by asking about the real owner. "Got it. You like to travel light and linger not so much. So back to the man who hired you. When will he arrive?"

He looked relieved and a bit shocked himself. "In the spring of next year. So we need to get busy."

He motioned to her with an impatient jabbing of his fingers in the air. Brenna turned away from the view outside to the reality of the man by her side. "Okay, so you're not the mysterious owner and you're not teasing me or trying to pull one over on me. I get that. So show me the rest of the house and give me the interior designer's phone number. I'll have to get with her and make sure I have a clear understanding of what she has planned."

He seemed to relax. Like a big cat, he'd almost pounced on her for being so nosy. But he'd pulled back, slinking away before he revealed anything too personal. "The designer knows she is to work with you in considering the art. Whatever you decide, she will work around it. Or make it work, per my instructions."

He once again reminded her of his authority.

But Brenna was known for always having the last word. "And just so we're clear, I'm only curious about the owner because I need to match the art to the person who will live here. But I have to say, Nick, you are every bit as mysterious as he-who-shall-not-be-mentioned-again. I'm sorry if I overstepped in being nosy. It's one of my flaws."

His dark eyebrows lifted. "Just one? You mean you have more?"

She saw that trace of a smile trying to pull at his lips. Saw that and so much that he didn't want her to see.

He didn't want to talk about the man who had bought Fleur House. But he especially didn't want to talk about himself, either. Which only made Brenna more curious.

Two hours later, Brenna waved goodbye to Nick and headed straight into town to her sister Alma's café. She needed comfort food and she needed some girl talk with Alma's right-hand woman and newly promoted manager, Winnie. And just to be sure, she called Callie, too. "I need to rant. Preferably over pie and coffee."

"Oh, I can't wait to hear all the details," Callie said. "I'll put Thelma at the front register and I'll be right over."

Brenna was about to disconnect but then she remembered. "Oh, Callie, Nick said he wants you to be in charge of all the landscaping once the house is done."

"Really?" Her sister squealed so loud Brenna had to hold her cell phone away. "I wanted to offer, but I chickened out and never applied. I dreamed about doing that, but I can't believe he actually asked for me. You didn't force him, did you?"

Brenna got an image of trying to force Nick Santiago into doing anything. Impossible. "Oh, no. He's not the kind to bend to the whims of a woman. He asked for you outright."

A brief memory of Nick telling her to make the mural beautiful fluttered through her mind. Okay, maybe he did bend to the whims of a woman every now and then.

Callie chatted on, excitement in every word. "Okay. I won't say anything until he brings it up. But I'll start playing with some garden designs. I know the layout of that acreage by heart, anyway."

"Yes, you've always wanted to live there and you've dreamed of cultivating that big garden. I know, I know. And after seeing the house, I can understand why. That's your thing, sis, not mine. I just get to help decorate the place."

She said goodbye, then again thought back over her sometimes-good, sometimes-bad conversation with Nick.

"Make it beautiful for me."

She'd seen the dare in his eyes when he'd said that. And she'd heard the gentleness in his request. Nick might not be the kind she could sweet-talk or force, but he could be the kind who would do something sweet and special simply because it pleased him. And he had done it for her, too, she sensed. But why? The man certainly presented a paradox. Too strange and spine-tingling for her to figure out right now, but too mysterious and intriguing for her to let go just yet.

"I'll need to read up on how to restore a mural," she said to get her mind off Nick and his "make it beautiful for me" lips. Then she pulled into a parking space across from the Fleur Café and hurried in to spill everything to Winnie and Callie.

* * *

Nick stood in the empty drawing room of Fleur House and sniffed the last of the sweet notes of Brenna's floral perfume. The smell of wisteria and jasmine hung in the air like a wedding veil, light and full of mystery.

And she thought he was the mysterious one.

He felt as empty as this big house.

Her laughter had echoed out over the quiet, still rooms like a rogue wind invading a hot house. Brenna seemed all buttoned-up and professional, but Nick thought there might be a free spirit hidden underneath that sensible facade. Did he dare encourage that side of her?

No, because he'd practically shouted at her to back off on trying to figure out what made him tick. He didn't have the right to encourage her in any aspect. He couldn't allow himself to get close to her, either. No time for that. He had to get this house in order and move on.

And where are you going?

The voice shouted into the silence of the afternoon and moved through the last of the sun's rays as he did one more walk-through of the house.

Tomorrow, the noise level would change and he wouldn't have to be alone with his silence. He'd be surrounded once again by hammers and drills and nail guns and saws. He'd hear the familiar sounds of workmen arguing and measuring, the noise of readjusting and tearing down. Demolition and restoration always signaled a change in the air, a forward movement of action. These were the sounds that soothed him. Not the laughter of a woman who seemed to be such a beautifully confusing contradiction. He'd smell the scent of sawdust and paint thinner, the scent of new paint and new wood, not the scent of wisteria and jasmine.

Tomorrow, he'd be in the thick of things again and then he could lose himself in his work, day and night.

Except for the times he'd lose himself in watching Brenna Blanchard making everything she touched beautiful.

He strolled toward the old mural that he'd saved after her last-minute plea. The genteel vista spoke of times gone by, times with smiling people walking along the bayou. The women wore colorful colliding frocks and the men looked dapper and distinguished in their waistcoats and top hats.

"Make it beautiful for me, Brenna," he said out loud, the echo of his solitude shouting back at him.

And he knew, she'd already made everything beautiful.

Too beautiful.

"He said that?" Winnie grabbed her coffee and took a long swig, her pecan-brown eyes going wide.

"He said exactly that," Brenna replied, her fork of bread pudding somewhere between her plate and her mouth. "And it was the way he said it, as if he'd never seen anything beautiful before."

"Must be some mural on that wall," Callie retorted through a mouthful of the creamy pudding. She finished chewing and let out a sigh. "It's so romantic."

"He is not romantic," Brenna said. "Didn't you hear the part about him living in a trailer and always being on the move? The man might as well wear a sign that says 'Don't bother. I ain't buying any.'"

"Or maybe the man protests too much," Winnie replied with her usual sweet smile. "And that in itself is highly romantic."

"He's not romantic," Brenna repeated, trying to convince herself. She couldn't do it, so she gave up. The man was like a walking Heathcliff—shuttered, disengaged, disturbing…and the total package, the kind of package a woman couldn't help but tear open. She wanted to dive right in and find the treasure. But she couldn't, wouldn't do that.

"I mean, the house is so romantic," Callie said with another sigh, completely ignoring Brenna's denial. "I hope I get to sneak in with you and see it all gussied up. I've always—"

"Wanted to live there," Brenna finished. "We all know that." She shrugged and shot her sister an indulging smile. "At least the new owner is single. He's a widower. You might have a chance."

"Oh, how tragic…and romantic," Callie said on another sigh. "At least we can understand how the man must feel. But why buy such a big house if he's all alone?" Her expression turned dreamy. "I know. He wants to wander around from room to room, lamenting his lost love. Tragic and poignant."

Brenna looked at her sister. "Have you ever considered writing a romance novel?"

Winnie brought some clarity to the situation. "Maybe he bought the house for his *new* bride."

Callie sat up straight, ignoring Brenna's question and Winnie's speculation. "I need to lose about ten pounds and do something about my sallow, washed-out skin and what about these laugh lines? What can

I do about that?" She pushed at her long curly golden hair. "And maybe a haircut."

"No," both Winnie and Brenna said.

"Don't cut your hair," Brenna told her sister. "It took you a while to get it long again."

Callie nodded, quiet now. "You're right. I do have good hair in spite of losing it all…before. And besides, what am I thinking? Winnie might be right. He's probably found a new wife already. Of course, I don't want to fool with another man. Too much trouble. I might be in remission, but I'm still too tired to tackle a relationship."

"Amen," Brenna said. "I don't mind you stepping out, but not me. So I had a little talk with myself on the way over here. I will remain professional and businesslike. I won't pry into Nick's life at all."

"Yeah, right," her sister said. Then she leaned close. "Might want to test that theory. Nick just walked in the door and he's headed straight for our table."

Brenna gasped. "Why is it that all the men in our life always wind up in this café? Remember how Julien hounded Alma every day, over pie and petulance?"

Winnie giggled. "And suga', we sure got both."

Callie looked up with mock-surprise on her face. "Nick Santiago. How in the world are you?"

"Hello, ladies." Nick couldn't help the grin that smeared the sternness off his face. "As if you don't already know that I'm demanding, surly and hard to work with. I'm sure your pretty sister has filled you in on all my bad qualities."

Callie didn't take the bait. "Actually, I've been the one filling her in—on what a nice man you *can* be.

I've sent enough flowers with your signature on them to know."

Nick really liked the Blanchard sisters, especially their somewhat sweet naïveté. "Sending flowers does not complete my résumé, Callie." He gave Brenna a direct stare.

Callie didn't let that stop her. "No, but I'm pretty good with getting it right with my regulars. You're the real deal, Nick."

Brenna cleared her throat. "This little mutual admiration society is endearing, but I have to get going. My boss *is* demanding." She shot Nick a daring smile. "Just passing through or did you need to speak to me?"

Nick wanted to keep sparring but duty called. "Actually, I wanted to see both you and Callie. And Winnie, too, for that matter."

Winnie slapped the table. "The highlight of my day, for true."

Brenna gave her sister a covert glance. "Have you changed your mind about hiring both of us?"

"No," Nick said, accepting the glass of water Winnie offered him. "I'm calling an impromptu meeting later this week. Kind of a town hall thing. I've had so many questions about what's happening with Fleur House, I thought I'd answer all of them in one fell swoop."

"Smart," Callie said. "What day and time?"

"Six-thirty Thursday, inside the church fellowship hall." He turned to Brenna. "And I want you there to take a few notes on ideas the people of Fleur might have about the house and gardens. We have a gem of a home right here in Fleur and my client wants to make sure everyone here is comfortable with what will probably become a tourist attraction. He hopes to open both the house and the gardens for tours at certain times when he's traveling on business."

"I'll be there," Brenna replied, touched that both Nick and he-who-she-couldn't-mention were willing to do this for the town.

Callie stood up. "Nick, you have to tell us about this man."

Nick shook his head. "I can't do that. My contract has a very precise confidentiality clause."

"Which we will honor," Brenna replied, sending her sister a warning look.

"Oh, all right." Callie made a face. "Want a bowl of bread pudding, Nick?"

Nick glanced at Brenna. "I shouldn't—"

"Oh, live a little, boss," Brenna said. "It might make you sweeter."

He laughed at that. "I'll have some, then. With some of that strong coffee Fleur seems to be famous for."

Callie brought him his pudding and coffee. "I have to get back to work. I'll see y'all later."

He watched as Brenna gathered her things, obviously in a hurry to get away from him. "What is this? I have to eat all alone?"

She stopped, glanced around. "I see a lot of people in here."

"I don't know them yet."

"You don't know me yet, either," she said. "I'll be at your meeting and I'll take copious notes, but right now I want to research some art for the house. I want to get this right as much as you do, believe it or not."

"I believe you," he said, wishing she'd stay while he willed her to go. "Go, get to work. I am paying you a lot of money, after all."

"Yes, sir."

He watched her walk away, that elusive fragrance following her. Then he looked up to find Winnie smiling down at him.

"I'm still here," she said with a grin.

Nick laughed at that because he was pretty sure Winnie was married and had four children. "Sit down and keep me company, then. And while you're at it, maybe you can tell me why I find that woman so fascinating."

Chapter Five

⤜◝

Brenna sat watching the people of Fleur as they filed into the bright church hall one by one. Of course, Winnie had sent cookies to go with the urn of coffee. Refreshments were always a requirement here in this big, loud room. The Fleur Café, right across the street, was happy to provide them.

Good thing she brought extra. Tonight the main attraction had drawn a record crowd. Whenever a stranger came to town and wanted a meeting, people came to listen. Especially people who were unemployed or late with last month's mortgage. Especially people who already had two and sometimes three jobs but could never rest because their families needed food and shelter. Not that Nick came bearing jobs or solutions, but he was here on a positive note. He was taking something they all treasured and admired and making it beautiful again.

A restoration.

Brenna let that thought rush through her like sparkling water as she scanned the crowd. Nick wasn't here yet. Why was she so nervous, so hopeful for this man?

What had he done to her to make her see beneath that facade of cool and calm he cloaked around himself?

"Make it beautiful for me."

His words echoed over the boisterous gathering, haunting her with a sweet intensity.

Did Nick create and re-create lovely aesthetic things because he needed to make the world more beautiful? For someone he loved? Or maybe for someone he'd lost? Was that why he traveled so light and lingered only as long as required? She thought about the young girl in the portrait she'd seen on the internet. What did Jessica mean to him? Was she a friend? Or someone he'd loved and lost?

Dear Lord, help me to understand this man. Help me to restore his soul to You.

The plea of that prayer poured over her as people gathered for the meeting. And somehow, Brenna knew that would be the echo she'd hear in her head each time she was around Nick Santiago.

For now, she smiled and waved to the full house. She spotted Julien's younger brother, Pierre, along with his girlfriend, Mollie. They were so cute together. Since Julien and Alma had gotten back together, the Blanchard family had embraced Julien's family, welcoming his mother and his brother as their own. Her father came through the door, Mrs. LeBlanc walking with him. It was funny how several of the widows in the church seemed to be always after her daddy. But Julien's mother was just a friend. She had made it clear after her husband died almost two years ago she would never fall in love again.

Maybe Nick had made that same pledge, Brenna thought as she surveyed the crowd.

Callie came in and waved, then slid into a seat up front.

Brenna walked over to her sister and dropped her briefcase on the floor. "He's not here yet."

"I'm sure he's on his way," Callie said. "Hey, I got a call from Alma. They are having so much fun. The ocean, the beach, the shops, the honeymoon. She might not ever come home from Florida."

"She's in love," Brenna said, glad for her sister. "Did you tell her about Fleur House?"

Callie giggled. "Yes, I told her all about your new love interest Nick Santiago, which is what you're really asking."

"I am not. What did she say?"

"She said good for you. On the job…and the man."

"She's in love. She can be optimistic."

"Yeah, that's true. We, on the other hand, are more cynical. So we have to be cautious."

Brenna nodded at that, as sad as it sounded. But when she turned and saw Nick strolling in as if he owned the place, his suit tailored and fitted, his hair combed and shimmering, she wanted to throw caution to the wind. Her heart actually did a backward flip.

Frances LaBorde, a staunch church lady and one to always notice everything going on around here, leaned up and touched Brenna on the arm. "He's mighty perty, ain't he?" She winked at Brenna, then settled back with a look of delight on her puffy cheeks.

"Yes, he sure is," Callie whispered to Brenna. "If you don't go for him, I just might have to."

"Go ahead," Brenna said, inhaling a deep breath. "Ours is a working relationship." She ignored the little green monsters of jealousy laughing in her head.

"Yeah, and we all believe that," Callie retorted. "I was just teasing about my going after him. But the way he looks at you, I think you have a definite shot."

Nick surveyed the crowd. The tough crowd. He hadn't expected this many people to show up. But this was a small town with a big grapevine. No need for online networking here. This network moved through clotheslines and crab traps and church prayer chains.

He was a stranger in a strange land.

Then he looked up and saw Brenna sitting there on the front row, prim and proper and prepared, wearing a pretty spring dress and cute little blue sweater. She gave him an encouraging, questioning smile.

Showtime.

"Hello, everyone," he said in a loud calm voice.

The whispers died down as people settled into their seats.

Nick took a breath. "I'm Nick Santiago. I've been here for a while, but I've been so busy I haven't had time to talk to very many of you. I'm supervising the renovation of the Dubois mansion, locally known as Fleur House."

Applause followed that introduction. Nick grinned at that.

"I wanted to let you know what this means for your community."

"Yeah, what does it mean?" came a shout from the back.

"Jobs?" someone else asked.

The conversations started up again, a mixture of English and Cajun-French that turned into chaos. Nick tried raising his hand, but they were off and running, taking his initial explanations and creating little detours that rippled like a swamp wake.

"Excuse me!"

Nick watched as Brenna stood up and clapped her hands.

"Mr. Santiago is doing us a favor by bringing us here tonight. Let's show him that famous Fleur hospitality by *listening,* please. He'll be glad to answer any questions when he's finished."

The room went quiet.

Nick gave Brenna a grateful glance, then started again.

"Last spring, my client bought Fleur House and the surrounding gardens. Because I'm an architect and on retainer for this particular client, he commissioned me to oversee the renovations. I've been here a few weeks now, and I've seen some of you riding by the house. I know you're wondering who this man is and what's going on with all the construction."

He took a breath and drank a sip of water from the cup Brenna had put on a table. "I can't tell you who the owner is yet. He's a very private man with a very public obligation. But I can tell you about me. I grew up in San Antonio, Texas. My parents still live there." He stopped, glanced at Brenna, prayed she wouldn't see his doubts. "I've always loved old buildings. That is my specialty, restoring old neglected places and making them new again."

"We're glad to have you."

Nick nodded at the robust man who'd shouted that out. "And I'm glad to be here. So we will get serious about putting the final touches on the house now that the toughest parts of the renovation are finished. I've hired Brenna Blanchard to oversee some of the decor for the house, mainly the artwork. My client loves art and buys several pieces a year. Brenna will pick some of the main pieces for the house." He glanced at Brenna and smiled. "She is highly qualified."

"And she's an artist, too," someone called out.

Surprised, Nick took another sip of water. "Really? She left that off her résumé."

While Brenna shifted in her seat and looked down, another person said, "She don't like to brag."

Everyone laughed at that. But Nick made a note to ask Brenna about her hidden talent. Was it coincidence that she was also an artist? Did he dare tell her he used to paint? That was a lifetime ago. It didn't matter much now.

"So, what other talents do we have in this room? We're a little behind on the renovations, so I need some extra hands. I'll need some extra construction workers—both experienced and nonexperienced. I'll need a couple more electricians and plumbers, and journeymen to add to my team. I'll need a qualified house inspector. I have a list of positions here on the table. Please feel free to take the information. Even though I have a team from Texas, I'll still need a lot of locals to help. I'll be back here tomorrow at noon to accept applications. Mainly, I'm here to make Fleur House fresh and new again so that we can show it off to the community and to tourists and visitors, too."

Everyone clapped, then Brenna stood up. "Now, if you have any questions—"

An hour later, Brenna shooed the last person out the door, then turned to Nick. "Welcome to Fleur."

He ran a hand over his hair and laughed. "I'm exhausted."

He did look adorably exhausted. She had to keep her fingers from brushing through his dark hair. "And hungry, I imagine."

"Yes, I am." He started gathering his notes and shoved them into his briefcase. "I didn't realize that until now, however."

Brenna waffled like a frog on a vine, then finally turned to him. "You're invited to my daddy's house for chicken perlo. It's my mama's recipe, but Papa has perfected it. It's always good on a crisp fall night."

"That sounds great." He touched her midback and guided her toward the door. "How did I do?"

Brenna didn't have to hide her reaction to that. "You were great. I had no idea you'd be able to offer people jobs. I guess I never asked."

She'd been too concerned about herself even to think of that. Once she'd been hired, she did her usual thing. She began to obsess about being perfect.

He gave her an indulgent smile. "I have my own crew, but we always try to hire locals and now that we're down to the wire, it makes sense. I should have explained that to you."

Interesting. "So you do this a lot. Find a house, renovate it and move on?"

"*Sí.* That's my job. My client keeps me busy year-round. He's mostly into industrial real estate, but he sometimes buys estates and renovates them. He's bought and sold some incredible homes."

More and more information. But she wanted to know more about Nick right now. "Is he your main employer?"

Nick held the door for her. Outside, the fall night held a hint of winter. While the winters here were mild, it was beginning to be chilly enough to wear a light jacket.

Brenna only had a light sweater. She shivered.

"I work for several different people, but mostly for him, *si*."

And that was the end of that.

She shivered again. Then she felt Nick's hands on her arms, felt the warmth of his soft wool suit jacket enveloping her shoulders. "You're cold."

And you are seriously...hot.

Brenna reeled in her treacherous reaction, the scent of soap and spice all around her. "Thank you. I have to remember to unpack my winter clothes."

"Do you need a ride?" he asked. Then he motioned to his car. Only she'd never seen a car like this one.

"What...what is that exactly?"

He grinned like a schoolboy. "That is a vintage 1969 GTO convertible with four-on-the-floor and a 400 horsepower engine with a turbo transmission."

Brenna looked at the baby blue automobile, then back at him. "A muscle car? You drive a muscle car?"

He looked surprised. "You know about muscle cars?"

"I've heard my papa and Julien and his brother, Pierre, talking about them, usually when they're watching a race on television. And now I've actually seen one."

He took her by the arm. "Not only seen one, but get to ride in one."

Brenna glanced around, then realized her father had left her! "I guess I do. I came with my daddy, but apparently both he and my sister forgot about me." On purpose, no doubt.

"Not a problem," he said, hurrying around to open the passenger-side door for her. "I would get lost without you."

Did the man realize he had a way with words? Did he even know that the way he said things with that exquisite hint of an accent went right to a woman's heart?

She could speak one thing and mean another, too. "I don't want you to get lost."

His dark eyes gleamed like midnight water. "Then let's go.

"Top down?"

She nodded. She needed the cold wind to make her snap out of this massive crush.

With that, he got in and cranked the motor. The car purred like a great cat. Nick shifted gears and Brenna held on for dear life, her breath caught in the cool night air. This man with all his fancy things had first reminded her of Jeffrey. But Nick Santiago was nothing like her shallow, self-centered, very ex-fiancé. As Callie had said, he seemed to be the real thing.

At least he felt real, driving this powerful machine, his hands only inches away from her. Brenna tried to focus on breathing. He was too close, way too close.

"Where am I going?" he asked.

Brenna came out of the fog surrounding her mind. "Oh, take a left at the next traffic light. Our house is a few miles out of town, on the Big Fleur Bayou. When you see the sign for Blanchard's Landing, you're there."

"What is chicken perlo?" he asked, grinning over at her.

"Well, it's chicken and rice and spices and we serve

it with corn bread and biscuits, all homemade. It's usually cooked in a big iron pot."

He hit a hand on the steering wheel. "The food down here is so good."

Brenna couldn't deny that. "But I've been to San Antonio. The food there is wonderful, too."

"Yes, and my mom is a good cook."

She wanted to know all about his family. "So you're an only child?"

He slowed the car as they reached the sign she'd mentioned, then turned into the next driveway.

"Yes." He parked the car in the long driveway leading to the white cottage and stared into the darkness. "I have been for a long time now. But I had a sister. She died when I was a teenager."

Shock hit at Brenna with the ticking of the car's cooling engine. She thought about the girl in the painting. "I'm so sorry. What happened?"

"It's complicated," he said. Then he got out and came around to open her door.

"I didn't mean to pry," Brenna said. "I'm sorry."

Nick stared down at her, his eyes shimmering dark in the moonlight over the bayou water. "It's okay. One day, I'll explain. But for now, I'd rather not discuss it."

"Then we won't." She took his hand, needing to show him some sort of comfort. "Let's go inside."

He nodded and remained quiet. But he didn't let go of her hand.

Chapter Six

⌒

Warmth enveloped Nick when he stepped inside the quaint cottage on the bayou. The house was bigger than it looked from the road. It went back a long way, starting with a big living room that led into an even bigger kitchen where paned windows and a set of French doors led to a big porch and an open view to the bayou beyond. Out on the boathouse and dock, white lights twinkled like fireflies in the night.

"Amazing," he said to Brenna as she called out to her father. "This is a nice house."

She smiled and handed him his coat back. "It's not Fleur House, but my papa built it with his own hands—and help from a lot of people, too. It started out small and grew with each daughter. Papa decided long ago that we all needed our own space."

Nick laughed at that. "So he just kept adding rooms?"

"All da way out to da water," Ramon Blanchard called from the kitchen. "Plum ran out of land."

Brenna pulled Nick toward the long white-tiled

kitchen counter. "Then he built a boathouse. We loved sleeping out there when we were growing up."

"Dat was fer your mama," Mr. Blanchard said. "She loved to sit out dere and read her 'woman novels' as she called dem." He threw his dish towel over his shoulder and held out his beefy hand to Nick. "Welcome. C'mon on in. We got plenty and den some."

Nick laughed while he caught up with Mr. Blanchard's heavy Cajun accent, then took the glass of sweet tea Callie handed him. "It sure smells great. Thanks for inviting me, Mr. Blanchard."

"It's Ramon. But most call me Papa."

"He's also Papa Noel at Christmastime," Callie said.

"I'll keep that in mind and try to stay off the naughty list," Nick replied. His gaze settled on Brenna. Her smile was small, but he caught the hint of dare in her eyes.

Mr. Blanchard's nod and mock-mean look made Nick think he might have to really be careful. A father always protected his daughters. Just the way his father had tried to protect his sister.

Callie tugged him toward the big long dining table between the kitchen and the den. "Don't look so afraid. His bark is much worse than his bite."

Brenna nodded on that. "And he forgives all us at Christmas and Easter."

Ramon let out a grunt. "It is my burden to bear, having three lovely daughters. I have to forgive and forget most every day of the week."

"And you love it," Brenna said, kissing her father on the cheek. "Now let's eat. I'm starving."

Nick waited for the women to sit, then pulled out a

chair. "This table is like a work of art. Did you build it, Ramon?"

"*Oui*. It's pure cypress. Built it for my own *mère* about fifty years ago. My papa and me, we built it together."

Nick admired the worn patina on the aged cypress planks of the long table. He imagined a lot of meals served on this mellow, dented wood. "You could feed an army on this thing."

"I've done dat, for sure," Ramon said with a belly-roll laugh. "Tonight, just us chickens."

The dinner progressed with good food and tall tales. The more Ramon Blanchard talked the more pronounced his Cajun-French became.

Brenna leaned close. "I'll have to explain most of that to you later."

Nick nodded and buttered another fat, flaky biscuit. Then he glanced over at the big stone fireplace on the long wall past the open counter. "Is that your mother?" he asked Brenna, nodding toward the portrait over the mantel of a beautiful blonde woman. She sat in a garden with the bayou behind her and cypress trees sheltering her.

"Yes," she said, the one word quieting the room. "Lila."

"Daughter Number Three painted that picture," Ramon said, his tone reverent and low but full of pride. "Bree always wanted to paint pretty pictures."

Nick shot Brenna a quick glance. "I heard someone mention that at the meeting. You didn't tell me that."

"I studied art," she said with a shrug. "Dabbling is a part of the procedure." She gave him another daring look.

"That is more than dabbling," Nick said, remembering how much he had once loved art, how he had once fancied himself an artist. He'd channeled that notion into creating and re-creating houses instead. But Brenna clearly had talent. "It's impressive."

She looked embarrassed, but her smile hid her obvious doubts. "Thank you. I am glad I painted our mother. It makes things easier now."

Everyone went quiet for a minute while Nick admired the portrait.

She'd captured the playfulness in her mother's face that spoke of the same spirit he'd seen in Callie and Brenna. He imagined Alma had some of it, too. But where Alma had darker hair and a petite frame, Callie was tall and blond, more like her mother. And Brenna seemed to possess some of both parents. A nice mix. An interesting mix.

A dangerous mix.

"More chicken and rice?" Callie asked, her knowing gaze trapping him.

"Yes." Nick took the big bowl and dipped more of the seasoned rice and tender chicken. "This is really good."

Brenna took a sip of her tea. "We have sweet potato pie for dessert."

Nick moaned. "After three biscuits, I'd better skip the pie."

"You can't do dat," Ramon said, his frown like a broken boat. "Dis pie makes people sweet. You gonna need to be sweet dealing with Daughter Number Three, trust me."

Nick laughed at that. "Maybe you're right."

He took the pie. And ate every bite.

An hour later, after they'd done the dishes, Ramon decided it was time for him to retire and Callie said she needed to get back to her own house.

Brenna watched her sister go, a look of dread mixed in with her smile. Did she not want to be alone with him? Then she turned to Nick. "Want to sit awhile?"

He checked his watch. He had a big day tomorrow and a lot of work waiting tonight. But he didn't want to leave yet.

"For a few minutes." He followed her to the big plaid sofa across from the massive hearth. "You must love coming home to this place every day."

Brenna glanced around. "I do, but I didn't like having to move back in. I love my papa, but I enjoyed being independent and out on my own." She shrugged. "I always wanted to move away from Fleur. So did Alma, but now she's changed that tune. She and Julien plan to build a house in a few years. For now, they'll be living in our *grandmère's* cottage behind Fleur Café. Alma loves that old place. I think after they build the house, she hopes to turn it into a tea room—an extension of the café but more private—for luncheons and parties."

Nick took in all the informal information she offered. "I have to say the Blanchard sisters are an enterprising bunch. And you? You wanted the big city and art? Do you still paint?"

She seemed to squirm a bit. "Not for a long time. Jeffrey—that's my ex-fiancé—convinced me that I couldn't be a good curator if I spent too much time working on my own art." She stopped, took a long sigh. "He was critical of everything I painted, so I just—"

"Gave up?" Nick wanted to throttle this Jeffrey person. But he'd given up on a lot of things himself. Being around Brenna made him wonder if he needed to go back and change some of that.

"Yes." She glanced up at her mother's portrait. "But, hey, I have more time on my hands now. Maybe I'll pick it back up. I want to paint Callie. She's the most expressive one in the bunch."

Nick got up to study the portrait. "I think you should. And you should never let anyone else talk you out of your dreams."

"Good advice," she said. "I didn't have enough confidence to fight him. I think being with him stripped me of a lot of myself, if that makes sense."

Nick nodded. "Makes perfect sense. But why did you allow that to happen?"

She looked down at her hands. "I thought if I acted the way he thought I should act, he'd love me. Isn't that the craziest notion? I was taught all about unconditional love, but I never felt that with Jeffrey. I had this image of what type of man I wanted to marry in my mind. He fit the image—on paper, but not in reality. I messed up big-time."

He turned to stare down at her, marveling at how open and honest she seemed. "And now?"

Brenna got up. "Now, I'm home and I'm safe and I might try my hand at painting again. I intend to find myself again."

"I like hearing that." He picked up his suit coat. "You know, the light in the sunroom at Fleur House lends itself to a painter's brush. Feel free to try it out— that is when the workers aren't milling around. We take Sundays off. That can be your time if you want it."

She looked shocked and grateful. "That's thoughtful of you, Nick."

"I can be thoughtful every now and then."

She smiled and walked him to the door. "Oh, that made me think about the mural. I've already called an expert I know in New Orleans. He's good at what he does, but expensive. I wanted to run that by you before I have him drive down."

"Money isn't an issue," Nick said. "Bring in your expert, bring in whatever experts you might need."

"Wow, an unlimited budget?"

"I didn't say that, but this is an estate renovation. We want everything to look rich but viewable. My client will probably sell it after a while, anyway. He travels too much to stay in one place."

"Same as you," she said, her hand on the doorknob.

Nick had lain down the law on how he liked to live, so he didn't try to deny it. "I hope I wasn't rude about that. People don't always understand." He shrugged. "And it's hard for me to explain."

"You're right, I don't understand," she said when they walked out onto the long, wide porch. "You seem to love working on homes. Why don't you have one?"

It was a valid question.

So he tried to give her a truthful answer. "I left home at an early age and just kept on moving. After a few years of hotel rooms, the construction trailer just seemed like a good idea. I've never thought much about that. Until now."

She stared up at him, her golden-green eyes questioning and confused. "I didn't think I ever wanted to come back to Fleur. Until now."

Nick didn't know what to say. "I think we're both

at a crossroad." And his seemed to be leading straight to her.

She leaned against a thick column. "Yes, I guess so. We'll see what happens, which way we both go."

A thick silence hung between them like a low, moss-draped cypress branch hanging over dark water.

"I enjoyed supper," he said, using the term her father had used. "I hope I can repay the favor one day."

"I enjoyed riding in that souped-up car," she replied. "Now go. I can tell you're eager to get to work."

"You know me already." Nick took her hand, held it there between them. "I'll see you tomorrow."

"Yes. Bright and early." She pulled away.

He wanted to bring her back. But then, she might get the impression that he wanted more.

And Nick wasn't sure he could give her more.

So he got in his car and cranked the engine.

When he turned to wave, she had already gone in the house.

Brenna woke early the next morning. She had not slept much, but she couldn't wait to get on with her new assignment. After the restraints of her job back in Baton Rouge and the constraints of trying to please Jeffrey, she felt a sense of relief in being able to try her hand at finding art for Fleur House. It would be a challenge, but it would also release all of her creative intuitions and give her days purpose.

"Mama always said we'd find our joy in our purpose," she replied to her reflection in the mirror.

She intended to do just that. She'd spent hours last night after Nick had left searching for information on Fleur House, both online and in a few of the history books her mother had loved. She was as prepared as possible for now. So she checked her white sweater and navy-blue full skirt, then threw on a strand of silver pearls and tugged on her dark gray knee-high boots. A light plaid jacket completed her look. Not too prissy but professional enough. Once she'd found all the pieces, she'd dress more casual for the installations. But she had a lot to do before that time came.

After a quick breakfast of fruit and toast, she called the mural expert in New Orleans and made arrangements for him to come to the house and see what he could do to restore the wall in the dining room. Then she printed out copies of various pieces of art, hoping to make some auction bids when the pieces were available.

She'd need to get the computer-generated charts of each room in the house so she could play with where to place each piece. Even though this was challenging, it reminded her of when she and her sisters had played with paper dolls.

Brenna smiled at the memory. Even back then, she would paint over the doll clothes to make them look better and more to her liking, which only infuriated her sisters. But Alma would cook imaginary food for the paper figures and of course, Callie would pick flowers to lay around the feet of the wobbly, thin pretend people. Funny how they all did the same things now but with real intentions and talents.

Yes, this was the real deal, Brenna reminded herself. And what a house! What a great blank canvas. She really did like this job and she liked Nick, too. A lot.

Work, Brenna. Work.

She thanked God for the opportunity and in the

same prayer, asked Him to give her the strength to focus on work.

And not on the man who'd hired her.

Nick heard saws grinding through wood. After going over the blueprints with the project foreman, he pulled on his jacket and hard hat and went out onto the wide front lawn of the property. From this spot, he had a good view of the front of the house.

The Italianate design boasted oval arches on the many balconies and porches and open arches surrounding the side portico which used to be the carriage driveway. This same pattern carried to the garages and outbuildings. He'd taken many pictures of the house, from all angles. But this morning, in the sunlight coming through the pines and old oaks, the house looked alive and glowing.

"It's smiling at us."

Nick turned to find Brenna standing a few feet away, looking all buttoned-up but ready to work.

"You think so?" he asked, motioning her from the shell-encrusted driveway to the cushiony grass.

"I'd be excited if I were getting a massive make-over," she said. Her high-heeled boots seemed to sink into the grass but she managed to make her way to him. She let out a sigh of contentment. "Even with all the flowers just about gone, this place is still beautiful." She pointed to the camellia bushes scattered through the yard. "I've tried to count those so I'll know if your men destroyed any of them."

"Oh, you want the camellia bushes to stay?"

"Not me," she said on a grin. "Callie made me promise to tell you that. She really has counted them and she knows the names of each variety—those funny scientific names. You have your winter camellias and your spring camellias and Callie loves all of them. Especially because they are 'old grown' as she likes to call them. She believes trees and bushes and blossoms can tell us stories if we listen."

Nick liked hearing about Callie and knew she'd make a great landscape director, but he especially loved listening to her sister talk—about anything at all. Brenna's accent was part Southern and part Cajun which made it endearing and enchanting.

"I love listening to your stories," he said. Then to clear up any misunderstandings, he added, "Your dad is a hoot. He has some good stories of his own."

"And spun with a few embellishments," she replied, her eyes ripe with an emotion Nick couldn't pinpoint. "We all do, I suppose."

Nick sensed she wanted to get to work. "Okay, so for now, you need to get to know the house, room by room. You have free rein, but if you are anywhere near construction, you need to wear a hard hat. Understood?"

"Yes, sir." Her burnished hair lifted in the chilly morning wind. "I thought I'd make some sketches of the focus walls in each room. And if you can give me notes and swatches on your paint samples and explain the overall style of the house, I'll have a better idea of what we're doing here."

Nick took her by the elbow. "We'll talk more about the overall theme of the renovations at lunch. I can show you the blueprints, too. I have those in my trailer."

She glanced up at him, her eyes going wide. "I'm anxious to see this famous trailer."

"It's not much, but it's home."

That statement hit him like the wind moving through the trees. He didn't really have a true home. Strolling across the lawn with Brenna, he wondered for the first time since he'd arrived in Fleur if maybe it was time for him to settle down and find one.

Chapter Seven

Nick's trailer was one part messy construction office and one part plush home away from home. It consisted of a big office filled with books and ledgers and pictures of the current project and a long desk covered with blueprints, notes and an open laptop.

Brenna glanced past the efficiency kitchen with the coffeepot and a big bowl of power bars and fruit to the combination sitting room/bedroom on the back side of the long building. The bedspread had been messily thrown toward the big pillows and the tiny room looked neat enough if she ignored the suit hanging on the door. She noticed coffee-table books on design and architecture stacked three feet high beside the bed. So Nick liked to do his homework, too. Set against the books, a picture of a beautiful dark-haired little girl caught her attention, reminding her of the portrait she'd found. His sister? Curiosity usually got Brenna in trouble, so she had to squelch the urge to dig deeper.

Turning to face him, she said, "I love what you've done with the place."

Nick grinned then offered her a chair. The only clear

chair apparently. "I'm not always this messy. Things get crazy once a project gets going."

"I can organize things for you," Brenna offered. "I'm good at that kind of thing."

He glanced around, then back at her. "Not a good idea. My foreman might flip out. He's the messy one, but it's kind of a system he has and it works for him. So, thanks, but no thanks."

Brenna sank down and tried to put the idea of a clean work environment out of her mind, right along with the image of Nick in jeans and a heavy canvas jacket and hard hat. Time to get down to business. "I think the best thing I can do for now is take it room by room on the art. I'll match the proportions by the size and scope of the rooms. I already have some ideas for the entryway and the upstairs landing."

Nick nodded, then cranked up the laptop. "Let's look at the model rooms. That way you can also see the color swatches for each room. I'll give you a thumb-drive so you'll have everything you see here."

"I had a note to ask you about that. I used computer models to set up exhibits at the museum, so I'm picturing this as a really big museum."

He motioned for her to roll her chair over close to his desk. "Not a problem. I've been working on this for six months now, so I know the rooms in and out."

Brenna wasn't surprised. Pulling out her electronic pad, she said, "It takes a lot of work to do something of this size and scope. I hope I don't disappoint you."

His dark-eyed gaze held her. "Why would you think that?"

Brenna thought it was obvious. "I've never done anything like this. A five-thousand-square-foot estate house at that, and for a mysterious owner who refuses to show his face. It's a challenge."

His gaze danced over her face. "You'll be fine. Your eyes light up whenever you start talking about this house."

She wasn't so sure. "Why do you believe in me, Nick?"

He grinned at that. "Because of that spark I see in your eyes. And both of your sisters recommended you."

"Wow." Brenna didn't know why that should bring tears to her eyes but it did. "My family has always supported my efforts."

"They believe in you, so you need to believe in yourself."

Touched, Brenna decided to be positive. Other than her papa, she'd never had a man encourage her in the way Nick had. Was that part of being the boss, or did he see something in her she wasn't even aware of herself? "Okay, enough about my concerns. I'm excited and I want this to work."

He gave her a look that seemed to say the same thing, but not exactly about this house and her professionalism. His eyes, so dark and mysterious, reminded her of the blackest bayou waters. She saw secrets there, but she was afraid to find out about those secrets. She'd let Jeffrey roll right along without being honest and that had only brought her heartache. Did she hide her head in the sand when it came to men?

Glancing toward the stack of books by his bed, she told herself this time, she would stick to the business side of things and keep her heart out of this.

"Any other questions?" Nick asked, his gaze moving over the computer screen before he looked up at her.

They sat staring at each other for a long minute, but Brenna still didn't have the answers she needed. Reminding herself about work and not obsessing over this man and his past, she looked down at her notes. "I think I'm ready, boss."

"Okay, then. Let's get on with things."

Over the next hour, Nick showed her the computer-generated models of the house, room by room, including theme and colors and a mock-up of furnishings. When he stopped to take a phone call, Brenna took more notes as the ideas poured into her head. She was involved in the work ahead, but she couldn't forget the scent of leather mixed with sawdust that surrounded Nick and this place. Nor could she forget the forlorn theme that echoed out over the tiny trailer, especially whenever she glanced toward that picture of the pretty dark-haired little girl.

Figuring Nick would tell her about his sister if he wanted her to know, Brenna started imagining things. Obviously, his sister had died and obviously, it had affected Nick in a strong way. Was he running from his grief?

This trailer spoke of a life on the run, a life unsettled and unstoppable. Why couldn't Nick stop and find some rest? Was he running from something or did he enjoy his work to the point of ignoring life?

Could she help him with that? Or should she stay clear of getting tangled with yet another career-focused man?

He hung up, then turned to her. "The designer is driving over from San Antonio for a couple of days, probably next week. You'll be working closely with Serena."

Brenna didn't know why, but she didn't like the idea of that. She'd left messages at the number Nick had given her, but had yet to hear from the mysterious Serena. "She's coming here?"

Nick smiled. "The interior designer I mentioned, yes. Serena Delrio. Top-of-the-line and very sought-after in Houston, Dallas and San Antonio."

Brenna suddenly felt small and insecure. "Sounds wonderful. What if I can't keep up?"

"Brenna, you'll work *with* her. Not for her."

"Of course." She snapped to and stood up. "It's just with an exotic name like that, she has to be…pretty and powerful, maybe hard to deal with."

He laughed. "You got all of that just from her name?"

"I'm imagining things," she replied. "I'm still nervous about the whole art and design thing. But it'll be good to work with an expert even though she's so busy she hasn't returned my calls."

"She's a beauty and yes, she stays busy," he readily admitted. "But bear with her. She'll get around to us in time. We've know each other for a long time. And yes, she can be a pistol, but I'm pretty sure you can handle her."

"Hmm." She let that filter through the haze of curiosity covering her brain. "This should be interesting."

He gave her a look that told her way more than words. "Oh, yes." Then he grabbed two hard hats. "C'mon, let's see what the crew's done in the kitchen this morning."

Brenna couldn't miss the excitement in his words. "You love this, don't you?"

He nodded, pushed a bright yellow hat on her head. "*Sí.* It's what I do. Why wouldn't I love it?"

Brenna didn't answer that rhetorical question. She didn't have to. This wasn't just his livelihood. This was his life.

And she didn't see much room in that life for anyone else.

Especially her.

"Serena. Even her name sounds beautiful."

Callie stopped walking down the long, wide middle aisle of Callie's Corner, her garden and landscaping nursery, and stared across at Brenna. "You have a nice name and you're cute."

Brenna gritted her teeth. She'd worked with Nick all last week and she'd gone back to Fleur House over the weekend. They'd talked a lot, laughed a lot and discussed the house from every aspect and angle. Now she had to worry about the next step in the process. "Cute won't cut it with someone who answers to the name Serena. She won't return my phone calls. I think I'm in over my head."

Elvis, the huge mutt of a dog her sister had taken in after her divorce, came traipsing up the aisle toward them, his big fluffy tail hitting at colorful mums and sweeping palm fronds. He woofed a hello at Brenna.

"Hello, you big baby," she said, holding him away. "Elvis, love me tender and don't mess up my clothes, okay?" Leaning over to pet the woolly dog, she glanced up at Callie. "Well, what do you think?"

Callie gave her a twisted smile. "I think you need to grow a backbone. It's not like you to cower in terror. You don't even know this person yet. Why borrow trouble?"

Brenna stood back up, dog hair on her hands and skirt. Elvis woofed again, clearly not finished saying hello. When the dog tried to jump up on her again, his wet paws inches from her shirt, Brenna held him away. "Elvis, go play in the fish pond and relive *Blue Hawaii*."

He glanced at her, tongue wagging, glanced at Callie then dropped and took off toward the back of the vast property.

Callie's frown didn't quite meet her eyes. "Great. He chases the koi. I've told you that."

"And he never actually goes all the way into the water," Brenna replied. "Maybe I'm like Elvis. I just enjoy staying on the edge, safe and secure."

Callie actually snorted. "You seriously need to dive right in and do the job you were hired to do. You always panic about things you're not sure about and then you somehow manage to become the perfectionist you are and do such a good job everyone wants to be you."

Brenna had to agree with her on the first part. "You're right, I am in a panic. I'm calling Alma to see what she thinks."

Callie grabbed Brenna's phone. "You will do no such thing. She's on her honeymoon. Not a good time for your theatrics."

Brenna frowned. "Theatrics? But Alma handles my meltdowns better than you do. She sometimes agrees with me."

"She talks you down so you can figure things out for yourself," Callie retorted, her fingers moving through an angel wing begonia. When she heard barking, she took off. "Great. Elvis is harassing my fish. Thanks."

Brenna wasn't through whining. She stared at a beautiful Japanese maple tree, wondering why her organization skills never made it to her love life.

"Wait," she said to the tree. "This is *not* my love life. This is my job. A temporary job that could lead to a bigger, better job." Instead of going into a panic about an interior designer named Serena, she should be thanking her lucky stars that she had this opportunity. Shaking her head, she whispered to the tree, "I hate it when my sister is right."

The tree sat still and regal, regarding her with a whisper of wind. Brenna stared through the branches toward the sky. *Lord, help me to stay focused and on target. And help me to remember what, not who, is the target.*

A butterfly fluttered by in shades of brown and gold.

Brenna tugged her notebook out of her tote and sketched the butterfly. Then she turned to see Callie laughing at Elvis as the big dog raced back and forth in front of the koi pond. The smile on her sister's face was so full of joy and contentment, Brenna had to capture it.

She quickly drew Callie's face and filled in her hair. She could see her sister sitting in a garden, wearing a pretty dress, with that smile on her face. Brenna wanted to paint that joy. She wanted Callie to find that joy again after overcoming breast cancer and a failed marriage.

She stopped, gasped and then grinned. "I think I've found myself again, *Mère,*" she said to the sky. Her heart swelled with love and gratitude.

Callie came back down the aisle. "What are you up to now?"

Brenna grinned. "I'm all better now. I've got to get home. I want to do some research and I want to get out my brush sets and clean them."

Callie squealed so loud that Elvis woofed a bark in reply. "You're going to start painting again?"

"I think I am," Brenna said.

"What made you decide?"

She smiled at her sister. "Let's just say a butterfly fluttered by at exactly the right time."

Callie shrugged. "At least it got your mind off that Serena woman."

Brenna turned and waved. "Yes. Yes, it did."

For now, Brenna thought. Tomorrow might be different.

Brenna pulled up the long driveway to Fleur House on Tuesday morning and immediately noticed the sleek black luxury car that sat like a slinking panther next to Nick's work truck.

"Okay, so she looks *so* Houston," Brenna mumbled before she got out of her squat little economy car. "I look Baton Rouge, so I can deal."

Taking a breath, Brenna asked for strength and wisdom. *And dear Lord, don't let me bring out the drama.*

Walking up onto the limestone loggia at the entryway to the house, Brenna smoothed her denim pencil skirt and adjusted her plaid wool wrap. Brown, pointy-toed flat-heeled boots completed her work ensemble.

No drama. All business.

Following the sound of workmen talking and tools tinkling, Brenna marveled at the house all over again.

This place would be a showpiece once it was completely renovated.

"Brenna, there you are."

She turned into the kitchen at the back of the long central hallway to find Nick standing next to a voluptuous older woman with rich black hair worn in a chignon. Dripping with gold jewelry, the woman looked as sophisticated as any art buyer Brenna had ever dealt with.

"Good morning," Brenna said, wondering who the visitor was. His mother maybe? Surely not Serena?

Nick stepped toward Brenna and tugged her into what would become the breakfast room. "Brenna, I want you to meet Serena. Serena Delrio, meet Brenna Blanchard."

"Lovely, *sí*," Serena said, smiling up at Nick while she took Brenna's hand and held it in hers. "Nicholas has told me so much about you, Brenna."

Brenna almost giggled in relief. "You're Serena?"

Serena looked confused, then a soft smile crested her wrinkle-free face. "*Sí.* I'm Nicholas's aunt. But sometimes he calls me *Abuela,* because I helped my younger sister raise the boy."

Brenna's gaze landed on Nick. He shrugged and smiled. "I told you you'd love her."

Brenna nodded. "It's nice to meet you, Ms. Delrio. Nick has told me a lot about you, too." But clearly, not enough.

Serena chuckled. "Call me Serena, please. I'm thinking he didn't tell you *everything* about me."

Nick grinned. "Where would be the fun in that, *Abuela?*"

Serena said something in rapid Spanish. "I think

you let this poor girl believe I was a tyrant. Of course, I'm not." She crossed her arms. "However, I am a perfectionist."

Brenna breathed another sigh of relief. "Then I can assure you, we'll get along just fine."

Nick grinned at both of them. "I told you this would be interesting." He turned to Brenna. "My aunt has been decorating houses for close to thirty years."

"I started out as a gofer for a large firm in Houston and worked my way up. I went to design school on the company's dime. When the owner retired, I took over. He's still a silent partner, but I'm *la jefa*."

"The boss," Nick explained.

"Got it," Brenna said, not so relieved now. Nick's aunt might not be young and tempting, but the woman was stylish, formidable and…intimidating. In an *abuela* kind of way.

Serena slapped her massive black leather satchel up onto the dusty counter. "Now, where do I find a good cup of coffee around here?"

Nick's eyes filled with panic, but Brenna took charge. "The coffee in Nick's trailer is more like swamp mud. But at my sister Alma's café in town, the coffee is rich and dark and good. I'd be glad to buy you a cup."

Serena's throaty laugh echoed out over the sound of hissing saws and heavy hammers. "Lead the way, *querida*."

"Hey, what about work?" Nick called.

"We are working," Serena answered. "You go on with your tearing down and rebuilding. We'll figure out the good stuff."

"That's what scares me," Nick said.

Brenna almost felt sorry for the man. Now he had two very opinionated women to deal with. And she had a feeling there *would* be drama. Lots of drama.

Chapter Eight

Brenna took Serena back behind the Fleur Café so she could see the Little Fleur Bayou and Alma's quaint cottage. Even though winter was coming, the walking trail along the bayou was still colorful and full of life. Palmetto palms swayed in the wind near the water's edge. Callie and her garden club friends had placed colorful pots of mums along the trail. She'd added pumpkins and hay bales here and there, giving the whole town a festive fall look. A chickadee frolicked in a red-leaf swamp maple while a snowy egret showed off underneath the vivid gold and rich red of a tallow tree.

"It's beautiful," Serena said. "Different from Houston and San Antonio." She held her coffee cup with both hands and breathed in the crisp air. "The cypress trees are lovely. I never knew they turned in the fall."

Brenna lifted her head. "The leaves are like old golden lace, or at least that's what my mother used to call them when they'd cushion the swamps. They completely disappear back into the earth. The winter trees stay draped in gray moss, but then in the spring, new leaves sprout out green."

"We must tell Callie to plant some cypress trees in the gardens at Fleur House, then," Serena said before taking a sip of her coffee. "And maybe more of those gorgeous maples, too."

"The old cypress trees that have been there for centuries are located down by the bayou," Brenna replied. "They're covered with Spanish moss. But I'm sure Callie will love to plant some fresh ones near the old fish pond and foundation in the back garden. And she loves swamp maples, too. She'll make sure the garden represents all of our plants and foliage."

"Good idea." Serena saw an old wooden bench underneath a moss-draped live oak. "Would you like to sit before we get back to work?"

Brenna nodded. "Yes. I've sure enjoyed talking to you about Fleur House. You already know as much about the house as I do."

Serena did her throaty laugh. "*Sí.* I love old estates. Such beauty. I cannot wait to get busy on decorating Fleur House. We'll have such fun together. We get the good job, traveling around for art and furnishings. I love my work."

Brenna liked Nick's aunt. "I have a confession to make," she said on a sheepish grin. "Nick didn't tell me you were his aunt. I imagined a young, attractive woman he'd probably dated or intended to date. Not that that mattered, except I felt threatened."

"I'm not young and attractive?" Serena quipped.

Brenna didn't know what to say until the older woman started laughing. "Nick has always had a mischievous side," she said. "I'm not so young and not so attractive, and I'm certainly not a threat. But why would you worry about such things?"

Brenna relaxed a little bit. "You are gorgeous and yes, attractive," she quickly clarified. "But you're also impressive. I can't wait to work with you." Then she shrugged. "I just came off a bad relationship, so my confidence, even in my career, is shaky."

"I see." Serena set down her empty coffee cup. "You worried that you'd be distracted by all the flirting and innuendos between Nick and this young, attractive woman?"

"That and what if she didn't like the art I wanted to place? What if she saw me as a threat to her and Nick? Silly things that aren't even important."

Serena's vivid dark eyes brightened. "Maybe not so silly. Have you already fallen for my nephew?"

That question threw Brenna. "No. I mean, he's hunky and intriguing, but I don't need a rebound relationship."

"Has he pursued you?"

"Pursued? No, we hardly know each other. And I made it clear that this would be a working relationship. So did he."

Very clear. So why was she telling his aunt all about it?

"Clear? Nick? That boy can't see the forest for the trees sometimes."

Brenna thought about that. "Actually, I haven't said that to him outright. I've mostly told myself that, in front of the mirror."

Serena cackled at that comment. "I'm not so worried about you, *querida*. But Nick, he hides his heart so well. He might try to persuade you, but then in the end, he'll be the one to bolt."

"I've already realized that," Brenna said. "And trust

me, that's why I talk to myself in the mirror. I can't go back into that pattern of my falling for the worldly, successful man who keeps things too close to the chest. Besides, that only happens in books or movies. Not in real life." She shook her head. "I don't know why I even brought this up, except I want to assure you that I'm sticking to business."

"Pity," Serena said. She stood and touched a hand to Brenna's shoulder. "Nick could use someone like you in his life. He blames himself for things he had no control over."

Was Serena referring to his sister's death? Brenna almost asked what things, but she refused to pry about Nick behind his back. If the man wanted to tell her about his past, he'd do it in his own good time. She had to respect that he wasn't ready to talk about his issues, even if she'd vowed to never fall for another secretive man. Meantime, she had work to do. "Are you ready to go back to the house?"

Serena let out a contented sigh. "I suppose so. I'll be staying at Fleur Inn. I've already booked a room, but I can check in later. I travel light—just one big bag."

Brenna almost asked Serena to stay at her house, but that might be awkward with her papa coming and going at all hours.

"The inn is very comfortable and most of the rooms have a good view of both the big and the tiny bayou. If you need anything, let me know."

"I'll be fine," Serena replied. "But we might both get fired if we don't get back to the task at hand, *si?*"

"So right on that," Brenna said. "Let's go get our stuff and get busy."

Together, they strolled back up to the café and entered through the back door.

Winnie was behind the counter, refilling the salad and pie cases. "Want dessert?"

Brenna glanced at Serena. "We could carry some back to the workers."

Serena chuckled. "The friendliest place on earth. And so generous!"

Winnie walked over to the glass-front cooler. "I have a fresh coconut pie and I just made a batch of oatmeal cookies."

"Both," Brenna replied. "I'll take some plates and plastic forks, too. And put it all on my tab. I'll be here later to work it off."

"Tell me you don't have two jobs?" Serena asked, her eyebrows quirking.

"Just until my sister Alma returns." She shrugged and looked sheepish. "I haven't really helped that much, not since Nick hired me, anyway."

"You do what you can, when you can." Winnie nodded. "Got it down on the order. And remind the construction crew that we can bring lunch out to them anytime if you call ahead and give us a count. Mollie and Pierre like to deliver on-site orders."

Mollie was a waitress here at the café and Pierre, who was Julien's younger brother, worked part-time here in the afternoons after he finished his welding job at the shipyard.

"They're saving up for their wedding in a year or so," she explained after telling Serena about the young couple and their recent struggles.

"I'm sure Nick and his crew will order a lot of lunches," Serena replied.

"Good idea," Brenna said. "I can help deliver when Pierre's not around. A win-win situation."

Serena winked at Winnie. "In oh, so many ways."

"Tia Serena likes you," Nick told Brenna the next day.

Serena was in the house, measuring windows with some of the construction workers. Brenna and Nick were back in the trailer, going over some changes that had to be made in the staircase to accommodate a powder room in the central hallway. Nick wanted art pieces centered on each landing and there were three of them with wide staircases between each. But he also wanted to put a roomy downstairs powder room below the first landing. Brenna suggested a small table with a smaller painting over it near the door to the powder room. Nick seemed to agree on that idea.

"I like her, too," Brenna said. "We had a great lunch. Now that I've gotten to know her, I'm sure we'll work together just fine. She's a delight."

Nick gave her that look that held everything back while seeing everything she was trying to hide. "I never had any doubt. My aunt is one of the kindest, most faithful women I've ever known."

Shocked at his sincerity, Brenna ventured forth. "Do you have faith, Nick?"

He dropped the papers he'd been going over and stared out the tiny trailer window. "I have faith in things I can see and touch—like this house and my crew. I have faith in the people I care about, like my aunt and my parents. I have faith in you because I saw your passion the first time we talked about art."

Brenna couldn't stop herself. "And God? Do you have faith in God?"

He looked down, a frown darkening his face. "Is that important?"

"It is to me. I couldn't have gotten through my mother's illness and death without faith."

"And yet, it didn't save her. God didn't save her."

"No. He healed her in His own way, though."

"And this brings you comfort."

"Most days," she replied, wondering why she had even dared to bring this up.

He moved close, his face a dark mask of disdain. "And other days?"

"Other days, I miss my mama so much I ache with the pain and I hate the unfairness of it."

He stared at her for a long time, his eyes going ebony with an emotion that caused Brenna's heart to race. "Those days are the worst," he said on a whisper. Then he glanced at the old clock on the wall. "Time to go home."

Brenna glanced around. "I guess it is, for me, at least. I'll swing by the café and help Winnie for a couple of hours. That's part of my home."

"And me? I guess I should head home, huh?"

She saw the twist of humor on his face. "You're already home, right?"

Nick's smile was sharp and quick. "Yes, I am."

Brenna gathered her things and headed toward the door. Nick followed her, his hand automatically reaching out to guide her down the steps. "I'll see you tomorrow."

Brenna turned once she was on solid ground. "Oh, I just realized it's Wednesday night. Potluck at the church. You're always welcome to come. I think your aunt said she'd be there. She wants to meet everyone."

He rubbed a hand down his chin. "I have a lot of work."

"Of course." She turned to leave. But then she turned around to stare back up at him. "If you change your mind—"

"I won't."

With that, he shut the door and left her standing there in the gloaming.

Nick sat down to work, but his mind couldn't focus on the blueprints and construction reports on his desk. He needed to check on the permits and work on the purchase orders.

And yet, he couldn't get the scent of flowers out of his head. He inhaled and smelled the sweetness that Brenna had left behind. Getting up to head to the kitchen, Nick opened the small refrigerator and found a leftover piece of coconut pie.

He slammed the door and turned to lean against it. "Why does everyone around here love pie so much?"

And why did this tiny town always seem to congregate at the church?

He knew the answer to that one, of course. The church brought them comfort and companionship and…hope. Things he'd shunned for a long, long time now.

Brenna had no right to do this to him. No right to ask him about his faith. What did she know about his pain?

She lost her mother.

And you lost your sister.

She knows about pain.

"But not my pain," he said out loud.

Then he turned and pulled out the pie.

Dinner.

"I invited Nick to come, but he had work to do."

Serena listened to Brenna while they walked through the receiving line. "I'm sure he did. My nephew is driven."

Brenna took that to mean "The boy is stubborn and tightly wound. He won't budge."

"Hey, Papa's here," Callie said as she hurried by Brenna. "I have to check on the lasagna."

"Need help?"

Callie shook her head. "No. You have a guest."

"I could help, too," Serena offered.

"Nonsense," Brenna said. "Callie is right. You're our guest."

"I enjoyed the devotional," Serena replied. "Your minister seems like a good man."

"The best," Brenna replied. "Reverend Guidry was right there with us when Mama got so sick. He stood by with us through her death and after. He's like a rock to us."

Serena glanced back over her shoulder. "You have a strong church family."

"Yes." Brenna didn't tell Serena that she'd all but abandoned that family when she moved to Baton Rouge. "It's good to be back in the fold."

Serena looked as if she wanted to say more, but hesitated.

"There's Daughter Number Three," Brenna's papa said behind her.

Brenna turned and grinned. "Are you trying to cut line, Papa?"

Her robust daddy chuckled and smiled over at Serena. "Maybe. I see we have a lovely guest tonight."

Serena actually batted her eyelashes. "*Si.* I'm Serena Delrio, Nicholas Santiago's aunt."

"Is that a fact?" Papa's interested expression was almost comical. "Brenna, where are your manners? Aren't you gonna introduce us?"

"Uh, Papa, Serena just introduced herself. Serena, this is my papa, Ramon Blanchard."

Ramon extended his meaty hand to Serena. Instead of shaking her hand, however, he held it and almost bowed over it. "So nice to meet you. So glad to have you here tonight."

Serena's smile said it all. And so did Papa's antics. Her daddy was flirting with Nick's aunt.

"Callie?" Brenna called, her hands suddenly sweaty. "I… I need to see you in the kitchen. Now."

Her sister put down the plate of French bread she'd carried to the buffet table and hurried into the kitchen.

"I'll be right back," Brenna told Serena and her daddy.

But neither was listening. Papa got in line behind Serena and explained the various Cajun dishes to her, and all with a smile on his face.

"What's the matter?" Callie said, her eyebrows shooting up.

"It's Papa," Brenna replied. "Look at him."

Callie took a covert glance out the pass-through window.

"He's in line, getting a meal."

"Look at him again and watch what he does each time he looks up at Nick's aunt."

Callie squinted and watched, then gasped. "Is our daddy flirting?"

"Yes," Brenna said. "He can't do that. He's not supposed to do that."

Callie looked again, then grinned big. "Says who?"

Brenna hit a palm on the old Formica counter. "Says me. I don't think it's right."

"Who are we to judge?" Callie asked, shrugging.

Brenna couldn't shrug this off. "I'm not judging. I'm just not comfortable with this."

Callie leaned close. "It's not about your happiness. If that woman makes our papa smile, then we need to leave them alone."

But Brenna couldn't do that. She wouldn't make a scene, but she'd sure have a talk with her daddy later.

And maybe Serena, too.

Callie must have sensed her intent. "Do not say anything, Bree. They're just talking."

"I won't embarrass you or them," Brenna said. "But I will talk to Papa later."

"Just be considerate," Callie said. "Please."

"I will."

She turned to go to the back of the line just as a few feet away a side door opened.

And in walked Nick Santiago.

Chapter Nine

Nick saw Brenna and walked toward her, all the while telling himself he only came to visit with his aunt.

Brenna's smile froze on her face. Was she mad because he'd turned her down earlier? Or was she upset that he'd shown up here, after all?

"Hola," he said, his discomfort making him itchy and nervous. "I'm a little late, but I'm hungry."

"You came to the right place, then," Brenna said. "We have lasagna, made with crawfish just for fun. And bread and salad and all kinds of side dishes."

"Can't wait." He saw his aunt with Brenna's daddy. "What's with those two?"

Brenna looked toward the round table where they'd settled with some other church members. "Well, they seem to have hit it off. My papa is a gentleman, so he probably felt obligated to make your aunt feel welcome."

"And my aunt is a lady, so she must have felt obligated to allow him that courtesy."

"Right."

Nick wasn't buying it. Brenna didn't look excited

about her daddy sitting with his aunt. "You don't approve?"

"What's to approve? I'm not in charge of my daddy."

"But you think you should be?"

She shrugged and grabbed a big empty plate. "Somebody has to watch out for him."

Nick lifted his own plate. "And who looks out for you?"

"Me?" She grabbed a slab of buttered bread. "I've always been able to take care of myself."

Nick could believe that. She seemed capable. But did she have a clue that she was so obviously lonely and heartbroken?

"But you came home."

She turned, the lasagna spatula in her hand. "Yes, I came home because I was tired and burned-out and laid off and frustrated. Home is where I come when I need to get away from everything else."

Nick thought about that for a minute. "See, I'm the opposite. I move on to the next job and don't worry too much about getting away from everything."

"Really?" She slapped a big slab of steaming lasagna onto his plate. "So you'd rather run away from home than let someone see your weaknesses?"

He took his plate, winked at her then whispered in her ear, "I don't have any weaknesses."

He was rewarded with a huffy sigh behind him as he headed toward his smiling aunt.

Callie stared at Brenna so hard that Brenna fairly sizzled. "What?" she growled to her older sister.

"You're doing the drama-queen thing. Not very becoming."

"I am not. I'm tired and I ate too much lasagna."

"And two pieces of bread and four snickerdoodles."

Brenna glared back at her sister. "But who's counting?"

Callie ignored that and leaned close. "And already, you're mad at your new boss. That's been oh, almost two weeks of work, tops."

Brenna looked over at Nick. He raised his plastic cup of tea in a salute. "Great meal, ladies."

Papa nodded his agreement. "And great company, too." He smiled so big at Serena that Brenna wondered if his crowned teeth were going to burst.

"Thank you," Callie replied when Brenna didn't respond. "Mrs. LaBorde and her sewing circle had kitchen duty tonight. But I miss Alma's cooking. She ordered Winnie to take it easy while she's away because Winnie is running the café."

"Daughter Number Two—always thinking of others," Papa said, his hands on his rounded stomach. "Next week, our Alma will be back and then it will be gumbo night."

"And she's now a married woman," Brenna said, surprising the whole table. "Mrs. Julien LeBlanc."

"Did somebody mention my brother?" Pierre said from behind Brenna. He and his girlfriend, Mollie, better known as Pretty Mollie, were helping to clear the tables.

"We miss them," Callie replied, smiling at Mollie. "The café stays busy."

Mollie nodded. "But Winnie does a great job of keeping us all on our toes. She doesn't mess around."

"You young folk need that kind of authority," Papa

said, but his smile was indulgent. "Have you met Nick's aunt Serena?"

"I met her at the café," Mollie said, waving across the table at Serena. "Pierre, this is Miss Serena, Nick's aunt. I told you about Nick, remember?"

Pierre reached out to shake Nick's hand. "I talked to him the other day. I might help do some of the welding around the house, if he needs me."

Nick gave Brenna a quick glance, then nodded. "I can always use experienced welders. I also hired some of those buddies you brought by the other day when I had the open call for jobs. I appreciate it."

"So do they," Mollie replied, slapping Pierre on the arm.

Papa grinned up at them. "I'm proud of you, Pierre. And I'm sure your *maman* is, too."

Pierre squirmed and tried to look sullen, but it didn't work. "She's waving at me now. Guess I'd better go see what she wants."

Nick laughed as they gathered dishes and hurried away. "I remember that age." He looked down at his plate.

Serena leaned back in her chair. "So do I. Thought your poor mama was going to have a breakdown."

"I did give her and daddy cause for a lot of worry," Nick replied. "I'm surprised they're still speaking to me."

The table went quiet while Brenna wondered with a burn that surpassed the tangy crawfish lasagna what had shaped Nick into the man he'd become. He was obviously successful and well-respected. His work crew hung on his every word and worked hard. But he also had a brooding quality that probably scared people away. Especially women.

Maybe her, she told herself. Or she'd be wise to realize that. She wondered about his sister and what had happened. Maybe Serena would tell her the truth, but she'd rather hear it from Nick.

Before she knew it, everyone had left the table and she was sitting there staring across at Nick.

"What are you thinking?" he asked. He got up to come around and sit next to her.

Brenna blinked, wondering what to say to him. "I was concerned earlier about Papa and your aunt. But I think I've decided I like the idea of their being friends. Papa hasn't smiled like that in a very long time."

"You can handle that, really?" His dark eyes told her he didn't believe her.

"I can. I know I'm bossy and interfering, but I also want my papa to be happy. I'd be selfish to stand in the way of that."

He laughed, then chewed on a chunk of crushed ice. "Relax. They've only just met. I think it will all work out."

Maybe that was a hint for her to back off on him, too.

"You think so?"

He touched a finger to her hair, then dropped his hand back onto his lap. "I think everything will work out for the best."

Brenna had to know. "Why did you decide to come to dinner?"

He shook his head. "I ate the last of the coconut pie but I needed more." His gaze swept over her face. "I was still hungry."

Brenna's pulse went up a notch, the beating against her temple merging with the shivers of heat moving through her system. "And now?"

He got up. "Let's go outside."

She glanced around, saw Callie giving her a questioning look. Her sister nodded and pointed to the doors. "Go," Callie mouthed.

"What about your aunt?"

"She knows her way back to the inn across the street."

"Or Papa will make sure she gets home."

"Right."

They went out the same side door he'd entered earlier.

Once they were alone underneath an ancient magnolia tree, she asked, "What's the matter, Nick? Can't breathe in there?"

He laughed. "I just needed some air."

Brenna pushed at her hair and adjusted her wrap. "It was a bit stifling inside. We had a big crowd tonight."

He looked back at the glowing lights on the church porch. "It's a welcoming place and I'm sorry about earlier. I didn't mean to disrespect your church or your faith."

"I understand." She waited, hoping he'd open up.

"Wanna walk for a while?"

Brenna knew she wasn't going to get much more out of the man. And what did it matter? He would only be here for a short time. Once the house was done, he'd pack up that trailer and drive away, off to another challenge.

And he'd forget all about her.

They walked along the piers and docks surrounding

the Big Fleur Bayou that was part of the Intracoastal Waterway. Brenna had grown up walking these trails and boardwalks. But tonight, with Nick beside her, everything looked new and mysterious.

Because she was with a new and mysterious man.

"We have to work together," Nick said, taking her hand in his. "I tell myself that, but—"

"You already regret hiring me?"

"No, not at all. You've been a big help these last few days. And you're a lot better looking than most of the construction crew. But I need you to understand... I don't normally react to women the way I've reacted to you."

Brenna's heart did a little bouncing flip. "Is that a good or bad reaction?"

He stopped underneath a tall palm tree and turned to stare down at her. "Both."

Brenna knew this was a defining moment in their fledging relationship. She decided to let him off the hook. "I don't expect anything from you, Nick. We have a working relationship. Nothing more."

"No, nothing more," he said. "It's better that way, I think." His tone sounded final while his eyes told her he wanted something more.

Brenna waited, wondering what she should do next. Turn and run. Stay and fight. Accept? Be professional and shake his hand? Forget work and go for the romance?

No. She knew how that would end. She needed this job more than she needed another brooding, hard-to-understand man in her life.

Nick lifted his hand, his fingers trailing through her bangs. "You should wear your hair down more often."

She smiled to hide the warmth shivering down her spine. "Is that a work requirement?"

"No, that's a Nick requirement. But then, that's part of the problem. I shouldn't be making such requests. It's distracting."

"To me or you?"

He repeated a word he'd used earlier. "Both."

Brenna had to smile at that. "I don't want to distract you. I want to make this restoration the best possible."

"So do I," he said. He held his hand in her hair.

Brenna felt the warmth and strength of his touch through her skin, through her heart. "Then we shouldn't worry about the rest, right?"

"Right." He pulled her close. "I just need to clear up one thing."

Brenna didn't know how to read this man. His eyes were shimmering and inky like the bayou waters. His smile was secretive and compelling, like the vast swamps that stretched to the Gulf. His touch was like the wind, both cool and warm at the same time.

"Nick?"

He leaned down and kissed her, the touch of his mouth on hers drawing her, molding her, branding her. He tasted like the mint tea from Alma's café. He stopped, his lips grazing hers, waiting, testing.

Brenna's mouth touched his and held tight. He responded by taking her into his arms. For a few precious seconds, she was out in that vast water, floating underneath a crescent moon, her life complete and at peace.

He pulled back to stare down at her, his eyes black with a new awareness. "Well, that didn't work."

"What was that?" she asked between quick breaths.

"That was me, trying to get you out of my head."

"And it didn't work?"

"Not so much."

"What do we do now?"

Brenna knew what she wanted to do. She wanted to kiss him again, but he wanted a working relationship, not a love affair.

"We keep on at it. We get the job done. That's all we can do." He touched his hand to her face. "That's all I can offer, Brenna."

She pulled away. "Relax. I wasn't expecting anything more."

He stared down at her and then dropped his hand away. "I shouldn't have kissed you."

Anger colored the night and hid her embarrassment and disappointment. "Then why did you?"

"I thought this…feeling…would burn itself out if I did."

"But that didn't work for you?"

"No." He turned and leaned over the iron railing and stared down into the water. "It only made this worse."

She understood what the man was trying to say. "*This* being you and me, kissing, being aware of each other. This won't help your goal—to restore this house and move on, right?'

He pivoted toward her. "Right. I have to do my job and I have obligations. I need you to understand."

"What I understand is that you just kissed me and now you're regretting that to the point that I'm insulted."

He looked shocked, then sheepish. "I didn't intend to insult you. I… I enjoyed kissing you. A lot."

"But you can't do it again because it will interfere with your carefully controlled plan, which is to do your job and then hook up your little trailer and get on down the road."

"Yes," he said, trying to reach for her again. "You mess with my head, Brenna. You mess with all of my carefully controlled plans. I'm not sure how to handle you."

Brenna had enough. She hadn't exactly thrown herself at him. "I get it, Nick. But like you said, we need to relax. This will all work itself out. You don't need to worry. I'm a big girl. I know the rules. And I don't spend every waking breath pining away for you. I don't really know you and I'm pretty sure that's the way you want to keep it. Because you don't want me to know you. You don't want the Lord to know you. That's why you didn't want to come to church. You felt exposed and vulnerable and afraid. And now, to make things worse, you kissed me when you really didn't want to. I understand."

"You don't understand," he said, anger making his accent more pronounced. "You will never understand."

"Probably not, but that doesn't mean I can't mind my own business and do my job. No more kissing the boss for me."

She pivoted to head back to her car. The wind had turned cold, but the shivers crawling down her back weren't coming from the cold air. This coldness poured over her heart with a solid, freezing pain. Nick Santiago didn't know how to love anyone else. Because he couldn't love himself.

Brenna heard footsteps behind her, heard him call her name. But she wasn't going to turn back. She wouldn't let this man break her heart so soon after Jeffrey had hurt her so badly.

"Help me, Lord," she whispered to the night. She still had a lot of spiritual growing to do. But falling back into a destructive pattern wouldn't help that growth.

Nick was a temptation. A temptation she had to avoid.

But the test would be working with him every day while she tried to overcome that way he made her feel.

"Brenna?" he called behind her. "Are you all right?"

She turned at her car. "I'm fine, Nick. I'll be okay. I think you need to ask yourself that question, though." She pulled her keys out and unlocked the door. "Tell your aunt good-night for me. I'll see you tomorrow."

She got in and sped away before he could answer. But his lonely shadow stood in the night, silhouetted by a bayou moon. She couldn't get that image out of her head.

Chapter Ten

The last week of October went by in a blur for Brenna. She hadn't been out to Fleur House much this week because she had a copy of the layout and she and Serena had gone over the color schemes for the main downstairs rooms and all of the bedrooms and baths. Serena would coordinate the decor of each room with Brenna, so that together they could create rooms that pleased both Nick and the new owner. Most of that could be done online and with lots of phone conversations for now.

She could shop and bid for art pieces online and have them ordered and ready when the rooms were completely finished. Because she had so many contacts, she'd already planned a trip to New Orleans and a weekend back in Baton Rouge to shop for interesting items and pieces. Callie and Alma had jumped on the New Orleans trip, wanting to make it a sister act. That was fine with Brenna as long as they let her do her job. When she'd asked Serena to go with her to Baton Rouge, Nick's aunt had clapped her hands together in glee.

"We can combine Christmas shopping with work. A perfect trip."

Brenna had to admit she really loved Nick's Tia Serena. Serena was a combination of Earth Mother and a flamboyant, eclectic "crazy aunt." Everyone should have somebody like Serena in their family, Brenna decided. Whether Nick called her *Tia* or *Abuela,* Brenna could tell how close they were.

Her papa might agree with that because he and Serena had spent a lot of time together over the past few days.

Now if she could only get along so well with the nephew. While their working relationship was polite and above reproach, something had shifted after Nick had tried to kiss her out of his mind.

She couldn't get him out of her mind.

And from the way she'd spot him staring at her, Brenna was pretty sure he hadn't managed to put her out of his thoughts, either. But they were both too stubborn to explore that little problem. So they worked— sometimes apart, sometimes together.

She'd hated to see Serena leave yesterday.

Serena had not divulged what had happened to Nick's sister, but she had given Brenna a parting warning about that one. "He's a brooder. He hurts, but hides his pain behind his work. He's driven, Brenna. Driven by regret and an unforgiving mind-set. He needs the love of Christ back in his heart. We can't put it there for him. He has to find it on his own. But we can certainly pray for him."

And so that's what Brenna was trying to do. Pray for Nick every day, while she prayed for her family and her own scorched heart. "I don't know, Lord. This is new and different and I don't remember praying this much for Jeffrey."

Maybe she should have. Or maybe Nick was different from Jeffrey, after all. Remembering how her mother had comforted her once after a high school breakup, Brenna thought about her mother's reassuring words.

"God puts people in our paths for a reason, belle. It's not your time to fall in love. You're young still. When the time is right, you'll know because it will be in God's plan for you."

Maybe, maybe. Or maybe she was reading all the signs wrong.

So here she sat on a Friday afternoon, out on the screened porch of her papa's house, her home, her safe place. Shuffling through her files, Brenna shut down her laptop and stared out at the beginnings of a brilliant sunset over the water. Fleur was known for throwing festivals in spring, summer, fall and winter. Tonight was the Harvest Festival at the church. It would spill out onto the main street through town, the street that followed the big bayou. Vendors would put out their wares and Alma, bless her heart, would cook up some of her famous gumbo. Brenna expected even more crowds of tourists for that because Alma had partnered with the famous chef and newspaper columnist Jacob Sonnier to mass-produce her gumbo to supermarkets across the South.

"Another hot night on the bayou in good ol' Fleur," Brenna said into the wind. Out on the water, a crappie jumped and splashed while blue jays chirped and fussed in the nearby swamp maple. "I need to go get some of that gumbo," she told the noisy little birds. "Pronto."

And she wouldn't worry about Nick and his Friday-night plans. She could picture him in that drab trailer, poring over blueprints and permits, his laptop buzzing with a glow of churning battery power, his fingers moving in a dance across the keyboard. He might look up and out at the big house that was slowly changing into a fine estate. He might even wonder what it would be like to have such a home or any home at all.

And he might even think of her.

Maybe, just maybe.

Brenna finished her work, then got up to change for the festival. She didn't intend to sit around pining away on such a lovely night. She needed people and laughter and some good zydeco. That's what she needed.

He needed to get some air.

Nick looked up and realized the sun was setting out beyond the open door of his trailer. Everyone else had left long ago and now the quiet was mocking him, taunting him with a humming buzz that sounded like cicadas. He got up to stare across at the house. The facade had changed from a muted grayish-white stone to a bright, gleaming fresh white that shimmered in the golden sunset. Even with scaffolding all around it, the house seemed to be happy and proud, ready to begin a new life with new memories.

That, he loved about his job. He liked to leave a place better than he'd found it. It was one of the biblical principles his parents had taught him.

Nick ran a hand down his neck. He hadn't thought about the Bible in a long time. He needed to call his mother. Maybe he needed to do a quick run to San Antonio for a visit.

But tonight, he felt restless and alone. Tonight, he needed…something. Remembering the big sign he'd seen earlier in town, he thought about the Harvest Festival going on at the church.

Did he want to get in the thick of things?

Or did he just want to be near Brenna?

Without thinking about it too much, he hurried to get a quick shower and a change of clothes. He'd heard a lot about Alma LeBlanc's gumbo. High time he tried it out for himself.

Brenna watched Alma dancing with Julien. They seemed so happy. Ashamed that she's had a flash of jealousy at her sister's wedding, Brenna lifted up a prayer of thanks that Alma was happily married and so far, safe from breast cancer. Callie hadn't been so lucky, but even after her divorce, she'd survived for five years now. Brenna had a mammogram every year like clockwork. They'd all promised their mother they'd do that for her. But the thought of inheriting the dreaded disease was always with them.

Watching Alma now, Brenna smiled and remembered how hard Julien had fought to win back Alma's heart. Brenna could only dream of having a man fight for her like that. Jeffrey certainly hadn't. She turned to go back inside the church to check on more baked goods to sell at the dessert booth.

Turned and saw a tall man wearing a leather jacket with jeans and cowboy boots walking through the crowd.

Nick Santiago.

Why did her heart lift and dance along with the feisty zydeco? Other than the necessary meetings, she'd tried to avoid him this week. They'd been polite and to the point regarding what was expected of her, but each time she'd been around the man, she'd felt an undercurrent between them that raged worse than the Mississippi River. Brenna didn't want to be taken under by that strong pull, but how could she avoid it?

Nick looked up and right into her eyes.

No way out now.

"Hello," she said, waiting as he walked toward her.

"Hi." His gaze swept over her, taking in her wool jacket and jeans over her flat-heeled boots. "Nice night. How's the festival going?"

"Big crowd," she said, hoping her anticipation and apprehension didn't show on her face. "I think the church will make a lot of money for the next mission trip to Grande Isle."

"What do they do down at Grand Isle?"

"Rebuild," she replied. "Always rebuild. Hurricanes love that little barrier island."

He put his hands in the pockets of his jeans. "I've never been there."

"Well, sign up for the trip. They're going in about two weeks."

He nodded. "Depends on how the house is going."

She doubted he'd go on any mission trip. Why should he? He had an air-tight alibi—he worked day and night. She might go on the trip because her hours were pretty much her own. "I've been a couple of times. It's a wonderful place. Not resort territory, but wild and beautiful all the same."

He stared at her, the words *wild and beautiful* echoing between them. He changed the subject to avoid the obvious. "I came for some gumbo."

"Oh, well, then let me take you to the gumbo booth over in the café parking lot. I haven't had any yet and I'm hungry, too."

He lifted his chin. "Then we can eat together."

She laughed. "Have you noticed everything revolves around food in our town?"

"Yep, but I kind of like that. A good meal always brings people together."

"It's never stopped my family from coming together that's for sure. When my mama was alive, we used to celebrate every holiday with a big meal. We'd invite lots of people because she always cooked too much food. Always."

"That sounds nice."

"It was. My papa can cook, too. It's great, but it's not the same."

He stopped her before they crossed the closed-off street. "Brenna, I'm sorry I've been so distant this week. I didn't mean to let this happen."

Bracing herself, Brenna asked, "What's happened, other than we decided we'd stick to a strictly professional relationship?"

He didn't answer at first. "Nothing's happened, but I don't feel as close to you as I did when I first hired you. I enjoyed our friendship. Do we still have a friendship?"

She didn't want to complicate things, but he'd set the stipulations so he had to deal with them. "We don't have to be best buddies, Nick. We have a job to do and that's what we're focusing on right now." At the look of defeat in his eyes, she added, "But we can be friends.

I'd like that. I don't usually work very well with someone who resents me."

"I don't resent you," he said, guiding her through the foot traffic. "I don't know what I feel."

Brenna didn't know what she felt, either. Except that each time she was around him, Nick made her get all gooey and soft-centered. He melted away that hard core she'd place around her heart after she and Jeffrey had parted ways. But it was too soon to tell if she was grasping at a relationship or if this could be something more. Was Nick the one her mother had promised would come?

"Look," she said before they went to order their gumbo, "we can agree that we're attracted to each other. Is that so difficult to admit?"

He shook his head. "No. I mean, I think that was clear last week after we…kissed each other."

She closed her eyes to that particular memory. "Okay. So we have to work together for a few months, at least. But what's to hold us apart after that?"

He stared down at her with those dark, probing eyes. "I don't know about that, either."

"Because you'll move on?"

"Yes. I always move on."

She had already figured that one out, so she shouldn't have even suggested anything else. "Then I guess we'll just chalk this up to bad timing and your definite lack of commitment."

He tugged her by her elbow. "Whoa. My lack of commitment? I thought you were just as confused as I am."

"Oh, I'm confused all right. But I'm willing to explore the possibilities even though I've been through a rough time in the love department. Nick, I'm not ready to rush into anything, but I don't mind getting to know you."

"But you don't *see* me getting to know you? You don't think I can relax in the moment?"

"No, I think you're afraid to hint at anything more because you're so afraid I might jump on you like a duck on a june bug."

He actually smiled at that. "A duck on a june bug? How does that work exactly?"

She started walking again. "You know what I mean. The duck eats the little bug. Then there's nothing left. I'm not quite that bad."

He caught up with her. "You're right. You're not quite that bad. You're more like a ladybug, flying in and settling down. If I remember correctly, ladybugs bring good luck."

"Not in this case," she said over her shoulder.

Stopping her again, he said, "Can we just start over? Maybe take things a little slow? I've never been good at rushing a project."

"Is that what I am to you, Nick? A project?"

"No, I didn't mean it that way. I... I need you to understand...this is new to me."

"And I'm an old pro at bad relationships?"

"No. I don't want to hurt you." He looked out over the crowd, then glanced back at her. "But I don't want to be hurt, either."

Brenna took in a breath. "Well, at least admitting that is the first step. We can agree on that, too."

He nodded, his expression relaxing. "Can we eat now? I'm starving."

"C'mon, cowboy. You'll feel better after some gumbo and corn bread. Everyone always does."

He grinned for the first time tonight. "That sounds good. Really good."

"So good, it'll make you want to slap your mama," she quipped. "In a good way, I mean."

He followed her to the big booth, then leaned close to whisper in her ear. "I'm glad we had this discussion. I think we've reached a new compromise. In a good way, I mean."

"We'll see," she said, her mind whirling with confusion and hope. Compromise, if she considered that he'd once again warned her away with excuses and man-type reasoning. Did it really matter? He'd be gone soon and she'd have to decide where she wanted to go from here. "Only time will tell."

But they didn't have a whole lot of time.

She sure intended to make the best of the time they did have, however. Brenna had fought against her curious nature to preserve her job status. But that might change now. She'd do a good job, she had no doubt about that. But if Nick had feelings for her, she'd also push to bring those feeling to the surface.

Because she couldn't let him walk away without exploring the feelings they had for each other. Giving up had never been her thing. Brenna would fight to the finish to get to the truth.

But that might mean going into Nick's past to figure out why he was so afraid of loving again.

Chapter Eleven

The next morning, Brenna was back on the porch with Alma and Callie. They'd agreed to have an early breakfast with their dad before they all went their separate ways on what looked to be a busy Saturday.

"Okay," Alma said, her quiet tone always soothing. "You've told us all about Fleur House and all about Aunt Serena. We want to hear more about Nick now."

Brenna played with her napkin. "But aren't you concerned about Papa getting so close to another woman?"

Callie made a face, then glanced at Alma. Pointing at Brenna, she said, "*She's* not so keen on Papa being with another woman is what she meant to say."

Brenna bristled. "Well, doesn't it bother y'all? Besides, I am trying to tolerate Papa and Serena together."

Alma put her hands under her chin and leaned on the table. "I have to admit, it seems strange. But it's been over five years since Mama died. He hasn't looked at another woman even though he's always polite and nice to the church widows who've tried to get his attention."

"So maybe he's just being nice to Serena," Callie offered. She nabbed another strawberry and nibbled on it. "She was visiting and he knows she'll be working with you, Bree."

Brenna took a sip of her coffee. "No, it's more than just being nice. I've seen his nice persona. This went beyond that. He saw Serena standing there at church the other night and, well, something changed in him. He had that look that he used to get when Mama would walk into a room." She shrugged. "I think that's what got to me."

"Are you sure it was 'the look'?" Alma asked, tossing her dark curls off her shoulder. "I mean there's a look and then there's 'the look.'"

Brenna thought about the way Julien looked at Alma, the way her daddy had looked at her mama. And the way Nick had looked at her once or twice. "It was a look—maybe not the same one he gave Mama, but still…he was interested. And Serena is an attractive woman."

"With Latin blood," Callie added. "I think they make a good match."

"You're a hopeless romantic, too," Alma retorted. "Bree, has Papa said anything to you about Serena?"

"Not really. We don't mention it. I've avoided the discussion because I didn't want to do what I usually do—make a mountain out of a molehill—as Mama used to say."

"Well, that's wise," Alma said. "Considering you have to work with both Nick and his aunt, if you got all upset about this, it could make things awkward for everyone."

"Not any more awkward than Nick kissing me and then telling me he regretted it."

Alma squealed. "Now we're getting somewhere. I have to hear more about this."

"Did you overreact to that?" Callie asked, her eyes burning with questions.

Brenna rubbed a finger down her coffee mug. "I tried not to, but it was hard. I'm working on getting better in the overreacting department. I really like Serena, though. I'm just trying to imagine Papa with someone else."

Alma looked from Callie to Brenna. "She's not going to tell us about Nick or that kiss until we settle this." She took Brenna's hand. "Listen, it'll be hard to see Papa with someone else, but I'd rather have him with someone and happy than alone and lonely. I mean, really happy. So we have to decide if we can handle this or…break his heart all over again."

"I vote we handle it," Callie said, raising her hand. "And I really need to get to the garden center, so you need to tell us more about Nick, and right now. I left Elvis with one of the workers and that dog knows how to sweet-bark all of 'em."

Alma got up, too. "I agree. I have to go, too. Let's get to Nick."

"What about him?" Brenna asked, already knowing the answer. "He's not ready for a relationship—end of discussion."

Alma started clearing away their dishes. "Oh, I don't know about that. I want to hear about how he met you at my wedding and you danced together and then he hired you right away. About how you two seem to sizzle like crawfish hitting boiling water whenever you're together. Let me see, did I forget anything, Callie?"

Brenna let out a groan. "Crawfish? Seriously? I can't believe you two. It's not like that."

Callie laughed while she gathered muffins and fruit to take back into the house. "Oh, yes, it is so that way. But you don't see it. Kinda like Alma and Julien and their ten years of ignoring each other on purpose. Yeah, right."

Alma grinned and looked all dreamy. "Yeah, right."

Brenna's gaze followed her prissy older sister. "I hope one day we get to pick on her and dissect her love life."

"Her turn will come," Alma said on a smile. "But, Bree, are you interested in Nick Santiago?"

"He's an interesting man," Brenna quipped. "Hard to miss."

"But are you really interested?"

Brenna opened the door so Alma could bring in the coffeepot. "I might be. But the subject in question has made it clear he does not feel the same. Our kiss was the best. We connected."

"If you locked lips, I'd say you sure did," Callie retorted with a grin. "Winnie said he called you *fascinating*."

That surprised Brenna. "Really? Maybe that's why he decided to kiss me—to see if I'm as fascinating as I seem."

Alma grinned at Callie. "Well, that's a start."

"But he got all upset about it and apologized and backpedaled around things. The man can't wait to get this job finished so he can move on to the next one."

"Really? That's a shame." Alma rinsed out the coffee decanter and made sure the coffeemaker was off. "He seems so intense. And so interested in you."

"Good word for it—*intense,*" Brenna replied. "Too intense. He's a bit commitment—shy, I think."

"Why is that?" Callie asked.

Brenna knew she could trust her sisters. "Something about his sister. She died when they were young. That's all I know, but I think it must have something to do with that."

"Oh, how tragic," Alma replied. "Maybe he's never gotten over losing her and so he's afraid to love again. Same as Papa. Love, even love between siblings, can do strange things when you throw grief into the mix."

"Or guilt," Callie added. "Maybe he feels somehow responsible?"

"I never thought of that," Brenna replied, her mind whirling. "And the one time we talked about it, he said it was complicated and he didn't want to discuss it." She shrugged. "And for once in my life, I didn't push the issue. I wanted to keep my job and honestly, I wanted to keep my friendship with Nick. But that was before he kissed me and made me see that he feels more than friendship. And that he's fighting how he feels."

"You might need to gently ask about the sister," Alma suggested. "At the right time, of course."

Callie stood by the stove, staring at them. "He's never mentioned a sister to me. He's close to his parents, but I only found that out when he came in to order flowers for his mother's birthday. I mean, he seemed close to them. But he did say he hasn't been very good about going home for visits."

"They are close," Brenna said. "But something happened back then and he's made it clear he doesn't want to talk about it or deal with it. He never goes home because he is a workaholic. He prefers work to getting into issues."

"I can do an online search," Callie suggested.

"No." Brenna glared at her sister. "I want him to trust me enough to tell me himself, so back off." Then she stared down at the floor. "Besides, I already vetted him when I agreed to work for him. The only thing I found was a picture—a painted portrait of a girl named Jessica. I'm pretty sure the portrait was of his little sister. I got interrupted and never went back to read the article. It seemed…intrusive."

"Our nosy little sister is growing up," Alma said with a smile. "But now we all want to know what's in that article, of course."

"No," Brenna said. "You both have to promise me you won't snoop. I really want him to trust me enough to tell me himself. I used to snoop on Jeffrey and that only brought heartache. I saw pictures of him online, remember? Him with other women, laughing and posing. He didn't even care if I saw them. He always brushed it off as friends having fun."

"Well, this is different," Alma said. "If he feels responsible for his sister's death, this could explain Nick's so-called issues."

"I said, leave it alone," Brenna replied. "I mean it."

Callie held up her hands. "Okay. My lips are zipped."

Alma nodded. "Mine, too. I promise."

"Thank you," Brenna said. "He'd never trust me if he finds out we've been snooping behind his back. He'd never trust any of us again."

"She's right." Alma started gathering her stuff. "Callie has a stake in this, too, because she'll be working on the gardens next spring. Me, I don't have time to spy. I have more gumbo to get out and a café to run. I've abused Winnie enough, making her do both her work and mine."

"She loves it," Brenna said. She waved bye to her sisters and turned to finish up the dishes. Papa had headed out right after breakfast to take a group of tourists on a swamp tour, which left her with the whole morning open.

She thought about doing some more online research. She wanted to find the perfect centerpiece to put on the heavy tiger oak table Serena had found for the entryway.

But when she pulled up Google, her mind wondered to Callie's earlier suggestion regarding Nick's sister. That picture and article might explain a whole lot. If the Jessica she'd glimpsed was even Nick's sister. It could be another Jessica Santiago. She ought to check to be sure.

"I can't do that," Brenna told herself. "I can't."

But why couldn't she? If she found something and never mentioned it to Nick, what would be the harm?

The harm would be in her withholding what she'd found. She couldn't do that to Nick. Maybe he'd talk about his sister in God's own time. Or maybe her death had nothing to do with his attitude now.

On the other hand, maybe Brenna would understand him a little better if she had some idea of what had happened. Besides, there might not be any information online. Did she dare check to see?

"No." She got up and headed upstairs. Instead of work, she decided she'd paint. So she took the sketch of Callie and played with it a bit. Maybe she'd drive out to Fleur House tomorrow afternoon and take advantage of the wonderful light in the sunroom. Callie against the gardens of Fleur House—that would make a nice gift for her sister's upcoming birthday. She'd paint Callie from the sketch and add in the flowers and garden later.

And that would be time well spent. Much better than trying to figure out Nick Santiago by doing an internet recon search.

She didn't want to do a search on Nick. She wanted Nick to feel comfortable enough around her to tell her everything about himself. After all, that kind of intimacy was what made a love affair special and timeless.

"When are you coming home for a visit?"

Nick held the phone away and smiled. It was a beautiful Sunday afternoon and he'd felt restless. So he'd called home, dreading this conversation, but enduring it each time he talked to his mother. "Soon, *Madre,* soon. I have a lot of work to do before I can leave the crew here alone." He used the same old excuses each time they talked, but his mother wouldn't give up.

"Nicky, you work too hard," his mother replied. "Serena told me how when she was there you didn't stop to eat, barely to sleep. Why do you insist on doing this to yourself?"

They'd been down this road before. If his mother had her way, Nick would stay in his little hacienda and eat all of his meals at home with his parents. Oh, and marry a nice girl from the local community, preferable handpicked by her. She wanted to make him happy, but they both knew only he could do that.

His parents worried about him, prayed for him, hoped for him. But they couldn't fix the part of him that was shattered and broken. And they pretended that they weren't the same.

But his whole family was still in a deep state of grief. And a deep state of denial.

"I like my work," he said, pushing away the dark memories. "I'm okay. I stay in shape because I'm always moving and climbing. I eat good food here. The best."

"Better than my tamales?"

"Not that good," he replied, laughing. "I hope to be home soon, I promise. Tomorrow, I have to do a walk-through with the roofers and later this week I have a plumber coming back to finish up with the piping for the bathrooms."

"Your mind, it's always spinning."

"Yes, it is," Nick agreed. "I promise to call more often and to come visit soon."

"Serena also told me about this woman—Brenna. Serena thinks you two would make a perfect match."

Nick had expected this. "Serena only saw us working together for the most part. Brenna is a nice woman, but she's not interested in me." Or, at least, he'd pushed Brenna away from being interested in him. He was having a much harder time following the same advice.

Jeanette Santiago let loose in rapid Spanish. Settle down, find a nice girl, make me some grandbabies before I become an old woman. "I think that's the other way around. You need to find a good woman, Nicky. Bring her and let me meet her. I will know in my heart if she is the one for you."

"Isn't it better if *I* know in *my* heart, Mama?"

"Your heart is too bruised and battered to see what could be something good in your life."

He'd certainly heard it all before. At least this time she'd left out the lecture about letting go of the past and things he couldn't change.

Only this time, Nick actually took his mother's words under consideration. Brenna was something good in his life. And if he messed things up with her, she'd go running in the other direction. Did he want that? Or did he want to finally admit he'd like to have some of those dreams his mother dreamed for him? He roamed around the big, empty house, checking walls, noticing new fixtures. His eyes landed on the mural Brenna loved so much. The mural he'd saved for her.

"I'll consider bringing her to meet you," he finally said. "That might be a good idea, just to see…"

"Serena was right, then. You do have feelings for this girl."

Nick didn't argue with his mother because he knew the truth. This woman was different. This time, he'd felt a little tug in his heart that had broken through some of his guilt and pain. But would a tug lead to something else? Nick still wasn't sure how to handle this, but he couldn't keep denying that he had feelings for Brenna. These past few weeks, being around her, getting to know her, had changed him.

After hanging up, he gathered some papers and decided he'd ride into town and find a nice booth at the back of Fleur Café. Maybe he could get some of this necessary paperwork out of the way if he got out of this trailer and away from the big house. A few weeks until Thanksgiving and things were a little behind, but they could make it up if they had good weather. And if he could keep his mind off Brenna Blanchard.

"At least we're just about done with hurricane season," he mumbled as he got in his car and headed into town.

Chapter Twelve

She'd again been at Fleur House all afternoon. Brenna had made sure Nick wasn't around before she'd unlocked the big house and went inside. This was the second Sunday she'd enjoyed the quiet sanctuary of the house while she painted. Alma's weekend crew had let it slip that Nick liked to come to the café on Sunday afternoons to work quietly and drink gallons of coffee.

"And he eats pie," Alma had confided. "He seems to like pie."

No one other than Alma knew she'd been coming here. Not even Nick. She really wanted to surprise Callie with this portrait. But she also wanted to do this one thing simply because it brought her joy and made her feel closer to God.

It had been such a long time since Brenna had taken things slow and easy and actually enjoyed the beauty of a Sunday afternoon after church and dinner with her family. This time helped her to relax and reflect and see that she'd been living a spiraling, stressed life in Baton Rouge. Being back home had seemed like the worst thing at first, but being here now and being a part of this important restoration had helped her to see that she needed to do her own restoration, too.

Today, however, the sun wasn't shining through the ceiling-to-floor arched windows. The weatherman had predicted rain beginning tomorrow and lasting all week. The outer bands of the tropical disturbance were stirring around out in the Gulf. Brenna finished up and gathered her brushes, easel and other supplies, glad that she'd had a couple of hours to touch up the portrait. She'd talked to Callie so much about which plants and flowers she favored that Brenna knew them by heart. No sunflowers, but Callie loved old magnolias and crape myrtles, moss-covered cypress trees and trailing bougainvilleas. Brenna had gathered this information on the pretense of taking notes for the owner regarding the garden. And she'd give those notes to Nick to pass on. But the portrait was growing more vivid each time she passed her brush over the canvas. She hoped to have it finished in time for Callie's December birthday.

The house would soon be finished, too. And Nick would move on. She kept telling herself that so she'd be prepared, so she could accept that his time here wasn't permanent. And neither was her job. They'd been working together comfortably, laughing, discussing, planning. No more kissing, though.

But every now and then, Brenna would look up and find Nick gazing at her, that intense expression pouring over his face. And she'd remember their kiss.

She stood staring out the windows now, wishing she could paint another picture. In that portrait, she'd be dancing in Nick's arms again. And this time, she'd be the sweetheart bride in the picture.

* * *

Another week had rolled by, but the image of her own wedding wouldn't leave Brenna's mind. Because it had rained off and on all week, she'd at least been spared seeing Nick every day. They'd mostly talked on the phone and through emails.

About work. About the weather. About sports. About food and movies and television. About her past, but never about his past.

Now she was in her room at home, doing a little more work on Callie's portrait. It was still a secret between Alma and Brenna. And painting had become her escape from her feelings for Nick.

Her cell phone rang, scaring Brenna. When she saw Nick's name pop up, she stared at the rain outside her window and took a deep breath. Why was he calling on a Saturday? "Hello," she said on a caught breath of guilt.

"You sound winded."

"I was…busy." For some reason, she wanted to tell him about the painting. "I… I've been painting again. I've gone out to Fleur House the last couple of Sundays to paint in the sunroom."

He chuckled. "The walls or a picture?"

She giggled. "A portrait. Of Callie."

He went silent. "A portrait of your sister?"

"Yes. I hope you don't mind—"

"No, no. I'm glad you're painting again."

Something in his voice caught at Bree's heart. Did he miss painting? Did he resent her or did he wish he could do the same?

"Nick?"

"Maybe this a bad time, then?"

Why? she wanted to shout. Not sure what to do or say, she rambled on. "No, no. I'm at home now. Just finishing up, adding hues and strokes here and there. I'm going to wash my brushes, then go back online to do some more preliminary searches for some sculptures and mixed media. Your aunt gave me some good ideas on how to coordinate things. I've found several paintings and fixtures that might work. I've explored primitives—Clementine Hunter to be specific—and I thought I'd see what kind of Southwestern art I can find."

"Good, good."

She waited, her heart beating a questioning thump. He didn't seem interested or inclined to ask her about the famous Louisiana artist who'd painted scenes of plantation life with a primitive but poignant flair.

"Did you need anything?" she finally asked.

"Well, I'm at the café, working. I called my office in San Antonio, just to check in. I have to make a run over there to clear up a complication with another project."

"Oh, okay. We'll hold down the fort here. When do you leave?"

"Tomorrow, but Brenna, I was wondering if you'd like to go with me. We'd be there a day or two at the most."

Brenna was so surprised that she couldn't speak for a full minute. How was she supposed to adhere to their work rules when the man had just asked her to go on a trip with him?

"Brenna?"

"I'm here. Just thinking."

He didn't speak for a couple of heartbeats, then finally said, "I know it's last minute, but it is strictly business. You can check out some of the galleries there, see what you think. And Tia Serena can meet us there. It makes sense for us to get with her to see what she's come up with so far."

Brenna doubted she'd be able to think clearly, let alone buy any art. "That does sound interesting."

And what timing because she'd planned to look at more art online later today, anyway.

"If you can't make it—"

"I… I can. Let me shift some things around. What time tomorrow?"

"I can wait until after church. I know how impor-tant that is to you."

Touched that he'd accepted that, she smiled to her-self. "Okay. Are we driving?" Because several hours in a car with him just might do her in for good.

"No, we'll fly over to save time. I can book two tickets after we hang up. And two rooms, of course. Oh, and I'll have to drop in and see my parents while we're there, but you don't need to go with me. Unless you want to, of course. My mother wants to meet you. Tia Serena has apparently praised you."

Flying to San Antonio with Nick Santiago. And pos-sibly meeting his family. Her day had sure changed in a hurry. "That's so nice. I wouldn't want to disappoint them, but I'd love to meet them, too. That's fine."

After telling him bye, she thought about it. "Well, I've been on other trips such as this, with other cowork-ers. So why are my palms all sweaty?" And why was her heart doing that rolling-over thing in her chest?

Was this really a business trip or Nick's way of pushing things between them to a new level? It might also be a good opportunity for him to tell her more about his past. And his little sister.

"I'm not so sure I like you going off with dis man."

Brenna leaned down to hug her papa's neck. "I'll be fine. It's business. I've traveled for business many, many times."

Papa bobbed his head, his thick neck red from years in the sun, his ruddy cheeks puffing in disapproval. His accent thickened with each word. "But I didn't have to know about those times, *chère*. Now I get images in my head that don't want to go away."

Brenna got some images in her head each time she thought about Nick, too. "Papa, honestly, you have to trust me. I'm a grown woman."

"I know that, but den so does he, *belle*."

"I have to go," she said on a gentle note. "And I can't be late. I'm meeting him at the house in a couple of hours and we'll drive to the New Orleans airport from there. Our flight leaves at three."

"Are you attending worship first?"

"Yes, of course. And if you don't quit giving me the third degree so I can finish getting dressed, we'll be late for that, too."

Papa got up, his face as gray and hardened as a majestic cypress tree. "Don't get how some highfaluting stranger can come into town and start ordering everyone around."

"I thought you liked Nick," Brenna said, her hands on her hips.

Her papa mimicked her by putting his beefy hands on his own hips. "I did until I saw the way he looks at you."

* * *

Brenna sat up front with her sisters in their usual church pew, located beside a beautiful fleur-de-lis stained-glass window her family had donated to the church in her mother's memory.

She was dressed in a bright green wool skirt and a white blouse with a cozy brown-and-green tinged sweater. Her boots today were slouchy but high-heeled. She'd put on a pair of brown tights to keep her legs warm. A cold front had come through last night, but the weatherman was predicting a warm turn and possibly more storms later this week. She never could plan her wardrobe around Louisiana weather. But she'd checked the San Antonio weather forecast online and found it would warm there this week. So she'd packed lightweight slacks and a dress and a matching wrap.

Other than that, she didn't know what to expect.

She'd argued with herself all day and night about her rationale for agreeing to go on this trip. Nick was her boss and he'd asked her to go, she needed to shop for art objects for the house and she wanted to get to know Nick better.

She kept remembering that she also wanted to know what had happened to his sister. Would his family talk about that? Probably not in front of a stranger.

Brenna wondered why she had to have such a curious personality. And why did it matter so much?

While Brenna stared at the window with the purple Louisiana iris shaped like a true fleur-de-lis centered in the frame with other flowers in colors of red and orange and yellow surrounding it, a whisper started up in the back of the church and weaved its way to her pew. Then her sisters started whispering and glancing around.

Curious as always, Brenna looked back to see what all the fuss was about.

Nick Santiago strolled up the aisle, his gaze on her, his smile soft and sure and intact. And he didn't stop walking until he'd found her pew. Then he whispered "Excuse me" to the bevy of church ladies staring in awe and appreciation at him and slipped into the pew and sat down beside Brenna.

"Hi," he said, as if sitting down next to her in church was a normal, everyday occurrence.

"Hello," she said, asking it more as a question than a statement. "What are you doing?"

He looked confused, but that smile was intact. "Well, I'm attending church. Is that allowed?"

"Of course. It's just that—"

"I thought it would save time," he replied, clearly trying to dismiss her surprise. And maybe her hope, too.

"That does make sense."

"I try to be sensible."

Papa glared down the aisle at them as the organist cranked up things with "Love Lifted Me." Everyone stood and started singing. Nick stood but looked lost, so she handed him her hymnal and pointed to the verses. He nodded in appreciation but he didn't sing. He seemed to be reading the words. When the song was over, Reverend Guidry announced greeting time.

"We say hello and hug each other," she explained to Nick. When was the last time the man had darkened any church doors? Or been hugged in Christian love for that matter?

"Okay," he said, grabbing her up into his arms. "Good morning." He hugged her nice and tight and held on long enough for her to really start enjoying herself. Then he let her go but kept his hands on her elbows and his eyes on her. "I think I like church."

Shocked, Brenna stepped back and patted her ponytail. "Good morning to you, too."

Beside her, Callie elbowed her in the ribs. "When's my turn?"

Nick grinned and kissed Callie on the cheek. "Hi."

"Glad you came," Callie said, laughing.

Then Nick reached around the sisters and shook Papa's hand. "Morning, Mr. Blanchard."

"Morning to you, too," Papa said, his voice vibrating with questions and quibbles.

Afraid her daddy would start interrogating Nick right then and there, Brenna steered Nick toward Alma and Julien. "And you've met my other sister, Alma. Have you met her husband, Julien?"

"Pierre's older brother," Nick replied, shaking Julien's hand. "Nice to meet you. Your brother speaks highly of you."

"Does he now?" Julien asked, grinning. "There was a time when he sure didn't."

"Brothers tend to be that way," Nick replied.

Brenna noticed the dark sadness haunting his eyes. Was he thinking of his sister? Did he wish for a brother?

Nick and Julien went on to talk about Fleur House while Brenna greeted several other people sitting nearby. All of the ladies wanted to know about her "new boyfriend."

"He's not my boyfriend. He's my boss."

But it was useless to try and explain. Let them think what they wanted. She didn't care. Nick was her boss. Nothing more.

But she couldn't help but think about more.

In fact, she thought about a lot of things during the service. Most of them involving Nick Santiago. But she did pray in earnest. Mostly about Nick Santiago.

Before she knew it, the last hymn had been sung and everyone was leaving the sanctuary. By now, she'd worked herself up into a nervous frenzy, wondering if she should go with Nick or just stay home. If this trip involved more hugging, she was in for a whole bushel of trouble.

"Are you ready?" he asked as everyone filed out onto the parking lot. "We can grab lunch in New Orleans before the flight, if that's okay."

Brenna glanced around. Her sisters had abandoned her again, so she couldn't get one of them to take her car. She'd have to leave it parked at the church. "Uh, I guess. Sure. I need to get my bag out of my car."

"You don't sound so sure," Nick replied, his hand cupping her elbow as he took the bag she lifted out of her trunk and then walked her to his car. "Having second thoughts?"

Brenna wouldn't chicken out. That wouldn't be professional. She waited until he'd settled the stuffed bag into the trunk of his GTO. At least he'd left the old work truck he sometimes drove at the construction site. "It's just people are whispering and talking. They think we're an item or something."

Nick laughed at that. "Let 'em talk. Besides, it's really none of their business, is it?"

"Try telling the church ladies that," she replied, watching as he helped her into the car and shut the door.

Nick got in and smiled over at her. "I see what you mean. We have an audience."

"Always." She glanced in the passenger-side mirror and saw a group of older ladies laughing and pointing. "That should keep them busy for a few days. They saw you put my overnight bag in the trunk, so obviously they can see that we're headed out of town together." She'd call Callie and have her park the car at her house, at least.

He looked at the rearview mirror. "Would that ruin your reputation?"

She turned back and stared straight ahead. "No more than it's already ruined. They know I broke up with Jeffrey and lost my job all in the same week. They sure know I'm living with Papa out on the bayou. Now, they'll have a field day discussing this."

"It's a business trip," he said. He must have been practicing that explanation a lot, too. "Want to ride by and shout that out the window?"

"Oh, never mind," Brenna retorted. "Let's just go."

Nick cranked the car and turned out of the parking lot. "I enjoyed the service."

Surprised, Brenna glanced over at him. "Good. I'm glad you came. I wasn't expecting you, but I'm glad you came all the same."

He shot her a black-eyed glance. "Worried about my soul, Brenna?"

She didn't want to preach him another sermon because they'd just heard a good one about second chances and walking within the light. Nick could certainly use some of that light of the gospel. She was worried, but she held out hope. "No, I'm just happy that you decided to come to church. I think you impressed Papa."

"Good. I respect your daddy, that's for sure."

"He's not as overbearing and snarly as he lets on."

"And neither are you."

She had to laugh at that. Sitting back, she relaxed a little now that they had reached the city limits sign. "I'm sorry if I seemed silly back there. It's hard sometimes, living in a small community. Everyone knows your business and what they don't know, they tend to make up."

"I understand that. My parents have neighbors who are like that. I guess it's human nature to want to gossip and speculate." His eyes went into that dark mode.

"Yes. They're good people, but they seem to love matchmaking."

He gave another one of those rich, dark stares. "We wouldn't be such a bad match, would we?"

Floored, Brenna didn't know how to respond. The man needed to make up his mind about things. Finally she said, "I'm thinking we don't need to go down that road. Work, Nick. We need to focus on work. I can't wait to explore some of the galleries along the River Walk in San Antonio."

"Right," he said, his eyes on the road. "Because my meetings are downtown, you'll be able to explore all you want."

Brenna was glad to hear that. If he stayed busy with his meetings, she could get more of her work done. "Sounds like a good plan."

"In the meantime," he said with a nod, "we have a few hours together on this trip. And no one else around to gossip about what we say. A good chance to really get to know each other."

Brenna realized too late that she hadn't factored in the long day alone with Nick. What should they talk about? Would he finally tell her what had happened with his sister? She'd resisted going back to the article she'd found. Or rather, she'd felt too guilty to look again.

Somehow, she had to make Nick see that he could trust her. Maybe if she opened up more, so would he. After all, he'd ventured into church this morning. That meant his heart might be calling to the Lord.

Or maybe his heart was only calling to her heart.

Either way, it was a first step toward what she hoped would bring about a new relationship with God and a new beginning in Nick's faith journey.

She could help with that. She wanted to help with that.

And she truly wanted to help him heal from the grief of losing a loved one. After all, she knew all about that sort of grief.

Chapter Thirteen

They had lunch at a greasy spoon near the airport. Country vegetables for Brenna and corn bread with peppered steak and mashed potatoes for Nick.

"Very good," Nick commented after they were back in the car. "Did you enjoy your food?"

Brenna rubbed her tummy. "I think so. I'm stuffed. I don't usually eat that much in one sitting."

"You seemed nervous." He waited a beat. "Is that because of me?"

She had to smile at that. So far, the chatter between them had been mostly small talk mixed in with discussing Fleur House. She hadn't gotten very far in her you-need-to-trust-me quest to make Nick open up. But she wasn't giving up.

"No. I mean maybe. Yes, okay, you make me nervous."

"Because I'm the big bad boss?"

"No, because you're…you." He gave her a Nick-glance, full of mystery and promise. "That—that right there makes me nervous."

He held his hands out, palms up. "What?"

"The way you look at me."

"I like looking at you, okay?"

"Okay. Let's change the subject."

"Let's get back to you eating. You manage to stay healthy in spite of all the pie and bread pudding you eat."

"My family loves to eat, what can I say?" she retorted. "We do try to eat healthy now and then. And for the most part, we are all healthy." It was her turn to go to dark memories.

"You're thinking about your mother, right?"

She nodded. "That and the threat of cancer for all of us."

He looked ahead at the road. "That must be hard to live with."

"It is, but then death and grief are not easy subjects for any of us."

She watched in amazement as he let that opening slide away.

His gaze skimmed her face, a look close to a plea centered in his expression. "I don't mean to… I mean, you don't seem to have any problems with that. You look like you're in great shape, so I hope you're taking care of yourself."

"I have regular checkups and mammograms," she replied, wishing there was a medical test for people who closed down in their grief.

"And you seem to get lots of exercise."

"I love to walk," she admitted, ignoring what she was pretty sure must have been his attempt at a compliment. "I used to walk everywhere in downtown Baton Rouge. I'd walk at the indoor track at the gym near my condo, too."

"I've seen you walking around the gardens at Fleur House," he replied. "I do that sometimes early in the morning. I like to jog when I have the time."

She pictured him up and out and running, running, his thoughts focused on what he needed to accomplish.

"Is that your thinking time?"

"I guess it is. That and late at night when I can't sleep."

"I do that." She found it endearing that they had some of the same habits at least. "I get a thought in my head and then I'm wide-awake."

"Same here." He didn't speak for a few minutes. "I've always been a loner. I don't need much sleep, so I do get a lot done. I like my quiet time."

Brenna wondered about that. She wanted to ask him why he no longer painted. But then he might figure out she'd seen that picture of Jessica on the internet. "Don't you ever get lonely?"

He took a deep breath and adjusted his foot on the gas pedal. "Sure. At times. Who doesn't?"

She catalogued that information and went headfirst into another question. "You don't seem to have much of a life outside of your work. I don't mean to sound condemning, but don't you get tired of traveling from place to place, rebuilding, then leaving all over again?"

His chuckle rumbled through the car. "I never have before," he said, glancing over at her. "But now I'm beginning to wonder about that."

Brenna was too shocked to say anything else. The way he'd looked at her just now made her feel all soft and warm and confused. "What makes you wonder?"

"You," he said, his expression full of questions. "I

thought that kiss might cure me of wondering, but I'm afraid it just made things worse."

Now they were getting down to the real business. She sat up against the seat. "I don't want to make things worse for you, Nick. Why did you ask me on this trip? Really, really ask me. We both know I can find what I need in New Orleans or anywhere in the world for that matter, and you certainly didn't need me for your meeting."

He slowed the car as they approached the busy Louis Armstrong International Airport, then glanced over at her again. "You're right. I didn't need you to come on this trip with me. But I wanted you with me all the same."

"I don't get it," Brenna admitted. "What's going on here?"

"That's what I'm trying to find out."

"Oh, so first you kiss me to find out what's going on and you try to get me off your mind. Now, you invited me on a road trip to test that theory even more?"

"Yeah, something like that."

"You're an interesting, confusing man."

"And you're a challenging, confusing woman."

"This is gonna be one mighty strange trip."

He touched his hand to hers. "Or it could turn out to be the best trip of our lives."

Brenna liked the whisper of a promise in his words.

But she still wanted him to open up to her, to trust her, to share the worst he had with her. She'd let Jeffrey slide by on the intimacy issues and look where that had gotten her—alone and heartbroken. She hadn't pushed enough with her ex. Or maybe she'd pushed too much. It didn't matter. Things were different with Nick. She liked him. A lot. So she wanted to be his friend and his confidante. She wanted him to know he had her in his corner and that God was right there with them.

But she wasn't so sure he was ready for that. And she had to wonder what kind of test he'd put her through before he would be willing to offer her more.

Surprising her yet again, he reached for her hand. "Brenna, promise me you'll take care of yourself."

And then she suddenly understood a lot more about the man beside her. He wasn't afraid of getting involved with a woman. He was afraid of falling for *her*. Because of her family history with cancer. And because he had already lost someone he loved.

Brenna held on to his hand. "I'm fine, Nick. You don't have to worry about me."

But he did. She could see it in his eyes before he let go of her hand.

Nick adjusted his seat and prepared for the flight. "Not long now," he said. "Just a few hours and we'll be there."

He wondered now if he'd been wise to bring Brenna with him. He'd stepped over a big boundary, telling her that he wanted to get her out of his mind. Telling her one thing and then doing another could only confuse her even more. And him, too.

He could admit it now, at least. He wanted Brenna in his life, but his fear of a lasting commitment crippled his clumsy attempts at making that happen. He'd had enough grief and loss in his life. Loving someone for a lifetime was asking more of him than he could bear.

"Where is our hotel?" Brenna asked, her head down as she stared out the plane's window.

Nick worried with his seat belt. "It's on the River Walk."

"Oh, that's convenient."

He grinned, glad to have something else besides his erratic, irrational fears to think about. "*Sí*. But, we have to go by and see my parents first. I can't go to San Antonio and not visit with my parents. They'd never forgive me."

"Okay." She squirmed and fidgeted, her big eyes touching on him before she glanced away.

"You don't have to go with me. I could drop you off at the hotel first."

"I don't mind," she replied. "I'd love to meet your family."

"You don't look too excited about it, though." He put a hand on hers. "All you have to do is relax and enjoy the next couple of days away from Fleur. We'll be home Tuesday morning and you'll be fine."

Wiggling, she adjusted her seat belt again. "I don't know your family. What if they don't like me? I guess I'm a little overwhelmed."

He tilted his head toward her. "I want you to get to know them. And they're already asking about you."

"But they don't know me, either. How could they ask questions?"

"My Tia Serena gave them a glowing report. That's why they insisted I come by the house. My mom wouldn't have it any other way."

She shook her head. "Aren't we just fueling the fire all over again? They don't think we're an item, do they?"

"Not that I can tell, but I'm sure Tia Serena thinks

we should be an item. So that means she's probably convinced the whole family, too."

Looking perturbed, Brenna gave him a light tap on his arm. "Is this another part of getting me out of your system? So you asked me here to test me on your parents?"

He couldn't hide his frown. "Well, when you put it that way—"

"Are you serious?" She glanced toward the front of the plane. "I have a good mind to get off this plane and go home."

Maybe she could bolt from a moving plane, after all.

"I'm teasing," he said to cover his worry. "I've explained that we work together. Nothing more."

"Good. Let's keep it that way."

"Fine. You'll only have to endure them for dinner tonight. Tomorrow, it's all business."

She gave him a skeptical glare. "I sure hope so."

Nick put his head back on the seat. He'd never brought a woman home before, especially not a woman who worked with him. And he'd worked with lots of beautiful women. Why was Brenna so different? Why did she make his heart do too much pumping? Why did she make him *want* to settle down and stick around?

And why did he keep her so close when he knew he should push her away? Anyone with a brain could see he'd purposely brought her on this business trip just so he could be with her. But would it hurt to have a little fun with a pretty woman, a woman he admired and appreciated? Already, she's helped him with several problems regarding Fleur House. She was good at her job and she was good at spotting issues.

Maybe that was why she sat with a tight-lipped pout

right now. She had discovered an issue with his methods of trying to woo her. Maybe he should just level with her and get it over and done with, tell her he was a coward and he couldn't handle anything more than friendship and working together.

"Brenna?"

"What?"

"I should have told you...about going to see my parents right away. I'm sorry."

"Okay, all right. You did tell me they wanted to meet me. Might as well get to that right up front. I'll be fine. Really."

The plane lifted in the air. At least she was still sitting there. "Looks like the weather will be great," he said, trying to make small talk.

She stared out the window. "Wonderful. Can't wait."

Nick took her hand again. "Now, *bonita,* don't be mad at me. I wanted to extend a bit of hospitality to you. You'll like my family. We're very close, but they tend to be stifling at times. They mean well, but they can't see that I'm a grown man."

She finally turned to look at him. "I can see that and so much more about you. Just like my family. Our mother's death brought all of us closer together. Then Callie got cancer and well...it's hard sometimes. I worry—"

His heart hit turbulence even though the takeoff had been smooth. "That it might happen to you?"

"Yes." Her eyes turned a rich greenish-brown. "Yes. It's hard on a relationship, so I can understand your being hesitant. Jeffrey always laughed off my worries about breast cancer, but then, he laughed off a lot of my concerns."

Nick's heart ached for what she'd been through. He knew that same ache. It tore through him each time he thought of his beautiful little sister. Before he could stop himself, he said, "Jessica's death changed all of us. Part of my soul is broken, always raw."

Brenna's expression softened, her pout disappearing as quickly as it had come. "I'm so sorry. You said you don't like to talk about her, but Nick, I understand that kind of grief. It's blinding and hard to shake. And it makes getting close to people even harder." She waited, the expectation in her pretty eyes bright with hope and that gentle understanding she'd mentioned. "I think I have that same little tear in my soul. Maybe that's why Jeffrey only pretended to love me. Maybe because I only pretended to love him."

Nick wanted to tell her everything, but he'd been silent on this subject for so long that he couldn't bring himself to reveal his feelings, even to Brenna. "We'd better get back to business for now, don't you think?"

Disappointment shadowed the hope he'd seen in her eyes. "Okay. You're right, of course. And I need to stop being pushy."

He didn't respond at first, but he didn't want to leave things this way when they'd started out. "About Jeffrey, maybe you needed him to love you more—enough so that your feelings and fears wouldn't be so hard to handle."

"Yes," she said, giving him one of her daring gazes. "That's the kind of love I want. Someone who helps me through the bad stuff instead of dismissing my feelings as irrational or unreal. Someone who can overcome fear to experience love, real love that fights through good and bad." She gave him a brief glance, then turned back to the window. "Yes, that's what I want."

Nick thought about her words. How would she feel if he ever did tell her the whole story about his sister? He never talked about that subject, not even with his own family. But he knew one thing: if his feelings for Brenna were as real as they seemed, he'd never let cancer or heartache or any pain come her way again. Never. And he'd need to be completely honest with her, too, or he'd lose her.

"I think we all want that kind of love," he finally said.

She sat there, staring over at him, her expression shifting in shades of sunlight and whitewashed clouds and finally, she smiled. "I can't wait to meet your family."

Chapter Fourteen

The Santiago home was settled on a nice cul-de-sac in an older neighborhood full of trees and pretty land-scaping. The house was stucco and two-storied with an inviting front porch and Spanish-style arches that reminded Brenna of Fleur House. Palm trees and old oaks surrounded the shaded yard.

Brenna took in the big house, her mind still reeling from their earlier conversation. He'd come so close to sharing his pain with her. Maybe if she kept gently prodding, she'd know the truth one day, but she was thankful she'd finally figured out part of his hesitation toward her. She said a tiny prayer, asking God to give her patience to wait and to give Nick the strength to trust her. What kind of pain had he held inside his heart all this time? So much that he couldn't let go and find someone to love?

"This is it—my parents' home," Nick said, his eyes shining with pride. And something else. Regret, maybe?

Brenna gave him a quick smile. "It's beautiful. So peaceful and neat."

"My dad loves puttering in the garden." He opened his door. "Ready for this?"

"As ready as I'll ever be." Brenna opened her door and hopped out of the rental car. "The weather forecast was right. It is warmer here."

"Just a little. It can get warm and humid, even in fall and winter. It's a lot like Louisiana."

"Then I was smart to pack a variety of clothes."

He gathered their bags and guided her up the curving walkway to the front door. But before they'd made it halfway, several people fell out the door, all talking at once in Spanish.

"They're discussing how pretty you are," Nick explained with a grin.

Brenna stepped back as a voluptuous woman grabbed Nick and held him tight. She heard the word *bebé* and figured this must be Nick's mother.

"And this must be your lovely Brenna," the woman said, her hands reaching out to Brenna. "Welcome to our home."

"Hi," Brenna said before she was engulfed in a strong hug. A mother's hug. Brenna clung tight and savored the feeling, memories of her mother's soothing touch coloring the confusion hovering over her brain. "You're Nick's mom?"

"Yes, *sí.* Jeanette," the woman said. She smelled of cinnamon and wore her gray-streaked dark hair up in a beautiful silver clip. "And this is my husband, Alberto."

"Nice to meet you," the man said to Brenna.

"Hi, Dad," Nick said, shaking his father's hand.

Even though his hair was almost white, the older man looked a lot like Nick and seemed just as stoic and quiet, too. "Nicky, good to have you home. And to bring us such a pretty *chiquita,* too. We are honored."

Brenna was then shepherded around and introduced to the other people who'd come out to greet them. Aunts and uncles and cousins and long-lost relatives. Apparently, Nick's coming home was a big deal. Or had they all come to inspect her?

When they finally got through the front door, she glanced up to view the rest of the house and was happy to see Tia Serena coming down the wide staircase.

The older lady, elegant and graceful, took Brenna by the arm. "You're here. I'm so glad. I think they invited the whole family, and Nick, your papa has grilled and cooked right along with Jeanette. Hope you're both hungry."

Brenna grinned as Serena swept both of them close and kissed them each on the cheek. "I asked him to bring you on this trip, so don't be angry. I wanted us to get some preliminary work done and I wanted everyone to meet you."

Brenna shot a quick glance at Nick. He hadn't told her Serena had requested her. He obviously wanted her here, but the mystery of what motivated him held her. He seemed happy, but she could still see that darkness in his eyes. "I'm not angry," she replied to Serena. "Just a little intimidated."

"We tend to do that to people," Serena explained. "But I'm here to filter things and keep everyone from poking too hard at you, *si?*"

"I appreciate that," Brenna said, meaning it. Normally, she didn't mind being the center of attention, but this was Nick. This was different. She couldn't forget that this man seemed to have a process—a method to

his madness. He'd brought her here for some reason and
it involved more than work. It rankled, but she wanted
to pass inspection. She thought about Jeffrey and how
she'd tried to pass muster with him.

This is different, she told herself. With Jeffrey, passing included wearing the right clothes and knowing the
right people, things that would move them up the all-
important corporate and social ladders. Passing Nick's
test was all about gaining trust and unlocking the secrets he held in his heart.

Wondering if she'd ever get an A-plus in the love
department, Brenna said a silent little prayer. *Only with
You, Lord. That's where it counts.*

Serena's calming voice lifted over the chatter.
"Nicky, show Brenna where to freshen up. We will
have a good supper waiting when you come down."

"Okay." Nick finished hugging and kissing everyone. Motioning to Brenna, he said, "I'll show the bathroom upstairs. You'll have more privacy there."

Nick took Brenna upstairs without a word. When
they reached the second door on the right, he pointed
to it. "The bigger, quieter bathroom, as promised. I'll
be downstairs."

Then he turned and headed down without another
word.

Now she really felt uncomfortable. Was he angry
that so many people had come to see him? Or was he
mad that his family had made the wrong assumption.
Brenna wanted to run downstairs and call a cab to
take her back to the airport. She cared about Nick a
lot, wanted to get to know him better, but this was al-

most too much. He'd brought her on this trip because according to him, he wanted her here.

But did he also bring her here so she could see his big, happy family? So she'd stop pestering him or trying to turn him back on the right path? Or to scare her away?

His entire family seemed to be a happy, carefree lot and yet, he seemed so tragic and sad at times. And to top it all off, she'd have to put on a good front and go with the questions and assumption. What was going on?

After she'd combed her hair and put on fresh lipstick, Brenna walked out into the hallway, her gaze falling on the room directly across from the upstairs bathroom.

A real girly-girl room.

Glancing around while she stood outside the door, she saw family pictures here and there and recognized Nick in them. And Jessica. Brenna leaned close to search a large family portrait. A skinny young girl sat with her arm over Nick's shoulder, her smile beaming and bright.

Jessica. And yes, this Jessica certainly looked like the girl she'd caught a glimpse of in that newspaper article.

"What are you doing?"

Her hand on the wall, Brenna whirled to find Nick standing on the stairs, glaring at her.

"I'm sorry. I... I couldn't help but notice—"

His expression changed from angry to miserable and embarrassed. "My family means well, but they're trying to make a point with me. They kept this room as some sort of shrine to my sister and they always make sure I remember it's still here."

Brenna didn't know what to say. "It's hard to let go. You saw the portrait of my mother over our mantel. I think it's okay to keep mementoes and photos of lost loved ones."

"*Sí.* I saw the portrait of your mother, but I didn't see a whole room dedicated to her memory."

"No, we have a whole house that's filled with memories of her. We remember her each and every day."

"But you don't force those memories. They're natural and true and pure."

"I think so. We…we loved her, so we celebrate her life and we rejoice that she's with God now."

He came to stand with her, but he didn't look into the room. "I haven't gotten over Jessica's death. I don't think I ever will, but they push and push and try to make everything bright and happy. It's a facade for my sake. After I leave, they go back to their quiet suffering."

"While you're still suffering out there alone?"

He nodded, lowered his head. "I haven't been in here since she died. The door is usually closed."

"But why would they want to force you to come in her room if it bothers you?"

He held her, his hands on her elbows. "They love me. I know that. So they think they can make everything better, even after all these years. They have such a strong faith. It isn't as hard for them to keep going." He looked into Brenna's eyes, his expression begging her to understand. "If I can stand here with you, then I can go on with my life—that's what they are hoping."

Brenna didn't stop to think. She pulled him into her

arms and hugged him close. "Nick, grief takes many forms and it's a process that works differently for every person. I can close the door for you." And open another door on hope, she thought.

"No, no." He pulled away but held her there. "I'm okay, really. Seeing you here, having you understand, has helped me a lot." He searched her face. "Sometimes, turning to a more objective person does help."

"I can be that person," she replied. "Whatever happened when Jessica died, I can be that person for you, Nick. Between God and me, you can heal."

"Did God help you when your mother died?"

"Yes," she said, touched that he was willing to discuss this. "Yes, my faith, my family's strong faith, got us through. Because we know, no matter our suffering here on earth, we'll see our mother one day again—in heaven. You have to trust in that, too."

He touched his forehead to hers. "Heaven seems so far away. So far."

Brenna looked up, saw the torment in his eyes and wondered why the good Lord had commissioned her to be this man's spiritual guidance counselor. She wasn't qualified but she wouldn't turn away, either. "Heaven is far away, but God is close. He's always right here." She touched a hand to Nick's heart and felt the erratic beating. It reminded her of a trapped bird trying to break free.

Nick put his hand over hers and stared down at her. "You're an amazing person."

Brenna felt humbled by his words. "Not really. I'm just a very determined person. And I'm determined to make you smile again. I mean really smile."

She pulled away and lifted her hand to encompass

the neat girly-girl room. "This is part of heaven. You have memories, people smiling and laughing together, Jessica's favorite things all around. This is what you hold on to, Nick."

"I'd rather hold on to you," he said, grabbing her to pull her back.

Brenna gladly went into his arms. But his desperate words left her feeling deflated instead of joyful. Was he holding on to her just to ease the pain of his grief? And if so, what would happen to her if he decided to let go?

Brenna sat on an intricately carved bench out in the backyard, a giant magnolia tree shading her from the late-day sun. In spite of the warmth, she couldn't help but shiver. There was a sadness shrouding this otherwise-happy home.

Nick brought her another glass of tea and sat down beside her. "Looks like we'll get to see a brilliant sunset."

She leaned back, relaxed from the good food and all the chatter of his family. Once she'd made it back downstairs and talked with everyone, she'd felt more at ease. But she couldn't forget the way Nick had held on to her, there by his sister's room. "You're blessed, you know."

"I do know." He glanced back to where his parents and the other were inside the courtyard patio clearing away the remains of their feast. "I should come home more often."

"We all should," she replied. "I wish now that I'd had more time with my mother."

He looked down at his hands. "Same here. I imagine

Jessica all grown up and beautiful. I'd probably test all of her prom dates for perfection."

"The way you're testing me?" she asked, trying to keep things light.

His head shot up. "Do you really think that's what I'm doing?"

"Aren't you?" She set her glass down in the soft grass, then turned to him. "You seem to have a method to all your actions."

"I do have a process for work," he admitted, "but when it comes to you—"

"You're using the same process. Kissing me to see where it would go, inviting me here to see how it would be having me around your family." Not to mention, still not telling her anything about what had happened to his sister. Not mentioning that his aunt also wanted her to visit. She needed him to be up front and honest with her. Maybe that would be the real test. "What's next for me?"

He took her hand in his. "I don't know. And I didn't deliberately plan all of my actions. I think things through, long and hard, before I make any kind of move. I guess I'm doing that with you, too."

"Serena said she also wanted me on this trip, but you never mentioned that."

He looked surprised. "Does it matter? I asked you to come and I am your direct supervisor."

"Oh, we're gonna play it like that now?" She shifted, stared off into the sunset. "Nick, I understand this is business and I'll do my part. But we both know this is also personal. Are you and your family so desperate that you'd parade me around like some prize?"

He stood and stared down at her. "No one here intended to make you feel as if you were on exhibit, Brenna."

"No, no. You've all been kind and wonderful, but there is a weird dynamic here. Your family is so different from mine."

He sat back down, let out a long sigh. "So you noticed?"

"Um, yes. But I can tell there's a lot of love here, too. You should focus on that. And you should learn to rely on your friends a little bit more."

He nodded, took her hand in his. "I'm not so good at that and I'm truly sorry for how this might look." He stared down at their joined fingers. "The bottom line is I really wanted you here with me. I'm sorry for everything else."

Brenna could see the sincerity in his eyes. "I don't mind so much as long as you're honest with me," she replied, her hand squeezing his. "And if you can learn to trust me."

"Ah, trust." He looked over his shoulder. "Everyone tells me I should trust and let go. That's a tall order for someone who has to program every step."

"You have to see things to believe in them?"

He looked into her eyes. "Yes. I see you sitting here and I believe I need to keep you around."

She laughed at that, and used his previous words. "Well, when you put it that way."

He groaned, then pushed a hand through his inky hair. "Tomorrow, after work, I want to take you to a special place."

"Dinner?"

"No, but you won't go hungry. It's the *hacienda*

pequeña—my home when I'm back here for long periods."

His little hacienda. "Your one true home?"

"As close to a home as I've had since I left home."

Brenna didn't know what to say. Nick taking her to such a private, personal place. Another test?

But she wouldn't say no. She wanted to see the little house she'd heard so much about. "That sounds nice. I'd love to see it."

Maybe he was beginning to trust her, after all. First, the family and now a place where he could be alone and away from everyone and everything. With her.

As if he knew what she was thinking, he leaned close and whispered, "Don't worry. You know, you need to trust me a little bit, too."

He was right. And she would try.

The next morning, Serena met Brenna at the hotel bright and early to explore the River Walk. Nick told them he'd meet them later for lunch and they'd all give updates.

Getting used to his procedures now, Brenna smiled and told him goodbye.

"How did you sleep?" Serena asked, her hand on Brenna's arm as they strolled along with their fresh coffee in hand.

"Is that a trick question?" Brenna replied.

Serena's smile filled with acceptance. "Ah, so you think we are one strange family, right?"

Brenna sipped her coffee. "No, not any different from most. You're all obviously still grieving Jessica. It's not my place to judge."

Serena guided her into an art gallery. "We only

want the best for Nicky. We want him happy and whole again."

"So you think you can give him the best by forcing him to stare at his sister's things left all around like a shrine?"

Serena gave Brenna a quick, appreciative glance. "You do care about my nephew."

Brenna wouldn't deny it. "Of course I do. He's a good man who obviously went through something traumatic, something that still haunts him."

"Still," Serena repeated. "It's been over fifteen years."

Fifteen years. Brenna thought about the newspaper article she'd found. That would have been the right time frame.

"What happened?" she finally asked.

Serena shook her head. "You have to let Nick tell you. He'd never forgive me if I said anything more."

Frustrated, Brenna watched tourist boats floating by on the long canal through the River Walk. "That's not fair. He brought me here for a reason other than work, but no one wants to explain the man to me. He's hurting. Can't anyone see that?"

"We all see it," Serena replied. "I helped raise that boy and I was there when the worst happened. Jessica's death was hard on everyone, but Nick took it the hardest. We all tried to help him through. But—"

"But he blames himself, right?" Brenna asked, the assumption clear in her head.

Serena didn't speak for a full minute. Then she said, "*Sí.* Nicky blames himself for his sister's death. And, unfortunately, that's all I can say on the matter."

Chapter Fifteen

The rest of the day went by in a blaze of shopping, lunch and strolling along the crowded sidewalks. Brenna loved how a canal ran through the city, complete with large gondoliers carrying tourists and locals from place to place. Serena took her to a wonderful art gallery where, using the computer-generated sketches of the layout of the house, she found some mixed-media renderings to use in a couple of bedrooms and exquisite sculpture pieces to place here and there. She asked to have the items shipped and used the company charge card Nick had given her to pay for everything.

"A good day's work," she told Serena. Nick had been unable to meet them for lunch, so after doing some shopping for themselves, they headed back toward the hotel lobby.

"I enjoyed this," Serena said, her expression calm as always. "And I enjoy working with you. You definitely have an eye for design."

Brenna basked in that compliment. "What can I say? It's the only thing I'm good at. I love to paint and I love to deal in art. I liked my job at the gallery, but it was a challenge at times."

"Have you ever considered becoming an independent art dealer?" Serena asked. "You'd be good at that."

Brenna shook her head. "No. But then, I had a good job and never considered leaving my position. I'll have to look into that. Sounds as if I could work for myself and still have a job I love."

"Exactly," Serena said. "You could travel and work wherever you want as long as you have a client list. And that wouldn't be hard at all. You'd have to do some promotion work and advertising to get your name out there. I have contacts, too, of course. I'd recommend you."

"I'd need that," Brenna replied. "I hadn't thought past Fleur House, but I probably should consider what might be next. The house is scheduled to be finished by next spring."

Serena laughed. "Nick put a rush on everything. He's determined to meet his deadlines."

"I'm sure he is," Brenna replied.

And then, he'd be gone out of her life.

She needed to consider what she'd do next, so she was grateful to Serena for making the suggestion. Brenna would need something to keep her focused so she wouldn't miss Nick so much.

"Sorry I missed lunch," Nick told her as they left the city later that afternoon and headed south. "Things got complicated and my meeting ran longer than I'd planned."

"That's okay," Brenna replied. "We managed to have fun without you."

"Good." His smile held a hint of fatigue. "It was a long day for me, but we ironed out the problems on our next project. I missed you."

Brenna fidgeted with the fringe on her white wrap, then adjusted the skirt of her blue jersey dress. "I kind of missed you, too."

He took her hand. "Just kind of?"

A lot. But she didn't tell him that. "Yes, kind of. I was busy working, you know."

"Right." He laughed and dropped her hand. "I saw all those packages piled in your room. "How will we get all of that onto the plane?"

She leaned close and grinned. "That's an old feminine secret. We know how to consolidate. It will all fit into my suitcase because I left extra room."

"Ah, so that's how it's done."

She nodded. "Throughout the centuries."

"You're amazing. A constant surprise."

"Is that a good or bad thing?"

He took her hand again. "Good. But bad for my head."

Before she could say anything, her cell phone buzzed.

"Callie, what's up?"

Her sister sounded out of breath. "Have you heard the weather report?"

"Uh, no. We were out all day. Why?"

"Remember that little tropical disturbance out in the Gulf? Well, it took a turn and regained speed and strength. Now it's headed our way."

"Wow." Brenna turned to Nick and relayed the message. "When is it due?"

"They're saying midweek at the earliest. I'm sure

Nick is aware, but I just wanted to let you know what I've heard."

"I'll check the radar and see. We'll be home tomorrow, anyway, so don't fret too much."

"Okay," Callie said. "Papa is pacing and worrying. That should make him feel better, knowing you'll get home safely."

"Okay. We'll keep tabs on it."

"Hey, Brenna, tell Nick he might want to consider what to do about Fleur House. It could sustain damage if those winds get as bad as they're predicting."

Brenna glanced over at Nick. "I'm sure he's thinking about that right now."

After she put her phone away, she turned to Nick. "A storm could wipe out a lot of the work you've already done on the house. Should we leave early tomorrow?"

He nodded. "We're almost to the hacienda. I'll start calling as soon as we pull off the highway. My foreman should know what to do, but we'll make sure all the same. I've had my eye on these approaching storms, but I didn't check today. I'm surprised he hasn't called me about this."

"I can make some calls right now," she offered. "He probably wanted to wait to make sure, but my sister didn't wait. We've been through this too many times, so she knows the drill."

Nick gave her a couple of names and numbers so she could change their flight and alert the project foreman. By the time she was finished, they'd turned into a gated driveway. Nick hit a remote and the gate swung open. He pulled up into the long dirt drive and shut off the rental car. "Let me get a couple more calls made and then I'll show you the hacienda."

"You don't seem too worried," she said, wondering how he managed to stay so calm.

"I've been through this before, too," he said. "Galveston's been through some of the same rough weather as your coastline in Louisiana. I have a lot of clients who lost their homes in the last hurricane."

She nodded, thinking he was one of the hardest-working men she'd ever met. They clicked in that respect. They both did their jobs with gusto and passion. Maybe because their work was all they had right now.

Thirty minutes later and just as the sun had begun its descent into the western sky, Nick pulled the car up to a white cottage-size house that indeed was a true miniature hacienda.

The front porch held arched columns a lot like the bigger ones at Fleur House. But this porch was more Southwestern in design, long and narrow and inviting. A red slate roof slanted down to meet the porch and palm trees and huge cactus plants graced the front yard. Off to one side, an ancient live oak stood like a sentinel, guarding the house.

"It's beautiful," Brenna said, a warmth seeping into her bones. "Timeless."

"It's close to one hundred and fifty years old," Nick said. "My great-grandparents lived here and over the years, relatives kept adding to it. It was in disrepair when it was passed to my family. I begged my dad to let me renovate it."

"Obviously, he agreed."

Nick nodded, his eyes full of that dark torment she'd seen before. "*Sí*. It was one of my first projects after

I'd been away at school for a while. Took me a whole year, but I had to make sure I kept it authentic."

Brenna looked at the cozy little house, wondering if this house had helped him with some of his grief. Maybe that feeling of diving into a project had stayed with him through each home he restored. That would explain his need to keep working.

"If this was your first restoration project, I'd sure like to see some of the others. It's gorgeous."

"Gracias." He stared up at the house. "This place means a lot to me."

Brenna could understand. The house reminded her of something out of a fairy tale. She expected to see a beautiful *señorita* wearing black lace and holding a fan, waiting for them at the door. "I can't wait to see the rest."

Nick hurried around to help her out, then held her hand as they stood there for a minute. "Let's watch the sunset," he said. "It's always beautiful here, this time of day."

Brenna glanced beyond the house to the vast acreage of trees and shrubs spread across the surrounding pasture land and watched as the sun faded away in a brilliant orange-yellow glimmering glow that set off the stark white of the house and left the whole world a shimmering, glittering bronze.

"Wow."

Nick pulled her into his arms and looked her in the eye, then reached up his hand to pull at a strand of her hair. "Wow, yourself. I'm glad you're here."

"Me, too," she said. She thought he would kiss her and she almost died with frustration when instead he took her by the hand again. "Let's go inside."

* * *

The little house was cozy and clean. While the furnishings were stark and minimalist, they echoed the Southwestern theme, complete with paintings of the desert and beautiful clay pots here and there. Chunky wooden hutches, rustic tables and massive armoires mingled with rich brown leathers, handwoven looms and exquisite throw rugs. A massive iron-and-glass chandelier centered in the high ceiling brightened the whole place. The white color carried through to the inside of the house in a predominant theme and shined brightly against the severe browns in the furnishing and the rich red tiles of the floor.

Brenna looked around, taking in the decor. Then her gaze moved up the fireplace wall and she almost gasped. She glanced briefly at Nick. His gaze was centered on the portrait she'd just noticed, but he dropped his head and moved away before she could see his reaction.

The portrait of Jessica she'd briefly glimpsed on the internet was hanging over the fireplace. She almost said something, but she didn't want to disrupt the closeness she felt toward Nick. Maybe he would explain the portrait. Had he brought her here for that reason?

Right now, he was preoccupied with turning on lights and lighting candles.

While Brenna wandered around the big open living room and absorbed yet another revelation, Nick lit a fire in the arched kiva fireplace, then turned to smile at her. "Are you hungry? I called ahead and had one of the ranch hands bring down some cheese and fruit. And I have coffee or soda."

"That would be nice," she said, not sure what to

do. "Coffee sounds wonderful. It's chilly now that the sun's gone down."

"Come stand by the fire," he said. "I'll get us something to eat."

Brenna walked across toward the fireplace and put her back to the growing flames. The kitchen was tucked in one corner, neat and bright with colorful blue tiles across the backsplash. She watched Nick prepare the coffee and food and then she sat down on the tiled ledge in front of the fireplace.

"You must love coming here. It's so quiet and peaceful."

Nick brought over a tray with coffee and their food, then took a seat by her. "*Sí.* It's nice to get away and relax, even if I only do it on rare occasions. The stars are a lot brighter out in this big pasture."

She nibbled on a few grapes and speared a chunk of white cheddar. "You mentioned a ranch hand. Is this a working ranch?"

He nodded. "My father still comes out here once or twice a week to oversee things. This land has been in my family for a long, long time. We used to love to come out and ride horses or just have a barbecue and relax—my parents and relatives still do that a lot. Our workers have their own homes on the land, so it's a good place for all of us."

"Why did your parents move into the city?"

His face went blank, like a shutter blocking out the light. He looked up at the portrait above the fireplace. "It was hard being here…after Jessica died."

Stunned, Brenna stared at him. "Is that her in the picture?"

He kept staring at the portrait. "Yes."

No explanation.

Brenna scrambled for the right thing to say. "But Jessica has a room at the house in the city."

He nodded. "That's why it's such a bone of contention between my parents and me. They set up that room when they moved there."

Brenna's heart ached for this family. "Nick, your parents are good people. Don't they see that this hurts you?"

He took a breath. "They only see a young girl frozen in life. She'll always be fifteen to them. I don't mind the room so much, but I do mind that they seem to want me to grieve in the same way they do. I can't. I won't. I will never stop grieving, but they expect me to let God heal me. They try to force the issue and I bolt every time."

"It makes you uncomfortable?"

"It makes me angry. Jessica shouldn't have died."

"No, but then, we don't get to make that choice."

His gaze hit against hers. "No, we don't. But God does. And I don't understand why."

Brenna knew she was treading on shaky ground. Explaining God's grace to someone who'd lost a loved one wasn't easy. No amount of words or platitudes could help that. And hadn't she felt the same when her mother died?

"You have a picture of her here, though."

"I do. I painted that picture. It's the only thing I have left of her. I know she's gone, but they...they seem to think she's still around. I don't like it."

Brenna tried to gently reason with him. "Maybe your way of dealing with it is not the same as how they handle things. They might be acknowledging her spirit and celebrating her time on earth while you're only dealing with her death."

He got up to pace around the room. "That's the main reason I stay here when I come to San Antonio." He pointed to the portrait. "This makes me remember and it reminds me of my anger and my regret. This is not a celebration for me, ever."

Brenna took a sip of the coffee and decided she wouldn't push him anymore right now about his sister. He was being honest with her, but he was also hinting for her to back off. "But you don't stay here a lot?"

He sat back down beside her and drank from his own cup. His expression seemed more guarded now, as if he didn't want to tell her anything else. "No. Only when I know I'll be in San Antonio for a while. My office is in town, but it's good to have this place. I'm a little too old to stay with my parents, regardless of how we're dealing with my sister's death."

"I'm too old to be living with my dad," she replied, shifting away from his family. "But I'm grateful to be home with my family for a while. My sisters and Papa have helped me through a lot of issues. Papa wants me to stay, but I'll need to decide if I'm going back to Baton Rouge one day."

"You and your family seem to handle your grief much better than my family. How's that possible?"

She put down her coffee mug and clasped her hands on her lap. "I can't explain, except that we have each other and we've always been a tight-knit family. Plus, we live in a small town where people truly love and respect each other. We had a whole community behind us when Mom died. And we have our faith."

"It always comes back to that, doesn't it?"

"For me, yes. Always." She wanted to say more, but she didn't. Nick was teaching her a new way to witness the power of Christ. She had to be patient. She had to wait. And pray.

He nibbled a chunk of cheese and a handful of grapes, more relaxed now that they weren't discussing him. "Have you considered staying in Fleur?"

Brenna didn't know the answer to that. "I honestly don't see how I can. I need a job. A long-term job." She bit into a cracker and nabbed a strawberry. "I appreciate the few months I'll be working for you, though. That'll help me through the holidays and I won't have to dip into my savings."

They sat for another minute, then he looked over at her, his expression full of hope. "Come and work for me."

Chapter Sixteen

❧

"What?" Brenna almost dropped her mug of coffee. "Are you serious?"

"Very," he replied. "I'm always looking for qualified designers and art experts. I'd have you in one very nice package."

She tilted her head to stare over at him. "Are you offering me a job or flirting with me?"

"Both," he said through a grin.

She let that slide but fretted about their earlier conversation. "But you'd pay me twice as much, right?"

He laughed then playfully tapped her nose. "Your salary is negotiable, *sí*. And you'd be worth every penny."

Brenna got up to stare into the fire. "Me, working for you—permanently? I don't know."

"What's not to know? You love what you do and you're good at it. You've taken charge at Fleur House, putting together rooms on spec even though the place isn't finished. You seem to know what kind of art goes in each room, what will make it perfect. That's a gift.

Tia Serena is very impressed with you and you two seem to get along. You'd work mostly with her."

"I've studied art long enough to be able to gauge things like that. Nothing special. I'm not so sure—"

"Don't sell yourself short, Brenna," he said, standing to tug her close. "You're special."

Brenna finally found the courage to look up and into his eyes. She inhaled a breath when she saw the longing and need there in the richness of his dark gaze. This man confused and excited her, but he also left her wondering. "What do you really want from me, Nick?"

"This." He pulled her close and lowered his mouth to hers. "Only this."

Brenna melted into his embrace, the warmth of the fire not as sweet and toasty as the feelings brewing inside her heart. Nick's touch lifted her into a new realm of awareness.

She liked being in his arms, even if it seemed too dangerous. Even if she knew she'd be free-falling once it was over.

He stopped kissing her, then stood back. "See how well we work together?"

"Hmm. I see that I'd never get any work done with you around. Wouldn't it be rather scandalous if a client saw me kissing the boss in every corner of a house?"

"Every corner?" He gave her a peck on the nose. "We're gonna need a bigger house."

Brenna closed her eyes and rested her head on his shoulder. She shouldn't be having so much fun in his arms. Fun kisses were one thing, but true intimacy and openness were both another. It *was* scandalous the way she seemed to be drawn to this man. That startled her, especially after she'd vowed to take her time the next time. But he had opened up to her tonight and she'd seen the horrible pain he held inside his heart.

Did she dare take on the task of soothing that pain? Working with him would be a dream, but it would also keep her in close proximity to the man. She wasn't sure she could keep that line between work and her feelings clear.

Lifting her head, she smiled up at him, hoping to hide her doubts and fears. "What is it with us? I mean, why does this feel so right?"

"You tell me," he said, his lips grazing her skin. "Sometimes people just work out together." Then he lifted his head to look into her eyes. "No matter the odds or the obstacles."

"Is that what we're doing, working out, clicking, getting along? Sharing our secrets? Have I passed another test?"

"No test," he replied, his hand touching her chin. "No test here and no secrets. This is a sure thing."

Brenna thought about Jeffrey and how she'd believed he was a sure thing. She thought about her beautiful mother who'd believed seeing her grandchildren born was a sure thing. She thought about Callie, her sweet older sister and how much Callie had tried to save her marriage while she fought against breast cancer. And she thought about Nick's little sister and wondered why Jessica hadn't lived to a ripe old age, surrounded by beautiful dark-headed grandchildren of her own.

"Nothing is for sure, Nick."

He held her chin, his gaze locking with hers. "I thought you were the one with the solid faith. Can't you have faith in us, in me?"

She wanted that. She'd prayed for that. But she'd

also asked God to show Nick how to heal. Did he want to heal? Or did he want to stay in that dark place that shielded him from the world? And her? If she gave in, she might win a part of him. But Brenna wanted more. She wanted a love that gave all, that accepted the good and the bad. How would she deal with loving him if his anger simmered and festered underneath that calm exterior but never completely healed? Would he turn on her, would he forget his promises and all the odds they'd overcome?

Brenna pulled away. "I don't know. I want to believe, but you're still holding out on me."

He backed up. "In what way?"

Brenna didn't want to ask, but she had to understand. "What happened with your sister?"

He shook his head, then pointed his finger at her. "You've been talking to my aunt and my mother too much."

"No, no, I haven't," Brenna replied. "I didn't say a thing about this to your mother and your aunt won't tell me the truth out of respect for you."

Anger darkened his features. "So you've been asking around, talking to my family?"

"Of course not. I asked your aunt this morning and that was only because I saw Jessica's room."

His beautiful smile had turned into that dark scowl she'd seen before. "I shouldn't have brought you here. I tried to force this on you and now the tables are turned."

"Your family loves you," she said. "And while I don't like the shock value of what they've done, I understand the concern I saw on their faces when we got here."

"They went too far," he replied. "And so did I. I rushed things between us. It's too soon."

"It's not too soon if you trust me. I want to understand what's caused you so much pain."

"What does it matter?" he asked. "That has nothing to do with you and me and how we feel."

"I think it has everything to do with us. It's here in this house and it's back at the work site in your trailer. Your grief is stifling you, Nick. I don't know if I can bring life back to your broken heart."

"You're right. No one can do that except me. And I don't know how. It's not right of me to expect that of you, either."

Hurt that he was backpedaling after offering her what amounted to one of those stars in the sky, Brenna decided it was time to end this. She grabbed her tote bag. "I think we need to get back to town."

He let out a frustrated sigh, his gaze full of remorse now. "I'm sorry. Really."

"But not sorry enough to let me in, to show me why you can be so mercurial, so unpredictable at times. You know all about my family, my grief, my life. Why is it so hard for me to know about you?"

He turned, his hands on his hips. "You do know a lot about my life and my family, and you do know me—the real me. Why would I bring you here if I didn't trust you, Brenna?"

"I don't know." She shrugged, grabbed her wrap. "Maybe you *want* someone to force the issue. Your relatives seem to try at every turn to help you, to hope you'll be okay. Maybe you need someone with a more objective view to finally make you see the light."

"See the light? Forgive and forget? Turn back to

God?" He shook his head. "I can't go that far. I can't forget. No one has to force that issue. It's just a fact, a part of my life."

"You could have a better life, Nick, if you talked to someone, tried to move past the pain I've seen in your eyes. I could help you with that. I'd *like* to help you but I don't know how. In the end, it has to be you. You have to want this."

"I am okay. I can handle this my way." He looked out the window. "And forcing me won't work. My family should realize that by now. You should realize that, too."

"I get it," she said. "I do get it, Nick. It's your business, your burden to bear. But let someone in. Let me in. Turn to God and ask Him to take away some of your pain and your guilt. I understand how you must feel, but I need to understand why you feel that way."

He whirled, anger sparking on a thread through his eyes. "You know nothing of this kind of guilt. Nothing. And I don't need your help."

No, he didn't need her to help him. He only wanted someone to help with his work, to keep him occupied and busy so he wouldn't have to think about the horror of his past, whatever that had been.

"I didn't mean to overstep," Brenna said. "I really wish you could trust someone."

"I told you, I'm okay," he said, the words ground out. "I don't know why this has to be an issue between us."

"No, you don't get it. But I do. I thought I was in love with Jeffrey, thought we'd have a life together. But he held back, never letting me in, never actually making me feel loved. Then he accused me of pushing too much or not pushing enough, you name it, I've been blamed for it. He blamed me while he partied and flirted with most of my friends and with women I didn't even know. He belittled my way of life and my family. That's not love. That's control and manipulation. I can't go through that again."

"I'm not like Jeffrey," he retorted. "I respect you, admire you. I like your way of life. I need you, Brenna."

"Yes, you need me to work with you, to keep you busy, to keep you distracted. But what happens when the sun goes down and you have me but you're still angry and bitter and suffering. What happens then, Nick?"

He stared at her, his eyes as dark as a raging river. "I'd still have you. I'd have that smile, that hope I see in your eyes. You make things better, Brenna."

Tears pricked at her eyes. "But I can't make things right. I can't change what happened in your past. I want to, I want to make everything better, but your pain can't be my pain, Nick. I'm more than willing to listen and discuss and understand—"

"You can't understand and I can't bring myself to explain it."

She gave him one last look, then said, "We have to keep this relationship professional. Business only. I won't push you and you can't keep testing me to see if I'll get it right. That's how it has to be."

When he just stood there staring at her with that heavy torment in his eyes, Brenna pushed past him to go outside. She stared up at the inky darkness and thought he was right about one thing: the stars were much brighter out here.

And so was his pain.

* * *

They left early the next morning. Reports of the storm brewing in the Gulf were scattered all over the airwaves and the internet. What had started out as a tropical disturbance that seemed to be running its course had turned into a late-season, unpredictable tropical storm. And it was headed right for the Gulf coast. Fleur could take a direct hit unless the storm turned.

Dark clouds covered the entire coast, but it was nothing compared to the dark cloud hanging over Brenna's head as she hugged Nick's aunt goodbye after Serena had met them for breakfast and she'd told Serena to thank his parents for their hospitality.

Nick sat next to her now, brooding and moody, his nose stuck in his BlackBerry. He'd barely spoken to her after they'd had words last night. This morning, he'd nodded to her in passing. Even though he'd laughed and made conversation during the meal, Brenna was pretty sure his aunt had picked up on the rift between them.

She now understood why he didn't go home very often. He didn't want to face his family's concern and worry. She couldn't blame him for that, because she felt horrible about trying to force the issue herself. But he also didn't want to face his grief or change how it was controlling his life. Why did grief take such a hold on people? Why did it have to color hearts with doubt and guilt and a deep hole of pain?

Why, Lord?

She didn't voice the prayer out loud, but she questioned things in her heart. Why?

Why had he pushed her away?

Nick wondered that after he'd dropped Brenna back

at her car, thought about it all the way home after she'd halfheartedly thanked him and left. He had a million things on his mind, he thought as he glanced at the cloudy, ominous skies, but he couldn't stop thinking about Brenna and how she made him feel. He should have known better than to take her to see his family, should have left her at the hotel while he stayed out at his house. His life was a facade and now that she'd seen that, she might not want to be around him anymore. She'd pushed him to tell her the truth but instead, he'd shoved the truth in her face with no explanations. Was he testing her again?

It sure looked that way.

But he wanted her with him, wanted her to see him with his family so she'd see that he wasn't all doom and despair. His parents grieved, yes, but they also laughed and talked and loved and they'd managed to go on with their lives. He thought he had, too. But now, after being with Brenna, he knew he'd only been sleepwalking through life. No wonder he couldn't make a commitment to a steady relationship. He was numb inside. Cold. Asleep. He needed to wake up. Really wake up.

Brenna certainly had jarred him out of his nice, safe little cocoon. Brenna made him feel alive again, forced him to face the things he'd been running from for so long. Brenna made everything beautiful. But maybe he wasn't ready to face a beautiful world, after all. Maybe he needed to punish himself for a while longer.

The time away had blown up in his face because Brenna Blanchard wanted more. She wanted all of him. She wanted the part that he'd held away from everyone for so long now.

How could he open that cut again, bleed out in front

of her while he watched the horror and disgust on her face? He couldn't do that. But it was too late, he knew. The gate to his emotions had been prodded open just enough to let her in.

Or rather, Brenna had forced her way in and refused to leave. Now he had to decide if he wanted to fight for her to stay, or fight with her until she got fed up and left.

Chapter Seventeen

The next morning, Brenna hurried with Callie around the nursery. The wind and rain had picked up overnight and Callie and her crew were checking for anything left that might go flying through the air. The forecast predicted the storm would hit sometime this afternoon or late tonight.

"The place looks great. Colorful."

Callie stopped and glanced over at her, rain hitting on their bright ponchos. "Bree, it's early November. The nursery is as drab as an old washcloth right now and a hurricane is brewing out in the Gulf, but I think it's coming faster than anyone could predict. What's the matter with you?"

Brenna snapped to and noticed the dark sky and the roaring wind. Adjusting her plastic rain poncho, she said, "I'm sorry. It's complicated."

"That is so cliché," Callie retorted, motioning for her to get under the eaves of a nearby potting shed. Holding the plastic hood of her poncho over her face, she said, "Give me something else to chew on."

Brenna shivered and held tight to her own wet poncho. "Okay, all right. It's Nick. There. Chew on that."

Elvis heard the word *chew* and came running, his woof of hopefulness endearing and annoying at the same time.

Callie patted her faithful, wet companion on the head. "Auntie Bree is in a mood today, Elvis. Don't give her a big, wet kiss."

Elvis immediately did the opposite of what his mistress had suggested. He jumped up on Brenna with two big, furry paws and tried to lick her face.

"Get off me, you ol' hound dog," Brenna said, making a face at his wet paws all over her. But she couldn't help smiling. Technically, Elvis wasn't a hound dog, but she loved using Elvis references when she was around him. "Why can't men be more like you, Elvis? All lovable and easy?"

Callie giggled. "And hairy?"

Brenna pushed the dog away and grinned. "Okay, maybe not exactly like Elvis." She took the dry towel her sister found inside the shed and handed her. "Nick doesn't like being pushed into anything. He has methods. He makes a plan and sticks to it. Apparently, that plan means he'll tell me what he wants me to know whenever he's good and ready."

"Typical male syndrome," Callie replied in a knowing tone while she scanned her domain. "What's *your* plan?"

"My plan?" Brenna squinted at her sister. "I don't have a plan. I'm going to finish the job I was hired to do and then move on."

"That is not a plan. That's a retreat."

"Yes, I'm retreating," Brenna admitted. "Look, I'm

not ready for another roller-coaster ride of a relationship. I want someone who'll love me and understand me and be there for me, but I need that someone to level with me and tell me the truth. I need someone to plan a life with, to grow old with, someone I can trust always."

Callie smiled, then whistled at Elvis. The big dog came barreling up the wide aisle of palm trees and fruit trees.

"Here's your man," Callie said. "You were right. Elvis is the perfect companion. Let's get him to the shelter quick."

"Very funny."

Giving Elvis a treat for his brilliant performance, Callie turned serious. "Bree, you've always let your heart get in the way of your head. Nick seems like a perfect candidate to mend your broken heart, unless he's just gonna contribute to the already-raw wound you're carrying around."

"Oh, he's contributing all right. One minute he's kissing me and offering me a job and the next, he's pushing me away and going all stonewall on me. It's confusing."

"The old mixed-message trick," Callie said. "I never liked that one."

"What woman does? I've tried to talk to him, bring him back to God. He's bitter about his sister's death, but he won't tell me exactly what happened."

"Did you ever go back to that article you found?"

"No. I want Nick to tell me. It matters to me, his past, his hurts, his issues. Jeffrey was always so tight-lipped about things and look where that got me. If I hadn't snooped around, trying to nail him, I wouldn't have even known how much he'd tricked me and lied to me. I won't go through that again. Even if I opt for the simple plan of just working for Nick, I'd still like to know what makes him tick."

"Do you hear yourself?" Callie asked as they headed for the storefront, bending together against the driving wind. "You're trying to make Nick into what you think he needs to be. You can't force someone back to God and you can't force grief or any other problem to disappear so the world will be all better. We both should know that from firsthand experience."

Brenna stopped walking and stared over at her sister, rain and wind hissing all around them. "You're right. I'm doing the same thing with Nick that I tried to do with Jeffrey—change him. Since we met, I've tried to force Nick at every turn. Exactly in the same way his concerned family tries to heal him and shock him into accepting what they think is best." She grabbed Callie's arm. "No wonder he doesn't want to talk to me. And, really, he's nothing like Jeffrey. Nick isn't lying about anything. He's just having a hard time with his grief, and of course, I've made that even worse. I have to go to the other plan on this."

"And what is the other plan?"

"The complicated, let's-figure-this-out plan. That one will take a lot more effort." She shrugged, glanced up at the gray, roving clouds. "Nick and I have to accept that we can weather the storms together, no matter what. He tried to tell me that, but I wouldn't listen to him. He needed me to do that. *Me.* That was his way of telling me he needed me. And what did I do? I walked away." She hit a hand against her wet hood. "I'm so dense sometimes."

Her sister stopped at the front counter inside the open nursery storefront to peel off her wet poncho. "Well, little sister, you have to decide which plan you *want* to fight for, which plan might work out best for you in the end. And going all philosophical on him might not work."

Brenna tugged at her poncho and brushed her damp hair into place. "Honestly, I don't know if either of us is up to figuring this out, but I have to try. I have to go and talk to Nick and tell him how sorry I am."

"What if he doesn't care? What if he was trying to send you away, trying to give you an out?"

"I have to try, anyway," Brenna said. "But right now, I have to get to him before this hurricane hits."

Callie shook her head, her hand in the air. "You can't go out to Fleur House. The bridge out of town is almost under water from that tide surge that's rolling in."

"I have to go," Brenna insisted. "This can't wait. He's out there all alone. He sent everyone else to safety. It's a perfect time to tell him how sorry I am."

Her sister's usually serene face held a frown of concern. "During a hurricane? Don't you think you should wait on that?"

Brenna bit at her bottom lip. "No, what better time—he'll have to listen."

"Papa will flip out if you go into a storm, Bree."

Brenna glanced at the dark sky and the steady rain. "I have to go, Callie. I have to. Maybe I can get him to come back to town with me. We can all be together in the designated shelter."

Callie grabbed a dry bright yellow raincoat off a peg. "Take this. It's thicker than that old poncho. And be careful. Call me and let me know you made it."

Brenna nodded. After changing into the heavy rain-coat, she said, "I'll call if I have service. But don't worry, I can tread water if I have to."

But once she was in her car and heading toward the curve in the Big Fleur Bayou, Brenna wondered if she'd made the right decision. The Bayou Bridge loomed ahead, old and creaky. Brenna took it slow, but she could see the angry, churning waters from the swampy river blending with the surge from the open Gulf. The water was beginning to merge over the bridge, wave by crashing wave.

Rain and wind lashed at Nick as he hurried across the yard at Fleur House. The crew had worked to secure the many windows and doors of the big house. Because they'd recently finished the major renovations inside and were now working on the outside, Nick wanted to make sure the house was secure.

Once things had been battened down, he'd sent all the workers home to be with their families, even those who'd traveled here from Texas. They could sit out the storm back in their homes instead of hotels out on the interstate.

But Nick didn't intend to leave. He had too much at stake here. He'd already reported to the owner that everything was under control. He intended to keep it that way.

His cell phone buzzed and he saw his aunt's number. Deciding to answer and reassure her before he lost cell power, he ran up on the porch to find shelter. "Hello."

"Nicky, we're all concerned about the storm. Why don't you come home?"

"You know I can't leave now, *Tia*. I have to watch over the house."

"It could be dangerous," Serena said. "That house is very close to the big water. Get somebody else to watch over it."

"This house has stood in this spot for close to two centuries and it's been through a lot of storms. I'll be fine, I promise." After promising his aunt that he'd seek cover, Nick thought of the many rooms in this big, old place. He could certainly get in the middle of the house if the wind and water got too bad. He hurried to get a weather radio, a flashlight and other supplies. He'd have those ready if he had to leave the trailer fast.

An hour later, he'd gone back over the house room by room and done everything he could to protect the huge windows and doors. Most of the windows had been shut tight with the built-in hurricane shutters he'd had installed for just such storms.

The house was dark now, the sound of the angry wind moaning around the tree branches and flying debris hissing and hitting at the mansion. Nick was headed back to his trailer when he heard a car approaching.

Who in their right mind would be out in this coming storm?

Brenna Blanchard.

Nick had only spoken to her a few times since they'd returned from San Antonio. They couldn't work with the storm approaching, so he'd told her to stay with her father and her family and to find a safe place.

She'd obviously ignored that suggestion.

Nick turned back toward the porch and waited for her. He intended to make her turn around and go home.

Brenna, dressed in a bright yellow trench coat and rain boots, hurried up the steps onto the deep porch. "Are you all right?" she asked, out of breath.

Nick's heart took a spin at seeing her again. "Yes. What are you doing here?"

She pulled off the scarf she'd wrapped around her head. "I was worried about you. I came to bring you back to the church gymnasium. It's the designated shelter." She tugged on his arm. "But we have to hurry. The surge is covering the roads and the big bridge."

"Hold on. I have plenty of shelter right here," he replied, pulling away. "But you need to get back to town. You can't stay here."

"I'm not going back without you," she said. "I mean it, Nick. I came to tell you I'm sorry for the way I've been acting. What can I do to help?"

Nick stared down at her, part of him wanting to tug her close while the other part of him wanted to send her on her merry way. "I think everything's under control." Except his heart. Then he looked into her eyes and said, "You don't need to apologize to me."

She stared up at him, her eyes a rich misty green-brown in the dark light. "I think I do. I've been pushing you since the day we met. Your faith and your life are none of my business. I'm so sorry."

Nick didn't know what to say. The woman had come through a storm to apologize to him when he was the one who should be explaining himself. "It's okay, Brenna. You need to go back to your family."

"I don't want to leave you out here alone. Are you sure everything is secure?"

He pointed to the windows. "We're prepared. All of the hurricane shutters are in place and all of the outside doors are shut tight. We taped over what we couldn't shutter."

"Where are you going to stay?"

He glanced toward his trailer.

Brenna followed his gaze. "No, not in there. It's too dangerous."

Nick looked up at the sky. He could tough this out. Sometimes the weather people got things wrong. "I've been through worse. I think I'll be fine. I have a weather radio. If it makes you feel better, I'll stay in the center of the house instead of my trailer."

"Have you seen the radar?" she asked, her hand motioning toward the sky. "This is a monster. It's covering the whole coast across Louisiana and Mississippi. They say it might become a Cat Three by nightfall. It's bad, Nick."

Nick checked the dark, roaring clouds, then glanced around. The rain and wind were definitely picking up. Even in a three, the surge could reach miles inland and destroy just about everything in its path. He could take care of himself, but he wouldn't be responsible for her. She should be with her family. He wouldn't risk something happening to her. He could not carry yet another burden of guilt by losing someone he loved.

Loved.

The realization tore through him with the same intensity as this storm. And because he did love her, he had to make her leave.

Tugging her toward the steps, his heart at war with his brain, he shouted, "All the more reason for you to turn around and go back to the shelter. Now, Brenna. Hurry."

Brenna watched the sky, then shook her head. Over

the roar of thunder and lightning and heavy winds, she shouted, "I don't think I can go back now. The road out here was already beginning to wash out from the surge. I barely got across the bridge. I'm pretty sure it's under water by now."

As if to back her up, the heavens burst forth with heavy, heaving rain and flashing shards of thunder and lightning. Nick looked from the sky back to Brenna. He couldn't send her out in this. But what if he couldn't protect her, either?

Chapter Eighteen

"You're where?"

Brenna held her cell phone away from her ear and hit the speaker button while her papa let out a string on angry words that cleared the static coming over the wireless. "I'm with Nick at Fleur House. I don't think I can make it back to town."

"Of course you can't make it," Papa said, his words rolling together like the big waves hitting the seawall down below the house. "Da roads are washed out, de big bridge is sitting in wader. Why on earth did you think it'd be smart to go out to dat house tonight of all nights?"

Brenna could hear him even with the sound of the storm raging through the house. "I wanted Nick to come back to town with me, but he refused. I can't leave him out here all alone, Papa."

Her papa didn't agree with that decision. "Of course you can't, 'cause you're just that stubborn and impulsive, Daughter Number Three. Let me talk to da man."

"He wants to speak to you." She handed Nick her phone.

"I can hear that," Nick said to her on a whisper. "Uh, hello, Mr. Blanchard."

"Listen to me and listen good," Ramon Blanchard said. "Dat dere is my baby girl. You better take good care of her, *mon ami*. If I find one hair on her head messed up, I'll take the law into my own hands."

Nick glanced at Brenna. "Of course I'll take care of her. I told her she should have stayed in town, but I can't let her leave now."

"*Non,* she's trapped dere with you. I expect you to make sure she's safe and sound." Mr. Blanchard went on for a few more seconds, lapsing in and out of Cajun-French.

"We should be okay, Mr. Blanchard. Fleur House is built up high and the yard has a slight incline toward the bayou and swamps."

"I'm not so worried about da incline, you understand? I'm more worried about you and my daughter out dere all alone."

Nick understood what Brenna's father was telling him. "You can trust me, sir. I'll look out for her and take care of her."

"See dat you do just dat."

Nick listened, then handed the phone back to Brenna. "He's not happy and neither am I."

Brenna glared at Nick, then tried to soothe her daddy's frazzled nerves. Taking off the speaker, she said, "Papa, this is a big, old house up on a hill. I'll be as safe here as I would be in that gym."

"You just make sure dat's the case, daughter. Now go somewhere away from de wind and water. And call me back every hour on de hour until morning."

"I will unless the cell towers go out," Brenna said. "I love you."

Her father responded in kind. "I love you, too. But me, I'm thinking you love someone else better now."

A few minutes later, Brenna turned to stare at the man who'd shoved her inside the big, empty house. She watched him building a fire in the sparkling clean and updated fireplace and thought about her papa's words.

Was she in love with Nick?

She did cross a raging canal of water to get to him so she could apologize. She did want more from him, more than just a job or a friendship. She wanted to know him on an intimate, mind-to-mind, heart-to-heart level.

She was alone in a storm with a man she'd barely known a full month. And yes, she was in love with him.

But he certainly didn't look in love with her. He kept glaring at her with those dark eyes, his expression as stormy and hard to predict as the rain and wind crashing around them.

"I'm sorry," she finally said. "I should have realized you can take care of yourself, and that you didn't want me here."

Nick nodded, kept glaring. "Yes, and you should have known better than to come out in this storm. Why didn't you stay in the shelter with your family?"

"I wanted you there, too," she finally said. "I couldn't leave you out here alone, Nick."

He lifted his hands in the air, then let them drop to his side. "Why not? Why can't you leave me alone?"

Hurt by his anger, Brenna turned and stared into the big empty fireplace. Nick had lit a fire to keep them dry and warm, but the heat of his rage burned worse than the fire.

"You're right," she said, grabbing her rain slicker and heading for the front door. "I'll go. I'm sure if I hurry I can make it back across the bridge. I'd rather take a chance on that than being with you in this mood."

Then she felt his hand on her arm. "I'm sorry, too. Sorry that you felt it necessary to worry about me, necessary to come out here. Brenna, you don't need to fix me. You need someone better in your life."

He let go of her and turned away.

She whirled, her face burning in embarrassment. "Fix you? Make you better? Is that what you think I'm trying to do?" She had to close her eyes to the truth she'd already seen. She had been trying to…help him. Wasn't that the reason she'd come through that storm? To tell him she was sorry.

He stood with his arms folded and stared over at her. "Well, yes. You want me to open up to you, to tell you all about the ugliness of my life. But I can't, and I'm not the kind of man who'll ever be able to open up completely. I don't want to talk about it because it's too painful to tell."

She tugged at her resentment and swallowed her pride. "And yet, you managed to get all the details of my past out of me."

"You offered all of that," he replied, pushing off a wall to come toward the fire. Then he said on a gentle note, "You're more open and honest than I'll ever be."

"Yes, yes, I am," she retorted. "I'm honest and I expect honesty in people I care about."

That brought his head up. "You care about me?"

"Of course I do. We've been working together for

weeks now. I care that you and I seem to share the same goals and we both love our work, work that seems to merge each time we're together. We complement each other. We understand each other."

"When it comes to work, you mean?"

She nodded. "But it ends there."

"And you want it to go deeper?"

"I don't know what I want," she admitted. "I don't know what I feel anymore, either." She went to the big front door and peeked through the one place he'd left open, a tiny pane of beveled glass. The yellow security light spotlighted the torrent of rain and wind. "It's getting worse out there."

"Come with me," he said, stalking toward her. "I left a weather radio in the kitchen." Then he took her hand. "And the crew set up a coffee bar in there as soon as we had power in the house. Hopefully we can find something to eat and drink before the electricity gets knocked out."

"You think it'll get really bad?" she asked, the warmth of his hand lessening the tension between them.

"Yes." He stopped and turned to her. "And even though you shouldn't have done it, I'm kinda glad I have you here with me."

Brenna took that statement and weighed it inside her heart. He tried to send her away to protect her. But he was afraid to love her. The man had to care a little bit, but she didn't know if he'd ever take things any further. And right now, she wasn't sure she even wanted that. Forcing someone to love her had never worked in her favor.

Maybe Papa was right. Had she gone off the deep end?

They made their way to the back of the house and the kitchen. "I have some candles somewhere in here," Nick said. "For ambiance. One of the locals gave me a hurricane kit."

"Good." Brenna let out a sigh of relief. "We all have a go-bag around here, filled with our most precious things and all our vital information."

Nick went to the big wide counter and found the heavy tote bag Pierre LeBlanc had brought by that morning. "Mrs. LeBlanc insisted I take this, according to Pierre. It's full of toiletries and a lot of other essentials."

"The women of the church put those together in case a hurricane comes through. Just makes things easier during and afterward."

Nick lit one of the candles and placed it on the counter. They stood silent for a while, then his eyes met Brenna's. "I'm sorry for what I said earlier. And I'm sorry our weekend ended on a bad note."

She nodded, stayed on her side of the room. "I shouldn't have forced myself on you during this storm. I really was concerned about you and I did want to apologize, too."

"You didn't force anything. I… I didn't think I needed to leave the house. I'm responsible for this place."

"And who's responsible for your safety and well-being, Nick?"

"Only me." He shrugged. "You don't need to take on that role."

"You don't want anyone to take on that role, do you?"

"No, I guess I don't. I've learned how to take care of myself and I've been on my own for a long time."

"Since Jessica died?"

The quiet mood disappeared. His face grew as dark as the night pushing through the rain outside. "I'm not going there, Brenna."

But Brenna was going there. She didn't know why, but she figured if he couldn't talk to her about his worst pain, then they'd never be able to get along, work or no work. And even though she'd tried to apologize and so had he, they were here together and neither could leave. Maybe now *was* the best time to get it all out there.

"I almost looked it up on the internet. I saw a newspaper article and a picture of a girl on a horse—the same portrait you have over your hacienda mantel."

"Stop it."

"I never went back to finish the article. I wanted to hear it from you."

"Why? What does it matter now?"

Unsure what to say or do, she came around the corner and touched a hand to his shoulder. "Because I care, Nick. Because I've been hurt by grief. Because I worry, yes, worry about you. And pray for you."

He didn't turn around, but she felt the tension coiling inside him, felt the heat of pain and despair radiating around him. "I…can't talk about it. I don't want people to know—"

She leaned close behind him, laid her head against his broad back and wrapped her arms tight around him. "Why? Because it will hurt? Because you're afraid I'll turn away? This is me, Nick. I don't do that. I don't turn away. I turn toward the things I want in life."

Then she heard a low, growling whisper. "Do you want me, then, in your life?"

"Yes, yes, I think I do. But I want all of you, not just the parts you want me to see." She held on to him. "I'm sorry, but I have to be honest. And I need you to be honest."

"You might not like what you see if I show you everything."

"Let me be the judge of that," she said. "Please, Nick?"

He turned then, his eyes a deep, dark pool of anger and grief. "I don't think—"

A crash outside brought them apart. Nick took her by the hand and tugged her upstairs. "There's a port window on the staircase. I left it uncovered but it's got tape across it. Maybe we can see out that."

Startled and disoriented, Brenna followed him and waited while he squinted into the dark night. "The security lights are still on." He turned back to her, his features a mixture of concern and regret. "But the seawall didn't hold back the surge. It looks like the whole front yard is flooded with water."

They lost electricity around midnight.

Brenna sat huddled with Nick in the upstairs sitting room. He'd assured her the floodwaters shouldn't reach them up here.

Now, she prayed the water wouldn't damage the bottom floor. But this was only a house. She also prayed that everyone she loved would be safe. All they could do was wait and watch. And continue to pray.

"I'm glad I called Callie earlier," she said. "They'd

all be so worried. And they don't need to know about the seawall breaking."

Nick sat with his hands resting on his knees. "If the water has reached that high, I'm pretty sure they've seen it in town, too. It's gonna be a long night."

Brenna saw the shadows moving across his face. The candlelight traced his fatigue. "I guess I should have stayed in town. Now you feel responsible for me, too."

He shook his head. "I didn't mean— I wasn't talking about your being here. This storm could rage for hours." He touched a finger to her still-damp curls. "It's as stubborn as you, I think."

"You're comparing me to a hurricane?"

"You do tend to push through walls and come crashing onto a scene."

She didn't respond to that because she knew it was true. "I don't always think things through."

He tugged at the strands he had around his finger. "And I don't always say what I really mean."

The house rattled. They heard more crashing sounds.

"Why don't we go check on the bottom floor?" she asked. "I promise I won't do anything crazy. I'll be right behind you."

He'd refused this idea earlier, telling her he couldn't risk her getting injured. Now he stared over at her with those dark eyes. "You amaze me."

Shocked, she drew her head back. "What? Me? Why?"

"You have this positive attitude, even in the middle of a hurricane. For every doubt I throw out there, you have a reassurance. It's one of the things I—admire about you."

Her heart hammered in a heavy cadence, so she tried to keep her words light. "Oh, there's more than one thing you admire about me?"

He leaned close. "Yes, lots more."

She swallowed, her throat going dry. "Then tell me."

He shifted, then touched her hair again. "I admire your hair." He pushed his fingers through her tangled locks.

"It's frizzing right now," she said, her heart doing that excited beat.

"You look good in frizzy hair."

She grinned at that. "Thank you."

He moved a little closer. "And I love those big ever-changing eyes." Then he held up her chin so he could feather her nose with kisses. "And I like this. Being with you like this, in spite of all the things that brought us here together in this storm, means the world to me."

Brenna drew back to stare up at him. "Nick, I need you to understand something."

He pressed a kiss to her temple. "But I'm not through admiring all your good qualities."

She put her hand on his face. "I don't have such good qualities. I've been pushy, nosy, demanding. When I go after something or someone, I *do* want it all. It's the way God wired me, but I'm trying to change. I think that's why Jeffrey and I didn't work."

Nick grabbed her hand in his. "Jeffrey was an idiot to treat you so badly and to let you get away."

"Or maybe he was smart to end things before he got trapped in a marriage with me."

"You can't be serious?"

"I am very serious. I'm seriously flawed. The whole time I've known you, I've badgered you about your past when really, all that matters is the future."

"Our future, you mean?"

"Do you want a future with someone like me in it?"

"No," he said, his expression solemn and unyielding.

Brenna's heart sank like a battered boat. "Well, then—"

"I don't want someone *like* you. I want *you* in my future."

A new shock wave flowed through her. "Working with you?"

He smiled, then kissed her hand. "That and more."

Brenna didn't know what to say. But Nick didn't give her time to speak. He tugged her into his arms and kissed her.

Brenna fell into that kiss with a feeling of falling into that raging water down below them. A floating sensation took over and purged all of her doubts and fears. She didn't need to know the truth about Nick's tragic past. She only knew one truth right now.

She loved him.

Nick lifted his head and hugged her. "Everything is going to work out for us, Brenna."

"What makes you so sure of that?"

"I have faith," he said, his smile soft and sure. "Because of you, I have faith in us."

She blinked at the tears pricking at her eyes. "I guess that's one of my positive attributes, huh?"

"*Sí.* The best one next to your sweet lips."

She couldn't speak, didn't understand the full meaning of his calm words. What had changed inside that fascinating mind? When he stood and reached down for her, she almost didn't get up. She wasn't sure she would be steady on her feet.

"Let's go check the water," he said. "If everything looks okay, we'll sit down and have a long talk."

"About us?" she had to ask. "About our future?"

He stopped on the landing. "No, about me. About my past."

Chapter Nineteen

Nick found a flashlight and guided Brenna down the stairs. Shining the wide beam ahead of them, he could hear the never-ending roar of the wind and water whirling with gale strength around the big house. The weather radio warning indicated the storm had made landfall dead-center between Louisiana and Mississippi. Things could have been much worse, but there would be millions of dollars of damage all the same.

"Steady," he said as he stayed in front of her. "Be careful."

"I'm right here," Brenna replied, her hand holding tight to his shirt.

Nick thought that certainly was an appropriate statement. Brenna had been right here from the beginning. She'd come home for her sister's wedding even when her own heart was breaking because she'd just called off things with her fiancé. Nick had danced with her at that wedding because he wanted to get to know her. The attraction was there even in those first awkward moments. He couldn't deny that. He'd offered her a job because of her expertise and experience, but he'd wanted her near so he could enjoy being around her.

And he realized now, as he thought about the mural she'd begged him to restore, that Brenna was a lot like that big, oversize depiction of a long-ago way of life. She was a bit tattered and torn, but she was larger-than-life and she held a deep beauty that couldn't be denied. He'd fallen for her that day when she'd stared up at that mural, probably had fallen for her when he'd look up and saw her at the wedding.

He'd tried to deny that, but he'd at least been honest when he'd told her what he wanted more than anything. "Make it beautiful for me."

She could do that and more. She could make his life new and fresh and full of hope and love instead of doubt and grief and regret.

But first, he had to be completely honest with her. Brenna demanded that above all else.

And he would tell her everything, as soon as he knew she'd be safe in this house. They made it to the landing above the first floor. The whole house seemed to be shaking and shimmying against the power of that wind. But from what he could tell from the long beam of light, the bottom floor was intact.

"No water down here so far," he said, glad for the distraction. "I'll need to check the basement."

"The basement!" She held even tighter to him. "You can't go down there. It's dark and spooky and if water is coming in, you might bump into snakes and alligators."

"I don't think they can make it through the new mesh screens we installed on the windows."

"You never know."

But he did know a lot of things now that he'd never

known before. Brenna kept pushing, pushing until he had to take a long hard look at himself and his own shaky faith.

Why did it have to take a storm to get him to stop and take a long, hard look at his life? And to realize he was truly in love for the first time, the last time if he had his way.

"Let's check the port window," he said, glancing behind him. He held the light up toward the round little window, but it was hard to see in the darkness. "I can't tell with the rain and wind blowing so hard. It's dark out there with no security lights."

"Let's keep going," she said, her hand on his arm.

When they reached the bottom floor, he turned to stare up at her. "Are you okay?"

"I'm fine," she said. "Just glad I'm here with you."

"What about your family?"

"They know I'll be all right."

"You trust me that much?"

She let out a breath. "Yes, I do."

"I don't deserve your trust."

"And I don't deserve you."

He helped her down the last stairstep, thinking she might change that assumption. The windows rattled and shook while the wind hit at the house like a construction worker with a sledgehammer. Nick heard debris pelting against the porches and the windows and wondered if anything would be left of the yard. Thankfully, he'd had his foreman move all the heavy machinery and tools to a safer location.

"Where's your car?" Brenna asked.

"Julien let me put it in his boat shop."

"That's good. I love that car."

Nick had to smile at her nervous chatter. He loved that car, too. "The car should be okay. Julien seems to have some experience with storms."

"Oh, yes. His brother and my papa got lost in one last spring, in a boat that Julien built."

"I've heard about that. They survived. We will, too."

She grabbed at him when they entered the big, empty dining room. "What if Fleur House doesn't survive?"

Once, just a few short weeks ago, Nick would have been devastated by that kind of talk. It would have painted him as a failure. Now, he looked around, shining the flashlight's beam here and there.

And he only saw one thing that mattered.

Brenna.

"I'm not worried about that. I only want you to survive."

She looked up at him, her eyes shining bright in the faint glow the flashlight provided. "I'm tough. It'll take more than a hurricane to sweep me off my feet."

Nick decided he wanted to be the one to sweep her away. He was tired of fighting his feelings, tired of carrying his heavy burden, so tired of living in the shadow of his guilt and shame. He might not deserve any happiness, but he couldn't fight this any longer. He needed Brenna in his life.

"Hold tight," he said, pulling her with him. "I'll need your help when we reach the basement door."

Brenna wasn't so sure about this. She'd never really liked basements. But then, she'd never really gone in a lot of basements, either. But Nick was with her and that did bring her a measure of security and calm.

The irony of their situation hit at her with the same force as the wind and rain pelting the house. Nick was going to open up to her so they could have a future together.

Maybe getting dirty in a dank basement was a metaphor for their relationship. They had to get into the thick of things to make it through. She'd certainly pushed him, fought with him, forced him to confront whatever he seemed to be holding him back.

And what about you? she asked herself. Hadn't she been holding back in her own life? She'd practically run away from Fleur to put the tragedy of her mother's death behind her. Then Callie had gotten sick and Brenna had poured herself into work and trying to please Jeffrey because she didn't want to face the fear of a dreaded disease. Callie was more upbeat and positive than any of them, and yet, Brenna had shied away from telling her brave, remarkable sister how proud she was of her.

And now, she'd found a man who could deal with her quirks and her fears, but he was afraid to confront his own shortcomings and guilt. Would she run from him, too?

They were at the basement door now.

Nick turned to her. "Are you ready?"

"I think so." She kissed him for good measure.

He listened through the massive door right off the new kitchen. "The workers haven't done much down here, but it's pretty sturdy. It's held up this house for a long, long time."

Brenna bobbed her head. Nick turned the doorknob and slowly pushed it open, then he shined the light down the stairs.

Brenna glanced over his shoulder. She heard it before they saw it. "Water."

"It's three steps away," Nick said. "Any higher and the bottom floor will be flooded."

"What can we do?"

"Hope the storm passes quickly so this can start receding," he replied.

"What about sandbags, a way to seal off the rest of the house?"

He shook his head. "We counted on the seawall to hold, so we put down only a few sandbags around the base of the house and obviously those didn't hold, either."

Brenna wasn't afraid for herself. They could go to the top of the house if they had to. But she hated to see this great old house go through a flood so soon after being renovated.

"Is this the only door to the basement?"

He nodded. "If the surge begins to recede, we'll be okay."

"This means the surge did reach the house," Brenna said. "I don't know if that's ever happened before."

"We'll rebuild the seawall," he replied as they turned toward the kitchen. "We'll make it stronger."

Brenna smiled in spite of her fears. Nick was in this for the long haul. Maybe he'd use that same declaration regarding their relationship, too.

They reached the kitchen and he motioned to two plastic chairs the construction guys had left behind. "Nothing we can do now but wait. Let's sit a minute. I'll check the water level again in a bit."

He offered her a banana he found on the counter. "You must be starving."

"I'm okay."

Brenna kept thinking about upstairs and how he'd reached for her, how he'd kissed her and told her he wanted her in his future. Had he only said those things because he was trapped here with her? Because this storm made him think of what could or could not happen?

They sat in silence for a few minutes while she finished her banana. The wind continued its assault against the house, the rain drowning out the rest of the world. Her phone didn't have any reception, but she wondered how Papa and Callie and the rest of her family and friends were faring. The water was so close, so very close.

Nick got up. "I'll check again."

Brenna closed her eyes and said a prayer for all the people she loved. Suddenly, she wanted her family near, wished she could have convinced Nick to go back to town with her.

But God had put her here for a reason, storm or no storm.

She didn't have it in her to abandon Nick, the same as when that other storm had hit and her papa and Pierre had gone missing. She'd driven through that storm to get home.

She'd driven through this storm to find her heart.

"Brenna?"

She opened her eyes to find Nick standing over her. "What?"

"I don't think the water's getting any higher. The surge probably pushed through the garden and grounds and met up with the bayou on the low end of the property. We'll have to keep watch, but if that rain settles down, I think maybe we'll be okay."

She nodded, tears pushing at her tired eyes.

He motioned to the dining room. "Let's go look at the mural."

Thinking this was an odd time for that, she got up, anyway.

Nick took her into the big, empty room, then pulled her close. "Let's dance."

"We don't have music."

"We don't need music."

He started humming a soft, sweet tune and she fell into his arms. "This is nice."

He kissed her near her temple. "The storm is out there, but we're okay in here."

She laid her head on his shoulder and closed her eyes. "Yes, we're okay."

They danced for a few minutes, then he stopped and looked down at her. "I… I blame myself for what happened to Jessica."

"I know," she said, her heart hurting for him.

"Is it that obvious?"

"Sometimes you look like you have the weight of the world on your shoulders."

"It feels that way at times."

She waited, patient now because she knew how much this had cost him.

He pulled her close again. "We still lived out on the ranch. Not in the hacienda, but in our house a few miles away. She was taking horseback riding lessons. She knew how to ride a horse, but this was for a competition, not a rodeo. But more formal."

"Dressage?"

"Yes. I was angry because she needed a ride to the stables where she was trained and Mom and Dad had gone into town to take care of some banking business. They expected me to take her to her lesson and they'd planned to meet her there later. Her horse was already there. We boarded him there away from the other animals. I had a date that night and I was in a mood, rushing her around, calling her names. I didn't want to give her a ride and when she finally got in the truck, she was pouting because her big brother had shouted at her."

Brenna closed her eyes, an image forming inside her head. But she didn't dare ask what had happened.

"She was late because of me. I was going through this phase where I resented everything my parents tried to do for us. It seemed they were spoiling Jessica. I told her that. She didn't want to get in trouble with her instructor, though, so she got in and just sat there, tears in her eyes." He paused, took a breath.

Brenna could hear the wind howling, pushing, fighting at the house. The rain hit harder and harder against the windows.

She held tight to the man in her arms, willing him to talk to her.

"I had planned to drop her off and leave, but she turned to me with those big brown eyes. 'Nicky, won't you stay and watch?'"

He stopped, stood back to slide his hand down his face. "She was fifteen, Brenna. Fifteen. I was eighteen and hotheaded, determined to get back at her for bothering me. I was selfish and in a hurry to get to my girl. I laughed and told her I didn't have time to sit around watching her on some stupid horse."

He walked to the mural and stared into the darkness.

"The funny thing is I'd painted a portrait of her on that very horse about a month before that. We wanted to give it to our parents for their anniversary."

Brenna put a hand to her mouth to stop the gasp of anguish.

"The picture hanging on your wall, the same one I saw on the internet?"

He nodded. "The local paper did a story on her, on her death, and my mother showed them the portrait. So tragic, such a waste of a young girl's dreams."

Brenna rushed to him. "Nick, don't. Don't say anything else."

But he was ready to talk now. "No, you need to understand. You need to see what kind of person I was then. I was selfish and I wanted more—I wanted the big city and money and I wanted to design great houses and buildings, but I was stuck on this ranch, working day and night and trying to finish school. We had to sacrifice to buy that horse for her. Always for her."

"Nick—"

He held up a hand. "I only painted the portrait because she wanted to surprise our parents, wanted to thank them for believing in her. So I painted her, hoping they'd be proud of me, too." He shook his head. "They were always proud of me, but I was too blind to see that."

He paced back and forth, then turned to face Brenna. "I walked back to my truck and I got inside even while she stood there crying." He stopped, put a hand to his face. "I left her there and peeled out, spewing rocks everywhere. The old truck backfired. It was so loud."

When he gulped a breath, Brenna grabbed at his hand and held it.

"All that noise spooked one of the horses and it came charging around the corner and... She was standing there, waving to me, but it kept coming and the horse reared back and kicked and kicked and—"

Brenna pulled him into her arms, held him while his body shuddered. "The horse kicked her in the head and kept running. I was at the end of the drive. I turned to look back, thinking I shouldn't leave her that way. I glanced over, debating whether to go back or not, and I saw the horse charging toward her, saw her trying to protect herself. I called out, then I got out of the truck and ran toward her, but it was too late, too late."

He held on to Brenna. "She died instantly, according to the doctors." He sniffed and stood back to wipe his eyes. "My mother found the portrait a week later in Jessica's closet."

He finally looked at Brenna. "I stopped painting after that. I didn't want to live after that. But I did live. My heart kept right on beating, so I finished college and I worked and worked, but I couldn't keep the memory of that day out of my mind. I build beautiful homes for families, for people to live in and play in and laugh in, but I didn't think I deserved such things. My parents kept telling me it wasn't my fault, but I knew it was. It was, Brenna. I caused my little sister's death."

"No," she said, trying to reach out to him. "No, Nick. You turned. You were going back."

"She never knew that. She was crying and then she tried to shield herself. I see that image every day, every night, and I have to live with that the rest of my life."

Brenna swiped at the tears streaming down her face. "So you live in a trailer to punish yourself?"

"No, I live in a trailer so I can keep moving."

"But you can't get away from this grief."

"No. And I can't get away from asking God why? Why Jessica? Why wasn't it me that day? Why am I still here when she's gone forever?"

Brenna grabbed for him, her fingers willing him to relax. "You're a good man, Nick. I can see that. Your family loves you. God loves you. I love you, too. And you will see Jessica again one day."

He shook his head, pulled away. "No. I was so angry at God for so long. I buried all that anger and pain in my work. But then, you came along and shattered everything I'd built around my heart. I wanted to get out of here and keep going. I didn't want to face you or God." He looked down at her, his heart in the dark torment of his eyes. "But now, I want you both in my life."

She reached for his hands and held them tight, her eyes searching his, tears falling down her face. "We're here. I'm here and God never turned from you. It's okay, you can rest now." She pulled him into her arms, her hand massaging his back. "You can stop running now, Nick."

Chapter Twenty

Nick woke with a start.

He was sitting against a wall in the second-floor hallway with Brenna in his arms, her raincoat covering her. She sighed and opened her eyes to look up at him.

"I don't hear rain," she said. She sat up and pushed at the coat. "Nick, I think it's over."

"It's morning," he said. "Early yet." He checked his watch. "Six-fifteen. It's still drizzling, but we should be okay now."

"I have to call Callie and Alma."

She lifted up before he could move to help her.

While she paced and waited to hear, Nick thought over the long night. Brenna loved him. She'd told him that.

She wanted him to stop running from his guilt. Could he do that? He'd never actually talked to anyone other than his family about that day and what had happened to Jessica. They kept telling him they didn't blame him, but in his heart he'd always felt that they did. His parents loved him, but how could they ever forgive him? How could he forgive himself?

He'd told Brenna everything, the whole ugly story.

And she hadn't turned away. She'd held him and comforted him and he knew she'd prayed for him. Did he deserve her? Did he deserve her understanding? Did he deserve God's love and forgiveness?

He kept remembering what she'd said once. She turned toward the things she wanted. Nick realized she was right. He ran from the things he really wanted—a home, a family, a faith-based life—because he didn't think he deserved those things. And with Brenna, he'd worried that if he loved her too much, God would somehow punish him by taking her away. What if she got breast cancer? Could he handle that now?

Brenna thought he was worth fighting for, and she believed that Christ thought he was worth fighting for. Could he really have the kind of life he'd only dreamed about?

Nick got up to see if he could get through to his parents. His phone signal was weak, but he could hear the phone ringing.

"Hello?"

"Mama, it's Nick. I'm okay. I haven't checked outside the house yet, but I think we made it."

"Oh, Nicky, I'm so thankful. I asked so many people to pray for all of you."

"Thanks, Mama." He glanced at Brenna. She was talking, her hands moving in animation. Her hair was down and falling all around her face, her shirt and jeans rumbled, her feet bare. She'd never looked more beautiful.

Nick talked to his mother a little longer. "I'd better go, but before I do, I need to tell you something."

"What is it?" his mother asked. "Are you sure you're okay?"

"I told Brenna about Jessica, Mama. I told her about that day and what really happened."

"Nicky." His mother lapsed into Spanish. She thanked God and everyone else she could think of. "I'm so glad. Brenna, she understands. She cares for you because she has the love of Christ in her heart. She is a good girl, *sí?*"

"*Sí,*" he replied. "She's special."

His mother's next words were shaky. "Nicky, we love you so much. All is forgiven. All, Nicky. It's time for you to forgive yourself."

"I think maybe you're right," he said. "It's so hard, but I'm trying. Brenna has helped me a lot with that."

He hung up and turned to stare at the woman at the other end of the long, dark hallway. Brenna put her phone away and came toward him. "They're all okay. They have some damage and leakage in the church gymnasium, the roads are still flooded and a few buildings and homes are damaged. But it's not nearly as bad as it could have been. Callie said they were getting reports of other areas that got the brunt of it. We'll need to help out there."

Nick didn't say anything. He just pulled her into his arms and held her. He wanted to say so many things. He wanted to tell her that he loved her, that he'd fallen for her the first time he'd seen her. But these feelings rushing through him were every bit as powerful as the storm that had bombarded them through the night. They'd been spared the worst of the hurricane, and he'd been spared the pain and agony of his guilt.

"Are you all right?" Brenna asked, lifting away to stare up at him.

"I'm good," he replied. "I feel lighter, less burdened."

"Confession is good for the soul," she replied. Then she took his hand in hers. "Nick, it wasn't your fault."

"It will always be my fault," he said. "My anger and refusal to stay, the truck backfiring, the skittish horse breaking loose—it all happened because of me. I know I can't change any of it, but Jessica would want me to be happy. She'd tell me I'm being silly, that I can't control the world."

"I wish I could have known her," Brenna replied.

"I do, too. She would have loved you." He kissed her, then looked her in the eye. "I love you."

Brenna's eyes filled with tears. "I love you, too." She smiled up at him. "We probably need to check on things."

"Yes. Let me get the radio and see what's being reported."

The new wasn't good. The worst of the storm had gone east of Fleur, but the spin-off had done enough damage to bring everything to a halt. Roads and homes were under water and several businesses had sustained considerable damage.

"We'd better stay here awhile longer," he said. "The bridge back to town might not be safe."

Brenna agreed. "I don't even know if my car is still around. But we don't have to worry. Someone will come and get us by boat if they have to."

"Probably your father," Nick replied, his thoughts somber. "And I can't say that I blame him."

"Papa knows he can trust me. And I think he must

trust you, too. If not, he would have come through that storm to fetch me home."

He laughed at that. "I have this image—"

"I'm serious. My papa means business."

"I believe you. But he *can* trust me. *You* can trust me."

Brenna had felt a bit awkward in the light of day, after hearing the tragic story of Jessica's death. But now, she turned to Nick and put her arms around him. "And now, you know you can trust me." She stood back to stare up at him. "It must have been awful, carrying around all that guilt for so long. I hope now you can begin to heal."

Nick pulled her close. "Yes, I think so." He kissed her on the nose. "There is so much I want to say to you. But right now, I need to check outside."

After eating granola bars and washing them down with tepid water, Brenna and Nick opened the front door to survey the grounds.

"Well, I'll definitely need Callie's help in restoring the gardens," he said.

The front yard was still standing in about a foot of water. Brenna could tell where the water had come and gone because some of the bushes and young saplings were bent and still leaning almost to the ground. The force of the water and wind had caused everything to shift, and in some places, trees and limbs lay broken.

Brenna moved from one side of the big porch to the other, looking for her car. She let out a gasp and forgot about that for now. "Nick, your trailer is gone."

Nick rushed down the steps to stand in the muddy water. "Unbelievable." He pointed out toward the back of the property where a small bayou was now overflowing and full of debris.

"It's sitting in the water in the middle of the little bayou. And your car is jammed up against it."

Brenna came down the steps. "The water carried the trailer and my car right into the stream."

He nodded. "That's probably what caused the crash we heard last night. That cypress stopped both from floating away."

"Did you have anything valuable in the trailer?"

He turned to look at her and her breath stopped. "Not as valuable as you," he said, his eyes moving over her face.

"I'm serious, Nick."

"So am I."

He took her hand. "I have my laptop and my files and blueprints inside the house, but honestly, right now I don't care about that. I'm just glad you're okay and that no one we know died in this storm."

"I feel the same." She glanced around. "But your trailer is totaled."

Nick put his hand on her face. "Brenna, I don't need that trailer anymore."

Brenna's heart hit at her rib cage. "You don't?"

He shook his head. "No." Then he brought her close. "I think I've found my home. It's wherever you are."

"Nick," she said on a soft sigh. "Nick."

He kissed her, then lifted her up and carried her back to the porch. Brenna didn't protest. Being in his arms felt right, no matter the circumstances.

When he set her down, she stared up at him. "Are you sure? I know how much you loved that trailer."

"No, you're wrong on that."

Surprised, she said, "But—"

"I never said I loved it," he interjected. "I thought I needed to live there. But Brenna, I needed so much more. I wanted so much more."

She nodded in understanding. "Just like me. I've always wanted more." Then she smiled. "But right now, I think I have exactly enough."

Then they heard a sound off in the distance. Brenna listened and waited as the low roar got closer. Through the trees, she spotted a boat with two men aboard slowly making its way through the murky flood waters.

Nick squinted through the muted sunlight. "I think the cavalry has arrived."

Brenna smiled. "It's Papa and Julien."

"Do they have guns?" Nick asked, grinning.

"Of course not." She waved at them. "Well, they might. You know there are all sorts of predators in these waters."

"You have a point," Nick replied.

Brenna waved. "Papa, we're here."

Her papa waved as Julien pulled up the motor and maneuvered the trolling boat up into the yard with paddles. "Dere's Daughter Number Three."

Julien grinned and called out. *"Bonjour!"*

Brenna couldn't hide the tears misting her eyes. Nick took her hand and squeezed it. "You're safe now."

But Brenna knew she'd found her heart. She'd always be safe with Nick. And she'd make sure she safeguarded his heart by showing him how much she loved him.

After greeting her father and her brother-in-law and assuring Papa that she was okay, Brenna gathered the things she and Nick needed while the men went down to survey the basement.

"It's still underwater," Nick told her when they came back up. "We'll have to pump it out, but I think the basement is still sound. We'll have to figure out what happens next, but I'll worry about that. We need to get you back to town."

"You're coming, too, right?"

"Course he is," Papa said, his gaze on Nick. "We'll need his help. Lots of things need our attention."

Nick readily agreed and soon they were on their way back up what used to be the main road into town. Along the way, Julien pointed out some of the worst of the damage.

"Papa, what about our house?" Brenna asked.

"Da carport is gone," Papa said with a shrug. "And the back porch is damaged. But we can fix dat. Again." He let out a little chuckle. "At least dis time, I know me some good decorators and architects." He winked at Nick. "Tell your aunt we'll be giving her some business real soon."

Nick laughed at that. "She'll be happy to help."

Brenna glanced from her papa to the man she loved.

As the sun rose pink and fresh over the flooded bayou, she lifted her head and thanked God for this beautiful day. And for the man who'd come into her life broken and burdened.

They could finish Fleur House together. Because they'd both been through their own restoration. And she knew even though there would be other storms and other challenges, God was still working on her and Nick. With His grace, they'd survive.

Epilogue

Two weeks later

Nick looked around the long table and smiled. Thanksgiving at the Blanchard house was different from any other Thanksgiving he'd ever attended. Different and so much better.

Brenna sat beside him, while Julien and Alma were next to her. Callie sat across from them, then his Tia Serena and his parents were on the other side of the table, along with Pierre and Molly and Mrs. LeBlanc. Papa Blanchard sat at the head, grinning big.

"Dis is the best Thanksgiving we've had in a month of Sundays," Mr. Blanchard declared. He glanced up at the picture of his deceased wife. "Lila, we know you're up dere pulling some strings for us, belle." He stopped, cleared his throat. "And we know you got a whole passel of angels with you." He glanced at Nick, then looked around the table. "We are a blessed bunch, *oui?*"

A chorus of *oui* and *sí* followed.

"Den let's eat us some turkey and dressing."

Callie nodded. "But first, we bless the food."

Elvis put his nose to the back door and barked.

After Mr. Blanchard said grace, the meal progressed. Nick had never seen so many side dishes or desserts. Two very distinctive cultures had come together for this meal, so no one would go hungry.

He glanced over at Brenna. "I'd like to talk to you after we eat. In private."

"Really? What's the big secret?"

He shrugged. "No secret. I just haven't had a minute alone with your since the storm."

"We have been busy," she said. "Okay, I'll meet you out back under the arbor after dessert."

Nick dived into the meal and thought about the last two weeks. They'd all been clearing, cleaning and rebuilding. His family had come earlier in the week to help out. Fleur House was back on track, but he'd offered to lend out several of his construction workers to help with other needs. His boss had been very generous in anonymously giving a huge donation to the town of Fleur. The money had been put to good use and they'd all worked hard to fix what needed fixing. He couldn't believe he could be so happy. He couldn't believe he'd finally found a real home.

So after the big meal, while everyone sat back and groaned at being so full, he walked outside and waited for Brenna underneath the white arbor. It was a crisp fall day, but the temperatures were pleasant and the sun was bright. Two squirrels fussed in the moss-covered oak that shaded most of the backyard.

He watched them until he heard a door open and shut.

Brenna came hurrying toward him, her long skirt swishing against her suede boots. "I'm here. What's the big deal?"

Nick pulled her into his arms. "You," he said. "You are a very big deal."

She grinned and slapped him on the chest. "I think you just wanted to be alone with me."

"I did."

"Me, too," she said. "I've missed this."

Nick had missed their alone time, too. "I think I have a way to remedy this situation," he said, his heart jumping and skipping.

She drew back, her eyes almost golden in the sunlight. "What's that?"

He pulled a black box out of his pocket, then got down on one knee. "*Te amo.* I love you."

Brenna let out a gasp, her hand going to her heart. "Nick?"

Nick looked at her beautiful face. "Brenna, you are my home, *mi corazón.*" He opened the box and took out the ring.

"Nick?"

He heard the joy in her voice, saw that same joy in her eyes. It reflected exactly how he felt.

He took her hand and said, "Will you marry me?"

Brenna gasped again, then sank down on her knees and hugged him close. "Yes, of course. I love you so much."

Nick breathed a sigh of relief and placed the antique ring on her finger. "This was my grandmother's ring.

My mother gave it to me when I told her I wanted to marry you. If you don't—"

"It's perfect," Brenna said. "Just perfect."

Nick kissed her. "I'm not perfect—just remember that."

"You are to me," she said.

He held her close, savoring the new joy that flowed like pure water through his soul. "Remember that day I told you to make it beautiful for me?"

"The mural, you mean? Yes, I remember."

He looked into her eyes and finally told her his last secret. "I wasn't talking about the mural."

"I know," she said with a smile. "How am I doing?"

"You make everything beautiful."

He kissed her again, then stood and helped her up.

They stayed that way for a few minutes, then turned to go inside and announce their good news.

But they didn't have to do that. Callie came running out, screaming and laughing and crying. "Let me see this ring I've been hearing about."

"You knew?" Brenna asked, wiping away tears. Alma was right behind her, tears on her face.

Callie hugged her sister close, her gaze on Nick. "Of course we knew about the ring, but *I* knew from the beginning."

Nick smiled. "*Sí,* your sister is very wise."

"Yes, I am," Callie said, giving him a hug, too.

Then the whole family spilled out into the yard, everyone laughing and crying and speaking in two different languages.

But Nick understood now. Restoration was good for the soul.

He looked up toward the trees and saw a golden-green butterfly fluttering through the air. And he could have sworn he felt the touch of an angel's wings caressing his face.

* * * * *

Dear Reader,

I hope you enjoyed this second story in my Cajun series. Brenna is a lot like me, I think (drama queen!). But she learned to reel in on overreacting to things. This helped her when it came to waiting for Nick to open up to her. She wanted to rush things along, but she also learned that sometimes things have to happen in God's own time.

Nick held back his emotions and his doubts because he thought he was unworthy in God's eyes. He couldn't share his deepest pain with anyone, but Brenna did bring him to a spot where he realized he had to let go of the past and his guilt.

These two opposite personalities came together through God's grace and a yearning inside both of them. I think we all yearn for something that we know is just out of our reach. But Christ is right there with us, lifting us up on our faith journey.

Soon comes Callie's happily ever after. I hope you'll bear with me until it's finished. She will meet the mysterious owner of Fleur House and change his life forever!

Until next time, may the angels watch over you—always.

Lenora Worth

YULETIDE TWINS

Renee Andrews

This novel is dedicated to and inspired by the precious twins I met years ago, Amber Gonzales Harrington and Angel Gonzales Stroop. I've watched you grow into young women with beautiful families of your own. You've touched my heart and my life.

Give, and it will be given to you. A good measure, pressed down, shaken together and running over, will be poured into your lap. For with the measure you use, it will be measured to you.

—*Luke* 6:38

Chapter One

Laura Holland climbed out of her jam-packed Volkswagen bug and squinted toward the windows of the bookstore across the Claremont town square. During the entire four-hour drive from Nashville to this tiny North Alabama town, she'd attempted to convince herself that she'd made the right decision. Staying with her parents, especially with her mother threatening to leave again, was out of the question. But now she wondered what made her think she could show up here, reconnect with her old friend and somehow convince him to give her a job?

What if David sent her packing? Then where would she go?

Laura took a step toward the bookstore but halted when an elderly gentleman made his way to the entrance. He stood out from the other shoppers with his slow and steady gait. A shadow passed in front of the window as someone went to greet him when he entered.

Was that David? Laura remembered the tall, dark-haired guy who'd been Jared's college roommate the entire time he and Laura dated. Nice-looking in a Clark Kent kind of way, David wore dark-rimmed glasses, dressed impeccably and jogged regularly. He would be twenty-five now, merely two years older than Laura, and yet he'd already "made it" in the world, was self-sufficient and running his own business. A far cry from where Laura was now. More shadows passed in front of the awning-covered window, and then a man carrying a briefcase entered. How many people were in the store? And did she really want an audience when she begged for a job?

Spotting a rack of free classifieds outside of the five-and-dime, Laura grabbed a copy and sat on a wrought-iron bench while she waited for a few of David's customers to leave. If—and that was a big if—David was willing to hire her in her current state, she'd also need somewhere to live.

The unseasonable weather was nice enough that she could probably sit and browse the paper until dark. In Nashville, it'd already turned too cold to spend time outside. But here the first Monday in November felt uncommonly pleasant, with merely a slight chill in the air. Then again, Laura stayed warmer these days due to the extra weight she carried. She wondered if David was still the same big-hearted guy he'd been in college. Would he be willing to help her out? She suspected—and hoped—that he hadn't changed.

Laura rubbed her swollen belly. She sure had.

David Presley flipped the page of the quarterly report his accountant personally delivered and saw the nasty numbers on the P&L sheet identifying the sad state of his bookstore. He closed the folder, but the image of those red numbers wouldn't go away.

"I'll borrow more from my line of credit." The muscles in his neck immediately tightened, and he shifted his shoulders to relieve a little stress.

"Can I be honest with you, David?" Milton Stott had inherited the bookstore's account when his father retired, in much the same way David had inherited A Likely Story when his grandmother passed away. However, Milton's inheritance gave him the accounts of most everyone in town, so it wouldn't be all that terrible if he lost the bookstore as a client. David's inheritance, on the other hand, plopped all of his eggs in one basket. A basket that was, based on these numbers, almost empty.

Somehow David managed a smile. "I'd love to think that you weren't being honest and that those numbers were lying, but I know I can count on you giving me the truth. And since you've already delivered a painful dose, you might as well add the rest."

A noise in the back of the store caused Milton to turn. "You have a customer?"

David nodded. "Zeb Shackleford, but he wouldn't spread news of my financial state even if he heard it."

Milton heaved a sigh. "Okay, then. I'm going to tell it to you straight. Your grandmother barely got by with the store. I told Vesta she should sell the thing before she passed away so the family wouldn't be burdened. Your parents weren't interested in it…."

"They were pretty excited when Dad got the job opportunity in Florida." David's folks had been thrilled about the potential for a year-round warm climate, but even if they hadn't been tempted by the beach, they wouldn't have taken over running A Likely Story. They'd never appreciated the old store on the square the way he had.

"Well, Vesta knew they didn't want it and insisted you could breathe life into the old place. Back then, I told her that probably wasn't possible," Milton said, then added somberly, "I'm sorry that it appears I was right." He placed his copy of David's financials back in his briefcase and snapped it shut. "I don't see how you can keep the place open more than a couple of months, and that's only if you get enough holiday business to boost your numbers."

David swallowed past the bitterness creeping up his throat. He'd tried so hard to make the bookstore work, but Milton was right. He lost money every day the doors were open. He scanned the multitude of shelves lining the walls, the tiny reading corners his grandmother had insisted on having for customers to sit and enjoy their books—all of them persistently empty—and his sole customer, Zeb, gingerly perusing the packed shelves. "I'm not ready to give up," he told the accountant. "My grandmother thought I could make this place work, really believed it could be done, and that I was the one to do it. You said so."

"I also said that it probably wasn't possible," Milton reminded.

Zeb rounded the end of one of the stacks and held up his plastic basket. "Found some good ones today," he said with a grin.

David's heart moved with a glimmer of hope. "I had several bags of used books turned in this week for credit, so I thought you'd be able to find quite a few."

Zeb's face cracked into more wrinkles as his smile

widened. Oddly, the weathered lines made him even more endearing. "Any of those suspense ones I've been looking for? Miss Tilly at the nursing home has been asking for some."

David pointed toward the other side of the store. "I think so. Look over there, about halfway down."

"Thanks." Zeb nodded at Milton. "Good to see you, Mil."

"You, too, Zeb." He waited for the old man to move a little farther away, lowered his voice and said, "Credit? You're still taking books for credit? I told your grandmother years ago that she should stop that. It makes no business sense whatsoever."

"That's the way used bookstores typically work. And I carry new books, too, but there are folks in Claremont, like Zeb, who like the used ones." David said a silent prayer that Zeb would take his time finding the books he wanted so Milton wouldn't also learn the elderly man got his books for free.

Milton tsked and tapped David's folder on the counter. "Listen, I'm not charging you for my services this quarter. I know you can't afford it right now."

"I can't let you do that," David began, but Milton shook his head.

"Nope, not taking a penny. But what I *am* going to do is start praying that you'll think about what I've said and consider other options. You're a smart young man with a business degree from a great university and your whole life ahead of you. There are other things you can do, businesses that can make a profit and keep your head above water." Milton turned to leave. "However, if you're determined to give it a go, I'll pray for your success."

David agreed that a prayer wouldn't hurt.

Help me out, Lord. Show me what I need to do to breathe life into this place. I could really use some guidance here.

The bell on the front door sounded as Milton exited, and Zeb Shackleford edged his way toward David with books balancing over the top of his red plastic basket. He gingerly placed the basket on the counter and then reached to his back pocket and pulled out a worn leather wallet. "Now, I'm gonna pay you today, David. Please don't fight me on this. I got a lot of books, and I know you can't afford to keep giving 'em to me for free."

David suspected Zeb had gotten the gist of his conversation with Milton, even if he might not have caught every word. He loved the old man and the way he took care of so many people around Claremont. Right now he was trying to take care of David, but there was no way David would take his money. "We've been through this before. Those books are a donation."

Zeb opened the wallet and moved a shaky thumb across the top of a few dollar bills. "Please, David. Let me pay."

David placed his hand on top of Zeb's, and the trembling ceased. "It'd be different if you were keeping those books yourself, but I know that you'll be hauling them over to the nursing home and to the hospital and then to the shut-ins around town. You'll read the books to them, and then if they like the story, you'll let them keep them, won't you?" When Zeb didn't answer, David added, "My grandmother's last days were so much better because of your visits. She loved listening to you read. You've got a way of bringing stories to life. She had that gift, too, before the cancer got the best of her. But with your visits, she could still enjoy a good story." He pointed to the books. "I'm not letting you pay for them."

"She never would take my money, either," Zeb huffed, folding the wallet and sliding it in his back pocket. Then he lifted his eyes and said, "I know you need the money."

David didn't want the older man to worry, even if his own anxiety made his stomach churn. He placed all of the man's books in two plastic bags. "I'll be fine."

Zeb placed a hand on David's forearm and squeezed. "You have a blessed day, son."

"I will." The words had barely left David's mouth when he heard someone moving through one of the aisles from the front of the store. He hadn't heard the bell sound, but he definitely had another customer. "Hello?"

Zeb turned so that he saw the pregnant woman at the same time as David. But David was certain Zeb didn't recognize the lady, since she wasn't from Claremont. David, however, did, and his heart squeezed in his chest the way it always had whenever he saw the stunning blonde in college. Infatuation had a way of doing that, lingering through the years, and David's had apparently hung around. "Laura?"

"Hey, David." She continued toward the counter. "I came in when the other man left," she said, which explained why David didn't hear the bell, "and then I didn't want to interrupt you while you were talking to a customer."

"Well, I'm about to leave." Zeb extended a hand.

"I'm Zebulon Shackleford, but folks around here call me Zeb."

"Laura Holland," she answered, shaking his hand and giving him a tender smile.

Holland. David didn't miss the fact that she was still Laura Holland. No married name. Why not? And who was the father of the baby she carried? So many questions, and he wanted to know the answers.

"I…" She hesitated. "I hope it's okay that I came here."

Shell-shocked, David realized he hadn't said anything more than her name. He mentally slapped himself out of the momentary stupor. "I'm sorry," he said. "Yes, of course it's okay." Though he suddenly wondered why she was here, in his bookstore, when he hadn't heard anything from her in over two years. The last time he'd seen her, in fact, she'd been very much in love with his college roommate.

Zeb slid his arms between the loops of the bags then pulled them off of the counter as he stepped away. "David, if it's okay with you, I might sit a spell and read in one of your nooks before I head out. I'm feeling a little weary and think it might do me good to rest a few minutes."

David had to forcibly move his gaze from Laura, still amazingly beautiful, to Zeb. "Sure, that's fine. And let me know if you want me to drive you home. It isn't a problem."

"Aw, I drove today, wasn't quite feeling up to walking this time. It's just that I parked on the other side of the square, and I think I'll handle that walk a little better if I sit a minute or two."

"Take all the time you need," he said, glad that his

mind began to work again, the surprise of seeing Laura finally settling in to reality.

She looked even prettier than he remembered. She had her straight blond hair pulled back, drawing even more attention to pale blue eyes and a heart-shaped face. Jared had often compared her to Reese Witherspoon, and David agreed they were similar, but Laura was… Laura. Back then, he'd found an instant attraction toward the striking beauty, but as usual, he'd fallen into the role of second fiddle when she dubbed him her friend, and Jared her love. Then again, David was wise enough now to realize that his fascination with her had been merely that, a fascination. But beyond the intriguing element that'd always been a part of his relationship with Laura, had been the friendship that David had found with Jared's girl. He was certain that friendship was what brought her here now, because David knew she was no longer with Jared. His buddy had married in June.

Laura forced a smile, blinked a couple of times and then seemed to struggle to focus on David, as though she were afraid if she looked directly at him, he'd see too much. Which was probably true.

In college, he mastered reading her eyes. If Jared had hurt her, David could see it in those telling eyes. He'd seen that look way too many times. Even though he was close to Jared, David never believed his old friend treated Laura the way she deserved. She had a kind heart and would do anything for anyone. Jared took advantage of that; he'd taken advantage of her love. David hated seeing that look of emotional pain in her eyes back then.

He studied her now and didn't see pain, but he saw something else that bothered him almost as much. Fear.

"Laura, is something wrong?" he asked, then quickly added, "I'm glad that you're here, but—" he decided it best to state the truth "—I haven't heard from you since I graduated from Tennessee, so to see you now, over two years later…" His gaze moved to her belly. "Do you need help?"

Her lip quivered, and then tears pushed free. She quickly brushed them away with two flicks of her hand. "I told myself I wouldn't cry."

David felt bad for causing her to release those tears, but he didn't know what else to say or do. However, he did know this—he would do whatever it took to help her. "Hey, it'll be okay." Rounding the counter, he did the only thing that seemed right—opened his arms and let her move inside his embrace. But he had no idea why she needed his comfort, so he said another silent prayer for God's guidance.

Laura let him hold her for a moment, but then he sensed her gaining her composure again, her shoulders rising as she sniffed then eased out of his hug. She looked up at him, and David suddenly felt taller than his six-one. He'd forgotten how petite she was, no more than five-four. Her size made him feel an even stronger urge to protect her from whatever had her so upset.

"I'm sorry I fell apart. I'll be okay." A lock of blond hair had escaped her barrette and rested along her cheek. She gently pushed it behind her ear. "It's been a long day."

David knew that was an understatement, but he'd maintain his patience and wait until she was ready to explain. He tried to think of what he could do to make her feel more comfortable. He had no idea where she'd parked or how far she'd walked to get to his store. Finding a spot at the square was sometimes difficult, so she could have walked a bit to get here, probably not all that easy with the pregnancy. "Why don't we sit and visit?" He pointed to the reading area nearest the counter. "I've got some lemonade in the kitchen. I'll get us a couple of glasses, and you can tell me what's going on."

She nodded. "Okay."

He went to the small kitchen in the back and poured two glasses of lemonade then returned to find her sitting in one of the oversize chairs pressing her hand against her belly and smiling.

"Here you go." He placed a glass on the table beside her and then took a seat on the sofa nearby. "Everything okay?" He indicated her hand, still rubbing against her stomach.

She nodded. "Yes, they get a little more active as it gets closer to night." A soft chuckle escaped when her hand actually edged out a little as something pushed—or kicked—from inside. "Makes sleeping quite a feat."

David would have said something about that kick, because he'd never seen anything like it, but instead he keyed in on the most important word in her statement. "They?"

Another nod, then she said, "Twins." She took a sip of the lemonade, swallowed and then announced, "Twin girls."

"Twin girls," he repeated, amazed.

Then, before he could ask anything like how far along she was, she added three words that put every question David may have had on hold.

"And they're Jared's."

He focused on her stomach. Twins were there. Jared's twins. His mind reeled at that. It'd been, what, over four months since he stood beside Jared as a groomsman at his wedding?

David continued staring at her swollen belly—he couldn't help it—and wondered how far along...

"Seven months," she whispered, obviously following his thought process. "I found out about the pregnancy the end of May, the week I graduated. By that time, our relationship had been over for two months, which was exactly how far along I was." She held the glass of lemonade, palms sliding up and down the clear column as her shaky voice continued. "I didn't know he'd been seeing Anita—seeing both of us—and then...he married her." Her attempted smile caused a couple of tears to fall free, and again she wiped them away. Then she seemed to gather the courage to tell him more and said, "He told me he'd pay to get rid of the baby." One shoulder lifted. "He had no idea there were two."

David's mouth opened, but no words came, and his opinion of his old roommate plummeted.

"My parents wanted me to put them up for adoption. They said it'd be better, you know, since I don't have a job or anything." She placed her glass on the table. "I got my early education degree, but schools aren't that interested in hiring a teacher who's going to have to miss work for doctor appointments and will be out for six weeks of maternity leave."

He tried to put the pieces together but still didn't see what had brought Laura here, to Claremont. However, he wanted to make sure that she knew, whatever she needed, he would try to help. "I hate it that you've had a hard time, and I'm really sorry that I haven't tried to contact you since I left." He'd thought of her often, but it didn't seem right calling Jared's girl, even after he knew they weren't together anymore. Plus he'd been seeing AnnElise Riley for the majority of that time, and she'd never have understood him reconnecting with an old, moreover attractive, female friend. Her jealousy had been over the top, which really made the fact that she'd cheated on David with her old boyfriend—and consequently left town with him—sting.

David shook away the bitter memory and concentrated on the woman in his bookstore. Now he wished he'd at least tried to check on her over the past couple of years.

"I didn't call you, either," she said softly, "so we're even."

That was true, but somehow it didn't help David's tinge of guilt. When Jared married Anita, he should have called to see if Laura was okay. And she was so not okay. She'd been several months pregnant when Anita walked down the aisle. David still couldn't get a handle on that fact. Why hadn't Jared at least mentioned it?

In any case, David would do what he'd always done back in college—help Laura after Jared had left her hurting. "Well, I'm glad that you've come here now, and I want you to know that if there's anything that I can do to help you, I will." He placed his glass next to hers then took her hands in his. "I mean that, Laura."

She blinked, nodded and then David saw pleading in those vivid blue eyes. "When my parents realized I wouldn't give up the babies and that I couldn't get a job in the school system, they offered to take care of everything. They wanted me to live with them, let them support me and the babies, for as long as I needed." One corner of her mouth lifted. "You remember how they were always fighting, how Mom was always threatening to leave or actually leaving. I didn't want my babies to grow up around that tension." Another sniff. "I want them to have a real home, somehow. And *I* want to take care of them."

David had met her parents a few times when they visited Laura in college. Her mother had always seemed angry or been pouting over one thing or another, and her father had tried to explain and make amends for her behavior. Laura had been even more independent because she didn't want to rely on them. "You didn't take them up on their offer."

She shook her head. "No, I couldn't. I've stayed with them the past few months, since I graduated, while I tried to find a job. At first I was able to substitute teach, but the schools don't even call me for that anymore. I think they're afraid I'll go into early labor." She gave him a soft smile. "Probably wouldn't be too great for my water to break in a classroom of first graders."

He grinned. "Yeah, probably not."

"But I want to show my folks that I'll be okay on my own. And I really didn't want to stay in Nashville." She touched her hand to her stomach, then added, "Jared and Anita live there."

David nodded. Jared and Anita were beginning their life in Laura's hometown, and he was certain she wouldn't want the slightest chance of running into her babies' father and his new bride.

"So, here goes." She took a deep breath, pushed it out. "I need a job. I want to support myself and my ba-

bies. And I thought of you and your bookstore, and—"
she scanned the surplus of books "—I would work really hard for you. I know I'm limited physically now,
but I can still sell books, and maybe I could help you
start some reading programs or something like that?
Something that would let me work with children, like I
would have been able to do with my teaching degree?"
She paused a beat then quietly added, "And I'll need
help finding somewhere to live. I have a little cash in
my savings, and I thought with this being a smaller
town and all, maybe the cost of living would be lower
than Nashville." She looked at him hopefully. "Do you
think I could help you out? Or, I guess what I'm asking
is, do you think you could help me out?"

He swallowed thickly through the lump lodging in
his throat. He'd seen the worst figures ever this afternoon on his P&L statement, had even wondered how
he'd stay in business past the holidays. Hiring someone wasn't something he'd have considered, at all. He
couldn't pay himself, much less someone else. But this
was Laura. And her baby girls. David knew the only
answer he could give, even if it didn't make sense and
even if it might give Milton Stott an early heart attack.

"Yes, I can use your help."

Chapter Two

Laura had been around David enough in college to know when something wasn't going right in his world. Right now, as he talked on the phone to the woman who owned the Claremont Bed-and-Breakfast, she could tell he wasn't getting the answer he wanted. He'd removed his glasses and placed them on the counter, then he pinched the bridge of his nose as he listened to what the lady had to say.

"No, Mrs. Tingle, I understand. I'd forgotten about the crafting folks coming in for the First Friday festival. They don't usually stay overnight, though, do they?" He flinched as she apparently delivered another bit of bad news, then his head slowly moved up and down. "That's right. I wasn't thinking about everything happening next week. Yes, the bookstore is going to offer some activities for the festival. I just haven't decided exactly what I'm doing yet." His jaw tensed. "Okay, I'll let Laura know you should have some rooms available in a couple of weeks."

Laura waited for him to look her way then mouthed, "No luck?"

He held up a palm and gave her a half smile in an apparent effort to let her know everything would be okay. But Laura's stomach quivered, and she began to think everything might not be okay. What if *every* room in town was booked for this festival he mentioned? For two weeks! Then what would she do?

"Yes, ma'am, we are having a book signing for Destiny Lee at the store next Saturday. That's the only thing I've officially set up so far, but it's definitely happening. It's her first signing and she's pretty excited about it." He nodded. "I'd heard she included a story about you and Mr. Tingle in the book. I look forward to reading it." He continued listening, then finally said, "That's okay, I'm sure we'll find something."

Laura didn't think he sounded so sure, and she wasn't feeling a whole lot of certainty, either. She waited for him to click the end button on his cell then asked, "Do you think all of the hotels in town are booked, too?"

He picked up his glasses and slid them back in place to rest on his nose. "See, that's the thing. Claremont doesn't *have* any hotels."

Laura felt her jaw drop. "None that have rooms, you mean?"

"None at all. The town's population is only 4,500. Usually the bed-and-breakfast offers more than enough room to house tourists...except when we have the crafting festivals."

"First Friday, that's a craft festival?" She'd heard him mention the term in his conversation.

"No, the First Friday festival happens every month, and it's basically a combination of crafters and performers, as well as a chance for all of the square's merchants to showcase their merchandise." He leaned against the counter. "First Friday brings in practically everyone from Claremont and the surrounding counties, but they don't typically stay overnight. However, November's First Friday is a little different, in that it leads into the annual Holiday Crafters Extravaganza, which lasts a full week. The crafters will have booths set up around the square through the following weekend, and each of the local stores coordinates activities for the festival, as well."

"And they've booked all of the rooms at the B and B," Laura said.

"As well as all of the hotel rooms in Stockville, which is the nearest city. Not that that would matter, though, since Stockville is a good twenty miles away, and you wouldn't want to drive that far." His brows lifted as he apparently thought of something, and then he asked, "About driving…how long will you be able to drive? I'm assuming there's a certain time when the doctors tell you to stop driving in pregnancy?" He glanced at her stomach and probably wondered how she could fit all of that behind the wheel. Laura had almost doubted the possibility herself, but she'd been able to pull it off by adjusting the steering wheel and seat.

"I don't have to stop driving," she said. "I did ask my doctor before taking the trip here today, not because I thought I couldn't drive but because I was traveling so far. She told me as long as I took periodic breaks to rest, I'd be fine, and I didn't have any problems." Laura had been amazed at how smoothly the trip had gone, but apparently the drive to Claremont wasn't her biggest dilemma. Thanks to the crafters in town, she had no place to stay. She'd been so worried about getting a job that she hadn't thought to consider locating a place to live before she traveled nearly four hundred miles. Her mother often said she acted too impulsively, and this was yet another time she'd be proving her right.

David must have noticed her anxiety because he moved to the seat next to hers and reached for her hand. The warmth of his large palm encircling hers reminded her of all the times he'd consoled her in college whenever Jared had let her down. Why couldn't her heart have fallen for someone like David instead of always tumbling head over heels for the one who'd treat her wrong? Even in high school, she'd been drawn to the bad boys. They just seemed so intriguing, dangerous and undeniably tempting.

"Some girls are just drawn to guys that treat them badly," her mother had said in an apparent effort to make Laura feel better about her situation. It didn't help. In fact, it only made her more resolute that she would *not* be hurt again, because she wasn't going to rely on a guy again.

Uh-huh, right. Then why did you come running here to David? her mind whispered.

Laura shook that thought away. She'd never thought of David "that" way. He was her friend and he'd always been there for her, just like he was now. This was a different situation entirely. She wasn't relying on a guy; she was counting on a friend.

"We'll find somewhere for you to stay," he said, solidifying the fact that she could, in fact, count on him. "Even if we don't find a place tonight, you have somewhere to go. You can stay in my apartment." He pointed to the ceiling. "It's above the bookstore."

Laura was touched that he'd offer, but she knew she

couldn't accept. Asking David for help with the job was one thing; living in his apartment would be something different entirely. She'd gotten too close to Jared without the boundaries of marriage, and she'd been left to raise her babies on her own. She was certain *that* wasn't what David was offering, but still…the two of them staying together in his apartment wouldn't give the right impression to the people around town, or to David, for that matter.

She didn't need him thinking that she wanted more. She didn't—not with David or with any guy. Not for a long, long time. The wound inflicted by Jared was still too raw. "David, I don't think that's a good idea, for us to stay together…." She searched for the right words but didn't have to say anything because David halted her progress.

"Oh, no—" he shook his head "—hey, that wasn't what I meant. *You* can stay in my apartment, and I'll stay with one of my friends in town."

She felt her cheeks flush. "Oh, I should have known that wasn't what you meant." A little surge of adrenaline, or something, pulsed through her veins as she tried to shake the embarrassment. She was seven months pregnant…with twins! "I'm sorry," she said, then added, "and embarrassed."

Still holding her hand, he tenderly squeezed her palm. "It's okay. A few years ago, those first three years of college, I'd have been exactly the kind of guy to ask a girl to stay at my place and wouldn't have thought a thing about it, but that's the old David."

His comment reminded her of the fact that he'd changed during his last year at UT. Something had happened that caused him to turn away from his wilder ways and back to his faith. Laura had been so wrapped up in Jared at the time that she hadn't thought a lot about what caused David's rapid transformation. But now she wished she could recall.

"So you don't have anything to worry about." He grinned, and Laura spotted a slight dimple creasing his left cheek. Funny, she'd never noticed it before, but she liked it, very much. And she liked David, even more for making her feel at ease with her crazy presumption.

She laughed at her foolishness and slid her palm from his. For some reason, it suddenly seemed a little too intimate for their current relationship, friend-to-friend and boss-to-employee. "Okay, then, if you don't mind, and since there doesn't seem to be another place in town, I'll take you up on your offer."

The bell on the door sounded as someone entered the shop. "Welcome to A Likely Story," David called toward the front. Then he stood and held out a hand to help Laura rise from the chair.

She occasionally had a little trouble off-balancing her weight when she stood, and the support of his strong hand was a welcome addition. "Thanks."

"Anytime," he said, and she knew he meant it. David would help her stand and help her with a job and even help her find a place to live. Already, in less than an hour, he'd done more for her than anyone else had in years, and the gratitude for that compassion washed over her at once. She blinked back the urge to cry.

Luckily, a blond little boy dashed through the aisle knocking a few books from the endcap as he circled and taking Laura's attention off of herself and the man currently taking her under his wing.

"Kaden, please, slow down." A pretty brunette

picked up the dislodged books and tucked them back in place then gave David an apologetic smile. "I told him we needed to hurry if we were going to make it to the bookstore before you closed at six, and I'm afraid he got the impression that we had to run all the way in."

"Not a problem at all," David said, tousling the boy's blond curls. "What ya so excited about, Kaden?"

"My teacher says I need some more books because I'm not—what did she say again, Mom?"

"Challenged," the lady said. "He's breezing through the sight word books and because of that, he's becoming a little disruptive during reading time at school."

"And we only get library day on Tuesday, and I can only check out one book for the whole entire week, and I really want more books than just one book, so Mom said we could come and buy some."

"I see," David said to Kaden.

Laura liked the way he didn't change his voice to talk to the boy. He spoke to him as though speaking to an adult, and Kaden nodded his head as if he totally believed David did see and understood his dilemma. Then he seemed to forget all about David as his attention zoned in on Laura. "Wow, how many babies are in *your* tummy?"

"Oh, my," his mother exclaimed. "Kaden, that isn't something that we ask…" She tapped her finger against her chin and seemed as though she didn't know how to complete her instruction to her son. Then she looked at Laura. "I'm so sorry. We have a baby at home—well, she's eighteen months now—but I had explained to Kaden when I was pregnant about how baby Mia was in my tummy. However, I forgot to explain how some women may not want to give the details…."

Kaden's brows drew together and he shrugged as though he couldn't figure out what he'd done wrong, and Laura laughed. "It's fine," she said. She pointed to her stomach and told Kaden, "Actually, there are two babies in my stomach. Two baby girls."

"Wow! Cool!"

This time David laughed, too, and Kaden's mother simply shook her head.

Kaden, undeterred, moved right on to his next pressing question. "So, can you help me find some books?" he asked, focused intently on David.

"Tell you what. This is my friend Miss Laura, and she just started working at the bookstore today." David tilted his head to Laura, and she smiled at Kaden, who turned his attention from David to her. "I think she will be able to help you find some really good books, and while she's helping you, I'm going to go get her things out of her car." He glanced to Laura. "Sound good?"

She felt a tinge of excitement at already being trusted to help a child. This was going to be...wonderful. "Sounds great." She'd dropped her purse on the table, so she turned, opened it and retrieved her keys. Handing them to David, she said, "It's the same Volkswagen I drove in school, and it's parked by the five-and-dime. I've got one large suitcase and a smaller makeup bag."

"That's it?" he asked.

"I brought some teaching supplies, just in case." She still hoped that she'd eventually get to teach. "But for now, I only need the two bags. I appreciate you getting them for me."

"No problem at all." David seemed to realize he'd forgotten introductions. "Mandy, this is Laura Holland. She's moved to Claremont and is going to be working here. Laura, this is Mandy Carter—Mandy Brantley, I mean. You'd think after all this time I'd get used to that."

"Not a problem," Mandy said.

"Mandy is married to the youth minister, Daniel Brantley, who also happens to be one of my best friends. And she owns Carter Photography on the square. She's a pretty amazing photographer. You'll have to check out her studio."

"Thanks," Mandy said. She smiled at Laura. "Nice to meet you."

"Nice to meet you, too."

"So, you ready to help me find books?" Kaden asked, grabbing Laura's hand and tugging her toward the children's area.

"Sure." Laura let him tug her away, but even though she listened to Kaden talk about the kinds of books he liked, she also heard David ask Mandy whether he could bunk at their house tonight. Laura hated making David move out of his own apartment, but she didn't know what else to do.

"Which ones do you think I should try?" Kaden squinted at the titles on the shelves with his hands on his hips.

"Well, let's see." Laura scanned the books and was pleased with the variety David offered. "How about these Dr. Seuss books?"

"Already read 'em."

"All of them?" Laura asked.

He bobbed his head. "Yep."

"Here's a good one. *Where the Wild Things Are*."

"Read it, too."

Mandy had finished talking with David and now walked to stand behind her son. "He loves to read."

"I can see that," Laura said, reaching for *Curious George's First Day of School*.

"I like Curious George, but I've read them already," Kaden said matter-of-factly. "But that one would be good for baby Mia." He pointed to the *Curious George Pat-A-Cake* board book.

"We'll get that one for her," Mandy said to Kaden, "but let's find some for you, too."

A hint of a memory crossed Laura's thoughts. David, talking about Mia from Claremont, and what a special person she was. But that wouldn't be this baby, since she hadn't even been born at the time. Laura tried to remember, but before she could bring the memory into focus, Kaden forged ahead in his search for books.

"What else do you have, Miss Laura?"

Laura ran a finger along the spines and then saw a group that she thought might appeal to Kaden, if he hadn't read them yet. She pulled out the first book in the series. "How about *The Boxcar Children*? Those were some of my favorite books when I was young."

"Mine, too," Mandy said.

Kaden took the book and studied the illustration of four children and a red boxcar on the cover. "Is it a girl book, or is it for boys, too?"

"It's a great book for both boys and girls," Laura said.

"That's true," Mandy agreed. "Our librarian, Miss Ivey, read the books to us when I was in elementary school. Everyone loved them, and then we'd go on the playground and pretend we were the boxcar children."

"What's it about?" Kaden asked.

Laura could tell his interest was piqued. "It's about four brothers and sisters who have run away and find a boxcar to live in."

"They have to take care of themselves? All by themselves?" Kaden asked.

"Yes, they do. And there are all of these books that tell you about their adventures."

"Okay, I want some of these books, Mom! I wonder if Nathan knows about them. He might like them, too, huh?"

"Nathan is one of Kaden's older friends," Mandy explained.

"He's nine," Kaden said.

Laura thought about the possibility of Kaden and his friends starting to read the series together. That could be a very good thing, not only for the kids, but also for her to prove herself as an asset to David's bookstore. "Why don't you see if Nathan, and maybe some of your other friends, would like to read the stories? I'm sure Mr. David would be happy to order more copies, and then all of you could read them together." Her mind kept churning, and she liked where her ideas were headed. "Maybe we could start a *Boxcar Children* club here, and you could all come talk about the books and the adventures."

David entered the children's area a little winded from his trek with the luggage, but he'd obviously heard Laura's idea. "That sounds good to me," he said.

"I've never thought about a book club for children, but given Kaden's appetite for reading, it'd be great for him. I'll call Nathan's parents tonight, as well as a few more of Kaden's friends," Mandy said. "Go ahead and get the first three books in the series, and we'll get that board book for Mia."

"How is the littlest Brantley?" David asked.

"Chattering up a storm now," Mandy said. "I'll bring her the next time I come."

"Sounds great," he said, then to Laura added, "I got your luggage. I put it by the checkout counter for now, but I'll carry it upstairs for you after Mandy and Kaden are done shopping."

"We're ready," Kaden said, grabbing the three books and clutching them to his chest. "I want to go read some before I have to go to bed."

"Okay, take the books up to the counter so we can pay," Mandy instructed, and Kaden ran off with his new books. Then she turned to David. "Daniel and I would love for you to stay with us, but I think I have a better idea. My apartment is open above my studio. I haven't lived there since Daniel and I married three years ago, but I kept the furnishings intact. Laura, you could stay there. It's clean and ready, and you could stay as long as you like."

"Oh, I couldn't take advantage of you that way," Laura said.

"Nonsense. It's just sitting there, and it'd be convenient for you if you're working at the bookstore. It's only a few doors down on the square. And then David wouldn't have to stay anywhere else, either. It'd be perfect."

"I'd want to pay you," Laura said.

"We'll work something out," Mandy promised. "I'll ask Daniel about payment, but really, we haven't been using it anyway."

"That would be convenient," David said, "if it sounds good to you, Laura."

"It sounds great, actually. Thank you, Mandy." She was a little stunned that someone she just met would offer her a place to stay, but she could already tell, not only from David, but also by the first people she met in Claremont, that people here were different, and she meant that in a very good way. Maybe, in Claremont, she and her babies would have a real home.

Chapter Three

David used the key Mandy gave them to unlock the door to her studio, then carried Laura's luggage through the gallery and toward the apartment. "All of the shops on the square are designed the same, with a kitchen in the back and then a small second-floor apartment. My grandparents lived above the bookstore when they first started out, but then they bought a farmhouse a little ways out from town when they had my mother."

He'd reached the kitchen and turned to make sure Laura was doing okay, but she wasn't there. Instead, she'd stopped to admire one of Mandy's photographs displayed on an easel. David put the luggage down and went to see what had her attention.

The photo was of Mandy, very pregnant, wearing a white dress with her hands cradling her stomach. Kaden and Daniel were on either side of her with their hands placed against hers and also appearing to cradle the new addition to their family.

Laura's hand was at her throat, her eyes glistening at the image. "It's beautiful, isn't it?" she whispered.

David swallowed, uncertain whether she was talking about the photo itself or the beauty of a complete family, something she didn't have for her little girls. His heart ached for her, and he longed to reach out and hold her, but he didn't want to make her uncomfortable. She'd balked earlier when he said she could stay in his apartment because she thought he was trying to cross the line into a personal relationship. But David had determined long ago that his relationship with Laura was strictly friendship. And right now she needed a friend.

"You're going to be a great mother, Laura. And your relationship with your girls will be beautiful, too," he said honestly.

She blinked a couple of times, moved her eyes from the photograph to David, and undeniable gratitude shone from the pale blue. "You think so, David? Really?"

He realized that she needed reassurance of the fact and that she probably hadn't received it from anyone else. Jared had asked her to end the pregnancy, and her parents practically begged her to put the babies up for adoption. But Laura wanted her girls, and David needed her to know that he believed in her. A single tear leaked from her right eye, and he placed a finger against the droplet on her cheek to softly wipe it away. "I know so," he said. "Just think about what you did tonight, talking with Kaden and helping him get excited about reading and sharing his books with his friends. You're a natural."

"He's six," she said, "a bit different than newborns, don't you think?"

"Motherhood instincts *are* there, and you *are* a natural. Like I said, you're going to be great, and they're going to love you."

She studied the photo another moment then said, "Thanks. I really needed to hear that."

"You're welcome. Now let's go get you settled in."

This time she followed him through the gallery. He picked up the luggage when they reached the kitchen and then stopped at the foot of the stairs. "You go first, and I'll follow."

She gave him a knowing glance. "You afraid I'll get off balance and fall? I'll have you know I've had to tackle some form of stairs nearly every day of the pregnancy, and they haven't gotten the best of me yet. And now that I'll be living here, I'll navigate these every day."

"Yeah," David said, eyeing the steepness of the stairwell. "And I'm not so sure that's a great thing. Maybe we should keep looking for other rental places, some that are on the first floor."

She smirked. "Never knew you to be such a worrier. I can still drive—the doctor said so—and I can still climb stairs." She stepped ahead and started up the first steps. "But if it will make you feel better, I always use the handrails." She placed a firm palm on the banister to prove her point. "See?"

"Yeah, I see," he said, but he still wasn't thrilled at the thought of her climbing all of the stairs every day. What if she did fall? More worries came to mind. What if she went into labor trying to make her way to the apartment? Or what if she went into labor in the apartment and then had to climb down the stairs to get to the hospital? As if he wanted to make certain she knew, he said, "When you go into labor, just call me. I'll make sure you get to the hospital in time."

Her smirk moved into a smile. "You're precious, you know that?"

"Precious, yep, that's me. *That's* what I go for." And that's what he'd always been to Laura, and to most every other girl before the relationships eventually ended. Precious. A friend.

She laughed, and even though he wasn't thrilled with his never-changing "best bud" status, he was glad to have given her that luxury. "You know what I mean," she said.

"Yeah, I do." It was the same thing Mia Carter had meant when she told him she'd fallen for Jacob Brantley. And then AnnElise Riley last year, when she'd left town with Gage Sommers. And, the most memorable of all, Laura herself, who'd fallen for his college roommate without even realizing David was captivated, as well.

And although David had experienced one semi-long-term relationship in college with a girl who did, in fact, think he hung the moon, he'd ended the relationship with Cassadee because she hadn't shared his faith.

And *that* was what David wanted—the kind of relationship that lasted for life, with God in its center—what he'd witnessed with his grandparents and parents. He'd never felt *that* toward Cassadee, or Laura, or any of the others, really. But he had no doubt he would, one day, in God's time. For now, though, he'd be a friend to the cute, very pregnant woman making her way up the stairs.

Laura slowed her progress as she examined several photographs. In the gallery, the only personal photo of Mandy's was the one Laura had noticed; however, all of the photos lining the stairwell were of Mandy's family. "Is that Mandy's husband?" She pointed to a photo of Mandy, Daniel and Kaden amid a group of children in Africa.

"Yes, they lead up a support effort in Malawi that our church funds, and they travel down every other year to check on the kids."

"That's so wonderful," she whispered, then took another couple of steps before she stopped again, her head tilting at the largest photo on the wall. "That's Kaden, right?" She pointed to the toddler between the couple. "And that's Mandy's husband, but that isn't Mandy, is it?"

David's chest caught a little when he looked at the image, the way it always did when he remembered his dear friends. "Actually, that isn't Daniel. It's his twin, Jacob. And that's Mandy's sister, Mia. They're Kaden's parents, but..."

Laura audibly inhaled. "I remember now. Mia, that was your friend you were so close to from home, and during your senior year at UT they were killed in a car accident."

"Hit by a drunk driver," David said, that painful memory slamming him the way it always did. "Kaden was only three, and Mandy adopted him."

"And Daniel?" she asked, glancing between the two pictures to see the powerful resemblance between the identical twins.

"He'd been serving as a full-time missionary in Africa, at the place the church supports, but came back to help Mandy raise Kaden."

"And they fell in love," Laura said, emotion flowing through her words. "What a sad—and beautiful—story."

David nodded, his own emotions not allowing him to say more. Then he cleared his throat and forced his attention away from the photos. "You want to head on up? The luggage is getting a little heavy here." David winced at the lie. He hadn't intended to tell it, but he hadn't expected to reminisce over painful memories tonight, either.

Laura gave him a look that said she knew he wasn't telling the truth but that she'd also let it go. Evidently she knew he was tired of thinking about Jacob's and Mia's deaths. "Sorry," she said softly, then completed the few steps left to reach the apartment.

She glanced in the first bedroom, a twin bed against one wall and bookshelves lining the remainder of the room. A baseball comforter covered the bed, and a long blue pillow with *Kaden* embroidered in red centered the headboard made of baseball bats. "Oh, how cute!" she said, taking it all in. "I want to have a neat room for my girls, too. I need to start thinking about that."

"Well, from what Mandy has told me, Kaden has an identical room to that one at their home. When she and Daniel married, they were going to move all of Kaden's things to the new place, but then Mandy said she knew he'd be spending a lot of time here with her, especially in the summer when school is out, so she kept his room intact. She also converted one of her studio rooms downstairs into a room for Mia."

"See, that's the thing that would be great about being a teacher. I could have my summers off to spend with the girls," Laura said. "I'll look at the room she did for Mia later. Maybe I can get some ideas for my girls. I want their room to be special, like this one is for Kaden."

"I've got some magazines at the bookstore that should help you out. I get several home design ones for the moms in town, some specifically for decorating children's rooms."

"That'd be great," she said, but her tone wasn't overly enthusiastic. Before David could ask why, she added, "Mandy said this apartment has two bedrooms. And I'm sure she won't want me changing things, since this is obviously Kaden's room."

David understood. She wanted a special place for her girls, and she wouldn't be able to decorate for them here, unless Mandy and Daniel allowed this to be something fairly permanent. David suspected they would offer, but he didn't know if that's what Laura wanted. "She has several studio rooms downstairs, and I don't think she uses them all. She may let you change one of them."

"Yeah," she said, "but still, I hope that eventually I'll have something more like—" she paused, swallowed "—a home." Then she looked to David and shook her head. "I'm sure that sounded like I'm not grateful Mandy gave me this place to stay, or rather is going to let me rent it. I *am* going to pay rent." She frowned. "I didn't ask what you'd pay me at the bookstore, and anything will be fine—I promise—but you'd know more than I do.... Will I be able to afford the rent here?"

David wished he could pay her what a college graduate deserved, but he wasn't sure how he was going to pay her at all. "I think Daniel and Mandy will give you a very reasonable rate." Of that he was certain, and whatever that rate was, David would make sure he gave her enough hours and enough pay for her to live here. Somehow. And he didn't want to worry about that anymore now. But the look on her face said she was uncertain, and she had enough on her plate without having to be concerned over how to pay her rent. "You'll be able to pay it." He smiled, and thankfully, she did, too.

"Well, let's go see the other rooms." She left Kaden's room and continued past a small bathroom and into a larger bedroom. "Oh, this is so nice."

David followed her into the room and placed the larger piece of luggage on the floor and her makeup bag on the dresser. The bed was an antique, beautifully carved and cloaked in a handmade quilt. Embroidered circular doilies decorated each nightstand with antique lamps in the center. Long, slender embroidered linen covered the dresser. And, looking a bit out of place amid the furnishings, a small flat-screen television topped a highboy chest of drawers. "You like it?"

Laura ran her hand along the bumpy quilt and smiled. "I love it. Granted, it may not be a permanent home for me and the babies, but it's a beautiful place to start, isn't it?"

"Yes, it is."

Like the remainder of the apartment, the room had an abundance of photographs on the walls, all of these black-and-white images, some landscapes and additional family photos. Laura spotted a framed photo at one end of the dresser. She picked it up and studied the image of Mandy and Mia, the two girls hugging tightly and smiling from ear to ear. "They were really close, weren't they?"

David blinked, nodded. "Yeah, they were."

"I hope my girls are that close, too." She kept looking at the picture, then glanced up at David, and her voice was barely above a whisper when she asked, "You loved Mia, didn't you?"

He honestly couldn't remember how much he'd shared with Laura that night at UT when he'd gotten the call that informed him Mia was gone. Maybe she already knew the answer. But even so, he wouldn't lie to her about it. "I was pretty sure I loved her in high school, you know, young love and all of that. I thought I'd marry her," he admitted. "But she was two years behind me in school, and when I left, she kept hanging around with all of our friends, and she and Jacob fell in love." David thought it was important to add, "And I was happy for them. Maybe not at first, but after I saw how much they meant to each other, and how happy Mia was, I *was* happy for them."

Laura's head moved subtly, as though she were putting the pieces together. "So those first years at UT, when I met you and you were dating so much and partying so much, you were trying to get over her."

It wasn't a question, so David didn't answer. There was no need. It was the truth. Except he wouldn't add that he would've dated Laura if she'd have looked at him the way she looked at Jared.

"And then, when she died, that's when you changed." Her head nodded more certainly now, as though she had no doubt whatsoever in the truth of her statement. "You turned to your faith after you lost your friends. I remember that. No more partying, no more dating everyone on campus."

David fought the impulse to tell her that the only girl he'd ever really wanted to date at UT was the one standing in this room. Instead, he said, "I realized I hadn't had any peace without my faith. And when I needed something to hold on to, something real, that's where I turned."

"I remember that," she said, placing the photo back on the dresser and turning toward David. "You found God, about the same time that I lost Him."

Her mouth flattened, and David sensed the sadness in her admission. Back in college, every now and then, particularly when she was upset, he'd had intense conversations with Laura, the kind where you wonder if you said too much, opened up too much, showed your pain too much. Then he would hold her until she was okay. He moved toward her with the intention of holding her again, but she stepped back and shook her head.

"I'll be okay," she said. "It's like that saying, if you find yourself farther from God, who moved?" She waited a beat and then whispered, "I did."

In spite of all the tough conversations David had with Laura before, he'd never said anything about faith, or God. At the time, that wasn't at the top of his priorities. Now, though, it was. "Laura, we have an amazing church here, full of people who understand God's love and His grace. Why don't you come with me Wednesday night for the midweek worship?"

The look she gave David resembled shock. Then she glanced down at her stomach and shook her head. "Trust me, I have no business in church right now."

"Laura—" he began, but she cleared her throat.

"Please, David. I don't want to talk about it. I just want to get my things unpacked and relax awhile. It's been a long day."

David knew when a conversation had been ended, and this one was done, in spite of how important he felt it was for her to find her faith again, for her to find the peace that he'd found again. "Sure," he said and turned to go, but he wasn't giving up. He'd already determined several ways he hoped to help Laura. He wanted to help her support her babies until she was able to get a teaching job, and he'd do that—somehow—at the bookstore. And he wanted to help her find her faith and the peace he'd experienced again since he'd turned his life back over to God. In other words, David wanted to help her have the two things she needed most—a friend and a Savior.

Chapter Four

"What's that you're working on?" Zeb Shackleford peered over Laura's shoulder at her pitiful sketch.

"We're starting a book club for kids," she said. "The first series we're reading is *The Boxcar Children*. I thought it'd be nice to decorate the children's area to look like a boxcar." She frowned at the plain red rectangle on the page. "I was going to do a sketch and then go to the craft store to see what materials I could use to create a big prop." She shook her head again at the image on the paper. "But my artistic skills are rather lacking."

He set the two books he'd been holding on a table nearby and gingerly lowered himself into the seat next to hers. "You know, my sweet Dolly used to say I had quite a knack with a pencil and paper. I used to draw all of the scenes for her classroom bulletin boards. You want me to give it a go for you?"

"Would you mind?" Laura gladly relinquished the sketch pad and colored pencils to the kind man.

"I'd be honored." He turned the page to a clean sheet, opened the box of pencils and selected the charcoal one. Laura had propped *The Boxcar Children* book on the table to use as a go-by, and he squinted at it for a few seconds then began to draw. It didn't take but a minute of watching him move the pencil around the page for Laura to see that he really did have a talent.

"Dolly," she said as he drew, "is she your wife?"

"For fifty-seven years before the Lord called her home." He paused, looked at Laura and said, "I'm looking forward to seeing her again."

Touched by the affection in his tone, Laura didn't know what to say. She'd met Zeb Monday, only four days ago, but already she'd grown very attached to the kindhearted man who visited the store each day.

"She was a teacher, too," Zeb said, then turned his attention back to sketching.

"I'm not a teacher yet." She'd talked to Zeb about her dream to become a teacher, as well as how she'd had to put that plan on hold until she had her babies and until schools were willing to hire her.

Zeb completed the boxcar—which looked amazing—and began to draw the children from the book cover. Laura didn't really need the children drawn, since she was only planning to design a big boxcar prop, but he was doing such an incredible job that she didn't want to stop him. "You know," he said, "the way I see it, teaching doesn't have to occur inside school walls." He pointed to the book. "Sounds like you're already working toward encouraging some of the kids around here to increase their joy of reading. That's teaching, any way you look at it."

Laura smiled. She *had* felt good about the responses they'd already received for the book club. "I guess it is." Several of Kaden's friends had signed up, and she anticipated adding more tonight if she got this display done and could advertise it properly for the First Friday event. "I've decided to hold the Boxcar Book Club gathering each Monday after school. I thought that'd be a good way to start each child's week, and I'm planning to bring in some of the activities from the book to make it more interactive."

"Dolly did the same thing, tried to give the kids more hands-on activities when they were learning. She said it helped them retain what they learned if they had an action associated with it." He put down the pencil and turned the page toward Laura. "I think she'd have liked this. Do you?"

The detail of the boxcar, as well as the four children, was astounding. "It's incredible."

"Okay, so to create this to scale, I believe you'll need six pieces of craft board, the thickest kind they sell. You'll also need to fix this door so it opens, because they'll probably want to go inside of it, don't you think?"

Laura nodded. "That's what I wanted."

He ran tiny dashes around the drawing to show how he believed the boards should be assembled. "Then all you'll need is some wood stands to hold it in place. I'm pretty sure David can get wood for you out of some of those crates that are always stacked behind the stores."

He handed her the sketch pad. "Take it over to Scraps and Crafts. It's straight across the square—you can't miss it. Diane Marsh owns the place and will be able to tell you exactly what you need to build a boxcar prop for the kids." He lifted a finger. "Her grandson is about Kaden's age. Have you got an Andy Marsh on your list of kids signed up?"

Laura remembered the name. "Yes, I do."

"Chances are, Diane will donate the materials if she knows it'll help Andy enjoy his reading. She's talked to me about that before, wanting him to learn to like books."

"I'm pretty sure it was his grandmother who called and signed him up," she said.

Zeb grinned. "Sounds like Diane. She loves those grandchildren. The other ones are older, teens I think. If you start something for teens, she'll probably sign them up, too."

Laura had been thinking the same thing, that if this book club was a success, she could start more. "I hope to do just that."

He pushed up from the chair and picked up the two books. Glancing at his watch, he said, "I'd go with you to see Diane, but I'm supposed to be at the hospital in a half hour so I'd better go."

"The hospital?"

"I read to the kids on the children's floor a couple of days each week during their lunch." He turned the books so Laura could see the titles, *Daniel and the Lion's Den* and *The Story of Moses*. "Picked a couple of Bible stories for today."

Laura's heart moved the way it did every time she heard about one of Zeb's regular activities. She'd never met anyone like him. "That's wonderful, Zeb. I'm sure they love having you read to them."

He leaned one of the books toward Laura and said, "You should go with me sometime, and David, too. I've got to tell you, they do way more for me than I do for them. Makes you really understand what Christ meant when He said it's more blessed to give than to receive, you know?"

Laura nodded. She did know, and yet that made her current situation all the more painful. David had asked her to go to his midweek Bible study on Wednesday at the Claremont Community Church, and she'd declined. And Mandy had invited her to a ladies' Bible study that she was hosting last night, and again, she'd declined. Now Zeb was reminding her subtly that…she missed church. But she'd so blatantly turned her back on God that she wasn't certain He'd want her. And she didn't know whether she could handle the guilt of entering a church and being surrounded by all of the people who "got it right."

Zeb had turned his attention to the two children's books in his hand and didn't notice Laura's discomposure. Instead, he flipped through the pages and smiled. "These illustrations are beautiful. The kids will love them." He moved toward the counter. "I'll leave the money over here so you don't have to get up."

"Don't leave any money, Mr. Zeb. David doesn't want you to pay, and neither do I. And I'm getting up anyway." She maneuvered her way out of the chair, then winced when one of the babies apparently kicked her for disturbing her sleep. "Whoa."

He quickly turned from the counter. "You okay?"

"Yes," she said, gritting her teeth as another kick matched the first, then exhaling when the twins finally settled down. "I'm fine. One of them is apparently attempting to teach the other one karate," she said with a laugh. "But I'm not taking your money."

He frowned. "I told you not to get up."

"I'm going to the craft store as soon as David gets

back from the post office, so I needed to get up anyway. And I want to walk you to the door." She gently steered him farther away from the checkout counter and toward the door.

"You're just trying to keep me from paying."

"And I'm doing a pretty good job of it, too, aren't I?" She smiled, gave him a hug and then opened the door for him to leave.

"One of these days I'm going to repay you," he said.

"You can repay me by letting me go with you to visit those kids one day. That sounds like a teacher's dream."

He smiled. "It is. You have a blessed day, Miss Laura."

"You, too."

Zeb exited, leaving Laura alone in the bookstore. That was something she'd noticed this week more than anything else; it was almost always empty. In the four days she'd been working, Laura had learned how to collect used books and log the credits in the computer, how to shelve the titles according to genre and author, how to select which books would appeal to readers in the various reading nooks and how to guide customers in their purchases. All of that could be considered part of her job description, but it wasn't the most important thing she learned during her first week on the job.

She learned David wasn't making any money.

Throughout the week, they'd received several bags of used books from customers who typically swapped out for other books during the same shopping trip. Then they had a few who came in and visited, browsed titles and perhaps even sat in a reading nook to peruse a book for a while before they placed it back on the shelf. Hence, no revenue. And while David did offer a few new books for purchase, the majority of the store was composed of trade-ins, and most of his sales were for credit. Or, in the case of Zeb Shackleford, free.

Laura didn't mind David giving so many books to the precious older man, but she didn't understand how he could continue running this business with virtually no income. And then this morning he'd given her a paycheck for her first week of employment, and he'd paid her well. Nothing excessive, but more than she'd expected considering the fact that he let her rest whenever she needed, let her go to her doctor's appointment yesterday and told her she could arrive late and leave early if she felt weary from the pregnancy.

But with the lack of customers and income that Laura had seen this week, she had no doubt David wasn't making enough money to support the store, much less to pay Laura as though everything were a-okay, hunky-dory.

And something else that wasn't a-okay or hunky-dory was the fact that her good-looking and nice guy of a boss was undeniably single. She'd paid attention throughout the week; he never texted, didn't phone anyone for quiet conversations, and even though several pretty ladies had stopped by the store over the past few days, he'd offered nothing more than a friendly smile. No flirting. No invitations for dinner or even coffee. And Laura got the impression that at least a couple of the twentysomething females had stopped by specifically to see the dashing owner and maybe even find themselves on the receiving end of his attention.

But David didn't appear to even notice he had a following. Then again, Laura had never actually realized how cute he was until this week. Maybe it was the pregnancy hormones kicking in. Or maybe he'd always been attractive, and she'd been too absorbed in Jared to notice. But in any case, he hadn't seemed the least bit interested in any of the single ladies of Claremont, which was a problem. A big one. Because Laura needed him to be interested in someone else. That would control this ridiculous notion that he might be interested in the very pregnant friend working in his shop. And it would also control her bizarre impulse to return the interest. Ever since their heart-to-heart Monday night, when he talked to her about loving and losing Mia, she'd felt even closer to David. And she wasn't ready for a relationship, at all.

Merely thinking about that day when she realized that she was pregnant and when Jared practically demanded that she end the pregnancy caused Laura's stomach to pitch. She'd jumped into that relationship headfirst and had been undeniably stupid. She wouldn't make that mistake again. Oh, no, it would be a long time before she handed her heart over. But when she did, she knew what she wanted. A guy who was honest. A guy who was faithful. A guy who loved her completely—no one else, just Laura—and a guy who she loved the very same way.

She flinched as an image of David carrying her luggage up the stairs overtook her thoughts. David, giving her a job. David, holding her hand to help her stand. That was the kind of guy she wanted next time, but she simply wasn't ready for that yet. Not that it mattered. There was still the fact that she'd dated his friend, was having his babies, in fact. And the fact that she didn't exactly look the part of a girl anyone would date, seven months pregnant and waddling. And, as far as David was concerned, she didn't share his faith. Not anymore. She'd given up on God because she assumed He'd given up on her.

Plenty of reasons for David not to look at her beyond friendship. Which was good. Exactly what she wanted.

Really.

The bell on the front door rang, and Laura turned to see the object of her thoughts entering with a big brown box tucked under one arm. He wore a black cashmere sweater over a blue-and-white striped button-down shirt, well-worn jeans and black boots. He scanned the store. "No customers?"

She shook her head then tucked a wayward lock of hair behind her ear. In spite of all of the cute maternity clothes her mother had bought her for the pregnancy, she never felt like she looked half as good as he did. Because right now, he looked very good. She stopped herself from attempting to check her reflection in the nearest window and tried to control the nervousness that had started occurring whenever her boss came around. "It's been a slow hour," she said. Truthfully, it'd been a slow week, but she wouldn't point out the obvious.

"That's okay. It'll give us time to check out what we got in the mail." A dark wave of brown hair shifted to cover one eye as he nudged the door shut with his shoulder. He jerked his head to the side to toss it back into place. Laura liked the way he managed to dress neat but also look rumpled, like he'd taken in a game of Frisbee on the square on his way to the post office. In college, he'd often played ultimate Frisbee with Jared and several of the other guys they hung around. Even though David gave the appearance of being Mr.

Studious, he'd surprised everyone with his athleticism and competitiveness on the quad. Laura had thought it funny that he'd turned out to be the superb athlete in the bunch, something Jared and the gang hadn't expected.

Funny…and impressive.

She shook the memory of David running and diving for those soaring discs and told herself she would stop recalling anything about him that might be considered overly appealing. He was appealing enough without being an athlete, too. But this was a business relationship between friends. He'd given her a job and helped her find a place to stay, and he'd watched over her since she arrived in Claremont like any good friend would do. So this emotion that kept creeping in was gratitude. That was it, gratitude. And she had to keep reminding herself of that fact.

"The *Boxcar* books came in today. I got a case, forty-eight books. You really think we might have that many kids show up?"

Laura had asked him to get the books Tuesday morning, before she realized that the bookstore didn't appear to hold its own moneywise. Now she feared if she didn't have that many kids to purchase those books, she'd end up costing him more than she made. She swallowed. David had helped her too much for her to hurt his business, so she *would* make this work; she had to. "Sure we will," she said, and did her best to sound upbeat, enthusiastic, excited even.

His smile said he bought it, and Laura breathed a sigh of relief. If David was right and the majority of the town showed up tonight for the First Friday event, she'd focus on finding kids to join that club…and selling their parents the book. David might not have had the time to figure out ways to make money for himself and his store, but Laura wasn't about to work here and not offer some sort of appreciation for the deal. And her appreciation would come in the form of more customers for her boss.

"You do realize that there's no way we could handle forty-eight kids in the children's area at once. I'd say we couldn't seat more than fifteen at the most," he said.

Laura hadn't thought about that, but he had a point. And if she sold all of those books, she'd need to make sure she had room for all of the kids. "What if we had the book club each day after school instead of only on Mondays?" She remembered what Zeb said about potentially starting a teen book club, too. "And if we did additional book clubs for teens or adults, we could put those later in the day."

"You're counting on this taking off, aren't you?" he asked.

"I am," she admitted. "It'd be a good thing for the store, wouldn't it?"

"Definitely a good thing." He picked up the list of kids who had already signed up for the book club. "Nine so far." His mouth slid to the side as he silently read the names. "I know all of these kids, and some of them aren't even close in age. Nathan and Autumn are both nine, maybe ten. And Kaden, Abi and Andy are all younger, six or seven, I'd say. Do you think we should divide them up by age?"

"That's a good idea," Laura said. "I'll call the ones on the list, get the specific ages and let them know we'll set up the book club so that each day of the week corresponds with a different age bracket. I think that'd be more enjoyable for the kids because that'd put them with their friends from school and most likely with those on the same reading level."

"Except for kids like Kaden, who need a challenge," David said, obviously remembering Mandy's comment.

Laura laughed. She'd been around Mandy and her family a good bit this week because they were often in the gallery when she went to her apartment at night. Kaden was an adorable little boy, but he was one of the most inquisitive children she'd ever met. Laura now understood what his teacher meant by saying he needed a challenge. "I think Kaden could probably go with an older group of kids, as far as the reading level, but since they will be reading the books on their own and mainly talking about what they've read here, I think he'll enjoy being with his own age, don't you?"

"Yeah, I do," David agreed. He looked at Laura, and his attention moved to her cheek, where that wayward lock of hair curled against her skin. Laura knew what he was about to do, so she could have quickly tucked the strands out of the way herself, but for some strange reason, she didn't. Instead she held her breath as David tenderly slid his finger against her skin and eased the lock in place. "You're going to be an excellent teacher."

A tingle of *something* echoed from the point where his finger touched her skin, ricocheting through her senses and then settling in her chest. Laura didn't know if the effect was from his compassionate touch or his earnest words. Or both.

Ready to get control of her emotions, she walked back to the children's area and said, "Zeb came by while you were gone. Come see what he did for us." She picked up the sketch pad from the table and turned it so David could see the drawing. "I'm going to make a boxcar to decorate the children's reading nook. If we use this design, they could climb inside and pretend they're on the actual boxcar while we talk about the story. We can use some of the beanbags and pillows already in the reading nook."

Even before she looked to verify the fact, she knew that David had moved closer to look at the drawing. She could sense the warmth of his body next to hers, and she turned to see that his face—as she suspected—was mere inches from her own. A hint of cologne teased the air, and she fought the urge to inhale...or move closer.

"It sounds like a great idea," he said. "Um, did Zeb mention how much he thought the materials would run?"

He couldn't disguise the worry in his tone, and it reinforced Laura's quest to make, rather than lose, money for his store. It also pulled her out of the uncomfortable moment of attraction that she was pretty sure only occurred on her side of this fence.

"He said since Diane Marsh's grandson is one of the kids participating in the book club, she'd probably donate the craft board and other materials we might need. And he said he thought you could make the wooden stands to hold the boxcar from crates that are usually kept behind the store."

The worry lines that'd shown on David's forehead as he'd looked at the drawing disappeared as his face slid into a grin. "Leave it to Zeb to get it all worked out. Zeb and you, I mean. This *is* a great idea, and if Diane will donate the materials, that'd make it even better."

"I'll go see her right now," Laura said. "I'd like to have it ready for First Friday."

David looked at the circular clock above the entrance showing straight-up noon. "You realize that's only six hours from now, right?"

"Then I'd better get busy." Laughing, she grabbed her purse and turned to leave, but then stopped when her cell started ringing the song "Daddy's Hands." "Hang on, that's my dad." Her father taught middle school history, and even though he was probably on his lunch break, she knew he never made personal calls from the school. She answered. "Daddy? Anything wrong?"

He exhaled thickly over the line. "Laura, I hate to bother you, and I sure don't want to worry you, but I need to ask…have you heard from your mother today?"

Laura had called her parents each night this week to let them know how things were going at the bookstore, how she was settling in, and then yesterday how the appointment with the new doctor had gone. But she hadn't heard from her mother since she hung up the phone with them last night. "I haven't. Did she leave again?"

"I don't know what's going on, hon, but it's been so much worse this year, since this summer. She isn't happy, and I honestly don't know what to do anymore. She wanted to go on that cruise in August, before I had to start back at the school, and I took her, but that still didn't help. And she wanted to go on regular dates, and we've been doing that, or trying to—she's been working more hours at the mall, you know." He sounded miserable, the way he always sounded whenever her mother did another round of leaving to "find herself."

"She isn't answering her cell?"

"Goes straight to voice mail. She must have it turned off."

"Was she supposed to work today?" Laura asked.

"She was, but Nan, the store manager, called me to see where she was this morning when she didn't show up at the store. I was afraid she'd had an accident or something, since she's never late for work, and I started trying to call her cell. And like I said, it went straight to voice mail. But I just called Nan back to see if she ever heard from her, and she said that your mother called in and said she was taking a personal day." He paused. "She'd assumed your mother would've called and told me."

"Of course she did," Laura said. Because that's what a normal wife would do. But something *was* different this time, because regardless of how many times Marjorie Holland had left without warning, she always planned her disappearances on her days off. She could leave Laura's father and Laura without any explanation whatsoever, but she would never miss a day of work and risk someone else taking her sales.

"I'll try calling her, but I'm sure you're right," Laura said. "If she doesn't want to talk to us, she won't."

"I know, dear. But, well, if you hear from her, will you call me, text me, whatever is more convenient? I just want to know that she's okay."

"I will, Daddy." She disconnected then immediately dialed her mother. Sure enough, it went straight to voice mail.

"She left again?" David asked.

Laura dropped the cell in her purse. "I don't know how he does it, goes through this over and over without any rhyme or reason to why she acts the way she does." For years, especially when she was younger, Laura would cry whenever her mother mysteriously disappeared. But those tears were done. Crying never helped, and Laura wasn't going to let her mother upset her now. It wasn't good for the babies if Laura was stressed, so she would *not* get stressed.

"You want to talk about it?" David asked, the concern in his voice evident.

She'd talked to David about her mother's peculiar behavior a few times when they were at UT, but she didn't want to spend their time today analyzing the mystery that was Marjorie Holland. "Nope. I want to go buy what we need to build a boxcar. Or rather, have it all donated to the cause."

He spotted a book out of order on a shelf, withdrew it and then began running his finger along the spines to find the correct spot. "Okay," he said, "but get some lunch while you're out. I don't want you forgetting to eat because you're trying to finish that boxcar."

"Don't worry." She pointed to her stomach. "They don't let me forget."

"That's good." He tapped a book as he apparently located where the misfiled one belonged, and then slid it into place. Then he leaned against the shelves and smiled. "And take your time. It shouldn't take all that long to make that prop, and I don't want you rushing to eat."

Laura liked his smile. "I won't rush," she promised.

Opening the door, she stepped outside, inhaled the crisp November air, took two steps down the sidewalk...and nearly ran smack-dab into her mom.

In a royal-blue pantsuit, gold jewelry and heels, Marjorie Holland looked as beautiful as ever. A peach Coach bag was draped over one shoulder. With her sleek blond hair and flawless complexion, she could easily pass for an older sister instead of Laura's mother. Then again, she was only seventeen years older and on top of that looked quite young for forty.

Her smile faltered a bit; she obviously was still preparing what she'd say when she found her daughter.

Laura waited and braced for the explanation.

She got none. Instead, Marjorie pulled out the beauty pageant smile, grabbed her in a hug and said, "Surprise!"

Chapter Five

Marjorie released Laura from the too-tight hug, leaned back and peered at her daughter. "Honey, pregnancy agrees with you. I believe you look even prettier."

"Thanks, Mom. But why didn't you tell me you were coming? Is everything okay?"

"Why, of course. I know you said that you were doing fine, but I just wanted to see for myself." She fingered the sleeve of Laura's dark green top. "Don't you love that blouse? I just knew it'd look adorable on you when I found it at the store. I got a great deal, you know."

"Thanks." Laura's mother had worked at Macy's, aka *the store*, for twenty years. She'd been the top salesperson in women's fashion for almost that long and lived for "great deals." The problem was, even with her employee discount, her addiction to sales typically ate up her paycheck. And Laura's father rarely said anything because she was always on the verge of leaving anyway without him giving her a reason to go. He'd often say that he was a timid personality and that Marjorie's fiery one was his perfect complement. Laura wasn't so sure.

"I brought you some more maternity clothes, also very stylish, for the last couple of months. You're going to *love* them," her mother said excitedly.

Laura already had so many clothes from Marjorie's previous purchases that she wasn't certain she'd be able to wear them all before the pregnancy was over. "Mom, I really have plenty already."

"Nonsense. You can never have too many clothes, or shoes." She held up her right leg for Laura to see her high-heeled boots. "How do you like these? The hue is called winter-peach. It's the latest complimentary color for the season. Fashion week paired it with everything. Aren't they amazing?"

"They're nice," Laura said, then shivered. She hadn't grabbed her cardigan because she'd planned to simply walk across the square to Scraps and Crafts. Little did she know she'd run into her mom and begin a lengthy chat session before she'd even crossed the sidewalk.

"Oh, my, why aren't you wearing that cute gold cardigan I bought you? You don't need to get chilled," her mother said.

"I have it in the store, but it's really not that cold, as long as you don't stay outside overly long." Laura pointed to the craft store. "I was going to Scraps and Crafts to get some things for a project I want to do today and also get some lunch."

"Well, why don't we do lunch first and then I'll help you get the craft items you need?"

"That sounds great." Despite her mother's quirks, Laura did enjoy spending time with her when she was in one of her happy moods, and she appeared to be in one today, in spite of—or maybe because of—the fact that she'd left Nashville without any word to her husband.

"Wonderful. I can drive. Where would you like to go? What's near here?" She dug around in her purse then withdrew her keys.

Laura smiled. "This—" she waved her hand toward the shops that composed the town square "—*is* what's around here."

Marjorie's blue eyes widened, and she plunked her keys back in her bag. "Well, okay, then." She scanned the storefronts. "So…where do we eat?"

"Come on, I'll show you." Laura led the way to Nelson's Variety Store, her mother's boots clicking the sidewalk with every step.

Marjorie stopped when they reached the tiny black-and-white tiles that formed the entrance to the five-and-dime. "Here?"

Laura opened the door. "Come on, it's really good."

Her mother visibly swallowed, her smile slipping again, but then she quickly recovered and headed in as though she owned the place.

"Well, hello, Miss Laura," Marvin Tolleson said as they entered. "Who's your friend?" He guided them to a red vinyl booth near the old-fashioned soda fountain.

"Mr. Marvin, this is my mother, Marjorie Holland. Mom, this is Marvin Tolleson. He and his wife, Mae, own the variety store, and they serve the best cheeseburger and sweet potato fries you'll ever taste." Laura and David had shared lunch here twice this week already, and she'd loved every bite.

"Cheeseburgers," Marjorie said, again fighting to hold her smile in place. "Why that sounds…delicious."

Laura couldn't remember ever seeing her mother eat a cheeseburger. In fact, the majority of the time she dined on a salad with grilled chicken and fat-free dressing. "They have salads, too," she said. "But the burgers are the best."

"We do have salads," Marvin agreed. "But they don't stick to your ribs like a good ol' burger. All Angus beef, too."

"You don't say." Marjorie lifted the laminated single page of the menu and flipped it, looking for the rest of the available items. There weren't any, so she slowly turned the page back over.

"Why don't I get your drinks while you're deciding," Marvin offered, unfazed by her mother's lack of enthusiasm.

"Water with lemon please," she said.

"Okay, and you want your extra large lemonade, Miss Laura?"

"You know I do." She'd grown very fond of Mr. Marvin, and of all the Claremont residents she'd met so far. They weren't pretentious, nothing showy or ostentatious. In fact, she'd say they were as down-to-earth as anyone she'd ever known. Her family wasn't rich, but you'd never know that by the way her mother dressed and carried herself. Her father, on the other hand, was proud of his teaching job and never put on a show. He was most comfortable in a pullover and jeans or khakis, and he didn't try to talk or act like he was something he wasn't.

"I'm going to the restroom, dear. If he comes back for the order, just get me a salad with the fat-free dressing, okay?"

Laura had hoped her mother *might* forego her routine for their day together, but she should've known better. "I will."

Marjorie clicked across the floor to the bathrooms with every head in the restaurant watching her move, and Laura waited for her to disappear before pulling her cell phone from her purse. She quickly sent a text to her father.

She's here. She's fine. I'll let you know when she starts back home. And I'll let you know if I figure out what's going on.

Marvin returned with the drinks and Laura ordered their food. Then her phone buzzed with a text from her father. Undoubtedly he was teaching a class, but he must have had his cell on hand in case he heard anything from his runaway wife.

I'm so glad she's okay. Please keep me posted. Love you.

Laura sent a quick text—I love you, too, Daddy—and dropped the phone back in her purse at the exact moment her mother exited the restroom. She felt so sorry for her dad, never being able to figure out the woman he loved so much. And part of her felt sorry for her mother, too, attempting to appear happy and content when obviously she was anything but.

Marjorie gracefully slid into the booth. She didn't do anything that looked unrehearsed, and even the way she sat appeared camera-ready. She'd won Miss Teen for Davidson County when she was merely sixteen, an accomplishment heralded in countless photos around their home. In Laura's opinion, her mother still acted as though she were being scored for poise on a daily basis. "Did you order?" she asked, unfolding the paper napkin and placing it on her lap.

"I did."

They sat for a moment in an awkward silence, Laura not knowing what to say and her mother smiling politely at each person who passed the booth but not speaking to anyone. She had a regal air about her, and she definitely stood out amid the others gathering for lunch in the five-and-dime. Most folks sitting in booths or at the soda fountain had on long-sleeved T-shirts or sweaters with a pair of jeans and sneakers. A few wore khakis, and one lady had on a plaid dress, but hardly any jobs on the square required a strict dress code. At Macy's, Marjorie dressed like she was ready for a photo shoot each day and was the most requested salesperson for help with style. However, even today, when she knew she wasn't going to work, she dressed the same way. She didn't have any dress-down clothes and probably wouldn't wear them even if she did.

The silence continued, until her mother obviously couldn't take it anymore. "I had to get away," she whispered. Then, as if in afterthought, she added, "And I did want to see how you were doing."

"Why did you have to get away?" Laura asked quietly. The booths and tables were all very close together so that customers could easily converse with those around them. When she and David had eaten here before, they'd almost always chatted with people at the other tables nearby. But there'd be no way anyone else could jump in on this conversation. Laura didn't even know what was going on with her mom; how would anyone else?

As if she also suspected someone was listening, Marjorie lowered her voice again. "I just did, you know. It's…hard to explain."

Obviously. She'd been doing it as long as Laura could remember, and no one had received an explanation yet.

Marjorie lifted her fork, inspected it as though looking for smudges, then returned it to the table. "So… how *are* you doing?"

"I'm fine," Laura said, choosing not to dwell on the subject her mother refused to talk about; it wouldn't help anyway. "I love it here, and I think the job at the bookstore is going to be perfect until I'm able to get hired in the school system."

A man at the booth behind her mother turned and leaned around the edge. "Sorry, but I couldn't help overhearing, and I thought you'd like to know that Mrs. Jackson, the kindergarten teacher, is retiring at the end of this year. You might want to go ahead and put your resumé in at the elementary school. Or if you're looking for something at the middle school, Mr. Nance, the eighth grade teacher, is leaving after this semester, so they'll need someone for his spot in January."

Laura felt her heartbeat increase at her excitement. There was no way she could take a teaching job in January, since she'd have just had the babies, but a kindergarten position starting next school year? That'd be perfect! "Thanks for letting me know.…" She knew she'd seen him before but couldn't remember the name.

"Aidan," he said. "Aidan Lee. And you're working with David at the bookstore, aren't you? I came by earlier this week to bring him the information for my sister-in-law's book signing next Saturday."

"Yes, I am," she said. "And I remember meeting you now. Aidan, this is my mother, Marjorie Holland."

He extended a hand. "Really? You're her mom. I'd have guessed sister."

Laura watched her mother beam.

"Aw, thank you," she said, her hand fluttering in front of her face the way it always did when she faked embarrassment. Laura knew she loved this, but Laura didn't mind; her mother was beautiful, and it was nice to see her look sincerely happy, even if it took a bout of flattery to make it happen.

"Well, I'll let y'all get back to your visit, and I'll try not to eavesdrop—" he grinned "—too much."

Laura and her mother laughed.

"Is everyone here that friendly?" Marjorie attempted to whisper, but Laura thought Aidan probably heard. Even so, he remained facing the other direction.

"They are. Just wait until you meet the people I'm renting my apartment from. They've been so nice."

"Maybe when we get done with lunch you can show it to me. I saw the Carter Photography building," Marjorie said. "That's the one you said you're staying at, right?"

"Yes, the apartment is above her gallery. I was thrilled that Mandy and Daniel offered it for rent. And they're only charging me two hundred a month."

"Seriously? How can they afford to rent it for so cheap?"

"I'm pretty sure they aren't doing it for extra money, but they knew I wouldn't accept it for free."

"Amazing," her mother said as Marvin returned

with a huge salad topped with bacon, boiled eggs and grilled chicken and placed the bowl in front of her. Then he gave Laura her plate, covered completely with a big juicy cheeseburger and a small mountain of sweet potato fries.

"That's…" Marjorie eased the bowl away a little, as though she couldn't take it all in while it was so close. "That's the biggest salad I've ever seen."

"Biggest one we make," Marvin said with a grin. Then he looked a little confused. "That is the one you ordered, isn't it, Miss Laura?"

Laura laughed. "Yes, it is."

"So y'all have everything you need?" he asked.

"We do," she said and waited for her mother's complaint. Marjorie didn't disappoint.

"Did you really think I could eat all of this?" she asked.

"I knew you'd never order the monster salad, but I also knew it wouldn't hurt you to splurge every now and then." To her relief, her mother's face split into a smile.

"I am hungry," she admitted.

Laura suspected her mother was often hungry, but she wouldn't say that now. Instead, she'd enjoy seeing her mother eat enough to fill her up for a change.

They chatted throughout the meal, with Laura carefully staying away from the subject of why Marjorie had really left Nashville this time, and when they were done, Laura was pleasantly surprised to see her mother had eaten every bite of her salad *and* a few of Laura's sweet potato fries.

"Oh, my, I'm absolutely stuffed," she said.

Laura nodded in agreement. "Same here, but it's a

good stuffed, and I'm pretty sure the twins are content. They aren't moving."

"You were that way," Marjorie said, "always quiet and still after I ate. And then, of course, you'd try to dance your way through the night."

Laura dabbed her napkin at her mouth and then tossed it on her empty plate. "They wake me up every now and then, too."

Marjorie picked up the check, glanced at the amount and then placed the cash on the table. "I've got this."

Laura knew better than to argue. "Thanks, Mom."

They started to leave, but Aidan climbed out of his booth. "Hey, before you go, I wanted to tell you something about Destiny's book signing."

"Okay." So far Laura had learned that Destiny had recently married Aidan's brother, Troy, and had her first book coming out this month. The book was a collection of love stories based in Claremont, and she had a contract to write several more love-story books for cities all across the South. Laura looked forward to meeting the new author and also to figuring out how she could best promote Destiny…and garner some sales for David's bookstore.

"I forgot to tell y'all the other day that she's got a Facebook page, and she's already got a few thousand fans just from the publicity her publisher has done and word of mouth."

"A few *thousand?* That's terrific." Laura sensed that next Saturday's book signing had the potential to be much bigger than the "small friends and family" gathering that David had said he anticipated for the event.

"Yeah, we're all pretty excited for her," Aidan said, "but the part I wanted to tell you about is that we set up an event for her book signing at A Likely Story. I haven't checked it today, but yesterday she already had two hundred people that said they were coming. Just wanted to make sure David ordered enough books."

Laura couldn't believe it. David hadn't ordered nearly that many books. This would be wonderful for business next week and also great exposure for the bookstore with all of those people coming in. Laura would definitely want to have book club information available for adults. Maybe she'd see about having the adult book club start out with Destiny's book, and Destiny could be a guest author for one of their meetings. "That's great news, Aidan! David's got a Facebook page for the bookstore, too. He hasn't done a lot with it, but we were talking about updating and promoting it better. He wanted me to work on it, and I'll get started right away."

"Cool," he said, then nodded to Marjorie. "Nice to meet you, Mrs. Holland."

"You, too." She waited until they were out of the store, then said, "That was a nice-looking young man, don't you think?"

"I'm not looking, Mom."

"As I recall, David is a nice-looking man also. Very nice-looking, I'd say. And he's been a real friend, hasn't he? Sounds like his bookstore is doing well, too."

Laura wasn't going to comment on David's attractiveness, particularly since she'd only recently noticed just how appealing her friend was…and because she didn't want her mother to think there was any chance of a relationship between them. They were friends, and that was that.

She walked beside her mom toward the craft store

and wondered whether she should address the other point of her mother's statement—David's business. She could voice her concerns for the financial state of the place, but she wouldn't. Laura needed her parents to feel good about her move here, and she also believed that David's store would become profitable, eventually. The book club was gaining kids by the day, and it appeared the book signing he'd lined up for Destiny Lee was going to bring in plenty of customers, too. Yes, with Laura's help, it would be just fine.

"I really enjoy working there. And I honestly believe the experience will help me be a better teacher. We're starting a children's book club. That's why I need the items from the craft store, to make a prop for their story area."

"I'm just glad you're happy," her mother said, and Laura could tell she meant every word. "David, well, he cares about you, Laura. A guy who'd help you the way he has this week, *that's* the kind you need to look for."

"I told you," Laura said, forcing a smile as she opened the door to Scraps and Crafts, "I'm not looking."

"I know, dear, but when you do, I want to make sure you find someone who cares about you. You want a man who chooses *you*."

The last few words didn't make sense to Laura. A man who chooses her? As opposed to…what? But before she could ask, an older woman standing amid the quilting supplies hurriedly crossed the store to meet them.

"Welcome to Scraps and Crafts," she said. "I'm Diane Marsh." She noticed Laura's tummy leading the way and smiled. "I'm guessing you're Laura Holland."

"I'm not the only pregnant woman in town, am I?"

"No, Hannah Graham is expecting, too, but you're the only one that I knew was pregnant and would be coming over to get supplies to make a boxcar."

"How did you know that?"

"Zeb. He called and asked if I could get the materials together for you because he was afraid you'd try to carry them to the bookstore yourself. He said you didn't need to be toting that kind of weight in your condition."

Laura grinned. "He never stops helping people, does he?"

"No, he doesn't. He also said that you're the one organizing that book club I signed my grandson Andy up for, and he asked if I'd be willing to donate the materials for your prop."

"Did he leave anything for me to do?" Laura asked.

"Yes, he said he wanted you to meet me!" Diane laughed, and Laura and Marjorie joined in.

"Well, it's nice to meet you," Laura said. "And this is my mother, Marjorie Holland."

"Pleasure to meet you," Marjorie said, shaking Diane's hand.

"You, too," Diane answered.

Laura could tell the lady was surprised at the fact that her mother was young. She'd seen that same look anytime she introduced her mother growing up, and she suspected that would never change. "I'll probably make my way over to the bookstore tonight during First Friday so I can see the boxcar once it's finished."

"Do you think I can get it done today?" Laura glanced at her watch. "It's twelve forty-five."

"Sure you can," Diane said, "especially since you'll have help."

"Help?"

"Hannah Graham, the woman I mentioned that is also expecting. She was in here shopping for supplies to decorate her nursery when Zeb called. I told her about the book club, but she'd already heard about it from Mandy and signed up her little Autumn. Anyway, Hannah's a stay-at-home mom now, but before that she would design all of the store windows in the square. She's very talented with props, and when I told her about the boxcar, she said she'd like to help. More than likely, she's already working on it." Diane smiled. "I saw her head to the bookstore when she left here."

"She carried the materials over?" Laura asked, wishing she and her mother had come to the craft store first.

"Oh, no, David picked those up for you. He was evidently on the same page as Zeb and didn't want you toting them."

"Everybody's watching out for me around here, aren't they?" Laura asked.

"That's what folks 'round here do," Diane said. "It makes us feel useful."

"Well, I should go help Hannah."

"Nah, you visit with your mom. Hannah is used to creating on her own, and she said she had a lot of energy to use up. She's only in her first trimester, but she's already nesting. I'm sure you haven't had a chance to decorate your nursery yet, since you just got to town. Let me know when you get ready, and I'll help you out. Hannah will, too, I'm sure, if you'd like additional input."

Laura didn't even know whether she had a nursery to decorate, but she nodded. "I'll let you know."

They left the craft shop and immediately saw that

several vendors were already setting up booths along the sidewalks and in the center of the square.

"Wow, what's going on?" her mother asked.

"Tonight is the First Friday event. David said they have it every month, and it's a chance for all of the local artists and entertainers to perform, as well as the merchants to showcase their items. That's why we're trying to get the boxcar prop done by tonight." Laura stopped to look at some colorful wooden puzzles an elderly man had already placed out for viewing. He sat behind the table steadily carving pieces. A woman with a silver bun and a patchwork dress sat beside him painting a completed ballerina puzzle. The pieces stood up from the stand, so little hands would easily be able to drop them in place. "That's so pretty."

The woman pulled her paintbrush across the edge of the ballerina's skirt and looked up at Laura. "Thank you, dear. We can put your baby's name on one if you'd like." She smiled. "You having a boy or a girl?"

"Two girls," Marjorie answered before Laura had a chance.

"Twins!" She put her paintbrush down and placed her palms together as though she were praying. "Well, that's a real Christmas present, isn't it?"

Laura nodded. "Yes, it is." She ran a finger along one of the ballerina puzzles that had already dried. "I still haven't picked the girls' names yet, but when I do, I'd like to get them these puzzles. They won't be able to put them together for a while, but when they can, I'd really like them to have these."

"Do you have a business card?" Marjorie asked.

"We sure do," the man said. He'd finished carving and pulled a small card from his shirt pocket. Handing it to Laura, he said, "I will pray for an easy delivery and two beautiful healthy babies. That's quite a blessing you've got there, young lady."

Laura smiled. "Thank you, and I know."

She and her mother continued across the square, all of the booths tempting them with every step.

"Look at those wreaths," her mother said. "I haven't seen anything like them. Are they made of ribbon, or is that something else?" She pointed to the red, green and gold Christmas wreaths that seemed to change color in the sunlight.

"I'm not sure." Laura realized she would love to browse all of the booths with her mother, but she needed to get back to the bookstore and build the boxcar. "Mom, why don't you spend the night tonight? We could see all of the First Friday booths, and then tomorrow the town is adding even more for the Holiday Crafters Extravaganza, with everything geared around Thanksgiving and Christmas." She knew she'd have to call and explain to her dad, but she also knew that he'd want her to spend some quality time with her mom, if Marjorie were willing to stay.

Which she wasn't.

"Oh, honey, I was going to tell you that I probably need to head on home after we get you back to the bookstore. I have to work in the morning, you know. I had thought I'd have a chance to take a peek at your apartment, but I don't think it's going to work this time."

"Right. I wasn't thinking."

"But I need to go get that bag of clothes for you out of the car. I'm parked behind the toy store. Why don't you head on back to the bookstore, and I'll grab it and bring it to you before I go. That way I can see David before I leave."

Laura didn't know why she thought her mother might actually want to spend more than a little time with her. "Sure, that'd be fine."

Marjorie clicked her way toward Tiny Tots Treasure Box and then disappeared down the sidewalk leading to the parking area, while Laura, feeling defeated, went back to A Likely Story. Entering, she was surprised that the first thing she saw was the top of what appeared to be a red boxcar peeking above the bookshelves in the back right corner of the store. "Oh, my!"

"Whoops, we're caught. She's back," David said.

Laura heard a child's laugh, then some scuffling as someone apparently tripped, and then he stepped around the nearest endcap grinning and looking guilty.

"You've already finished it?" Laura asked.

"Not all of it," he said. "We were trying to get it done and surprise you, but you got back quicker than we thought. I figured you'd spend a little more time with your mom."

"You knew Mom was coming?" she asked, shocked.

He shook his head. "No, but Aidan Lee came by to see if I'd gotten in that graphics book he needed for school, and he mentioned that he'd met your mother at Nelson's."

"Did he tell you about Destiny Lee's event page for the signing?" she asked.

"He did, and I ordered more books. I have to admit, it surprised me, but in a good way."

She liked the way his eyes held a glint of excitement when he told her about ordering those books. She wanted to give him lots of reasons to look like that, and she hoped to start tonight when she signed up a bunch of kids for the book club. "And so you decided you'd surprise *me* in a good way by building the box-car on your own?"

"Nope, we're helping!"

Laura recognized Kaden's voice, and then he peeked from behind a book stack to verify the fact. "You're helping?" she asked.

He nodded. "Yep." He motioned for Laura to follow him, and she did. "See, me and Autumn are helping my mom and Miss Hannah. Miss Hannah is the best at drawing and painting and stuff, but Autumn and I have been really good at making the nail marks, haven't we, Miss Hannah?"

A woman with short brown hair and a streak of brown paint on her cheek stood up from where she and Mandy had been painting the lower half of a ladder extending down the right side of the boxcar.

"Hey, I'm Hannah Graham. I hope you don't mind us working on your reading prop. I used to be a window designer for the square before I married Matt, and this project reminded me of how much fun it is."

"I don't mind at all."

"And I'm Autumn." A beautiful little girl sat beside the boxcar with a black marker in hand.

"Nice to meet you, Autumn, and thank you for helping with the boxcar," Laura said.

"You're welcome," she said, then turned her attention back to the nail marks she'd been making with the marker.

"Hey, Laura," Mandy said with a wave of a paint-splattered hand.

"Hi, Mandy. Thanks for helping."

"Kaden hasn't stopped talking about the book club. When he found out there was the possibility of a box-car they could climb in, he wanted to make certain that happened. And the kids only had a half day of school today, so this gave us something to do."

"That's right," Kaden said, pumping a fist in the air. "Fall break starts today!"

"Fall break for Claremont coincides with the Holi-day Crafters Extravaganza," Hannah explained.

Laura noticed Hannah and Autumn wore matching pink overalls. Hannah's had a stretchy pouch for a po-tentially expanding stomach, but her pregnancy was barely showing. "Diane told me you're also expecting," Laura said, "but I think I've got you beat in the baby bump department."

Hannah laughed. "Check back with me in seven months."

"In seven months, I'm hoping we'll swap looks. You can go for this—" she pointed to her tummy "—and I'll be happy with that."

They all laughed, with David's masculine rum-ble standing out from the rest. Laura quieted her own laughter so she could listen to the beauty of his. He seemed to notice where her attention had landed be-cause his eyes caught hers, and she felt her cheeks blush before she turned her attention to the others. Then, as the chuckles died down, Laura heard the bell on the door and then the telltale clicking of her mother's heels working their way through the store.

"Laura?" she called. She found them all in the chil-dren's area and gave her best smile. "Well, hello." She held up an oversize Macy's bag dangling from her right arm. "Got your clothes."

"Wow, that's a bunch of clothes," Kaden said.

Laura explained, "She buys me too much, I think," and then before she hurt her mom's feelings, she added, "but I do appreciate them, Mom. Thanks."

"You're welcome," Marjorie said. Then Laura began the introductions.

"Everyone, this is my mom, Marjorie Holland. Mom, this is Hannah, Mandy, Kaden and Autumn. And you already know David."

Her mother said a brief hello to the others and then turned her entire attention on David. "It's so good to see you again," she said. "And it—well, it means so much to us that you're helping Laura get settled here. We'd have loved for her to stay in Nashville, you know, but she wanted a fresh start. And I have to admit, from everything I've seen so far of Claremont, this is a wonderful place to have a family."

David looked from Marjorie to Laura. "I was very happy that she knew she could come here."

Laura swallowed. His words said so much. She hadn't been certain that she'd made the right choice when she'd arrived in Claremont. She hadn't *known* that she could come here. She'd *hoped*, but she hadn't known. However, throughout the week, with every passing day, she learned and believed without a doubt that she had come to the right place. "Thank you, David."

"Okay, I think we're done," Hannah said, snapping the lid on a small paint can.

"But I can put lots more nail marks," Kaden said.

"I know you can," Mandy responded, "but it's got just the right amount now, so we don't want to overdo it. And we need to get ready for First Friday. You promised to help me at the shop, remember?"

"Oh, yeah, right." Kaden grabbed up his markers and handed them to Hannah. "Thanks for teaching me how to make nail marks, Miss Hannah."

"You're welcome," she said.

Autumn followed suit, handing her markers to her mother. Hannah put all of the markers and paints in a big green tote, hoisted it on her arm and then took Autumn's hand. "Okay, we'll see all of you at First Friday." She took another look at the boxcar. "Turned out great. Tell Zeb he did a super job on the design."

"I will," Laura said.

Marjorie said goodbye to each of them and promised she'd see them again on her next visit to Claremont. Then David walked them all to the door while Marjorie and Laura marveled at the incredible reading area. "It looks terrific, Laura. And it was so nice of your new friends to do all of this for you."

"I know." She was overwhelmed with gratitude. An hour ago, she hadn't been certain the boxcar would have been done by the time First Friday started. But now, it wasn't even 2:00 p.m. and it was finished. "This is amazing."

"That's what I think, too," David said, returning to stand beside them.

Laura turned to see his reaction to the completed boxcar, but he wasn't looking at the prop. Instead, he was focused intently…on her. And Laura was pretty sure she wasn't the only one who noticed. Her mother's perfectly arched brows lifted and her blue eyes studied Laura's friend-slash-boss.

A whistle sounded from the kitchen, breaking the

tension in the room and giving Laura the impression that she'd literally been saved by the bell.

"I guess Mandy forgot that she'd wanted some tea. I'll go take care of the kettle," David said, turning and heading to the back of the store and leaving Laura alone to deal with her mother.

"Anything you want to tell me?" Marjorie asked.

"No." Laura wondered if short and to-the-point would work.

It didn't. Her mother forged ahead with the interrogation. "Didn't you see the way he looked at you? And in case you're wondering what you look like when you look at him, it's pretty much the same thing."

"I'm emotional now," Laura said. "That's all. And he's protective, like any good friend would be for a friend that's pregnant."

A buzz sounded from her mother's purse, and Marjorie placed the bag of clothes on the nearest table and then fished out her cell. She glanced at the display. "That was Thomas. He's called eight times today, left five messages."

Laura wished she'd texted her father and given him another update, but she hadn't had time since lunch. He was probably finishing his school day now and wondering if he'd have a wife at home tonight. "Why didn't you tell Daddy you were coming here?" Laura figured it didn't hurt to ask what she really wanted to know. If her mother got mad, she was about to leave anyway.

But rather than telling Laura she should mind her own business, Marjorie merely turned and walked toward the front of the store. Laura followed, thinking that she was going to walk out without answering the question. But her mother stopped, peered toward the back and apparently realized that David was still occupied in the kitchen…and the two of them were completely alone.

"I'm sorry," Laura said, uncertain whether she meant the apology or not, but this was the way it went. Her mother got mad or got her feelings hurt, and Laura—or, more typically, her father—apologized.

"This year has been tougher than all the others," Marjorie whispered, staring out the window at the crafters setting up their booths.

"Why?" Laura asked.

Her head shook slightly, but she didn't answer her daughter's question. Instead, she continued, "Did I ever tell you your daddy took me to the fair? It was on our first date. He spent every dollar in his pocket trying to win me this big white teddy bear, and on the last throw, he did." She smiled, and a single tear flitted its way across her cheekbone. She didn't wipe it away, and it traced a slow path toward her neck, while Laura watched in awe.

She'd seen her mother mad, seen her upset. But she'd *never* seen her cry. "Mom?"

"I'd say I fell in love with Thomas when he finally won that bear, but I'd loved him well before that. I think I loved him the first time I saw him, you know. On the playground in junior high. I'd just moved to Nashville and it was my first day at a new school, and I saw him, and it was… I just knew." Another sad smile. "I've loved him ever since, I suppose."

Laura had never been more confused. Her head pounded, and her mind raced for the right words. But nothing her mother said made sense. She'd kept her father on edge for years with her running away, coming back, being sad, being happy. She was like Forrest Gump's box of chocolates—you never knew what you were going to get.

"This year, with you, the pregnancy and Jared… It's just—been hard for me. I'm so sorry. I'm happy for you, and I want you happy. I want you to have…everything you want. I'd have loved for you to stay with us, but I understand. It would be hard to start a life where Jared is starting his new one. I wouldn't want to do it." Still looking away from Laura and toward the square, she shrugged one shoulder. "But I wouldn't know about starting on my own. I'm glad, though. I'm glad that you didn't end up with Jared. You deserve to be the one somebody chooses. If you aren't, then—" another shrug "—then you always wonder, don't you?"

"Mom? Are you talking about Daddy? Or…what?"

Marjorie turned, and both of her eyes were now swimming in tears, wet smudges of mascara marring her perfect makeup. "David. You may not see it yet, and you may not even want it yet, but that boy…he would choose you."

Laura's head was reeling, and she felt exactly the same way she did when she'd had the morning sickness so terribly. But this wasn't the babies making her queasy. It was her mother. "Mama, Daddy chose you. He married you, and he loves you. He told me so today."

She smiled again, but like before, it didn't reach her eyes. "I knew he'd call you. He's precious, isn't he?"

"Yes, he is," Laura said, and immediately recalled that she'd used the exact same word to describe David. "Why do you keep leaving him the way you do? He doesn't know, but he wants to. If you tell him what's wrong, I honestly believe he'll fix it."

She shook her head again. "He can't. And after all of the reminders of this year are done, I'll be better again. I feel sure of it."

"You're saying you don't think Daddy chose you when he married you? If he didn't then who did he choose?"

Marjorie turned, hugged Laura tightly again and kissed her cheek. "I'm going home now." Then, without another word, she walked out the door.

Shaken, Laura watched the blue pantsuit disappear in the crowd, her mother's head bowed and looking at the ground as she walked, her posture a direct opposite of her typical confident gait. What had just happened? Laura felt like she'd finally glimpsed a little of what her mother kept hidden so well, but she still didn't understand, not at all. And that realization sucker punched her. She grabbed a gasp of air, turned to release her cry…and sank into David's embrace.

"Shhh," he soothed, holding her close and running a hand up and down her spine. "I'm here. I'm right here."

Chapter Six

David had returned from the kitchen in time to hear the last of Marjorie's disjointed conversation, see her walk out the door and then witness Laura's reaction. Holding her in his arms seemed the natural thing to do, to provide comfort to his friend when she was hurting. Before this week, he'd never felt gratitude for his store being empty, but he did now. Because with the solitude came the ability to hold her as long as she needed. He ran his palm gently down her hair, while her face was still buried against his chest.

"It'll be okay," he said, and he prayed that it would. Laura had mentioned her mother's moodiness through college, but what David saw a moment ago was more than moodiness. Marjorie Holland was an emotional roller coaster. No wonder Laura didn't want to stay there to raise her little girls.

She shifted her head to the side, wiped her hand beneath her eyes and inhaled deeply. Then she wiggled out of his embrace and swiped under her eyes again. "Some employee I'm turning out to be, huh? Bursting into tears the first week on the job." One corner of her mouth lifted in a half smile. "Ready to fire me?"

David wished she'd have let him hold her a little longer. He could tell she was still upset, but he could also tell she was ready to move on. He'd let her. "Why would I fire the one person who's been able to bring paying customers? I've never had that much success at it. Just ask my accountant." He hadn't intended to say anything that would indicate his business wasn't going well, so he attempted a laugh and changed the subject. "Hey, I made that tea for Mandy. Might as well drink it. You want some?"

"Sure."

He started toward the back.

"And David?"

He stopped, turned. "Yeah?"

"Thanks. Not just for the tea, but for…everything."

"You're welcome." He prepared the tea and returned to find her sitting in front of the boxcar and talking on her phone.

"Yes, she left a few minutes ago. She should be there in about four hours. No, she didn't tell me," she said into the cell. Looking up, she mouthed "thanks" when he placed the tea on the table beside her.

Wanting to give her privacy, he went to the computer at the counter and checked on the number of people registered to attend Destiny Lee's signing. When he'd looked this afternoon, the number was just over 200. Now it was 283. "Wow."

"What is it?" Laura asked when she'd hung up, leaning over the counter to see the monitor.

"There are nearly three hundred people registered for Destiny's signing next Saturday. We'll need to set up the tent outside and have them line up on the side-walk."

"That's awesome." She smiled and looked like she was feeling better, her eyes clearing up from her tears.

"You talked to your dad?"

She took a sip of her tea and nodded. "Yes. Mom said something about him not choosing her. I have no idea what she was talking about, but it didn't seem like something to ask him on the phone. But he said he's coming here the day after Thanksgiving. We can talk then."

"The day *after* Thanksgiving? Aren't your parents coming here for the holiday to see you? Or are you not going there?"

She took another sip of tea. "Our family has never done the typical Thanksgiving thing because Mom doesn't want to have to cook a big dinner and get exhausted on Thanksgiving and then work all day on Black Friday. And she refuses to take off on Black Friday because it's the biggest sale day of the year. Macy's opens at midnight Thanksgiving night and stays open for twenty-three hours straight. It's a pretty big deal for Mom."

David thought Thanksgiving was a pretty big deal for most moms, but he wouldn't point that out. Instead, he asked, "So you'll be here for Thanksgiving?"

"Yeah, I don't want to drive all the way to Nashville and back when they aren't doing anything for the holiday. Our family dinner is just three people anyway— my grandparents have all passed on, and I'm an only child. Plus Dad is driving here on Black Friday since she'll be working all day. I told him I was sure we'd have a big sale at the bookstore, too, and he offered to help us out."

"You don't have to work that day," David said. "You can visit with him."

"I know I don't have to. I want to. We're liable to sell all sorts of books that people can give for Christmas presents. We'll want to stock up with the most popular ones, you know."

He grinned. He may not have known how he could pay her, but it appeared if all of her sales ideas were right, she might actually save his business. "Okay, but if you're staying here for Thanksgiving you're going to have a real dinner. My folks are coming in for the holiday."

"Oh, no, I am *not* going to intrude on your family dinner."

He shook his head. "You aren't. Mom isn't about to travel all the way from South Florida and then cook, and I'm pathetic in the kitchen."

She held up her cup. "Your tea is good."

"I can handle tea and eggs. And grilling. Any guy can grill, but that's it."

"So do y'all go out to eat on Thanksgiving?" she asked.

"Nah, we join the others in town who have dinner at the church. Everybody brings a dish, and we all share. It's fun, and we have some amazing cooks in Claremont. The best way to go for Thanksgiving. Trust me, you'll like it."

She looked skeptical. "But I'm not a church member there. And I haven't even visited."

"That isn't a prerequisite," he said, liking the idea of helping her have her first "real" Thanksgiving dinner.

"It's for the community, and you're part of the Claremont community now."

"Yeah, I guess I am, aren't I?"

The bell on the front door sounded, and two dark-
haired boys darted in, ran past David and Laura at the
counter and made a beeline for the boxcar.

"Look, there it is!" one said.

"Yep, Kaden was right," the other answered, while
Clint Hayes entered the bookstore smiling and shaking his head.

"Hey, David, I'm assuming Matthew and Daniel
found their way to the boxcar?" he asked.

"They ran by so fast I can't for certain say it was
the twins," David said.

"That pretty much guarantees it was them." He
looked to Laura. "Clint Hayes. Please forgive my boys.
I'd like to say this isn't normal, but that'd be lying.
Their mother jokes that we spent a lot of their first year
trying to work them up to walking and we've spent the
next nine trying to get them to slow down."

Laura laughed. "They look adorable, from what I
saw of them. David's right, though, they moved pretty
fast."

The boys chatted away as they climbed in and
around the boxcar, while their dad picked up a couple of
Boxcar Children books from the stack by the register.

"They're excited about the book club," he said.
"That's a great idea, David." He withdrew his wallet
and gave David the money for the books.

"The idea was Laura's. She and I went to UT together, and she's helping me out at the bookstore until
she begins teaching. She's hoping to get a job at Claremont Elementary after she has her babies."

"Babies? You're having twins?"

"I am," Laura said.

"Twins are cool!" one of the boys called from the reading nook.

"Twin boys?" the other one yelled.

Laura laughed. "Actually, twin girls."

One of the kids emitted an "Eww," and Clint quickly responded. "Matthew, that's enough."

"Well, at least it's twins, even if it's girls," the other one added.

Laura laughed again, and David liked hearing it, especially after she'd been so upset by her mother's unusual departure.

"Twins are a lot of fun, even if they can be a handful," Clint said, taking his change from David. "By the way, the boys said all of the kids in their class at school were going to join your boxcar club. I think the majority of them are coming in tonight. That's why we came early. My wife thought it'd be smart to beat the rush."

"That's a good idea," Laura said. "And because we do expect a lot of kids to sign up, we're going to offer the book club each weekday after school. It'll start at three-thirty and last an hour." She reached past David to a stack of clipboards with signup sheets. David hadn't realized she'd already prepared the sheets, but she had each one labeled and ready to go. He'd been impressed with her organizational skills throughout the week and now she'd impressed him again.

"You really are going to be an amazing teacher," he said, as she handed Clint a pen to sign up the twins.

Clint put both of the kids on the Monday sheet. "We'll go with Monday, since that one says it's for nine-and ten-year-olds. The boys are ten. Plus Nathan and Autumn are down for that day. They're in the boys' class at school."

"Sounds good," Laura said.

"Cool! We're with Nathan and Autumn," Matthew told Daniel, still playing inside the boxcar.

"Awesome!" Daniel yelled.

"Okay, boys, we've got to go pick up your mom at the school. Let's go. You can come back here tonight and play in the boxcar during First Friday."

"Awwww," one of the boys grumbled.

"It won't be long," Clint stressed. Then he said to Laura, "My wife teaches fourth grade. I'll let her know you're looking for a job and have her stop by to meet you tonight. She can tell you what you need to do to apply when you're ready. And congratulations again on your twins. They really are a lot of fun."

"Thanks," Laura said as the boys ran by in a flash.

"Bye!" they yelled, brushing past their father as they flew out the door. "Last one to the fountain is a rotten egg!"

"And here we go. Pray for all of the vendors, and that my kids won't take out too many booths," Clint said, heading out the door.

"That's two different people who've tried to help me today with finding a job at the school," she said.

"Nothing unusual about that. People help each other out. That's what we're supposed to do." David grabbed two *Boxcar Children* books from the case behind the counter and replaced the two he'd just sold Clint on the display stacks.

"It might be usual for you, but it's new to me," she said. "And I have to admit, I like it."

"Claremont growing on you, huh?" he asked.

"Yeah, it is."

The bell sounded again on the door, and this time, three families charged inside, all of them chatting about the cold and the new book club they'd heard about for their kids.

"That's a good thing," David said, "because it looks like you're going to meet the majority of the town tonight." He smiled at the new customers and at the additional families entering the bookstore behind them. "Welcome to A Likely Story!"

Chapter Seven

"I'm looking forward to meeting your friend Laura."
Brother Henry shook David's hand as he exited the
church Sunday morning. "Zeb told me about her moving here and working at the bookstore." He gave David
a friendly smile. "That's a good thing you're doing for
that young lady, giving her a place to work and helping
her out when she's on her own and expecting."

"I did what any friend would do," David said.

Brother Henry nodded. "A true friend would," he
agreed. "Daniel and Mandy mentioned they invited her
to church this morning. Maybe she'll come worship
with us eventually. We'd love to have her."

"I invited her, as well," David said. "And I'm praying she'll come, too."

"That's good. That's what works," Brother Henry
answered, then turned to shake the next person's hand.

David started down the church steps with Laura
on his mind. They'd had such an amazing weekend,
selling all of the *Boxcar Children* books Friday night
and filling each of her sign-up sheets with kids for
the book club. Thanks to Laura, the bookstore would

have a record number of children in every week, and hopefully their parents would shop for books while the kids participated in the book club. His business could sure use the shot in the arm, but David wondered if it was enough.

As if he knew where David's thoughts had headed, Milton Stott waited for his client at the bottom of the steps.

"Morning, David," Milton said. "Nice service, wasn't it?"

"It was. Brother Henry always does a great job." David started toward his car and hoped that Milton wouldn't bring up business, but the accountant joined in to walk with him across the parking lot.

"David, I wanted to ask you about something I heard," he said.

Checking to make sure no one was close enough to overhear their conversation, David leaned against his car and braced for Milton's question. "Okay."

"My daughter mentioned meeting a new girl in town. Said she's expecting twins, that's she a nice lady *and* that she's working for you at the bookstore."

"She is a nice lady, a friend of mine from college, and she is expecting twins," David said. "I'd hoped to bring her to church with me this morning—maybe she'll come next week." David knew none of those things were what the accountant wanted to hear about, but he thought maybe it'd let him see that David didn't want to talk about her employment status.

Milton didn't seem to care.

"And she works for you at the bookstore?" Milton asked.

David should've known it wouldn't be that easy.

"She does," he said, "and she's already brought in several new customers. We've started a book club for kids that has maxed out, and it hasn't even officially started yet. And we're expecting a large turnout for Destiny Lee's first book signing next Saturday." David attempted to control his tone so that it didn't sound like he was tossing out a sales pitch for his new employee, even if that was, for the most part, exactly what he was doing.

Milton smiled and nodded at Bo and Maura Taylor as they walked by, and David, thankful his accountant waited for them to pass before continuing this conversation, did the same. As soon as the couple got in the car next to David's and left, Milton forged ahead.

"David," he said, frowning, "I'm glad that you're making some headway in the business, and I think it's admirable that you're willing to try to help that girl out, especially given the state of your financials. But even with those sales, I just don't see how you're going to get out of the red."

"We haven't even seen how many sales I can generate with the book signing. And the craft extravaganza is this week. That will also boost my numbers." David was grasping at straws, and the look on Milton's face said he knew it.

"Your grandmother left you two things—that bookstore and her farmhouse. The bookstore isn't making it, and every time you borrow more money against your line of credit to try to save it, you're risking losing the farmhouse, too."

When David got the line of credit and used the farmhouse as collateral, it hadn't seemed like that big of a risk. But, as Milton had pointed out, he'd been borrowing against it nearly every month in an effort to save the bookstore. Now he owed nearly as much as the place was worth, and he wasn't even living there.

"I think you need to consider two options, son. And I'm not trying to worry you. I'm just trying to save you from losing both. You need to either decide that you can make the bookstore work—somehow—and sell the farmhouse. Or you need to let the bookstore go, cut your losses and keep your grandmother's home."

"I plan to live in that house one day when I have a family," David said.

Milton grunted. "I suspected that. Well, then, I've got to tell you, I'd recommend putting the bookstore on the market. Residential real estate isn't selling all that great now, but commercial property on the square is always a sure thing."

David's heart felt heavy in his chest. "She thought I could make the store work. I can't let her down." And he didn't want to let Laura down, either.

"Personally, I think it would've let her down more if she'd have thought you'd lose the bookstore *and* the house." Milton sighed, obviously realizing David wasn't ready to throw in the towel. "Just promise me you'll think about what I've said. It's my job to watch out for your business, and I am trying."

"I know, and I appreciate that," David said. "And I promise to think about it." He'd have no trouble keeping that promise. The fear of losing the store, and now the house, hovered in his thoughts nonstop.

"All right, then. Let me know if you need to talk."

Once Milton had left, David unlocked his door and started to get in but stopped when someone called his name.

Chad Martin had his window rolled down as he pulled up in his old BMW. "Hey, we're all heading to Stockville to try out that new Country Junction buffet. You wanna come?"

Chad's wife, Jessica, waved from the passenger seat. Their son, Nathan, sat in the backseat beside his little sister, Lainey. He also rolled his window down and told David, "I've already read up to chapter six in *The Boxcar Children*. I'll be done before our club meets."

Chad grinned. "Nathan's pretty excited about being in a club."

Jessica leaned toward her husband so that she could see David clearly and added, "We figure if he's going to join a club, a book club is a good way to go."

"Yeah, it is," David said. "So who all is going to the buffet?"

"Us, Troy and Destiny, Matt, Hannah and Autumn, Mitch and his girls, Daniel, Mandy, Kaden and Mia."

"We invited the Cutters, but Eden had already fixed lunch for all of them to eat together at her farm," Jessica said. "We're going on to the restaurant to get the table. Matt needed to run by his office on the way, and Daniel and Mandy are going by her gallery to see if the lady renting from them wants to come. Mandy said she's a friend of yours from college?"

David was thrilled they remembered Laura, and he prayed she'd come. "Yes, she is."

"So, you coming?" Chad asked.

A moment ago he was debating it, but now, the decision was easy. "Sure."

Laura still felt odd waking on a Sunday morning and not going to church. True, she'd stopped halfway through her years at UT, but she'd never gotten over that automatic impulse to get dressed, drive to the nearest church building and worship. When she first stopped, it was because none of her friends attended any service on campus and most of them—including Laura—stayed up too late on Saturday night to even consider waking up early for a church service Sunday morning.

But since she graduated, she'd thought more about church again, thought more about faith again. And nowadays, she didn't attend for totally different reasons than those in college. Now she didn't go because of guilt. She'd left God behind and ended up single and pregnant. Not only that, but she also wasn't certain parents would want her attending a worship service with their kids. What kind of example was she for teens? Then again, they might want to use her as an example of what *not* to do.

She'd eaten a bagel for breakfast, but it was nearly noon, and her stomach said the babies were hungry. She started down the stairs to the kitchen to fix a PB&J... or two...and had just peeked in the refrigerator when the back door flew open and Kaden entered.

"What ya doing? You didn't eat yet, did you? Mom said we wanted to catch you before you ate lunch, but you didn't answer your phone, so I ran in!"

"I think my phone is still by my bed upstairs," she said. "Why did you want to catch me before I ate?"

"'Cause everybody is going to the new place to eat in Stockville, and Dad and Mom wanted you to come, too. You are going to come, aren't you? 'Cause I'm hungry and we need to go."

Mandy entered the kitchen and rubbed a hand over

Kaden's sandy curls. "We'd really like for you to join us," she said. "It's just a small group from church, but I'd like for you to meet them."

Laura noticed Mandy's sweaterdress, scarf and boots. Kaden wore a dark green polo shirt and khakis. She glanced down at her Titans T-shirt and maternity pajama pants. "I'm not exactly dressed for it. Maybe I'll go next time."

Mandy ran her hand down to Kaden's neck and tenderly turned him toward the door. "Kaden, go on and tell your daddy that we'll be out in a minute. We need to give Laura a second to change."

"But—" Laura began.

Neither listened.

"Okay!" Kaden ran to the door, leaped from the top stair to the pavement and then continued to their minivan shouting to his father that Laura was coming.

Mandy crossed the room, took Laura's hand from the refrigerator handle and then eased the door shut. "I want you to go. You've been either working at the bookstore or cooped up in here all week. You need to get out, and I want you to meet our friends."

"Your *church* friends," Laura said.

"Same difference."

"I don't belong with a church group now. It doesn't feel right for me to go. After I have the babies, I plan to start back. I want them to grow up knowing God, but now…"

"Now is the perfect time for you to start back."

"I've made so many mistakes. Mistakes that are—" she glanced at her growing stomach "—rather obvious." Then she thought about how that sounded and said, "I don't mean that my babies are a mistake. I'm excited about having them and hopeful that I'll do a good job as a new mom."

"I believe you will," Mandy interjected.

"But," Laura continued, "I'm afraid people will look at me and feel like I shouldn't be in church."

"Maybe *you* don't feel like you should be, but I think people will surprise you. Come eat lunch with us today," Mandy said. "You need to meet some of the folks that you think won't want you in church. Then tell me what you think. And besides, I have something to talk to you about over lunch. Another book club idea for the bookstore."

"Couldn't we talk about it here?" Laura asked.

"Nope. Now get dressed, please. I'm hungry." Mandy smiled and pointed to the stairs. "Go on."

"Are you always this bossy?"

"That's a question for my husband," she answered with a laugh.

Laura went to her room and changed into one of the new outfits her mother had brought. The mocha color-block dress had zigzagging diagonal stripes of chocolate and red accenting the skirt and flowed beautifully to Laura's ankles. She added the red jewelry her mother had bought to match the dress and chocolate flats. After running a brush through her hair and putting on a little mascara and lip gloss, she grabbed her purse and phone.

Before leaving, she took a final glance in the mirror. She still wasn't used to the new shape of her body, but even so, she did think pregnancy agreed with her. Her cheeks were rosy without blush, and her hair was healthier, too, probably due to the prenatal vitamins. Wearing the maternity clothes was also fun, especially when she had so many to choose from, thanks to her mom. She thought of her mom and sure hoped her dad would be able to help Laura figure out what was wrong. Laura looked forward to his visit after Thanksgiving.

She ran her hand along the fabric covering her stomach and smiled when one of the girls kicked toward her palm. "Don't worry. I'm feeding you soon." Then she left to join her friends in the van.

Mia was in her car seat in the middle section, a pacifier in her mouth. Kaden sat buckled in the very back.

"Wow, you look really pretty!" he said as Laura climbed in.

"That's my boy," Daniel said from the driver's seat. "Already knows how to compliment the ladies."

Mandy laughed, and Laura grinned. "Well, thank you, Kaden. You just made my day."

"Cool!"

"You do look very nice," Mandy agreed, "and we're glad you decided to come."

"Me, too," Laura admitted. It did feel good to get out with friends, and she found herself looking forward to meeting the others at the restaurant. She'd met quite a few of Claremont's residents over the past week and with each person she met, she grew a little fonder of her new town. It seemed the perfect place to raise her girls.

Her phone buzzed in her purse and she withdrew it to see she'd missed three messages. The first two were from Mandy.

Mandy Brantley: Hey, we're leaving church now. Want to come get you to go eat. Okay?

Mandy Brantley: Didn't hear back from you but we're on our way anyway ;) We want you to meet our friends.

She smiled at Mandy's persistence and then noticed that the third message was from David. She opened it.

David Presley: Mandy is inviting you to lunch. Say yes. See you there.

Laura hadn't known that David was part of the group going to lunch. She fiddled with the red beads on her necklace and wondered if, like Kaden, David might think she looked pretty, too.

During the twenty-minute drive to Stockville, Kaden told her all about everything he already liked about *The Boxcar Children* and how he had read more than any of the other kids in his class, but that he wouldn't tell what happened before they got to it. And while she listened to Kaden, she entertained Mia.

The baby withdrew her pacifier, tiny lips smacking with the action, tossed it in Laura's lap and giggled.

"Binky," she said, reaching for it.

Laura handed it back, and Mia proceeded to toss it again, her blue eyes glittering with mischief.

After the third toss, Laura realized the game wasn't ending, and she didn't care. To hear that baby belly laugh warmed her heart.

"She's got your number," Mandy said, looking around her seat to see her little princess. "Don't you." She squeezed Mia's knee, and the baby laughed even harder.

By the time they got to Stockville, Laura had re-trieved Mia's binky at least a couple dozen times. Her own babies were restless in her tummy, and Laura wondered what it'd be like to hear her little girls laugh the way Mia laughed now. She couldn't wait.

She walked behind Daniel and Mandy as they entered the restaurant. Daniel carried Mia and snagged a high chair as he headed toward a long table with several people already seated. "We brought Miss Laura!" Kaden announced.

Everyone said hello, and Mandy performed a quick introduction. "Laura, this is Mitch Gillespie and his daughters, Dee and Emmie." Mitch had reddish hair and a nice smile, reminding Laura of Prince Harry. Dee and Emmie both had strawberry curls, with Dee looking to be around two or three and Emmie about the same age as Mia.

"Nice to meet you," she said.

Mitch unwrapped a pack of crackers for Emmie and placed a few on her high-chair tray. "You, too," he said.

Daniel put Mia in a high chair next to Emmie's, and the two immediately started chattering and eating the crackers.

"And this is Dr. Matt Graham. You already met his wife, Hannah, and daughter, Autumn," Mandy said. "Then there's Troy and Destiny Lee. Destiny is our new local author and will be doing the book signing at A Likely Story next Saturday."

"Nice to meet you," Laura said, and then turned to the only person Mandy hadn't yet introduced.

"And of course you know David," Mandy said, grinning. "So, who wants to head to the buffet?"

Everyone answered in agreement and started toward the long tables of food in the center of the restaurant. Everyone, that is, except for the man wearing a black cashmere sweater over a pale blue polo shirt and black dress pants. The guy whose cologne again teased her senses because he stood so near. Her friend. Her employer. And right now, the guy making her heart beat so hard it was probably deafening her children.

Laura did not want to have a relationship again. Not yet. So why did every ounce of her being act like she wanted one now? Right here. Right now. She licked her lips and wondered what to say and whether he was thinking anything at all like what she was thinking.

He moved even closer, brought his mouth near her left ear and said, "You look amazing." His warm breath against her neck sent a patch of goose bumps down her arm, and she was thankful that the new dress had long sleeves.

"Thanks."

"I'm glad you came," he said.

She smiled. "Me, too."

"Y'all coming, or not?" Kaden called from the line by the food.

"We're coming." David waved a hand in front of her. "Ladies first."

Her stomach growled loudly, and she laughed. "And it's a good thing, because these ladies are hungry."

Laura filled her plate with roast beef, black-eyed peas, turnip greens and cornbread. David went for the meat loaf, potatoes, sweet peas and a roll.

Returning to the table, Daniel offered grace and they began eating, the kids chattering noisily and the adults talking about the delicious food, which Hannah described as "good ol' family-reunion-style cooking." Laura had never had enough family to have a family reunion, but she imagined if she did, it would be something like this. Everyone eating and laughing and chatting. They treated Laura as if she belonged here, with all of them, regardless of the fact that they'd all attended church this morning and she'd stayed home. Not once did anyone ask anything about the father of her children or why she was on her own. In fact, the only questions they asked were ones that would allow them to get to know her better…and even help her out.

"So, if you're going to keep working after the babies are born, have you found a place for them to stay?" Jessica asked between bites of chicken and dumplings. "Because I work at the Claremont day care, and I have to say, we have an amazing nursery program."

"You'd say all of your programs are amazing, wouldn't you?" her husband asked.

She took another bite, grinned. "It's the truth."

"She's right, the day care is top-notch," Hannah said. "I decided to stay home with Autumn, but if I did send my kids anywhere, that's where they'd go."

"I haven't decided what I'm doing yet," Laura said honestly. She had planned to look and see what was available, but since she'd only been in Claremont for a week, she hadn't had a chance. "I hope to spend a few weeks with them before I have to take them anywhere." She hadn't asked David about that, and she also wasn't sure how she'd stay with her girls if she wasn't working.

Suddenly her meal didn't look as appealing, and her stomach churned for another reason. What if she couldn't afford to spend a little time with the girls before going back to work? And how hard would it be to leave them if they were merely weeks old? Then another worry—how would she afford to pay for day care?

The majority of the table moved ahead with conversation, but David, sitting in the next chair, leaned toward Laura. "I don't have a problem with you bringing them to the bookstore. We'll work it out."

And just like that, her worries eased up a little. She still knew that she'd need to find something for the girls eventually, but if he'd let her start out bringing them with her to the bookstore, that would help. "Thank you," she whispered.

"Don't worry," he said.

She couldn't make that promise, because even now, she continued to think of her concerns, but she smiled, nodded and began to eat again.

"I wanted to talk to both of you about a book club for women that I'd like y'all to start at the bookstore. I think it'd be very popular, and I know it'd be beneficial to all of us," Mandy said. "Daniel has recommended the women at church spending more time together away from the regular church services, and I agree that it's a great idea. I was thinking about a book club that focused on women of the Bible, specifically the women in the lineage of Christ."

"Oh, I've seen those books, the series, I mean. Is that what you're talking about?" Destiny asked. "It starts with Tamar, then Rahab, Ruth, Bathsheba and Mary, right?"

Mandy nodded. "That's the one. David, it's called *The Lineage of Grace.* Could you order those for us? And Laura, do you think you could kind of lead us in the book club? I think there are study questions we could use, but I'll admit that I've never been in a book club before."

"I can order the books tomorrow," David said.

"And I'd be happy to help lead it," Laura said, excited that they were starting yet another book club to help David's store. "When were y'all thinking you'd want to meet?"

"Maybe Tuesday evenings?" Mandy said. "How about seven-thirty, so we'd have time to get the kids fed and done with homework and all. Would that work?"

"That's after the bookstore closes, but I think after hours for the adult book clubs would be better anyway. Less interruptions. It sounds great." Laura's appetite had completely returned now, and she turned her attention back to the delicious roast and gravy. She also found herself easily chatting with the others at the table and could tell that no one seemed to think any less of her or judge her or…anything. In fact, she realized that the "church friends" weren't so bad.

Maybe, with David's encouragement and with the friendships that she'd begun to develop with those seated at this table, she might actually find her way back to church again, too.

Chapter Eight

David's store was more packed than it'd ever been, with parents browsing—and buying—while their kids were busy enjoying the book club with Laura. He stayed attuned to his customers' needs but also peeked at what was happening in the children's area at every opportunity.

"I could totally live in a boxcar," Kaden said. "I like these berries a lot." He popped another couple of blueberries in his mouth and grinned at Laura, who proceeded to explain that the kids in the book didn't only live on berries. Then she also reminded Kaden of how good he had it to be able to live with his parents.

"Yeah, I know," Kaden said, "but still, I think I'm gonna ask Mom to get us lots of berries from the grocery. I do really like 'em."

The other kids in the group joined in with their comments of berries, questions about the children in the book and about boxcars in general.

"This is wonderful for Kaden," Mandy said as she moved to stand near David and see the interaction. "For all of the kids really." Then she lowered her voice and added, "And it's good for Laura, too, don't you think?"

"I do," he agreed. Indeed, Laura had been just as excited, or maybe even more, than the children about beginning the book club this week. Tonight was only the second night, but both evenings had filled the bookstore and also had the kids talking about looking forward to their next meeting. Consequently, David had his highest weekday sales ever.

"She showed me some pamphlets she printed out online about the train station in Stockville. Said she wanted to take the children on a field trip in the spring to look at real boxcars."

"I know. She mentioned that to me yesterday, and I think it's a great idea," David said, liking the notion of Laura still being here in the spring and praying his business continued to pick up so he could ensure that they still had a bookstore to run.

"She'd be a great schoolteacher," Mandy said, "but I can't help but think she's also very good at what she does here. I can't see her doing both, but if she does eventually take a job in the school system, maybe you could find someone else for this position?"

"Maybe so," David said, but he felt the same as Mandy; Laura was perfect for the bookstore. "Or maybe she'd decide to just work here." If he could pay her.

Mandy nudged him with her shoulder. "That's what I'm talking about."

David knew it was a long shot, but he thought it would be wonderful if the bookstore could eventually hold its own.

"So did those books for the women's book club come

in yet?" Mandy asked. "I was hoping to get started on the first one."

"They'll be here tomorrow."

"Awesome. I'll pick them up and hand them out to everyone at church tomorrow night." She looked again at Laura. "Think she'd want to come to church with us for the midweek study?"

"I asked, and she said she still didn't think she was ready. But it wouldn't hurt for you to ask, too." He loved it that Mandy and several others in town had taken an interest in Laura, not only personally but also spiritually. She had that quality, the ability to draw you in and make you care about her, probably because she cared so much for others. Now, in fact, she'd taken little Savannah Jameson in her lap and was letting her help turn the pages in the book.

"Look at that, isn't that precious," Mandy said, watching Savannah's eyes widen as she looked up at Laura telling the story. The little girl turned the page and then moved her hand to rest on Laura's tummy. "Hold these books," Mandy said, passing the stack in her arms to David. "I've got my camera in my purse."

David took the books and watched as Mandy quietly got her camera ready then raised it to take several pictures of Laura surrounded by the children. Laura was so into the discussion that she didn't notice.

"It's moments like that you can't get in a studio," Mandy said. "I'm predicting that will be a gallery favorite."

"I'd like a copy," David said, then when Mandy smiled knowingly, he added, "for the bookstore. It'll be good for customers to see the book club in action."

"Uh-huh," Mandy said, still grinning, but David

didn't acknowledge anything. Laura didn't feel that way about him; she never had, or she'd have noticed his attention when they first met back in college instead of zeroing in on Jared. And the next time David had a relationship, he wanted someone who wanted *him*.

"You ready for me to ring you up?" He indicated the books balanced in his arms.

"Sure." Mandy obviously decided to drop her suspicions for now, and he was grateful. He didn't need all of the customers browsing the bookstore to think there was something going on between him and his employee.

They moved to the checkout counter and David took her payment while Titus Jameson stood nearby. Mandy paid, said hello to Titus and then returned to the children's reading area to continue watching Kaden and the other kids.

"Anything I can help you find, Titus?" David asked.

"No, I just wanted to thank you for this book club that you've started. Savannah, well, she loves reading, but she hasn't seemed to enjoy it as much ever since her mom left." He nodded toward the big boxcar prop and all of the children sitting around it. "She's really taken to this story and to Laura." His mouth flattened, and David could tell the guy was holding back on his emotions. Titus was only a couple of years older than David, but he'd been through a lot this year with his wife leaving him for someone else and then heading out of town with the new guy. From what David had heard, she hadn't even seen Savannah since she left.

David swallowed past his own emotions and said, "Well, it looks like Laura has taken to Savannah, too."

Titus nodded. "I can see that, and I appreciate it

more than you could know." He ran a hand across his chin and said, "Something else, David."

"What's that?"

"Business has been down, you know. Not a lot of people building right now with the economy the way it is." Titus owned the only construction company in town and had always seemed to do very well with his business, but David hadn't seen any new houses going up lately or renovations, for that matter. "I was wondering," Titus continued, "if you might have any work you'd like to get done."

David shook his head. "I wish I could help you," he said. "The truth is that I am wanting to make some changes to one of the rooms in my apartment upstairs, but I was thinking my dad and I would work on that when he's here for Thanksgiving."

"I understand," Titus said solemnly.

"The thing is, I'd much rather hire someone to do it, and for that matter, I'd love to hire someone to fix up the old farmhouse I inherited from my grandmother. It needs, well, pretty much everything. But I just can't do it right now." He didn't explain that the economy was also killing him, but Titus's knowing nod said he understood.

"No problem," he said. "Something will work out. Hey, could I put a couple of flyers up in your window? Maybe someone needs work done. It's getting close to Christmas, you know, and I want Savannah to have a good one, especially with everything she's been through this year."

"Sure."

"I'll go get a couple from my truck and put them up tonight if that's okay."

"That's fine," David said, "and if I hear of anyone needing work done, I'll tell them to call you."

"I'd appreciate that," Titus said.

"I'll do the same." Zeb Shackleford had moved to the counter with a small stack of books and heard the last of their conversation.

Titus gave the older man a smile. "Thank you, Zeb."

Zeb's mouth slid to the side as he watched Titus make his way out of the store. "That boy's had a tough year."

"I know. I wish I could help him out," David said.

"I know you do," Zeb said.

David looked at the four books Zeb had on the counter and watched the man withdraw his worn wallet. He quietly whispered, "Don't. I'm not taking it."

Zeb whispered back, "One day, I'm repaying you." He pointed to David. "You can count on it. Somehow, I will."

"Laura said you were going to repay us by letting us go with you for some of your visits to read to the kids."

Zeb's face split into a smile and sent his wrinkles branching in all new directions. "I was going to ask y'all about that tonight. I know you're busy this month with the extravaganza, Destiny's book signing, Thanksgiving and all. Hoping y'all will be real busy for Black Friday."

"Me, too," David said.

"But how about in December y'all can come with me to the hospital? I try to go each night that month, since the kids are thinking about Christmas and all. It's easy for them to get sad during the holidays." He shrugged. "I try to help 'em stay happy."

"That sounds great," David said.

"Good deal." Zeb took his books off the counter. "Tell Laura I said good-night. I'm heading home."

"I will."

Laura loved every minute of her time with the kids and also enjoyed chancing a glance at David every now and again to see him smiling, obviously thrilled with the customers filling his store. When the book club hour ended, she found that the kids lingered, wanting to talk to her more about Henry, Violet, Jessie and Benny, the four children in the story. Laura was especially taken with Savannah Jameson. The little girl continued to ask questions about Violet and seemed to drink in every word. Laura had dreamed of teaching children who were that eager to learn, and it was just as wonderful as she'd thought it would be.

By the time they were down to the last customer, it was ten minutes past closing time. The pretty lady lingered at the doorway chatting with David while Laura tidied up the children's area and tried not to look overly interested in the fact that they were talking. The woman's name was Haley Calhoun, and Laura had learned that she was one of the two town vets. Haley had stopped by to pick up a couple of books David had ordered her about quarter horses, and she was nice to Laura, but in Laura's opinion, she was a bit nicer to David. She talked about church and about the fact that she thought David should have a puppy or a kitten in the bookstore, and Laura couldn't help but notice that she and David seemed to get along very well. And they looked good together, too.

Haley wore a fitted white jacket, black riding pants and black boots. She'd explained that she'd come straight from riding because she'd remembered that the bookstore closed at 6:00 p.m. The fact that she looked absolutely stunning in her riding gear only added to Laura's discomfort at watching her stick around and talk to David.

David laughed at something she said, and Laura did a one-eighty to keep from staring and dropping her jaw. Instead she moved as far away from the front of the store as possible and checked the author names for alphabetization.

She hardly paid attention to the books, however, because she was too busy silently chastising herself. She *wanted* David to be interested in someone. She didn't want to have a relationship herself, so why should she care that he was showing another female attention? She shouldn't.

Moving from the A's to the B's, she caught sight of a C book, yanked it out, found the correct location and jabbed it into place with as much force as she could muster.

"Easy there, slugger. They tend to sell better if they are still in one piece."

She'd been so absorbed in her thoughts/jealousy/ whatever that she hadn't heard him *finally* tell Haley goodbye. Her cheeks flamed and from the way his brows lifted and his glasses followed suit, he could tell.

"You upset about something?"

"No, of course not." She forced a laugh. "I'm just happy that everything went so well tonight, aren't you?" Did that sound *too* enthusiastic? Because she was happy, but she was also angry, and she wasn't about to admit why.

"I am. Best sales night on a weekday ever, excluding

holidays," he said, reaching past her to push another book in place. His arm brushed her side, and Laura fought the urge to lean into it.

These hormones were getting the best of her. She needed David to be dating someone so he'd officially be off-limits and stop messing with her head.

"Why aren't you dating anyone?" she blurted and then wished that she could push the words back in. But the widening of his eyes and the slight drop in his jaw said that there was no going back now. He'd heard what was on her mind, and he looked…more than a little surprised. Well, Laura had lost some of her filter for saying what was on her mind over the past few months. Maybe it *was* the pregnancy hormones in action, or maybe it was simply the fact that she didn't understand the bizarreness of her old friend, her attractive and kind and nice—okay, a little more gorgeous than she remembered—old friend being *so* single.

When he didn't readily offer a response, Laura, being Laura, couldn't stand the silence and decided to fill the vacant air with words. "You're a good-looking guy, you own your own business—" granted, it wasn't anywhere near what one would consider a thriving business, but Laura was in the process of fixing that "—you're nice to an extreme, honest to a fault…" She paused because the look on his face had shifted from surprise…to shock. "I just don't get it," she continued. "Several of the girls—women—who've been in the shop this week are interested in you. I'm pretty sure the one that just left could also be counted in that number. I don't know how you can't see it. I mean, do you want me to kind of, I don't know, find out if they want to go out with you or something?" At the moment, the thought of fixing David up didn't sound so appealing, but it'd sure help ease the tension between the two of them and control some of this infatuation she'd suddenly discovered toward her old friend.

His brows dipped, and he looked as though he were holding back a laugh. "I appreciate the offer," he said, "but to be completely honest, I think I have already been out with every single lady that visited the store this week."

That wasn't what she expected. "You have?"

He set that laugh free. "Don't sound so surprised."

"No, I didn't mean it like that," she said, then frowned. How did she mean it? "Well, then, why aren't you dating any of them, like, seriously?"

"Because I haven't felt *seriously* about any of them," he said, as though this conversation had run its course.

Laura didn't think it had. "But you like dating one person. You liked being serious," she said, recalling how committed he was to his girlfriend in college. "You dated Cassadee nearly two years when we were at UT." Then Laura recalled the reason they'd broken up. David had returned home to Claremont for Mia's funeral, started thinking about life and religion and all of the other things that come to mind after the loss of a loved one, and then he decided he had messed up by letting his faith go in college. "You two broke up because she didn't share your faith." She glanced up at him. "Is that why you haven't gotten serious with the girls you've dated here? Because they don't share your faith?"

"I only went out with the ones that do share my faith," he said, "but the truth is, I didn't feel 'that way' about them. Sharing faith is important to me, but you need…" He appeared to search for the word and then said, "You need more."

Laura knew what "more" he referred to. Attraction, that spark that simply happens when two people are together and know that they could have something special. *That* was what he meant. And unfortunately, Laura was pretty sure *that* was exactly what she was beginning to feel. But fortunately, the other statement he made reminded her that even if she did want any type of relationship, it would never happen with David.

I only went out with the ones that do share my faith.

And that eliminated Laura from any equation involving David. Twice he'd asked her if she wanted to join him at church, and twice she'd declined. And he'd already invited her to tomorrow night's midweek worship, and already, she'd declined. Not necessarily because she didn't share his faith, but because she still wasn't certain she'd be welcomed there. She'd been able to handle the lunch last Sunday with Mandy's friends, but she still felt like too much of a hypocrite to go and mingle with the real Christians full-time.

Laura realized she'd been sitting silently while he waited for her next question. And she felt a little badly for the bold interrogation regarding his dating habits. "Sorry, I was being nosy."

"Sometimes that's what friends do, right?" He leaned against the bookshelves and looked mighty nice doing it. "We are still friends, aren't we, Laura? Or… are we something else?" His eyes were so focused on her hers that Laura felt her breath catch. And she noticed that they weren't merely brown; they were chocolate. With tiny gold flecks near the center. They were exquisite, and she found that she couldn't stop looking at them. "Laura?" he prodded.

She didn't want a relationship. She didn't. She'd made a conscious decision that she wouldn't pursue anyone, or allow anyone to pursue her, which, of course, David wasn't doing. At all. So she should be happy, ecstatic even. Why had she even brought up this whole "why aren't you dating?" thing? And why had she gotten so jealous when she saw him talking to Haley Calhoun?

Uncomfortable with the fact that her emotions were trying to trump her mind, she took a step back, bumped her behind against a bookshelf and managed a smile. "We're still friends," she said, then she promptly turned away from those knowing eyes and made a beeline for home.

Chapter Nine

David rang up sale after sale as the entire Claremont community, as well as those from the surrounding counties, lined up for their autographed copies of *Southern Love in Claremont*. With Destiny Lee featuring over fifty Claremont love stories, practically everyone knew someone in the book. Luckily for David, it appeared everyone who was in the book or knew someone in the book wanted a copy or two.

By the end of the night, he'd sold all but twenty copies.

"Wow," Destiny said, beaming as she capped her pen, "that was incredible."

"I'll say it was," Troy said, undeniably happy for his wife. "You were awesome."

"And you were awesome, Laura," Destiny said as Laura picked up the empty plates and bottles around the signing area. "I hadn't considered having anything for them to snack on while they waited. Those cookies were a hit, and the bottled water kept them happy, too."

"I read up on how to have a successful book sign-

ing," Laura said. "The number-one thing the sites recommended was plenty of snacks and water."

"Well, it worked," Destiny said.

David joined Laura in picking up the trash. She
seemed to notice he was helping but didn't look in his
direction. She'd avoided eye contact like the plague
since her questions about his dating status on Tuesday; however, David had felt her gaze on more than
one occasion.

He reached for an empty water bottle at the same
time that Laura noticed it, and their hands collided on
the plastic. David didn't move his, but she jerked hers
away as though she'd been scalded.

He smiled. She blushed. And David wondered what
was happening between himself and his new employee.

Destiny cleared her throat, and David knew by looking at the lady that she'd seen the odd reaction. Then
she laughed out loud.

Laura looked up. "Everything okay?"

Troy put his arm around his wife. "Yeah," Troy
said, apparently watching everything, "my wife is just
happy. I think I'll take her out to dinner to celebrate.
How about Messina's?"

"Sounds yummy." Destiny gave David and Laura
a finger wave. "Y'all have a great night, and thanks
again."

"You're welcome," they both said, and then continued cleaning up while the couple left the bookstore.

After tossing the last paper plate in the trash, Laura
walked behind the counter to get her purse. The past
three nights, David let her say her quick goodbye and
rush to exit. But he didn't feel like letting her run away
again tonight. He moved to stand between the end of

the counter and the wall, essentially blocking her in. "Where are you headed?"

She slid the strap of her purse a little higher on her shoulder and then ran her fingers across the beads of her necklace. "Just going on home to eat and go to sleep. Been a long day." She took a small step toward him and waited for him to move.

David didn't budge. Her hand continued flitting across the red and gold beads of the long necklace. She looked beautiful, as always, wearing a long black dress that nearly met the floor, a red jacket and red and gold dangly earrings that matched her necklace. Red flat shoes similar to ballerina slippers peeked beneath the hem of her dress.

"Excuse me, please." She attempted another step, and again he stood his ground.

"I'm not letting you go home before we celebrate."

Her eyes widened, and her mouth opened in a little *O*. Then she cleared her throat and asked, "Celebrate? Celebrate what?"

"This was the best sales night in the history of the bookstore, or at least as long as I've owned it," he said. "If that doesn't call for a celebration, I don't know what does."

She seemed to consider his invitation but then shook her head. "I really do need to get home. It's been a long day, and I think I'll just eat a sandwich and go on to bed."

"All right then," he said. "Coffee and a sandwich it is." He turned and waved her through the opening to exit the counter area.

"Coffee and a sandwich?" she asked, and he was glad to see she appeared to be holding back a smile.

"Have you been to The Grind yet? It's delicious."

"The coffee shop? No," she said. "Do they have more than coffee? I mean, I like coffee, even if I'm only drinking decaffeinated now for the babies, but you said coffee and a sandwich."

"Reubens, turkey and brie, roast beef, pecan chicken salad, BLT with applewood bacon." He took a breath to keep going, but she held up a hand.

"You had me at turkey and brie."

He laughed and was pleased to see her join in. She'd been nervous and jittery around him ever since their awkward conversation Tuesday night, when she'd shocked him by showing a hint of jealousy. The emotion didn't coincide with the type of relationship he'd believed they had, and if she were jealous…what did that mean? Was Laura actually feeling something toward him beyond friend and employer?

"So, sandwich and coffee with the boss," she said, stepping ahead of him toward the door, "to celebrate our big night."

David was pretty sure she clarified because she didn't want this to appear like a date. Which was fine. He didn't, either. He simply wanted to celebrate, and he also wasn't quite ready to send Laura home.

Fifteen minutes later, they were seated at one of the cozy bistro tables near the fireplace inside The Grind sipping on vanilla lattes and listening to the band More Than This playing contemporary Christian music. Laura ordered the turkey and brie, of course, and David had his traditional Reuben. Both had the homemade sweet potato chips on the side.

Laura hummed her contentment through the first bite, and David nodded.

"Told you it was good."

"You were telling the truth," she said.

"I always try to."

The band finished playing "Lifted High" and then went to take a break. David and Laura clapped along with the others in the coffee house.

"They're really good," she said.

"I know. It's amazing how much talent we have locally, for a town this small."

She took another bite of her sandwich and hummed again.

He grinned, and she blushed.

"Sorry. It's just *so* good."

"I'm glad you're enjoying it," he said, "and I'm glad you agreed to come out with me."

Her eyes widened as she chewed, then she tapped beneath her throat as she swallowed. "But—this isn't a date," she said, "is it?"

David shook his head. "Just a celebration."

"I knew that." She took another bite, smiling through her chewing.

"I hope you know how much I appreciate everything you've done at the store this week. The book club is a hit, and the signing today was so much better because of you. Destiny was right—you did a great job keeping the crowd happy while they waited."

"It only took a few searches on the internet," she said, plucking a sweet potato chip from her plate and taking a bite.

"But you took the time to do it, and it worked. I appreciate that."

She ate another chip. "Hence our celebration."

"Exactly." He polished off his sandwich and then listened to the band tune their instruments to get ready for another song. Soon they'd started into "Where You Are," and David softly sang along.

When the song ended, he turned to see Laura had finished everything on her plate and was looking at him with a strange expression.

"What?" he asked.

"You sing, too. Is there anything you can't do?"

"I told you before, I can't cook, nothing more than eggs and anything grilled. I'm fairly hopeless in the kitchen."

"Sure you are," she said, tossing her napkin on the table.

Grinning, David caught the attention of their waitress. "Rhonda, which cookies do you have fresh out of the oven?"

"They just finished making the white-chocolate macadamia-nut cookies," she said.

"Awesome. We'll take four cookies and two lattes to go please, and the check."

She pulled her notepad out of her pocket, jotted down the additional items and handed him the ticket. "There you go. I'll be right back with your cookies and lattes."

"What if I don't want cookies?" Laura asked.

"Then there will be more for me," David said. "You don't want warm, gooey, fresh-out-of-the-oven white-chocolate macadamia-nut cookies?"

She smirked. "You know I do."

"That's what I thought," he said.

Rhonda returned, placed the cups on the table and

handed David a small white bag that smelled incredible. He thanked her, paid her and then asked Laura, "Ready to go?"

Laura couldn't remember ever feeling quite this special. David opened the door for her as they left the coffee house, and she worked to pull her jacket tighter with her free hand. David noticed and reached for her cup.

"Let me hold it while you tighten your coat," he said, his fingers grazing hers as he wrapped them around the cup and slid it away.

Laura attempted to ignore the sensation that zinged through her at the mere contact, drew her jacket closer around her and tightened the belt. "Thanks," she said, reaching for the coffee, their fingers brushing again with the exchange.

"Just wait until you try this." He withdrew a steaming cookie from the bag.

Laura reached for the treat, but it was so warm and gooey that it bent in half and broke, the majority of it landing with a plop on the sidewalk.

"No way," David said, frowning.

Laura looked at the goo on the sidewalk and the disappointment on his face and burst out laughing.

"Hey now, this isn't funny." He still had a small dab of cookie in his fingers, and it appeared to be melting to the touch.

"Oh, I beg to differ," she said, laughing so hard she nearly spilled her coffee, "it's very funny."

Obviously seeing what happened, Rhonda darted out of the restaurant with enough napkins to choke a horse and shoved them at David. "Here you go!" she said.

Which only made Laura laugh harder. And even

though her coffee had a lid, it still sloshed through the drink hole, and for some reason, she found that quite hysterical, too.

David used a napkin to get the mess off the sidewalk, tossed it in a nearby can and then made another effort to pull a cookie from the sack, this time with a napkin.

He handed the napkin-encased cookie to Laura, and she happily took a bite.

The sweet white chocolate melted on her tongue. "Oh, wow, you were right. These are amazing."

"Thanks," Rhonda said, then she headed back into the coffee house.

David and Laura started walking down the sidewalk, and he pulled another cookie from the bag. It started folding over, and this time, he tossed the whole thing in his mouth.

"Kinda hard to take your time enjoying it that way, isn't it?" she asked.

He smirked. "Oh, I enjoyed it."

They neared Carter Photography, and she glanced at the white sack. "Okay, I'm ready for my other one," she said.

He grinned. "Your other one was the one I dropped on the sidewalk. This one's mine." He lifted the last cookie, which, maybe because it'd had a little time to cool, stayed together.

"Hey, I'm eating for three here," she said.

"You have a point." He handed her the cookie.

Laura propped her coffee in the crook of her arm so she could break the cookie in half, then handed part to David. "Here."

He took it. "You sure?" he asked, tossing it in his mouth.

She laughed. "Well, I guess I'd better be, huh?"

"Looks that way."

She ate the last bite of hers. "Thanks for the celebration dinner and for walking me home."

"You're welcome." He stepped beneath the awning and watched as she found her keys in her purse and then moved to unlock the door. "I'll make sure you get inside safely."

Laura nodded and fumbled to slide the key into the lock. Finally, it clicked, and she turned the knob. It almost felt like the end of a date, like the moment when she'd stall, hold her breath and wait for their first kiss. She looked back at the man who'd already touched her heart in ways that no one else ever had. "But this isn't a date?" She'd meant it to come out as a statement, but the question was there, just the same. Why couldn't she stop her mouth from blurting whatever traipsed across her heart? She was practically *asking* for this to be a date, and that wasn't what she wanted.

Remember Jared. Remember how much relationships hurt. Remember how you promised—promised—yourself that you would not jump into another one too soon!

But this is David. He's perfect, her heart whispered, and her mind quickly screamed, *You thought Jared was perfect, too!*

He stepped closer, and Laura braced for a kiss that she was pretty sure would rock her to her toes. A kiss she did *not* want. Really.

"This isn't a date," he whispered.

Stunned, she blinked, nodded. "Have a good night," she said, opening the door.

"And, Laura…"

She looked back into those dark eyes, at the gold flecks catching the porch light. "Yes?"

"If I took you on a date, you wouldn't have to ask. You'd know."

Chapter Ten

Laura set aside Sunday to read the remainder of Destiny's book and to get started on the Tamar novel that the women's book club would discuss on Tuesday evening. With the past two weeks being so busy, she hadn't been able to read more than a couple of the love stories in Destiny's book, but she was already hooked. She fixed a cup of coffee, grabbed a quilt and the book then headed out to the balcony to read.

Most all of the apartments on the square had balconies overlooking the center area, where the three-tiered fountain flowed and a few geese ambled around the wrought-iron benches, where the elderly typically sat with bread. But unlike every other morning of the week, today the square was primarily empty, probably because people were home getting ready for church.

Laura assumed everyone she went to lunch with last Sunday would gather at the Claremont Community Church today, as would David.

She sipped her oversize mug of coffee. The crisp taste instantly reminded her of the lattes she'd shared with him a week ago and that parting comment that had teased her ever since.

She'd hardly been able to sleep for remembering his words and wondering what it would be like to go on a real date with David Presley.

A shiver passed over her, and it had nothing to do with the cold. She focused on the book and tried to tune out the memory of how badly she'd wanted to be kissed. And how he hadn't even tried. She turned the page and attempted to focus on the next story. It was interesting to read about couples she'd already met in town.

The first story was about Marvin and Mae Tolleson, the older couple who owned the variety store. And she'd read about Mandy and Daniel, learned how they'd started out basically despising one another because both of them wanted to adopt Kaden when his parents passed away. This morning she started into the third story, about Chad and Jessica. Soaking in the pages, Laura learned that Jessica was pregnant with Chad's baby when she ran away from Claremont as a teen, and she didn't tell him for six years. The story of how they reunited and how he forgave her for leaving touched Laura's heart. She thought of adorable little Nathan in the book club and realized that he was that precious baby who finally met his daddy.

Tears trickled down Laura's cheeks. Her little girls would never have a relationship with their biological father. Jared had made certain she knew that he didn't want any part of this pregnancy or their lives. But Laura wanted them to have a daddy, eventually.

A steady thumping caught her attention. She wiped the tears away and looked for the source of the noise, growing louder. Then she saw the jogger entering the square from Main Street. David ran steadily down the sidewalk, his tennis shoes producing the pounding she'd heard. Oddly, the even thudding of his shoes reminded her of the sounds she heard at each doctor's visit, her babies' heartbeats.

Laura's heart kicked it up a notch, too. He wore a gray T-shirt and navy sweatpants. An iPod was strapped around his right bicep with a white cord connecting the earphones. His shirt wasn't overly tight, but it still managed to emphasize the hard planes of his chest, flexing and releasing with each breath.

She continued staring until he reached the bookstore. He held one hand out to brace against the brick wall and checked his watch. Then he nodded, apparently satisfied with his time. He pulled the earphones out and then started to go into the store but, to Laura's surprise, he tossed a glance over his shoulder, locked eyes with her and smiled.

She should have waved, or yelled hello, or *something*. But instead she clutched the book, gathered the quilt and the coffee and retreated inside. She glanced at her closet. Several dresses hung there that would be perfect to wear to church today. A tiny whisper told her to get dressed and go. But while that voice whispered, her fear screamed louder. What if Mandy's friends weren't typical, and the remainder of the people there would rather a single, very pregnant lady not show up in the middle of their small community church? Laura couldn't deny she was starting to have serious feelings toward David, and he wanted—needed—a woman who shared his faith. If he'd have patience, Laura would get there again. As soon as she thought

God was ready for her. She figured He'd let her know somehow when the time was right.

"So, did you finish reading the book?" Hannah asked Mandy as they each plopped down in one of the cozy chairs at the front of the bookstore.

"I read it in two days," Mandy said, placing a hand over her heart. "It was amazing."

"I have to admit that I'd never really thought about the story from Tamar's point of view, and I found myself rooting for her more than any character I've ever read about," Hannah said.

Several more ladies came in and filled the chairs and sofas that David had arranged for the night's meeting. Laura said hello to Destiny and Jessica and met a sweet older lady named Mary, who said she was married to the preacher at the church. Then Eden Sanders came in and introduced herself, as well as her daughter, Georgiana Cutter, and Georgiana's sister-in-law, Dana. Laura noticed Georgiana holding Dana's forearm, and it didn't take but a moment for her to realize the pretty strawberry-haired woman was blind.

"We got the book on CD for Georgiana," Dana explained as they sat down.

"Yes, and I'm so glad we did," Georgiana said. "Tamar's story touched my heart."

"Mine, too," Laura admitted, taking her seat in the center chair and preparing to lead the discussion. "I started reading it Sunday afternoon and couldn't go to sleep that night until I was done, well after two o'clock."

Mandy sat next to Laura. They'd grown very close over the past few weeks, with Laura visiting Mandy nearly every day at the photography studio. She leaned toward Laura and said softly, "I really wanted you to read that story."

"I appreciate that," Laura said, "more than you could know."

She'd never read the story of Tamar, either, and she had no idea how terribly the lady had been treated by the men she tried to love. Nor did she know about the way Tamar had tricked her father-in-law into fathering her child. But in spite of her trickery, God favored her for attaining her natural rights when she'd been wronged by Judah's sons. And she ended up being one of only five women listed in the lineage of Christ.

Laura cleared her throat. "So, we have some discussion questions here. I'd like to get your thoughts on these. Question one, Tamar was abused, abandoned and neglected. She ended up taking matters into her own hands and having a difficult time of it. Have you ever felt like this?"

To Laura's relief, the women in the group were very open, with several of them bringing up instances in their lives where they'd experienced a hard time, often because they were trying to handle things on their own. Jessica spoke up first and talked about her fear when she'd become pregnant as a teen and how she'd hidden the pregnancy from Chad so he wouldn't give up his college scholarship.

"If I'd have told him the truth and hadn't run away, we'd have had six more years together raising Nathan. But I thought I'd messed up, and I didn't want to mess up his life, too." She brushed a tear away then added, "But Nathan completes his life, completes our lives. He and Lainey are the best parts of our world."

"I tried running away from God," Mandy said softly, "after Mia died. I know now that I was blaming Him. But He wanted me back—" she pointed to the book in her hand "—the same way He wanted Tamar."

"Enough to put her in the lineage of His Son," Mary said. "I think that's a beautiful image of how very much He wants us, don't you? Even when we feel we've messed up?"

All of the women agreed, and Laura swallowed thickly through the lump in her throat. She'd come to the same realization reading Tamar's story, but to hear her thoughts voiced by all of the other women, and to learn that they'd had moments where they felt like they'd turned their backs on God, too…overwhelmed her.

She glanced up and saw David leaning against one of the endcaps looking toward the group but undeniably focused on her. He tilted his head, held up the okay symbol with his hand and mouthed, *You okay?*

Laura's heart was filled with compassion toward Mandy, for convincing her to read this story, and toward David, for seeing her through the past few weeks and encouraging her to come back to God without shoving her through the church door. *Very okay,* she mouthed.

He smiled then turned and went to the counter apparently convinced that she would be fine. And, through question after question and discussion after discussion, she was. In fact, she was more than fine. For the first time in as long as she could remember, Laura felt…blessed.

Chapter Eleven

Laura checked the clock in her bedroom—11:45 a.m. David and his parents would be here any minute to pick her up to go to the church Thanksgiving dinner, and she couldn't decide what to wear. Four complete outfits were strewn haphazardly across the bed, and none of them had seemed right for meeting David's parents.

It wasn't as if she hadn't met them before. She'd met them plenty of times at UT when they visited David on campus; however, she'd never been nearly eight months pregnant with twins when she saw them. And she'd never really been trying to make an impression. But today, she was.

Last night, she'd attended the midweek Bible study with David at the church, and like Mandy had promised, everyone welcomed her with open arms. She'd felt accepted, forgiven, loved. David never left her side and introduced her to anyone she hadn't already met. Laura had enjoyed Brother Henry's class about grace and felt right at home in the small community church. In fact, she wondered why she'd stayed away from church, away from God, so long. And she wondered why she'd never realized how amazing David was when they were in school. He'd always been a dear friend, but she'd never thought of him beyond that. Now, as much as she'd fought it, she couldn't *stop* thinking about him that way, and she wondered if they'd ever have a real date.

Then again, she shouldn't have to wonder. He said if it happened, she'd know. Would it ever happen?

She heard the door downstairs and then a female voice calling, "Laura?"

"Oh, dear." Taking a look in the mirror, she saw that she'd ended up in a long stretchy navy dress. She'd yet to accessorize, and she had no idea about shoes.

"Laura, you here, dear?"

David's mother. Laura couldn't start their day together by keeping her waiting, so she headed down the stairs.

"I'm so sorry. I'm running behind," she said, entering the kitchen to find Mrs. Presley waving her hand through the smoke and attempting to turn down the knob on the oven. "Oh, no, I forgot all about the pie!" Laura hurried to help the lady as she opened the oven door, and more smoke came rolling out to fill the kitchen. And then, naturally, the smoke detector emitted a deafening screech.

"Where are your pot holders?" Mrs. Presley asked, all calm and cool in spite of the incessant blast, which seemed to be getting louder.

Laura coughed. "Over there, on the counter by the refrigerator."

David and his father entered the smoky room and quickly evaluated the situation. "Laura, Mom, y'all get out of this smoke," David said. "Dad, can you—"

"Open the doors and windows?" his father asked. "One step ahead of you." He'd already flung the back door open, and he unlocked a window and pushed it up, then moved to the next and did the same.

Thankfully, the smoke thinned out fairly quickly, and nothing was actually flaming.

"I'm so sorry," Laura said. "I wanted to make a pie for the lunch and then I was having a hard time picking out what to wear, and I forgot all about it."

David waved a hand above the charred meringue. "Well, it looks like it would have been—" he hesitated "—real good. What was it, chocolate?"

"Lemon," Laura said miserably. "Lemon icebox."

David's father was the first one to smother his laugh, but David couldn't hold his back, and it rolled out with gusto. His mother's lips were pressed together as though she were afraid to open them or she'd also set a laugh free.

Laura frowned. "I was just going to brown the meringue for a second."

"Well, it *is* brown," David said, pointing to the blackened mound of what used to be fluffy white topping. Then he laughed again, and this time, Laura joined in.

Apparently, Mrs. Presley was simply waiting for Laura's cue, because she released a giggle that Laura was pretty certain had a bit of a snort in the middle.

When they finally finished laughing and the room cleared of most of the smoke, David glanced at Laura's feet, sticking out beneath the dress. "Laura, were you planning to go without shoes?"

"No," she said. "I couldn't decide on what to wear, and I was in the middle of considering this dress when your mom came in and then I remembered the pie. Or rather, I never remembered it, I smelled it."

David's mother wrapped an arm around her and started toward the stairs. "Tell you what. You guys finish cleaning up and airing this place out down here. I'll help Laura get ready. Sound good?"

David and his father nodded in unison, and Laura let the lady guide her to her room.

"You'll have to forgive the mess," she said. "I was having a tough time deciding."

"This isn't a mess," Mrs. Presley said as she looked at the discarded clothes, "it's the sign of a woman getting ready."

"Thanks. I'm so sorry that we're going to be late. I'll hurry and pick something out."

"I like the dress you have on," she said.

"You do?" Laura ran a hand along the jersey fabric. "I did, too, to tell you the truth, but I wasn't sure what to put with it."

"How about this?" She picked the gold cardigan from Laura's closet. "And you have these matching flats. How about a chunky bracelet to go with it, maybe a red one?"

Laura moved to her jewelry box and withdrew a red cuff bracelet. "Like this one?"

"Perfect," she said, smiling as Laura snapped the bracelet in place. "And you know, I have a beautiful new red infinity scarf in the car. We'll add that when we go outside, and I think that'll tie it all together very nicely."

Laura was amazed. Her mother often coordinated clothes and usually gave Laura complete ensembles so that she never had to worry about mixing and matching items on her own. But watching Mrs. Presley in action was fun. "You're very good at that," she said.

David's mother spotted some gold earrings on the dresser and handed them to Laura. She tilted her head as Laura put the earrings on and then nodded her approval. "I've never had a daughter to shop with or to help dress. This is fun." She looked at Laura and didn't hide the fact that she noticed her tummy.

"Mrs. Presley," Laura began, feeling that she should explain.

David's mother spoke before Laura had a chance. "We're very happy for you," she said tenderly, "and your babies. Children are a gift from God, you know."

Laura's heart tugged in her chest. "I know."

"And we're glad you came to David. He told us about you working at the store and how you've boosted his business. I'll be honest, we've been worried that the bookstore wasn't going to make it, not because of anything he's said, but because it didn't seem to have a lot happening anytime we would visit. It's good to see that it's working again. And I'm grateful to you for helping that happen."

"I enjoy working there," Laura said. "And I'm very grateful for all of David's help. I, well, I don't know what I'd have done—or what I'd do—without him." She hadn't meant to say so much, but it was hard to talk about David now without attempting to explain how much he was beginning to mean to her, almost even more because she hadn't wanted to feel anything toward her boss, toward her friend. But she was definitely starting to feel something.

His mother ran a finger along her cheek and smiled. "You're helping him, too, dear. And in case you've

wondered about it, I don't want you to have any mis-
conceptions. David's father and I are very happy about
that. Whatever happens between you and our son, we
are happy about it." Her smile eased up a notch. "You
understand?"

Laura did understand, and the realization that David's mother had essentially said that she was happy
about a relationship between Laura and her son both
shocked and thrilled her. "I do understand, and thank
you."

"No, thank you. We haven't seen him this happy in
a very long time," she said, "and from what he says,
you haven't even been on a real date."

Laura couldn't control her surprise. "He told you
that?"

"Not voluntarily, but as a mother, I've learned what
questions to ask. I bet you'll figure out how to do the
same with your girls."

Laura thought about the future conversations she'd
have with her daughters. "I'm sure I will." They left
the bedroom and found the two men waiting at the bottom of the stairs.

"I get it," David said. "I told you I couldn't cook,
and you were trying to make me feel better."

"Very funny." Laura tried to stomp past him, but he
tossed an arm around her and pulled her close.

"It was sweet of you to want to fix a pie, but they
will have plenty of food. I bet they won't even miss it,"
he said as they passed through the semi-smoky kitchen
and walked outside. "But I bet you'll make some stray
cat's day." He pointed to the garbage can behind the
studio and the charred pie balanced on top of the bags.

Laura laughed, with David and his parents joining

in, and then they drove to the church and she had her best Thanksgiving dinner ever.

The next morning, the bookstore opened at 8:00 a.m. to join in the Black Friday "Sales on the Square." Laura's father called shortly after and said he was on his way, and she looked forward to him arriving and being part of today's fun. Customers filled the store and were steadily purchasing all of the inspirational gift books Laura had recommended David order for the holidays, as well as many other books in the store.

"The Christmas favorites display is a hit," David said, placing a large stuffed snowman in the chair beside the display. "I've always advertised the classics at Christmas, but you were right—putting the modern stories here as well has really been popular."

"Adults love the classics, but the teens are typically looking for something a little more trendy," his mother said. "Laura got it right."

"Thanks." Laura helped another customer looking for Destiny's book. "And it looks like *Southern Love in Claremont* is going to be a popular stocking stuffer this year."

"That'll make Destiny happy," David said.

Mr. Presley stayed behind the counter ringing up and visiting with customers while Laura, David and Mrs. Presley replenished the items on the displays and helped customers find their desired books. It didn't seem like four hours had passed when Laura's dad walked in.

She didn't realize how much she'd missed him until she saw him enter the store. "Daddy!" Laura hurried to him and hugged him tightly.

He kissed her cheek. "Hey, princess. How's it going?"

"It was going good, but now that you're here it's going great!" she said.

"Now that's a smile I've missed seeing," he said. "I can't wait to tell your mom how good you're doing."

Laura was often mesmerized by her father's love toward her mom. Obviously, Marjorie Holland wasn't easy to love, but that never stopped either of them from loving her just the same. "Mom called me this morning," Laura said. "Just to let me know she was sorry she couldn't come with you and that she'd call me again tonight after she got done at work."

He nodded. "I wish she could've come, too."

"Mr. Holland," David said. It took him a moment to maneuver past the children crowding around the box-car to get to Laura's dad. He extended a hand. "We're glad you're here."

"Thanks, David. I'm glad to be here, especially because I get to see my Laura smiling again," he said. "Thank you for that."

"Happy to help." David winked at Laura then glanced down to see the child tugging at his arm.

"Hey, Mr. David, can you come help us?"

Laura recognized the boy as Matthew Hayes, one of the twins. "Matthew, is there something I can help you with?" she asked.

"Nah, I just threw one of the pillows up high and it got stuck on the top shelf. Can you get it down, Mr. David, like, before Daddy sees it?"

David laughed. "Duty calls," he said, following Matthew to the scene of the crime. "I'll be right back."

"I like that young man," her father said as they

watched David retrieve the pillow and then hand it back to the kids.

"I do, too." And that had become a major understatement over the past few days.

Laura watched as David made certain the kids knew the pillows should stay at ground level then returned smiling. "Hey, since my folks are here to help me out in the store, why don't you go show your dad around the square? Take some time to visit, and go have lunch or something."

Laura did want to spend some time alone with her dad, but she didn't want to abandon David on the busy sale day. "You sure?"

"Of course. Besides, my dad and I need to run to the building supply store later for a project I've got going upstairs, so we'll trade. You and your dad can help my mom out here when we leave, and we'll call it even."

"When does your mom get a break?" Laura asked.

"Are you kidding? She's on cloud nine around all of these kids." He pointed to Mrs. Presley, sitting in the children's area and animatedly reading to the kids, who were captivated with her rendition of *Frosty the Snowman*. "I'll be lucky if I can talk her into retreating to the kitchen long enough to eat a sandwich."

Laura had to agree. David's mom appeared to be having a blast. "Okay, then, we'll head out and then tag team with you and your dad in an hour or so."

"Make it two hours. It's going to be a long day, and you'll want that extra break," he said. Then to Laura's dad, he said, "Don't let her overdo it on the walking. I try to watch and make sure she sits down and rests often, but she doesn't always listen."

"Sounds like he's got you pegged." Her dad wrapped

an arm around her and then looked back to David. "Don't worry, we won't overdo it."

Laura liked the fact that both of them wanted to take care of her. "Thanks, but I will stop if I get tired."

"And we'll make sure you keep that promise," her father said.

Laura didn't argue. There had been a couple of afternoons that David practically had to force her to take a break. She'd wanted everything perfect for the sale today and hadn't wanted to waste any time. But they were right. She was at the point in the pregnancy where she had to be careful and not overexert. Early labor was always a possibility with twins.

"So, you ready?" her dad asked.

"I am." She led him out of the bookstore and into the square. People filled the sidewalk, and signage advertising each merchant's Black Friday sales covered the storefronts. "What do you think?" she asked.

"I think your mother should've come," he said. "She would've loved all of this. Marjorie has spent so many Black Fridays at Macy's that she doesn't even realize there are more activities going on, like this type of old-fashioned thing. Look at that fountain and the geese. And all of these detailed storefronts. The architecture is remarkable. It's like someone plucked the entire town out of the fifties."

"I know. I love it here," she admitted.

"I'm glad for that. I really am. I meant what I told David. It's wonderful to see you smile again."

"I've been smiling a lot lately," she said, saying hello to several shoppers that she recognized from the bookstore and church as they walked down the sidewalk. Everyone was so friendly, and she realized that she already felt at home in Claremont. "So for lunch, how about one of the best cheeseburgers you'll ever taste?" She pointed across the square. "You're going to love Nelson's."

"Lead the way." He walked beside her, and when they reached the variety store, Marvin Tolleson met them at the door.

"Miss Laura, great to see you!" he said. "I've had several customers come in with bags from the bookstore. Looks like y'all are having a good day."

"We are." She nodded toward the packed booths and soda fountain. "And it looks like you are, too."

"God is blessing us," he agreed, "but don't worry. We have an open booth in the back for you. And I don't believe we've met." He smiled at Laura's father.

"Thomas Holland. I'm Laura's dad."

"Well, then, I believe I met your wife here a few weeks back," Marvin said, ushering them toward the only vacant booth. "Nice lady, but I'll admit, I thought she was Miss Laura's sister when she first came in."

Her father grinned. "We get that a lot, but I take it as a compliment, as does she."

"Well, here are your menus." He handed them each a laminated sheet. "Do you know what you want to drink?"

"I'll have sweet tea," her dad said.

"I'll have the large lemonade," Laura said, "and we can go ahead and order, if that's okay."

"The babies hungry?" her father asked.

Laura grinned. "Always."

"Well, we can take care of that," Marvin said. "What would you like?"

"Cheeseburger and sweet potato fries." It'd become one of her favorite meals.

"I'll have the same," her dad said as his phone started up with the "Rocky Top" ring tone. He withdrew it from his pocket and glanced at the display. Laura knew before he answered that it was her mom.

"Hey, how's work going?" He nodded a few times as she apparently told him about her morning, or night would be more accurate, since the sale started at midnight. "I'm sitting at a table with her right now for lunch. Yes, it is really nice here."

He continued talking for a few minutes and then said, "You get yourself something to eat while you have a chance. I'm glad you're having a good sales day." Another nod. "I'll tell her." He smiled. "I love you, too. 'Bye." He pocketed the phone. "She wanted me to tell you she loves you and misses you, and that she'll be back down here soon."

"I'd like that," Laura said as Marvin's wife, Mae, hurried toward the table with two plates of food.

"Marvin said your babies are hungry—" she placed a plate in front of each of them "—so we moved your order to the top."

Laura laughed. "I could've waited." She plucked a fry from the plate and started eating it.

"But we didn't want you to," Mae said. "And Marvin told me you're Laura's dad. We're glad you're here."

"Glad to be here," he said.

They started eating, but Laura didn't have her food on her mind. True, she was hungry, and she'd eat, but she also wanted to talk about what had been bothering her ever since her mother's visit. "Dad, when Mom came down, she seemed to really enjoy herself and we had a great day," she said.

"That's what she said. I wished she'd have told me she was coming down here, but I am glad you two enjoyed some time together."

"Me, too, but—" she decided just to tell him what happened "—but before she left, she said some things that confused me."

He was about to take another bite of cheeseburger, but he placed the sandwich back on his plate. "Something about why she keeps leaving? Because I asked her, again, and I got the same answer."

"What answer?"

"That she had to get away." He shrugged. "Same answer she's been giving me for nearly twenty-four years. Did she tell you something different?"

The eagerness in his tone hurt Laura. He so wanted to know what caused his wife to head out every now and then, and Laura wanted to know, too. Over the past few weeks, ever since she spent that day with her mom, she'd thought about the best words to convey everything her mother said, and she selected them carefully now. "She started off talking about you, the two of you, and how you were the love of her life, and that she thought she fell in love with you the first time she saw you."

His mouth flattened, and he nodded. "She's told me that before, and I believe her. I felt the same way. There's something to be said for love at first sight."

Laura imagined her parents young and so in love, and she liked the image. She almost didn't want to tell him the rest, but she knew how desperately he wanted to figure out what caused her mother to run. "But then she said something else through the day that I couldn't stop thinking about, something I didn't understand."

"What'd she say?" He'd pushed his plate forward, having lost all interest in eating until he and Laura had this conversation.

"She said that she wanted me to find someone who chose *me*. A couple of times she mentioned how important it was to be with someone who chose you." Laura shook her head, not understanding it any more now than she did that day. "Is there something that has happened in your marriage to make her think she wasn't your first choice? Or when you were dating?" Laura asked. "That's all I can think of."

He sat there for a second then ran his hand down his face while Laura took in his instant reaction. Maybe he did know what was going on with her mom.

"Daddy?" she asked while he straightened in the booth then leaned his head back against the seat and whispered something to the ceiling.

Laura couldn't hear his words for all of the chatter in the five-and-dime, but she read his lips.

"Oh, Marjorie, what do I have to do to make you believe me?"

Laura leaned forward in her seat and lowered her voice, though that hardly mattered with the crowd and the noise today. Even so, she didn't want to draw undue attention to whatever her father was about to say. "Daddy, did you—was there someone else that you loved?"

He slid his hand across the table, took Laura's in his and squeezed. "Honey, there has never been anyone else. Like I said earlier, I think I fell in love with your mom the first time I saw her."

"Then what is she talking about, wanting to be the one someone chooses? Why doesn't she feel like you chose her?" Laura was so thankful for Marvin's crowd now. Normally, it'd be impossible to have this conversation at the restaurant, but thanks to the Black Friday shoppers, that wasn't a problem. And Laura was glad; she didn't want to wait to hear his answer.

"She isn't talking about another woman," he said. "She's talking about…you."

Chapter Twelve

"Me?" Laura didn't see that coming. Her mother had never seemed jealous of her relationship with her father; she was certain of it. They were all close in spite of her mother's quirks. But surely if her mom didn't like the fact that Laura and her dad were close, Laura would have been able to tell, right? "What do you mean…me?"

He took a deep breath, let it out. Then he glanced at the surrounding tables to apparently make sure no one was listening to their conversation.

No one was. Everyone was busily chatting and eating and absorbed in discussing the activities of the day.

"Daddy, tell me what you're talking about."

He nodded. "Honey, you know that your mom was several months pregnant when we married."

Laura, of course, knew. Her parents were married in August, and Laura was born in February. It hadn't been a secret. She nodded and waited for him to continue.

"Back then, when she told me, and I said we'd get married, she said she didn't want me to marry her just because she was pregnant."

The pieces clicked into place, and Laura suddenly felt sorry for her mom. "She didn't think you would have married her if she hadn't been pregnant." Laura knew times had changed over the years. Back then, when a girl was pregnant, the couple typically married. Nowadays, for example with Jared, marrying Laura hadn't even occurred to him; he'd merely wanted her to end the pregnancy.

"I told her then that I had already known I wanted to marry her. Sure, it was quicker than we planned. She was only seventeen, and I was eighteen. But we would have married anyway. I'm sure of it, and I told her so. I thought she believed me." He shook his head. "All of these years, *that* was why she kept running away?"

Laura remembered more of what her mother said during her visit. "She said that everything had been harder this year, because of me and Jared. I didn't understand what she meant, but now I do. Me getting pregnant, and then Jared not even considering marriage to me—even marrying someone else—probably made her wonder if that's what you wanted back then."

"But it isn't, Laura. I always wanted your mother. I've always loved her, and I always will." He exhaled thickly. "I just don't know what I have to do to prove it to her."

Laura had pushed her plate to the center of the table, but she pulled it back and picked up a fry. She felt better, somehow, at least knowing what was going on in her mother's mind. And she was determined to help her father show his wife that he'd always chosen *her*. Pointing the fry at her dad, she said, "Well, then, that's our goal today, to figure out how you can prove it."

He'd looked miserable a moment ago, but his eyes

lit up, and one corner of his mouth lifted as he also reached for his discarded plate. "You have any ideas?"

She ate another fry then picked up her burger. "Not yet, but I'm not letting you leave here today until we figure something out."

He laughed. "Your determination. You get that from her, you know."

Laura smiled. "I know."

"And your good looks from me," he said with a wink, which caused both of them to laugh. Laura was the spitting image of her mother, and her father would be the first one to say so.

"I love you, Daddy," she said, then continued working on her cheeseburger.

"Love you right back," he said, then did the same.

They talked about things that might let Marjorie see how much he cared.

"How about a nice vacation, something like a second honeymoon?" Laura asked.

"That's what the cruise was supposed to be, and obviously that didn't do the trick."

"Jewelry?"

"I gave her a new necklace for her birthday, and she liked it, but no, I don't think that's the answer. She usually buys jewelry to match the clothes she gets at the store, so that isn't typically something she wants."

"Flowers," Laura said. She couldn't ever remember her father sending her mother flowers.

He shook his head. "Your mother never has liked flowers. She said they just die and remind her of funerals."

Laura squished her nose at that. "Gee, thanks for ruining the way I think of them, Mom."

He grinned at that. "There's got to be something I can do."

Laura pondered it while she ate but wasn't coming up with anything. She was still thinking about it when a cute Asian girl bounced up to the booth. Laura had noticed her moving around the restaurant from table to table, but she'd been too absorbed in her thoughts about her mother to pay much attention. The girl was a teen, sixteen or seventeen, Laura would guess.

"Hi," she said, "do you have any Secret Santa stories you'd like to share for the *Claremont News*?" Then she looked up from her small notepad and said, "Oh, hey, you're not from Claremont, are you?"

"I'm not," Laura's father said, "but my daughter moved here a few weeks ago." He pointed to Laura.

"Oh, yeah, I met you Wednesday night at church," she said. "I'm Nadia Berry. Brother Henry is my grandfather."

Laura nodded, the memory clicking into place. "I remember now." Then she asked, "You said something about a Secret Santa?"

"Oh, yes," Nadia said. "See, I'm hoping to get a degree in journalism after high school. I'm a senior now. And the newspaper is letting me intern there. They're letting me do a seasonal story on Claremont's Secret Santa. Have you not heard about our Secret Santa yet?"

Laura shook her head.

"Oh, well, it's pretty awesome," Nadia said. "See, several years ago—we can't figure out exactly when it started, which is something I'm trying to determine for my article—a Secret Santa started helping folks out in Claremont at Christmastime. Usually, the things start happening the day after Thanksgiving, which is today, and that's why I wanted to write a story about it."

"What kind of things?" Laura's father asked.

"Clothes for kids that need them, groceries and things like that. But also bigger things," she said, glancing at her notepad. "One man said that he couldn't make his mortgage one Christmas and didn't know how his kids were even going to have a Christmas, and Secret Santa paid his note and delivered toys for the kids. Another lady said she had hospital bills that she couldn't pay, and when she called in December to get the balance, she learned it'd been paid by Secret Santa. He's known to do big things like that, but also little things, like leaving candy canes for people to find and so they'll see where he's been. But I'm pretty sure lots of folks put the candy canes out now, just because it's fun and to throw people off his trail." Nadia grinned. "See, we really don't want to know who it is. We just like talking about it. It's fun for it to be a mystery, don't you think?"

"Yes, I do," Laura said, amazed at all of the uniqueness of this small Alabama town. A Secret Santa.

"Everyone loves surprises," Nadia continued, "especially when it means something special or helps you out in a big way." She looked at her notes. "It's like Mandy Brantley said earlier, 'It doesn't have to be anything huge, just something to let a person know someone cares and understands how they feel.'" Nadia looked up from the pad. "Mandy said Secret Santa sent her a card the first Christmas after she lost Mia and also sent a Bible storybook for Kaden that became his favorite. It was the story of Moses," Nadia said. "I'm definitely going to include that in my article."

"Well, I don't have a Secret Santa story to share since I just moved here," Laura said, "but I look forward to your article. It sounds like you're going to do a great job."

"Thanks!" Nadia exclaimed, and then said to Laura's father, "Nice to meet you."

"You, too," he said, finishing off his fries and smiling.

"What is it?" Laura asked.

"I think I have an idea for what I should do for your mom."

Ten minutes later they were back on the square. "What's your idea?" she asked.

"I thought I spotted…" He scanned the storefronts. "Yep, there it is. I knew I saw one. Come on." He walked purposefully, but Laura had no clue where they were headed.

"Where are we going?"

"You'll see."

She spotted the Tiny Tots Treasure Box toy store, Gina Brown's Art Gallery, The Grind coffee shop and The Sweet Stop candy shop in their path. But she didn't think any of those would have something that he'd want to buy her mother.

Then he stopped in front of the Claremont Jewelry Store and gazed at a collection of rings in the window.

"I thought you said she didn't like jewelry," Laura said as he moved toward the door and walked in.

"She doesn't like any ol' jewelry," he said. "But everyone likes surprises, especially when they mean something special," he added, quoting Nadia.

Laura wasn't sure what he had in mind, but she followed him over to the ring cases. There was only one gentleman working at the store. Laura remembered meeting him at church Wednesday night and again yesterday at the Thanksgiving dinner but couldn't recall his name. He finished up with another customer, then moved to the opposite side of the jewelry case from Laura and her dad.

"Well, hello. It's Laura, isn't it?" he said. His voice was so kind and friendly, and again Laura struggled to remember the name.

"I'm so sorry," she said. "I met so many people at church…."

"No problem," he said with a smile, "there are a lot of people to meet in Claremont. A lot of folks have told me about what a good job you're doing at the bookstore. My grandson comes to the book club with you on Mondays, and he's loving it." Then he shook his head and added, "I'm Marvin, by the way. Marvin Grier. And I own the jewelry store here. Is there anything I can help you with?"

"Wedding rings," her father said.

"Okay. Are we looking for an anniversary type band or a traditional set?"

"Traditional set."

Laura watched in amazement as Mr. Grier withdrew two satin-lined trays of stunning wedding rings. The bell on the door sounded as another customer came in behind them, and Mr. Grier said, "I'm going to help him and give you a little privacy while you make your decision. Just let me know if you have any questions."

"We will," Thomas said. He waited for Mr. Grier to move farther away and then explained, "When we first got married, I didn't have any money to pay for a nice ring. I asked her on our ten-year and then our twenty-year anniversary if she wanted a nicer one, but she said she didn't, that she loved the one I gave her in the beginning."

"I'm sure she does," Laura said.

"But our wedding was so quiet and low-key, and so was our engagement. We just wanted to get everything done quickly and be married. It didn't really give her the chance to enjoy the moment, you know." He frowned. "I asked her to marry me, but there was no surprise to it. She went with me to pick out the ring, and then we put it on her hand right there in the store. And then we went to the courthouse and got married."

Laura had never really thought about the details of her parents' wedding before, and now it seemed like it wasn't all that special.

"I want to give her a ring that tells her if I had a chance to do it all again, I'd choose her, and I'd give her a ring like this." He picked up a huge marquise solitaire. "She always liked this cut." He handed it to Laura. "Try it on for me, will you? Y'all wear the same size ring, don't you?"

"Yes," Laura said, and before she could stop him, he slid the ring on her finger. She stared at the sparkling huge stone. "Wow, Daddy. That's really something."

"You think she'll like it?"

"It looks like Mom," Laura admitted, taking another glance and then sliding the ring from her finger.

"I think so, too." He held it up to the light and admired the way it shone. Then he checked the price tag and winced.

"You don't have to get something so big," Laura said, knowing he didn't make a lot of money and prob-

ably didn't have that kind of cash lying around to purchase an extravagant ring.

"Yeah, I do," he said, "and I've been tucking away
money into savings over the years. I can't think of any
better reason to spend some of it." He grinned. "I'm
going to do it right this time, down on one knee, the
whole nine yards. And I'm going to make sure Marjorie knows that I chose her then, and I'd choose her all
over again. Thinking I'll give it to her on Christmas,
so keep it a secret, okay?"

"Okay." Laura nodded. "That's a wonderful idea,
Daddy."

Thomas kept looking at the ring he'd selected, while
Laura's attention focused on another set. The ring had
two small stones on either side of one a little larger,
nowhere near as big as the one her father had selected,
but in Laura's opinion, quite elegant. Beautiful.

"You want to try that one on?" Mr. Grier asked, and
Laura realized that she'd been so enthralled with the
pretty ring that she hadn't heard him return.

"Oh, no, I don't have any reason to," she said, but
her father and Mr. Grier urged her.

"Try it on," her dad said, and Mr. Grier lifted the
ring and slid it on her finger.

"A perfect fit, don't you think?" he said as the bell
on the door sounded and another customer must have
entered. Laura didn't turn to verify the fact, her attention unable to veer from the sight of that ring. She'd
never had a wedding ring on her finger before, but she
couldn't deny it looked good there. Felt good there, too.

"That's right pretty on you, Miss Laura."

She turned to see Zeb Shackleford standing behind
her and peering at the ring.

"Oh, I was just, I don't know, trying one on since my dad is looking at one for my mom," she stammered. "Mr. Zeb, this is my dad, Thomas Shackelford." She shook her head. "Thomas Holland, I mean. Sorry."

"Nice to meet you," Zeb said.

"You, too," her father answered, then turned his attention to Mr. Grier to discuss payment options.

Laura slipped the ring off and fumbled to put it back in the tray. "Don't know what I was thinking," she said, attempting a laugh toward Zeb.

The older man simply nodded as though he knew exactly what she was thinking, dreaming.

While her father continued surveying the ring in the light and attempting to make his final decision, Mr. Grier touched the one Laura had tried on. "Those are princess-cut diamonds," he said. "The three stones represent the past, present and future trio of your love."

As if the ring wasn't already calling Laura's name, she was even more drawn to it because of the symbolization. "That's beautiful," she said, then she turned her attention back to the person actually planning to purchase a ring today. "So, Daddy, what did you decide?"

"I'll take it," he said.

"That's great," Mr. Grier answered, and then they walked toward the back of the store to let Laura's father pay for his purchase.

"No harm in trying on wedding rings and dreaming a bit," Zeb said softly.

"I suppose not," she said, sneaking another peek at the ring before looking into Zeb's kind face. "What are you shopping for, Mr. Zeb?" He mentioned nearly every day that his sweet Dolly had passed on and that he looked forward to seeing her again. He also mentioned that they hadn't had any children, which was why he was so attached to all of the kids he read to each week. So Laura wondered who he was buying jewelry for.

"One of the girls at the hospital, her name is Faith," he said. "She has a charm bracelet and wanted some new charms for Christmas. I asked Mr. Grier to order one that I thought she'd like."

Mr. Grier had apparently finished taking her father's payment because the two of them made their way back to where Zeb and Laura stood by the display case.

"Zeb, your charm came in yesterday," Mr. Grier said, reaching beneath the counter and pulling out a small white box.

"You want to see it?" Zeb asked Laura.

"Sure."

Mr. Grier opened the box to reveal a tiny pink heart charm.

Zeb's mouth rolled in as he looked at the tiny charm. "We call Faith a little sweetheart," he said. "She wasn't supposed to make it this long, but God had other plans. She's still hanging on and touches all of our hearts every time we see her." He touched the delicate heart. "And her favorite color is pink. So I thought this was perfect."

Laura was moved by the elderly man's thoughtfulness. "It's incredible," she said. "David and I are still going with you next week to read to the children at the hospital, right?"

"I'd hoped you would. I'd like for you to meet them, and for them to meet you."

"I'm looking forward to meeting Faith," she said.

"I'm looking forward to you meeting her, too. Faith, well, Faith will change your life."

Chapter Thirteen

Whimsical murals from stories in the Bible covered the walls of the children's floor at Claremont Hospital. Zeb led Laura and David past the floor's lobby, which displayed a huge Noah's Ark scene, complete with fun, colorful animals lining up in pairs to hop on the boat. In the distance, a bright rainbow filled the sky, and the words *I have set my rainbow in the clouds* hovered in the center.

"That's gorgeous," Laura said.

"Why, thanks." A nurse wearing scrubs covered in teddy bears stepped away from the nurse's station to greet them. Her name tag read Shea Farmer. "We got the murals two years ago. As a matter of fact, they'll be mentioned in the paper this week in an article Nadia Berry is working on about Secret Santa."

"Secret Santa painted your murals?" David asked. "Didn't you kind of figure out who it was when you saw them painting?"

The lady laughed. "No, Secret Santa didn't paint them, but he sent the money to a woman who did the work. And it was pretty awesome, because she had been several months without employment, and she said the money she received for the murals helped her catch up on her bills and also allowed her family to have a real Christmas."

"That's wonderful," Laura said.

"I know," she said. "So, Zeb, the kids have been especially looking forward to tonight's visit, since you told them you were bringing some friends."

"Are they all in the playroom, Shea?" Zeb asked.

"Everyone except Faith," she said. "I told her you'd visit her room."

Laura recognized the name from the jewelry store. The little girl for whom Zeb bought the charm and whose favorite color was pink.

"She had a rough day?" Zeb asked.

"The day after chemo is always rough," Shea said, "but I know it'll cheer her up to see you."

Zeb nodded and then continued down the hall to a large room with toys and books bordering the walls and a group of children seated in the center.

"Hey, Mr. Zeb!" a little boy called. He looked about the same age as Kaden, but his skin didn't have the rosy glow that Kaden's had. Instead it was pale, if not tinged slightly yellow. "Are those your friends?"

"Yes, Avery, this is Mr. David and Miss Laura, who I told you about. Mr. David owns the bookstore that gives y'all the books we read."

"Cool!" another boy said. He sat in a wheelchair with a portable IV hooked up to a rolling pole. He had red hair and freckles and a beautiful smile.

"What's your name?" Laura asked.

"I'm Timothy, but you can call me Timmy if you want. That's what everyone else does. I'm seven."

"Well it's nice to meet you, Timmy," she said.

Zeb addressed the kids. "Now, like I told you last week, Mr. David and Miss Laura are going to start coming with me sometimes and will be reading to you from the *Boxcar Children* books. They've been reading them with some other kids at their bookstore each week and thought you might enjoy them, too."

Laura held up her copy of the book. "Ready to get started?"

They all nodded or answered "Yes!" and Laura took a seat in the middle of the group then opened the book to the first page.

"If it's okay with all of you," Zeb said, "Mr. David and I are going to walk down the hall and visit Faith while Miss Laura reads."

A little girl with brown pigtails bobbed her head. "Faith will like that," she said.

"That good for you?" David asked Laura.

She nodded. "Yes, it's fine." More than fine, really, because these children were undeniably anxious to hear the story, and she realized as she read that they were even happier about sharing the story than the kids in her weekly book club. The boys and girls surrounding her were confined to a hospital room the majority of their day. But now, as they leaned forward to hear every word about the story, they escaped their sickness, escaped their pain and lost themselves in the world of the *Boxcar Children*.

Laura read for an hour, answering questions whenever any child raised their hand, and she loved every minute. When Shea reappeared, Laura was saddened that it was time to leave, but the nurse explained amid the children's groans of disappointment that it was time for them to go to bed.

"I'll come back tomorrow if you like," Laura said.

They all clapped, and she smiled, happy to have this opportunity and grateful to Zeb for giving it to her. "Where is Faith's room, Shea?"

The nurse had started wheeling Timothy out, and the little boy answered, "She's at two twenty-four," he said, still smiling. He hadn't stopped smiling for the past hour.

"Thank you, Timmy," Laura said, then headed toward the room.

She found David and Zeb sitting on each side of the bed holding cards. The little girl, wearing a sequined pink cap to cover her lack of hair, plucked a card from David's hand.

"Another match for me," she said, then noticed Laura. "Hey, are you Miss Laura?"

Laura neared the bed. "I am."

"Mr. Zeb said you'll read to me next time and catch me up on what I missed with the *Boxcar Children*."

"I'd love to," Laura said. "I think I'm coming back tomorrow night. Maybe I can come in here first and read to you before I read to the others."

Faith's smile beamed. "That sounds great!" She watched as David grabbed a card from Zeb's hand, and then giggled when Zeb had to take one from hers. "I've only got two left," she said, "and guess what one of them is."

Zeb held his finger in front of one, tilted his head as he watched her eyes, blinking mischievously, and then took the other card.

Faith's giggle filled the room. "Old maid for you," she said.

Laura watched them continue until, sure enough, Zeb's last card was the unwanted lady.

"You lose again, Mr. Zeb," Faith said.

"And so I do," he said.

A young woman who looked to be in her early thirties walked in, her eyes bloodshot and undeniably tired, but she gave them all a smile. "Did you let Zeb win tonight, honey?"

"Nope," Faith said.

"I wouldn't know what to do if I won," Zeb answered, and Faith grinned.

"Thank you for playing with me," she said, "and you, too, Mr. David."

"It was my pleasure," David said.

"And you must be Laura," the woman said. "I'm Sharon Mulberry, Faith's mom."

"Wonderful to meet you," Laura said.

Faith stretched her jaw wide in a huge yawn, and her mother stepped forward to gather the cards from the bed.

"I think that's your clue that you need to sleep now," she said.

"I know. Thanks again for coming, Mr. Zeb, and Mr. David and Miss Laura, too." She shimmied down in the bed and tugged the covers to her neck. "I love y'all."

"We love you, too," Zeb answered, giving her another smile and patting the top of her hand. "We'll be back tomorrow night."

"Awesome," Faith whispered, her eyes growing heavy and another yawn slipping free.

Laura and David walked back down the hall passing murals of David and Goliath, Moses and the Ten Commandments, the Garden of Eden and then Noah's Ark again as they neared the elevator.

"Thank y'all for coming," Shea called from the nurses' station.

"We were glad to," Zeb said, and Laura and David nodded in agreement.

Laura waited until they were on the elevator and the doors slid closed, then she said, "Bless their little hearts."

Zeb nodded. "I feel the same way. This means a lot to them, to have people care enough to visit and spend time with them on a regular basis."

"It meant a lot to us, too," David said. He stood next to Laura in the elevator, and she felt his hand slide against her palm, then his fingers clasp with hers. The motion was sweet, tender, like the precious moments they just spent together with those children.

"I needed someone to help me out here," Zeb said. "I couldn't spend enough time with the group and also with Faith, or any of the others when they're unable to leave their rooms. Tonight, having your help meant the world to me."

"You can count on us, anytime," David said.

The elevator door opened at the first-floor lobby and they stepped out, with Zeb stopping a moment to look at them. "That's what I was just thinking," he said. "I *can* count on you." He took a step in the opposite direction. "I'm going to say hello to the lady that runs the flower shop before I leave."

"You want us to wait on you?" Laura asked.

"Nah, y'all go on home. I know you and those babies need your rest." He nodded his goodbye and then walked away.

Laura and David started out of the hospital, and he said what she felt.

"That was one of the most rewarding things I've ever done." He let go of her hand to open the door for her as they exited the hospital, and Laura immediately missed the contact of his skin against hers.

"I can't believe I've never thought to visit the kids on the children's floor before," she said. "Reading to them was incredible. They were so into the story and so appreciative of us coming to see them. I'm looking forward to coming back tomorrow."

"Me, too." He opened the passenger's door of his car.

Laura slid into the seat and then waited for him to shut the door, but he didn't. "Everything okay?" she asked.

David leaned into the car, took the seat belt and gently draped it across her and then snapped it into place, his face so close to hers she could smell a hint of peppermint on his breath. "You're amazing," he said. "You know that?"

Embarrassed, she felt her cheeks blush. "You really think so?"

"I know so." He still leaned into the car, so close that Laura would merely have to move forward a couple of inches to have her lips touch his.

She could feel her heart beating solidly in her chest as she waited for...whatever he planned to do.

"Remember when I told you that you'd know if I took you on a date?" he asked.

She blinked. "Was this a date?"

His smile broke free. "No, this is me, asking you for a date, tomorrow night after we visit the kids here. So, Laura, would you like to go out with me, on an official date, tomorrow night?"

She didn't hesitate, and she didn't let her promise to herself not to get in another relationship hinder her words. This was David, a completely different kind of guy than she'd ever gone out with before, a guy who'd been there for her when she needed him most, and a guy who made her feel something so special that she didn't want to miss the chance to see exactly where the feelings would lead. "I'd love to."

"That's what I was hoping you'd say." He slowly eased out of the car, shut her door, rounded the front and climbed in the driver's seat. Then he started the engine but didn't back up.

She glanced behind them and didn't see anything blocking his path. "Everything okay?" she asked again.

He turned to face her. "No, everything isn't."

"What's wrong?"

"I'm thinking that the whole time we're on our date tomorrow night we're going to keep wondering about something, and that wondering is probably going to make it where we can't enjoy our date," he said smoothly.

"Wondering about what?"

He smiled, leaned closer. "This." Laura hadn't been kissed in eight months, and she wasn't all that sure she remembered how, but David certainly did. His mouth was soft and inviting, teasing her lips and every last one of her senses.

When he pulled away, he must have been satisfied with the awestruck look on her face because he gave her a confident smile and said, "Now we won't have to wonder."

But Laura was already wondering…how long she'd have to wait to experience another kiss like that again.

Chapter Fourteen

David couldn't be happier with his choice of locations for their first date. The food at Messina's was amazing, as evidenced by Laura humming her contentment with nearly every bite. He pinched his lips together to keep from laughing, and she noticed.

"I'm doing it again," she said, shrugging. "I don't think I ever made noises when I ate before I got pregnant." She picked up another bite of lasagna with her fork and grinned. "But I also don't remember enjoying eating quite this much before."

"Personally, I think it's cute," he said. "In fact, I think several things you do fall into the 'cute' category."

She paused her fork in midair and then slowly placed it back on the plate, one corner of her mouth lifting as she turned all of her attention to David. "Several things?"

He nodded, enjoying the flirtatious banter of their first date. "Several."

"You realize you can't make a statement like that

without elaborating," she challenged. "So…what things?"

"What things do you do that I find cute?" he asked.

The other side of her mouth joined the first to give him a full smile. "Yes. Tell me."

"Okay." He wasted no time with his list. "The way your eyes glisten when you talk about your baby girls. The way you glance away at the bookstore when you catch me looking at you. The way your voice softens when you read to the kids in the book club, and the way I know that it'll do the same thing one day when you read to your little girls. And the way the base of your neck blushes when you're embarrassed, or flattered, or whatever it is that you are…right now."

Her hand touched that small pink spot at her neck, and she looked down at her plate. "You sure do notice a lot, don't you?"

"When I find something interesting."

She lifted her eyes back to his. "You find me interesting?"

"I always have."

"I've always found you interesting, too." She cleared her throat, and David thought for a moment that she'd say more, but then she pushed her plate away. "I'm done. Actually, I think I was done three bites ago, but it was too good to stop."

He understood that they'd gotten a little more personal than she'd planned for their first date. But he was satisfied, sensing that they were growing closer, step by step. He finished off the last of his own lasagna and nodded. "Agreed, but I kept going, too."

"It is that good, isn't it?" the waitress said, nearing

the table with a tray of assorted desserts. "We have our famous tiramisu, pignoli nut pie and cassata."

"Oh, I can't hold another bite," Laura said, "but those do look amazing."

"They are," the woman said.

"We'll take a tiramisu to go." David handed his credit card to her. Then to Laura he said, "You know you'll want it later."

She laughed. "Didn't take you long to figure that out."

The waitress nodded her approval then left the table to tally their check and get their dessert. A few minutes later she returned with the tiramisu boxed and bagged, David's card and receipt.

Laura started to stand, and David hurried to get up and help her out of her chair.

"I'm attempting to be a gentleman here."

"And I'm getting more and more used to having one around," she admitted. She leaned into him as they left the restaurant, the two of them admiring the elegant décor and also saying hello to a few people they recognized from town.

When they neared the exit, David opened the door and a blast of cold air pushed inside.

"Oh, my." Laura turned her head away from the chilly wind.

David pulled the door shut. "Wait here. I'll go get the car."

She nodded. "I'm not going to argue with you."

Laura watched through the window as David walked across the parking lot toward his car.

"Excuse me."

She turned toward the man. She'd seen him before at church but didn't remember ever being introduced. "Hello."

"I'm Milton Stott," he said. "David's accountant for the bookstore. You're the lady he hired, aren't you?"

Laura nodded. "I am. I love working there." She glanced out the window and saw that someone had stopped David in the parking lot to talk, but she couldn't identify the man. She wished David would hurry. Milton seemed harmless enough, but he was definitely crowding into her three feet of personal space.

Then she realized why. He wanted to tell her something in private. His voice wasn't a whisper but just louder than one.

"I'm not trying to interfere in another person's business," he said softly, "but when I saw you tonight, I couldn't live with myself if I didn't warn you. A woman in your condition and all."

Laura turned her attention to the man. "Warn me? Warn me about what?"

"The bookstore," he said. "I'm assuming you're, well, relying on it as your source of income?"

She blinked. "Yes, I am." That was all she had for income until something came through at one of the school systems, which she didn't see happening before next fall. Then it hit her; this was David's accountant. He knew the true financial state of David's business. Laura had suspected that it wasn't doing well when she first arrived, but lately things had seemed so much better. "We've been doing very well," she said, in case the guy hadn't checked the books in a while.

"I'm sorry, miss." He shook his head, opened his mouth as though he were going to say something else, then stopped and pointed out the window. "Your ride is here." And this time it was a whisper, then he returned to his table in the dining room.

Even though the man hadn't directly said anything about the stability of David's business, he'd certainly implied that things weren't going well. And if anyone would know, it'd be the accountant, right? Laura felt like she'd been kicked in the stomach. What else could she do if things didn't work out at the bookstore? Especially after she had the babies?

She stepped into the cold, and the wind made her eyes water and drip. Or that's what she would tell David, if he asked. Because now the fairy tale she'd begun to see was starting to disintegrate before her eyes.

David hopped out of the car and moved to open the door. "I've got another surprise for tonight," he said. "I can't wait to take you…"

She forced a smile. "David, it's been such a long day, with work and then visiting the kids at the hospital and all. Would you mind taking me on home?"

David didn't know what had happened, but from the moment he'd helped Laura in the car at the restaurant, her disposition had turned a one-eighty. She'd been laughing, even flirty, throughout dinner, and now she stared out the window and didn't say a single word during the entire drive to her apartment. He parked the car by the rear entrance to Carter Photography. "You want to share the tiramisu before we end the night? That would at least put a little something special at the end of the date. I'd planned to take you to see the Christmas lights at Hydrangea Park, but tiramisu will do."

She'd finally turned her attention away from the window, and David was fairly certain she'd passed her hand across her cheeks before facing him. Was she crying? A few rapid blinks and a forced smile told him she had been, and he couldn't fathom why.

"Hey, what's going on?" he asked. "I thought our date was going well. Did I do something, say something wrong?"

She shook her head and did that rapid-blink thing again to ward off her burgeoning tears. "Tonight," she said, her voice raspy and raw, "was one of the best nights of my life. You didn't do anything wrong. You haven't done anything wrong at all, from the first day I came to Claremont." Then she sighed and added, "You've never done anything wrong toward me, from the time that we first met at UT. In fact, everything you've ever done has been," she sniffed, bit her lower lip and then finally said, "perfect."

"Okay…" he said, confused beyond measure. "Then why are you so upset?"

"The pregnancy hormones, they make me emotional."

"That's it? Because you seemed to be really enjoying yourself at the restaurant." He'd noticed her sensitivity over the past few weeks, the way she bonded so intensely with the children and the way she'd worried about her parents. However, he'd never seen her emotions change this quickly, and he suspected there was a reason. But he had no clue what it was.

"David, I…" She hesitated. "I need to ask you something, and I want you to tell me the truth."

As if he'd ever give her anything less than the truth. "Anything."

"You'll tell me the truth, even if you don't think I want to hear it?"

He'd always told Laura the truth, even when she didn't want to hear it, like in college when he told her Jared wasn't right for her. Back then she didn't listen, but now, he could tell that she would. "I can't imagine what you don't already know, but yes, I'll tell you the truth. I promise."

"You always have," she said, reiterating David's very thoughts.

"So ask me what you need to know," he said.

"The bookstore. Is it not doing well? And are you paying me when you can't afford it?"

Her questions blindsided him. He ran his hand through his hair, his jaw tensing as he instantly dreaded giving her the truth this time. "Why are you asking?"

"Your accountant was at the restaurant tonight," she said. "He came to talk to me when you went to get the car, and he hinted that things weren't going well at the bookstore…at all."

David was floored. He hadn't seen Milton at Messina's, but the restaurant by nature had several dimly lit areas to provide the customers with privacy. But this time, it'd given his accountant a chance to hide…until he apparently found a chance to speak to Laura alone. "What did he say, exactly?"

"He said he felt like he should warn me, and he asked if I was relying on the bookstore as a source of income. I think he was trying to help me."

"Milton had no right." David plunged his hand through his hair again then moved his fingers down to his neck and pushed against the tension spreading like wildfire.

"I'm sorry if I upset you," she said.

"You didn't. He did."

She fidgeted with the strap of her purse. "Is it true?"

"The bookstore has been doing better than ever since you came. I've told you that, and I meant it," he said, keeping his voice calm in spite of his anger toward his accountant. He didn't want Laura feeling as though she'd done anything wrong by asking about the state of his business. Because of her, David thought he might actually make it into the black again by spring. "It's been amazing since you've put your touch on the place."

Laura lifted her brows and tilted her head as though waiting for the "but" that she knew was coming. And in order to tell her the truth, David had to say it.

"*But* the problem is, it hasn't been doing that good for the past couple of years, ever since I inherited it. Or truthfully, it'd started going down years before. People are moving into the ebook market, and a lot of folks stopped shopping at a brick-and-mortar store. Or that's what I'd thought. It turned out, they just needed the place to offer events of interest, get books they wanted to read and promote them. Everything you've been doing. If I'd have started that two years ago, everything would be different now."

"You're saying that our recent sales aren't enough, though," she said.

"You shouldn't be worried about any of this," David said. "And Milton may have just lost himself a client."

"I really think he was only trying to help, David," she said. "And I've…" She took an audible breath. "I've decided what I'm going to do."

"What do you mean, what you're going to do?"

David feared what she was about to offer, for her to stop working at the bookstore, because that was the exact opposite of what needed to happen. He *needed* her there. More than that, he *wanted* her there. "You don't need to do or change anything. You just need to keep helping me make it happen. We can do it together, Laura."

He'd just started thinking that there could be something between them, more than friendship, more than a boss-employee relationship. This had been their first date! And, because of Milton, it'd gone from perfect to the perfect storm. Because he could see it in her eyes. Laura had made up her mind.

"You can run the things at the store on your own, and I can eliminate all of the expenses associated with my employment. Besides, I wasn't going to be able to keep coming in during those weeks after I have the babies, and honestly, I still didn't know how I was going to afford to put them in day care whenever I could start back to work," she said, telling him exactly what he didn't want to hear.

"I told you..." he said.

She interrupted him. "I know you said I could bring them to the bookstore, but there's really no place there for babies, and I can't do that to you." Another deep breath, and then she set her thoughts free. "I'm going back to Nashville, to my parents' home. Everything is going to be more settled there now that my dad has finally figured out what's been bothering Mom all these years. And they're happy to support me until I get a teaching job somewhere."

"Laura, that's not what you need to do," he said, but

she opened the car door and started out without waiting for David to help her this time.

"I'm sorry, David. I'm going home." And then she closed the door to the car…and slammed the door of his heart.

Chapter Fifteen

Laura should've called her mother last night, but she didn't feel like talking about everything and only wanted to cry herself to sleep, which she did. Reluctantly, she dialed the number this morning. The phone rang once, twice and then Marjorie picked up.

"Laura, how are you, dear!"

Laura moved the phone away from her ear to make sure she dialed the right number. Her mother always had a polite greeting, but today she was practically singing. Sure enough, the display showed she'd dialed *Mom*.

"I'm—" she didn't want to lie to her mom "—I've been better."

"Oh, honey, what's wrong? Is it the babies? I can come right now. Early labor? What are you feeling? Have you called the doctor?"

Laura should've thought about how close she was to her delivery date, merely a month away, before she said she wasn't doing well. "It isn't anything physically, Mom."

"Aw, bless your heart. It's David?"

Over the past weeks, her mother had insisted that Laura had feelings for David. Laura never denied it, but she didn't specify the extent of those feelings before. Today, however, she would.

"I think I may love him."

Her mother got silent on the other end and for a second, Laura thought she'd lost the connection. Then her mother's sigh echoed through the line. "Oh, honey, that's wonderful. I'd been so afraid that your heart was so torn by Jared that you wouldn't be able to fall in love again, at least not for quite a while. This, well, like I said, it's wonderful. Does he feel the same?"

"I don't know. I think he may feel the beginnings of something because he asked me out on a date."

"When are you going out?" her mother asked.

"We went out, last night," Laura said, and before her mother had a chance to start celebrating, she added quickly, "and it didn't end well."

"Wh-what? How did it not end well? What do you mean?"

"I'm fairly certain that he took me in as a charity case. The bookstore has apparently had some rough years, and it doesn't look like he's going to catch up. I don't think he can afford to pay me. In fact, I don't think he's ever been able to afford it, but he's been doing it anyway."

"The bookstore seemed to be doing well when I was there," her mother said, "and your father said it was packed on Black Friday."

"It is doing well now," Laura said, "but his accountant hinted that it happened too late. And from the way David acted when I asked him how the business was doing, I'm afraid it's true." She'd walked to the kitchen while they were talking then opened the refrigerator and stood there. Nothing looked appealing, and she thought she knew why. She didn't want to go back to Nashville, but she also didn't want to hurt David in any way. "Mom, I'm coming back home."

"Here? To Nashville?"

"Yes. It's still okay for me to stay with y'all, isn't it? Until I have the babies and then find a job?"

Laura waited, and when her mother didn't readily answer, she asked again, "Mom? It is okay, right?"

"Well, yes," her mother said. "Or, it would be-e…" She drew the word out. "I was going to wait and surprise you with our news, but now I'm not sure how we'd surprise you. We thought you loved Claremont and would be there for Christmas, and then stay there when the babies are born. We were kind of counting on it."

"Counting on it?" Laura asked, closing the refrigerator door. "What does that mean?"

"I guess I'll start with the first part of our news," her mother said. "I quit!"

"You quit what? Your job?"

"Yes, after twenty-one years of service, I left. Told them just last night. And I am so surprised at how great it feels to retire!" She paused. "Can you call it retiring if you're only forty? Anyway, whatever it is, I did it, and I'm thrilled!"

Laura was floored. Her mother quit work? "I'm glad you're happy, Mom, but why did you quit?"

"And that's the second part of our news. Your dad," she giggled, "it sounds so funny to say this, but your daddy asked me to marry him again! I know you saw the ring and all—he told me you were with him when he picked it out. But you should've seen the proposal.

He took me to the Opryland Hotel night before last and got down on one knee right there in the middle by that big fountain. Then he announced to everyone that he loved me and wanted to spend the rest of his life with me." She laughed. "Can you believe that, Laura?"

"Yes, but I thought he was going to wait until Christmas. He told me to keep the secret."

"That's the rest of our news. I quit because we want to enjoy each other more, and we want to enjoy those grandbabies we're about to have. So I was planning to come to Claremont for Christmas and stay there to help you until the babies came and then also stay after they were born for a while. If I don't have a job, I can do that. And your dad went ahead and asked me so I'd know his plans, and then I could decide whether I wanted to quit work and spend all of the holidays with you in Claremont. And—this is the best part—we're going to renew our vows at the little community church there that you said you love so much!"

"Here? In Claremont?"

"Yes. Your father called and reserved the church this morning. It's going to be extremely small, with the preacher there, Brother Henry I believe was his name, and you as my maid of honor and then David as the best man."

"David?" Laura's head spun. "Dad is asking *David* to be the best man?"

"It seemed only natural, since we're having the ceremony in Claremont. Your dad has some good friends here, but none that want to travel to Claremont for us to renew our vows on Christmas. Everyone spends Christmas with family, and we're going to spend it with you."

"And David." Laura didn't plan to stay here more

than long enough to pack her things. She couldn't be here at Christmas. She couldn't continue hurting David's business—or David, period—by sticking around. And she couldn't help but wonder if this wasn't the best thing anyway, her leaving town and severing this "relationship" or whatever it was with him before it really got started. His business was struggling, and he loved that bookstore, and he didn't need a dependent— a woman who was about to have two dependents of her own, no less. Talk about baggage.

"Honestly, when your dad mentioned him, I thought it'd be a great idea, since you two have been getting so close. Your dad is going to call him this morning. He may already have called, in fact. And you did say you think you may love him."

"I also said I'm hurting him financially, and I have no way to fix that. David—" she swallowed "—he deserves so much." Way more than she had to offer. Laura plopped down at the kitchen table and shook her head. What would she do now? "I can't let him take me in like a charity case."

"You aren't a charity case." David's voice came from behind her, and Laura whirled around to see he'd entered the kitchen from the front of the store.

"Oh, is that David? Tell him I said hello," Marjorie said.

"Mom says hi," she said miserably. This phone call was supposed to cement her return home; instead, it seemed her mother wasn't interested in doing anything but coming here. "I'm not going to stay and cause you to go further in the hole. I'm going home."

"Oh, Laura, do you really think…" her mother began, but Laura cut her off.

"I'll call you back later, Mom. I have to go." She disconnected and looked at the tall gorgeous man invading her kitchen. "How did you get in?"

"It's ten o'clock. Mandy opens the front door at ten, and I was waiting for her when she arrived. You're supposed to be arriving at the bookstore now, by the way." He smirked. "You're late."

"I just need to get my coffee mug," Mandy said, entering the kitchen. She stopped in her tracks when she took a look at Laura. "Oh, uh, are you not working today?"

"No." Laura then remembered looking in the mirror before she'd started down the stairs. Her hair was sticking out like a troll doll, and she'd been so upset last night that she hadn't taken time to match her pajama top to her pants. Consequently, her hot pink and neon green plaid maternity pajama pants clashed severely with her oversize Vols orange nightshirt and purple slippers. But Laura didn't care. She wasn't going to work, and she didn't invite David over. He could take her the way she came, which was messy. And fairly gross. Maybe this would convince him that he didn't want to keep her around after all.

"Yes, she's coming to work," David said, deflating that idea, "if I have to drag her there."

"You wouldn't dare," Laura challenged.

"You think just because you're a little pregnant that I couldn't toss you over my shoulder and haul you down the street if I wanted?"

Mandy's laugh came out with force, and Laura shot her a look that promptly shut her up.

"S-sorry, Laura," she said. "But the thought of you,

as pregnant as you are, being hauled down the street on his shoulder…"

"It's not happening," Laura said.

Mandy looked to David as if wanting affirmation.

"I'm not hauling her anywhere, especially when she's dressed like that," he said.

"Hey!" Laura snapped, and Mandy laughed again, then grabbed her coffee mug and retreated to the gallery.

"I need you to work," he said, "at least until Christmas."

"David, your accountant insinuated that you didn't need to hire me, you don't need to pay me. If I went back home, that would help you. You can still do everything without me."

"No, I can't. I need someone to run the *Boxcar Children* book clubs. I need someone to lead the women in their discussion this week about Rahab. They don't want to listen to me do it, and you know you're enjoying those meetings. Plus, there are the kids at the hospital. They look forward to you reading to them."

"You could do that," she said.

"Not like you. Are you really going to let them down? Could you live with yourself if you let Faith down? She looks forward to our visits each week, and she'll ask why you aren't with us. Seems to me she's gotten even more attached to you, probably since you're female, or maybe it's because you're having the babies. But in any case, I can tell Faith really likes you and enjoys your visits. *I'm* not going to tell her that you aren't coming back. If you're going to Nashville, you'll have to be the one to tell her."

"You know I can't do that. I can't hurt her."

"But you can hurt me?"

"I am hurting you, your business, every day I stay."

"We've still got the holiday season. You never know what could happen at Christmas," he said. "What if we sold enough for me to catch up on my line of credit and even see the bookstore make a profit? What if we could make it work…together? There is a possibility, but there isn't if I have to do it all on my own."

"Milton Stott didn't think so," she reminded.

"Then that's what we'll pray for."

She grabbed an apple from the bowl of fruit on the table, rolled it between her palms as she thought about his suggestion. "You want me to stay until Christmas."

"I do. And you really should anyway. It'd be a shame for you to miss your parents' wedding."

She cut her eyes at him. "Daddy already called you?"

"I'm the best man. Of course he called." He sat beside her at the table smiling as though he'd won first prize at the fair, then he reached for the apple in her hand, brought it to his mouth and took a bite.

"That's mine," she said.

"Say you'll come to work, and I'll give it back."

She glared at the apple. She hadn't really been all that hungry for it before, but now that David was teasing her, she wanted it. Now. "Just until Christmas. I don't want to let the kids down."

He handed her the apple. "That'll work," he said, "for now. And get dressed. You're late."

Laura chomped a big bite of the apple, and he laughed, then turned and left the kitchen.

Chapter Sixteen

"I brought a Barbie for my book buddy." Savannah Jameson placed her wrapped gift beneath the Christmas tree in the children's area. "Daddy and I picked the one wearing a pink dress, since Faith's favorite color is pink. And I made her a pink card, too, with a snowman on it."

"She's going to love that, Savannah." Laura had been so excited about her idea to pair the kids at the hospital with the book-club children for Christmas. Each child that came to book club received the name and information about one of the children in the hospital and was told they could give their "book buddy" something for Christmas. It could be something they made, like a card or a poster, or a bought present. So far, each child brought both, something handmade and something purchased. She couldn't wait to deliver the gifts later tonight with David and Zeb.

"I got Timmy some Hot Wheels cars," Kaden said, sticking his gift under the tree, "and I drew him a cool car picture, too, that looks like one of the cars in the pack."

"He'll love that, Kaden." Laura waited for all of the children to place their gifts under the tree and then opened the *Boxcar Children* book. But before she said anything about the book, she stared at the tree, her mouth falling open. "Hey, did any of you put all of those candy canes on the Christmas tree?"

Their answers came back in a flurry of excitement, because everyone in town knew what candy canes meant.

"I didn't," one said.

"Nope!" yelled Kaden.

"Wow, he was here!" Savannah gasped then placed her hand over her broad smile.

Laura held up her palms. "Now, wait a minute. Let me ask Mr. David." She leaned out from the group and called toward the counter, where David was busily checking out customers. "David, did you put all of these candy canes on the tree?"

"Candy canes?" he answered, the same way he'd answered every other night when Laura had done the very same thing with the previous book-club meetings. "No, I didn't put candy canes on the tree."

"Well, I guess someone left them there for all of you," she said, and the kids scurried to the tree and grabbed their candy canes from Secret Santa. Their eyes were alive with wonder as they ate the candy, particularly since Christmas was merely three days away.

Laura smiled and began reading, and as soon as David had finished with the customers, he came over to listen and gave her a thumbs-up for pulling off the candy-cane scene again. She'd put the candy canes on the tree because she loved the idea of Secret Santa and wanted to help whoever it was keep his secret. Laura wasn't alone. Over the past few weeks, candy canes had shown up everywhere. On each table at Nelson's. On each photo in Mandy's shop. On the doors of each store. Under the windshields of parked cars. The entire town got in on trying to protect Secret Santa's identity, or maybe they just enjoyed getting in on the fun, but Laura loved every minute of it, especially bringing the fun to her book clubs.

When the book club had finished, Zeb showed up ready to ride with them to the hospital. The older man hadn't been feeling well and had started taking David up on his offer to drive him each night instead of Zeb taking his own vehicle. But Mr. Zeb wouldn't miss the trips to the hospital, especially tonight's visit, when the children were having their Christmas party and they'd distribute the presents from their book buddies.

Laura started toward the tree to gather the presents, but Zeb stopped her.

"Now, hold on, Miss Laura. You're going to have to stop lifting things. Those babies look like they're getting mighty close to an arrival, and we don't want you to overdo it and give them any reason to make an early appearance," Zeb said, stepping past her to pick up the gifts.

David laughed. "I'm trying to watch her, but she tends to do what she wants." He picked up the large bag he'd already started filling with gifts and joined Zeb at the tree to add the rest to the sack.

Laura placed a hand on her stomach. "I have to admit, getting up and down is becoming more and more difficult. But they aren't kicking anymore. Every now and then, they'll shift a little, but no more kicks."

"That's probably because they've run out of room," David said.

Laura pinched his bicep. "Very funny." She and David had grown so close over the past few weeks, and she couldn't imagine leaving in merely a few days. Being with him simply felt "right," and she didn't want to be away from him, definitely didn't want to leave.

But she would. She had to. She couldn't stay in Claremont as David's charity case, and she knew David would never leave his beloved town. He'd told her about his grandmother's farmhouse and indicated he'd live there one day. He hadn't added "with his family," but it'd definitely been implied. Laura would have her own family soon, and even if she had to live with her folks for a while until she found a teaching job, she'd eventually find a way to support herself and her babies. And in the meantime, David would probably realize that one of the pretty single ladies in Claremont would be a perfect companion for him for life. A woman who wasn't such a burden. That's what he deserved. Not an unemployed single mother of twins.

"Ready to go?" David asked, snapping her out of her silent pity party.

"Sure."

David carried the oversize bag filled with gifts down the hallway on the children's floor, anticipating the moment he finally got to see the kids. He and Laura enjoyed their time together at the bookstore each day, but nothing beat the moment when the day ended and they came to the hospital. She'd attempted to keep her distance from him over the past few weeks, reminding him every so often that she'd need to leave after the holiday, but even so, these nightly visits to the hospital were so special for both of them that they'd ended up growing even closer because of the love they'd developed together for these kids.

And, whether Laura admitted it to herself or not, David thought she had also felt the connection between the two of them. As though they were one. He'd held his tongue when it came to telling her how he felt because he wanted to wait until the sales numbers came through from the Christmas season and then show her that the bookstore would be okay…and the two of them had no reason not to pursue a life together. According to Milton, the books looked "a little better," but still weren't going to put him in the black anytime soon.

However, David's hope for a relationship with Laura was now on the line, and one way or another, he would convince her to stay in Claremont. He just didn't know how.

Swallowing past the lump in his throat, he nodded to Shea Farmer and the other nurses. "They ready for us?" he asked.

She laughed at the bag David had borrowed from Mr. Feazell, the owner of the Tiny Tots Treasure Box. Red velvet and lined with white fur, it qualified as a real Santa sack. "They're going to love that!"

"That's the goal," he said. "And what about the hats?" He'd purchased three Santa hats from Mr. Feazell, and he, Laura and Zeb each wore one.

Shea gave him the okay sign. "Perfect."

As they walked down the hall, Laura started laughing.

"What is it?" David asked.

She pointed to her stomach. "We should've rented

an entire Santa suit. I could've pulled it off without any stuffing."

"You'd be the cutest Santa around," he said.

"I'll second that," Zeb agreed as they heard the Christmas music blaring ahead.

"We let them turn it up loud tonight, since they're all in the playroom," Shea said. She and a few of the other nurses were following them to the party.

"Even Faith?" Laura asked.

"She didn't want to miss the party, and she's having a good day. A good month, really. Her parents haven't told her yet, but they think she may get to go home for Christmas."

David's steps faltered, and he looked to Laura. Her hand had moved to her heart. That was exactly what they'd been praying for. "That's wonderful," he said.

Faith had been in the hospital longer than any of the other kids, and David got the impression that her parents hadn't been certain she'd be able to go home again. But she was.

Thank You, God.

"Mr. David! Miss Laura! Mr. Zeb!" The kids yelled their names as they entered, big smiles on every face. Their parents were also here for the event, and they lined the walls taking photos with their phones and cameras as the trio entered.

"I'm going to miss them so much," Laura whispered, almost so quietly that it wouldn't be heard. But David did hear.

Please God, help me figure out a way to keep her here.

He got a grip on his emotions and smiled at the kids.

"Well, hello. Guess what. Your book buddies sent each of you Christmas presents!"

The clapping and cheering consumed the room as David, Laura and Zeb handed out the gifts. Along with the nurses, they helped the kids open their presents, each child thrilled with the gifts from their new friends.

David spoke to each of the kids, but he spent a little extra time with Faith before the party ended. "You look like you're feeling better today," he said.

"I am," she said. "I'm so glad I got to come be with everybody at the party. This was great, wasn't it?"

"Yes, it was."

"Did you see my candy cane? Secret Santa brought them for all of us." She held up a candy cane. "Isn't that neat?"

"Very neat," David said, smiling toward Shea, who he assumed bestowed the candy canes on the kids.

"Okay, everyone, we're going to need to get you all back to your rooms," Shea announced, "but don't worry. We'll have another party tomorrow when the church comes to visit, and then another one on Christmas day."

The kids cheered. "Lots of parties!"

Shea laughed. "That's right. This is party central, right here."

Zeb, Laura and David stood at the doorway to tell each child good-night as they headed out. Since the parents were in attendance, most of the kids were taken back to their rooms by their folks, and all but a couple of the nurses followed Zeb, Laura and David down the hallway as they left.

"Did you give them the candy canes?" David asked Shea.

"We've been doing that, too, at the bookstore," Laura said. "The kids love it, don't they?"

Shea nodded. "They do love it, but I didn't do it. The candy canes were delivered with a note asking us to give every child a candy cane from Secret Santa." She smiled. "He does that every year. And one of my friends that works at the nursing home says he sends them to every patient there, too, and all the nurses." She pointed to the nurses' station. "He sent them to us, too. That's mine, by my computer. I plan on snacking on it later," she said, "and thinking about Secret Santa, of course."

"That's wonderful," Laura said.

"I know."

As they started to turn toward the elevator and Shea returned to the nurses' station, she said, "David, can I see you for a moment?"

"Sure," he said.

"We'll go on to the elevator and wait for you," Zeb said.

"Okay." David followed Shea to her desk. "Everything all right?"

"Yes. I'm just following orders."

"Orders?"

She nodded, then glanced toward the elevator where Zeb and Laura were talking about the kids. "I am supposed to give these to all of you from Secret Santa. That's what his note said. But the note said this letter is for you only and that you're supposed to read it in private." She handed three candy canes and a small envelope to David.

Bewildered, he looked at the envelope, and sure enough, his name was written on the outside. He didn't recognize the handwriting, but the block letters would've made that practically impossible. "Thanks." He looked up to see Laura had turned toward him, and he held up the candy canes with one hand, while he slid the letter in his pocket with the other.

She smiled. "For us?"

"For us." Then to Shea, he said, "Thanks."

"You're welcome. I don't know what it is, but it was fun to help him out."

David didn't know what it was, either, and he looked forward to the moment when he got home and found out what Secret Santa had to say.

Chapter Seventeen

David read the note as soon as he returned home then had a difficult time sleeping, anxious to follow through with Secret Santa's instructions. The next morning, he woke early, ate breakfast and then waited for Laura to arrive.

She came in looking wistful, last night's cheer gone. "Those kids—they're amazing, aren't they?" she asked, obviously unable to get the children from the hospital off of her mind. But instead of looking happy about what they'd accomplished, providing a Christmas party and gifts for the kids, she looked miserable.

"They are amazing," he agreed and waited to see if she'd explain what had happened between last night and this morning to change her outlook.

She glanced around the bookstore, empty as usual for the morning. Thankfully it'd been filling up as each day progressed, but the mornings often reminded him of the fact that the place had been empty for several years before it'd been steadily filled. "You've done a lot of good here. I hate to think about it closing," she said.

"I do, too," he said. Milton had delivered updated

financial reports on Monday, and this time David had shared them with Laura. On Tuesday, they agreed that he shouldn't borrow any more money from his line of credit and risk losing the farmhouse. He would close the doors December 31 and attempt to find another job in Claremont. He'd already been looking unofficially but had come up with nothing. If he had something lined up, maybe he could convince Laura to stay, to let him support her until she found a teaching job. Because the thought of Laura leaving didn't sit well, at all. And it was about time for him to tell her why.

"Laura, I don't want you to—" His words were cut short when the bell on the door sounded.

Zeb, wearing the Santa hat from last night, slowly entered.

"What were you saying?" she whispered.

David didn't want an audience for this conversation. "I'll tell you later."

"Still feeling good about those kids," Zeb said. "That was a great party, wasn't it?"

"Yes, it was," Laura said.

He started to smile but winced midway through.

"You feeling okay, Zeb?" David asked.

"For my age, if I get out of bed and can move around a bit, I'm feeling okay," the older man answered. "I'm heading over to the nursing home this morning and wanted to take a few more of those suspense novels for Miss Tilly. Can y'all help me get a few together?"

"I've got to leave for a few minutes," David said, "but Laura will help you out."

She reached for his forearm, and he wished his long sleeves didn't keep her skin from touching his. They'd kept everything low-key, done their jobs and been

friends, ever since that date night. But David wanted
to feel that closeness again. He wanted to hold her,
and to kiss her, and to tell her how he felt—that he'd
fallen in love with her—and then he wanted to tell her
that she should stay in Claremont, and somehow they'd
work everything out.

"You'll tell me whatever you were going to say?"
she asked. "Later?"

David nodded. "Definitely."

For the first time this morning, she gave him a soft
smile, and David prayed that everything would be all
right. Somehow. But before he could work out the details, he needed to find out more about the note from
Secret Santa. "I'll be back in a little while, and then
we'll talk."

"Getting more building supplies?" she asked. "What
are you building up there, anyway?"

"Nah, I finished up with my apartment last week,
and it was just a little renovating," he said. Actually, it
was a lot of renovating, and it appeared all of his work
was in vain. The new room would probably never be
used.

He ran a finger over the note in his pocket. "I'm
going to the coffee shop," he said. "Y'all want anything?"

"Already had three cups," Zeb said. "And I won't
be here but a few minutes. Just going to pick up the
books and then head on. Brother Henry offered to drive
me to the nursing home this morning, and we're leaving soon."

"Okay, how about you, Laura?"

"Oh, yes, a mocha latte please."

"You've got it." He left the bookstore and made a

mental note to go by the coffee shop after he followed the instructions on the note.

Waving to Laura and Zeb as he left, he did a double take to make sure she'd turned her attention to locating the older man's books and didn't watch where he headed. When they disappeared toward the rear of the store, David walked purposefully down the street and stopped in front of Claremont Jewelry before reading the note again.

Tomorrow morning, go to Claremont Jewelry.
Tell Marvin Grier I sent you. S.S.

"Okay, Santa, here goes," David said, opening the door and walking inside.

Mr. Grier was at the checkout counter ringing up the only customer in the store, Chad Martin. "Every year I've tried to surprise Jessica with her present, and every year she finds out before Christmas." Chad accepted the small bag from the man then pointed a warning finger to David. "You tell her you saw me in here, and I'll tell Laura the same."

"Oh, I'm not shopping," David clarified, even though he'd love to be able to shop for Laura in this store—would love to buy a ring that she'd wear for life, a ring that would proclaim she loved him as much as he loved her, truth be told. But that wasn't why he was here. "I just came in to see Mr. Grier."

"Sure you did," Chad said, grinning. "Don't worry, I'll keep your secret…but don't you forget to keep mine. Just two days until Christmas. Maybe I'll actually pull off the surprise this year."

"Maybe so," David said, tired of trying to explain

why he was here, which was impossible, since he had no idea.

But Mr. Grier did. The minute Chad exited and the door snapped shut, he said, "I've been expecting you, David."

"You have?"

He nodded. "Each year, Secret Santa typically purchases one or two things from me. I'll find an envelope with cash and instructions by the register, and I never see who puts it there. Same thing every year. And this year, I got an envelope with instructions for you."

"For me? I mean, I like your store and all, but I don't really need any jewelry."

"Obviously Secret Santa thought you did." Mr. Grier handed David a small box and an envelope with his name written in the same block letters.

David opened the envelope and read...

This is not a gift. I am repaying a debt. S.S.

He ran a thumb over the top of the black velvet box then lifted the lid.

"No way."

The ring was stunning, three diamonds centering an elegant band. Exactly the type he'd buy for Laura, if he could.

"Laura tried that one on," Mr. Grier said.

"She did?" David was shocked.

"When her father was looking for the new wedding set for her mother," he explained. "It fits, by the way, in case you're wondering."

"But I can't accept this. And he says it's repayment for a debt? No one owes me anything."

"Well, Secret Santa must think he does because that's a beautiful ring, and it's paid for." He looked behind the counter. "Hold on a minute. Yes, here are the appraisal papers for it. You'll want that for insurance."

David flipped through the papers, saw the value of the ring and gasped. "Definitely no one owes me that much!"

"You'll have to take that up with Secret Santa," Mr. Grier said, "assuming you figure out who he is." He smiled. "I'm guessing you won't." Then he looked at the ring. "And I'm guessing you might be getting yourself a fiancée for Christmas. I really like Laura, you know."

"I really like her, too." David lifted the ring out of the box and held it up to the light. It was amazing.

"The three diamonds are princess cut," Mr. Grier explained, "and they represent the past, present and future of your love."

"And it's paid for," David said, finding it hard to believe.

"Paid for and yours."

He folded the appraisal papers and slid them into his back pocket. Then he put the ring box in his front right pocket. Maybe this was a sign—a sign that everything would work out. Somehow he'd find a way to make a living in Claremont…and keep Laura here, too. As his wife, if she said yes. "Thank you, Mr. Grier," he said, leaving the jewelry store in a state of disbelief. He, David Presley, had an engagement ring in his pocket…and a woman he wanted to give it to.

"Don't thank me," Mr. Grier called, "thank Santa."

Chapter Eighteen

David had started back to the bookstore but then remembered he was supposed to get coffee and backtracked across the square. Funny how a diamond ring in his pocket made him forget pretty much everything else. He opened the door to The Grind and was met by the warmth of the fireplace filling the room along with the crisp scent of coffee coupled with the sweet scent of fresh baked cookies.

"Merry Christmas Eve Eve," Rhonda said as he entered. Several people from town sat on the sofas and at the tables spaced sporadically around the coffeehouse and most all of them waved a hand or fingertips to David.

"Merry Christmas Eve Eve to you, too," he said, feeling as chipper as she looked in her green-and-red sequined Christmas cap and matching Christmas ornament earrings.

"There's a table open by the fireplace," she said, "or do you want something to go?"

"Two mocha lattes to go," he said.

She smiled knowingly as she jotted down the order. "For you and Laura?"

"Yes," he said, already liking the ring of that. David and Laura. It sounded really good. Felt even better.

"Want cookies, too? We made iced sugar cookies today."

"Why not? Give me four."

"All righty. They're shaped like Christmas trees, wreaths, stockings and snowmen. You have a preference for which ones you get?"

"One of each," he said, looking forward to watching Laura enjoy the treat. In college, he never saw her eat sweets; however, her pregnancy had her craving a bit of sugar almost every day. David was happy to oblige, just to see her smile. He really liked seeing her smile.

Rhonda moved behind the pastry counter and started getting David's cookies while the barista prepared the lattes. The band More Than This played Christmas music beside a decorated tree on one side of the shop, and David enjoyed the songs so much that he nearly didn't hear Rhonda's comment.

"So, was that Laura's brother looking for her earlier?" she asked. "I sent him over to the bookstore to find her."

David turned away from the band to look at the waitress. "Laura's brother?" He shook his head. "Laura's an only child. Someone was looking for her?"

She checked the white sack to see the cookies she'd already placed inside and then reached for a snowman one to add to the bag. "Yeah, not long ago. I know I've never seen him before. I'd have remembered. He kind of favored her, so I thought he might be her brother. You know, blond, nice features," she said, and she blushed. "Tall. I was actually going to ask if her brother was moving here, maybe." She slid a stocking cookie in the bag and then folded the top down. "And, you know, whether he was single?"

Obviously Rhonda had taken a quick interest in whoever this guy was, a tall, nice-looking blond dude who wasn't from around here and was looking for Laura. His old roommate's image came to mind.

"He, um, had the greenest eyes I've ever seen," she said. "Maybe that'll help you figure out who it is? You know anybody like that?"

I think the first thing that caught my attention was his eyes. And it's still so hard for me to look at his eyes and not just melt. Laura's confession from college, on a night when she'd been hurt by Jared's flirting with one of her friends, had clued David in on the effect of his buddy's unique eyes on women.

Obviously, Rhonda wasn't immune.

"You know who he is?" she asked, and David realized she'd been scrutinizing his response to every tidbit of information she revealed.

"I think I do." And he wondered why Jared had come here, to Claremont. "Was anyone with him?" Like, say, his wife?

"No," she said. "He was by himself. And he said he needed to find Laura as soon as possible because he'd made a terrible mistake and he wanted to fix it. I figured it was one of those sibling arguments, you know, like me and my brother have. Figured he came here to apologize in person. He seemed like the kind of guy that would do that," she said dreamily.

Great. Yet another one taken with Jared. And Jared, apparently, was currently with Laura.

"So…is he single?" Rhonda asked, sliding the sack of cookies across the glass counter toward the two white cups holding their lattes.

"No, he isn't," David said.

"Right," she answered disappointedly, while David took his coffees and cookies then headed toward the door…wondering if he'd just told a lie. Was Jared single now? Did the "mistake" he was talking about include leaving Laura, the mother of his twins, and marrying someone else? Would he have left Anita already and decided he had made a mistake, that he still loved Laura? That he should've married Laura?

The brisk December cold hit him even harder, an abrupt change from the warmth of the coffeehouse. Or maybe it merely felt colder because of the cold reality that the father of Laura's babies had come to town. The guy Laura had loved first.

He looked toward the bookstore and saw the door open. David took a step back to stand beneath the coffeehouse's awning and prayed that the two wouldn't look his way. He didn't want to talk to Jared, but he wanted to see—no, he didn't want to, but he needed to see—him interact with Laura. Did she still want him?

Sure enough, Jared stepped outside with Laura standing within the open door. David watched as his old friend reached out and ran the backs of his fingers along her cheek. He saw Laura turn her head into Jared's touch.

David couldn't watch anymore. Jared was here, and he obviously wanted her back. And from all appearances, Laura wanted him, too. Well, of course she did. This was the guy she'd loved throughout college, and this was the father of her babies. They *should* be together. David felt a sharp stab of pity for Anita, the woman Jared had apparently married on a whim and then dumped to be with the woman…he never should have left.

The woman David loved.

"Hey, Mr. David, did your friend find you?" Kaden asked, running down the sidewalk toward David.

"My friend?" David asked.

Kaden nodded exuberantly while Mandy, carrying Mia, tried to catch up with her son.

"Kaden, you need to slow down," she said breathlessly, and then to David, "your old roommate from college came into the bookstore while we were there. He asked where you were."

"Did he?" David glanced past Mandy to see Jared walking away from the bookstore, and from David's vantage, he appeared to be smiling. If he'd actually been interested in seeing David, he'd have stuck around until he returned, wouldn't he? But he hadn't. And David knew that was because he hadn't really been searching for his old roommate. He'd been looking for the girl he'd loved, the mother of his babies.

"Yeah," Kaden said, unaware of the tumult this conversation was inflicting on David, "but then he said he really wanted to just talk to Miss Laura, and then they started talking about her babies and stuff."

Mandy ran a hand across Kaden's curls. "That's enough, Kaden. We didn't mean to eavesdrop," she explained. "And we left so they could talk without an audience." She tilted her head toward Kaden.

David wondered what Jared had said that the boy had overheard.

"We aren't a audience," Kaden said with shrug. "Mr. David, is that guy her boyfriend?"

"Did he say he was?" David asked.

"Kinda."

David's skin bristled. "How do you mean?"

"'Cause he said he missed her and he hugged her and stuff, like if he was her boyfriend. Adam at my school has a girlfriend, but he doesn't hug her or anything. They just play on the monkey bars and the seesaw instead of Adam playing tag with us boys." Kaden shook his head. "I don't want a girlfriend, 'cause I like to play tag."

David weeded through the information and zeroed in on what was important in his world. "He said he missed her."

Mandy nervously cleared her throat. "He mentioned that he'd missed Laura and that he had been thinking about her," she said. "But then we left."

"But remember? Miss Laura said she'd been thinking about him, too," Kaden added, unknowingly twisting the knife.

"Yes, I remember," Mandy admitted, her cheeks turning even more red. "And then we left." She gave David what she probably thought was a reassuring smile.

He didn't feel reassured. "Well, y'all have a good day." Turning away from the uncomfortable conversation, he reentered the coffeehouse and took a seat. More Than This started playing "Blue Christmas." David couldn't think of a more fitting song.

Laura couldn't believe how much had changed in the span of a few hours. Jared's offer was so heartfelt,

so meaningful, so…unexpected. He wasn't the same
guy that she'd known in the spring. This wasn't a man
who would tell her to end a pregnancy. No, this guy
already loved her babies because they were his, too.
This guy had offered her a Nashville apartment to live
in until she found a job. And he said he'd help her pay
for everything, from now on, for the girls, even though
Laura hadn't asked.

And all because he'd finally found faith…with
Anita. His story had made Laura cry because now
she understood. She'd found her faith again, too, because of David. But she'd been so touched listening
to Jared describe how his eyes had been opened and
how Anita had encouraged him to do what was right,
especially since she was now pregnant, too. Jared and
his new wife didn't want his twins not knowing the
sibling they would have next summer.

Laura had promised to think about Jared's offer and
consider it. Either way he would help her support the
girls, whether she moved back to Nashville or stayed
here. His offer would help her stay here…if that's what
David wanted.

She prayed it was, that he would still want her in
Claremont and with him even if the bookstore wasn't a
factor. Because she knew she loved him. The thought of
leaving him in two days had made her sick this morning, but now Jared had promised to help her out until
she found a job. And she would find a job, eventually.
No, it wouldn't be at the bookstore, but surely she could
find something here to hold her over until she was able
to get a position teaching at the school.

She simply needed David to tell her he wanted her
to stay. And she suspected he'd been about to say that

very thing this morning before they were interrupted by Zeb. Maybe he was even going to say more. The three words that she wanted to hear so desperately.

The bookstore door opened, and she turned to see David entering carrying two coffee cups and a small white bag. She smiled. "You just can't get coffee without cookies, can you?"

He didn't give her the smile she expected, but instead walked past her to place the items on the counter. "I guess not."

Laura started to tell him about Jared's visit and his offer, but there was something she wanted to cover first, something she hadn't stopped thinking about since he left. "You said you'd tell me what you were going to say this morning," she reminded, grabbing her mocha latte and taking a delicious sip. "So...tell." And then she'd tell him her news, too, that Jared would be helping financially.

David picked up his coffee, took a long sip and then swallowed.

Laura's skin tingled, she was so anxious. "So...what were you going to tell me? You said, 'Laura, I don't want you to...' and then Zeb walked in. You don't want me to—what?" She knew what he was going to say, that he didn't want her to leave. That he felt as strongly toward her as she felt toward him, and he wanted her to stay in Claremont and the two of them to work through everything together. Now and forever. She took another sip of her latte, let the rich mocha tease her tongue while she waited to hear him tell her how he felt.

"I don't want you to," he began again, then visibly swallowed and added, "stay in Claremont."

The coffee lodged in her throat and she forced herself to swallow it down. "Wh-what? You want me to leave?"

"The bookstore is closing. I tried to help you out, but I won't be able to anymore," he said, his words clipped and firm, without even a hint of compassion. "Your life is in Nashville. Mine is here." He took another sip of his coffee. "We're still friends, though," he added. "If you ever need me, and if I can help, I'll be here."

"Of course you will," she said, shaken by this change of events, "because that's what friends do, help you out when you need it…and then send you on your way." She waited for him to refute the statement, to tell her that wasn't what he was doing at all, but he nodded once, placed his coffee cup on the counter and then left her sitting alone.

Chapter Nineteen

David hadn't been able to find a way to back out of his commitment to be best man at this wedding. For the past two days, he'd only spoken to Laura when absolutely necessary, not wanting to make things even more awkward than they already were by trying to talk her out of leaving.

He'd told her to go, and after her parents said "I do," she'd do just that. Leave…and go back to Jared.

David had been shocked that she still hadn't even told him about Jared's visit, but then again, what good would telling him do? It wouldn't change the fact that Jared had shown up and now she was returning to Nashville, where she could be with the father of her babies.

David should be happy things worked out the way Laura wanted.

He *should* be.

Marjorie wore a fitted cream dress and carried a bouquet of poinsettias. Thomas and David wore suits, as did Brother Henry. The only people present who weren't in the wedding party were Brother Henry's wife, Mary, who sat in the second row and dripped tears through the ceremony as though it were her own daughter getting married for the first time, and David's parents, thrilled to spend part of their holiday attending a vow renewal. None of them realized the pain he endured, attending a wedding with Laura present and knowing that the wedding he most wanted, the one between the two of them, would never happen.

"I just love this," Mary whispered repeatedly.

Several times, Marjorie, never taking her eyes from her husband, agreed, "I do, too."

But all of the others faded into the background for David. The only person he saw wore a pretty red dress and a smile that seemed forced. Laura had her hair pulled up and held in place with some decorative barrettes, a curled blond tendril hanging down on each side of her face. David wondered if she'd have worn her hair that way for *their* wedding day. Or if she'd wear it that way when she wed Jared.

He stuck his hand in his pocket, felt the ring Thomas had purchased for Marjorie and thought of the ring David had, courtesy of Secret Santa, in the opposite pocket. He hadn't wanted to leave it in his apartment. He hadn't wanted to leave it anywhere period. He'd wanted to put it on Laura's finger. And now that she was leaving, he should probably give it back.

But he had no idea who'd given it to him. The town was so protective of Secret Santa that David didn't have a clue to the guy's identity. How could he return the ring?

Laura gazed at her parents as they completed their vows, but as soon as they finished, she looked at David, her eyes filled with unanswered questions.

David couldn't look at her, so he focused on Thomas and Marjorie, finishing the ceremony with a kiss. Their show of affection went on a little too long for comfort, and Mary's tears turned to giggles. Brother Henry also chuckled, and Laura returned her attention to her parents.

"Sorry, but this is just so wonderful!" Marjorie gushed.

"I totally agree, Mom," Laura said. "It is wonderful. I'm so—" she brushed away a tear "—happy for both of you." Glancing at David, she frowned a little, then took a step toward her mom to hug her, and stopped. "Oh! Oh, my!" She grabbed at her stomach and winced.

"Laura, what is it?" Marjorie asked, while David rushed to her side.

"Laura? Is it the babies?" he asked.

Still wincing, she nodded, and David realized she was holding her breath. He forgot about the fact that they were barely speaking, forgot about the fact that his heart had been broken and solely concentrated on helping the woman he loved—whether she loved him back or not. "Breathe, honey. Hold on to me." He took her hands and she squeezed them nearly hard enough to break bone. Then she eased up, released her breath and said, "Not—not false labor."

"We'll go get the car and pull it around to the door," her father said, darting toward the church exit with his wife at his side. "David, you help her out."

Everyone in the church moved into action. Brother Henry and Mary rushed to open the doors as David guided Laura down the aisle and outside. His parents followed Laura's folks out so they could also head to the hospital. And David held his arm around Laura as she slowly progressed toward the vehicle.

Another hard contraction slammed her when they were merely feet from the car, and she latched on to David and yelled through the onslaught. It killed him to see her in so much pain, but what hurt even more were her words, directed to him in the midst of that horrible contraction.

As her faced flexed with pain, her arms clung to David and tears fell freely, Laura asked, "What—what happened to us?"

Marjorie, holding the back car door open for her daughter, locked eyes with David, her mouth flattening and her eyes suddenly filled with sorrow. Obviously she'd heard Laura's question, even though her daughter's yelp with yet another contraction kept David from having to answer.

He eased her into the backseat, and Marjorie slid in to sit beside her, draping her arm around Laura and still looking at David as though she didn't understand.

"I'll be right behind you," he said, closing the door without addressing Marjorie's questioning eyes. And without answering Laura's question.

Because he didn't understand, either.

Chapter Twenty

"They're beautiful," David's mother said, standing beside him at the nursery window while Grace and Joy slept peacefully in their pink blanket cocoons. Laura had said the names came easily after she went into labor in the church on Christmas day.

"They are, aren't they?" he agreed. The girls came two weeks early but were perfectly healthy. And now, merely two days old, they were doing great.

"What a Christmas present," she said.

"I couldn't have said it better myself," Zeb said as he neared the nursery. "How's the little mama?" he asked.

"She's amazing," David said. And she was. Laura had endured four hours of labor before delivering Grace and then three minutes later, Joy. Seeing her hold the baby girls, talk to them and love them over the past two days had touched David's heart like nothing he'd ever witnessed before and he wanted to tell her, but the timing had never been right. Someone was always in the room, and then on top of that, David kept wondering when Jared would show up to see his new daughters. If David were a smart man, he wouldn't stick around waiting for the inevitable, when another man waltzed in and claimed what he wanted so much. But David couldn't help himself; he wanted to be near Laura.

Zeb had been at the hospital several times over the past couple of days, not only to check on Laura but also to see all of the kids on the children's floor for Christmas. David had gone down to see them, as well, and had taken photos of the babies along. All of the kids had made cards for Laura, and they were displayed in her room. Zeb nudged David. "Whatever is going on between you two needs to be fixed."

"What?" David asked, but he knew exactly what the older man referred to.

"You and Miss Laura. You were meant to be together, and I think you know it. You two—" he pointed to the babies "—and those two." He nodded for emphasis. "Together."

"Zeb, you don't know what's happened," David said, and he didn't want to discuss the girls' daddy now, especially since Laura's parents were walking toward them.

"Laura still sleeping?" Marjorie asked as they joined David and Zeb at the window.

"I think so." David looked at the couple, their arms around each other as if they were newlyweds. Then again, in a way, they were.

Marjorie held up a bag. "I've got a gift. Why don't you walk with me and we can go see if she's up? I think she's going to like this." She gave her husband a look that told David this "walk with me" thing was a setup. Obviously she wanted to talk to David alone, and all of the people huddled around the nursery window apparently knew it...and went along with it.

David looked again at the babies, their little mouths open as they slept with tiny fists near their lips. He'd been surprised Marjorie hadn't already asked him about Laura's comment on the way to the hospital, but again, the past two days had been a flurry of emotion with hardly any chances for private conversations. Until now. He prayed he was ready. "Okay."

They turned the corner and walked far enough away from the nursery that the group couldn't hear, and then Marjorie slowed her steps. "Laura is supposed to leave the hospital in an hour," she said.

"I know."

"Well, then, I think it's time we figure out where she's going, don't you?" She raised one intimidating brow to David.

"Where she's going?"

"Yes. Is she going home with us...or staying here with you?" Before David could respond, she added, "She asked you what happened to the two of you, and from what I can tell, you still haven't given her an answer."

"I haven't had a chance to talk to her privately since we got here," David said, feeling like a kid who'd been called into the principal's office.

She handed over the gift. "Here. You can deliver my gift, and you can talk to her. Now. This is your chance. Because as much as I'd love for her to live with us, I refuse to drive her back to Nashville when I honestly believe her heart is—and will always be—in Claremont."

"What about Jared?" David knew he shouldn't have

asked, but the question came out before he had a chance to filter his thoughts.

Now both brows popped up, her eyes widened and then she shook her head for good measure. "*That's* what this is about?" She gave him a small shove toward Laura's room. "Oh, you definitely need to go talk to my daughter. And in the future, that's the way the two of you should handle things. Talk things out. I went more than two decades keeping my thoughts and fears from Thomas. I was stupid. And you are, too, if you don't figure out what's what." Then she abruptly turned on her heel and started back toward the nursery.

While David, not knowing what was about to happen, continued toward Laura's room.

She was sitting up in the bed and smiling at her phone when he entered, and David felt a sharp stab of jealousy wondering whether Jared had texted something that made her smile like that.

She glanced up and that confused look that had crossed her face every time she'd seen him since Jared came to town returned. Then she cleared her throat, turned the phone so he could see the image of the babies on the screen and said, "I love all of the pictures everyone has already put up of the girls."

David mentally kicked himself for, as Marjorie said, being stupid. He had to stop assuming things and start asking what he wanted to know. Starting right now. "They're beautiful." He held up the gift bag. "Your mom sent another gift."

Laura reached for the bag, and David handed it over, their fingers touching in the exchange. She hesitated as skin met skin, looked at him and then slowly took the gift. Peeking inside, she said, "These are the kind of pacifiers the nurse said the girls like best."

David nodded, his thoughts more focused on what he was about to say than on Marjorie's gift, and Laura seemed to understand. She placed the bag on the nightstand and then watched him pull a chair near the bed and sit down.

"So, are you going to tell me now?" she asked, her voice barely above a whisper, as though she also dreaded this conversation. "What happened?"

David hated seeing her upset because of him, but the whole point of sending her to Nashville was to give her what she wanted and make certain she was happy. "I know how much you loved Jared, how you wanted him to marry you and the two of you to raise Grace and Joy together. And I know how much it hurt you when he didn't," he said.

"David…"

He shook his head. "Let me finish. I've held this in, and I should have told you when I saw the two of you together again."

"Oh, wait, David, you don't—"

"Laura, please," he said, and she stopped. David glanced at the door, still closed, and was thankful they finally had the privacy he needed to tell her everything in his heart. "I saw him leaving the bookstore and the way you looked at him. I could see that you love him, and I could also see that the two of you appeared to be working things out. Which is great. For the girls. I know that's what you want, and I won't stand in your way of that." He took a deep breath, let it out. "I just wish you'd have told me."

A different look came over her face, one David couldn't read, and then finally, she asked, "Why?"

"Why?" he repeated.

"Yes, why do you wish I'd have told you? Why would you care that Jared came to see me? And on top of that, why did you show up at the bookstore, barely speak to me and treat me as though you couldn't stand to look at me ever since? Why?" When he didn't readily answer, she persisted, "You said you've held it in ever since that day. You didn't tell me what you wanted to say, what I believe you were about to say that morning before you left. Why?"

David had no choice but to answer. "Because I couldn't stand to see him with you."

She blinked. And the fire that'd been in her eyes merely a second ago converted to a warmth as she looked at him. Then she seemed to fight a smile as she asked once more, "Why?"

David decided he might as well go for broke. He'd already started down the rabbit hole, might as well fall in. "Because I know you love him, Laura, and I wanted…"

"You wanted what?" She reached for his hand and tenderly laced her fingers between his. "What is it that you wanted, David?"

"I wanted you to love me."

Her eyes glistened, and several tears fell free. "Oh, David," she said. "I will always care for Jared because he's the girls' father. But his life is with Anita, and with the baby she's carrying."

"With the baby she's carrying?"

Laura nodded, her tears still falling, but her smile sending them in awkward paths along her cheeks and neck. "That's why he came, to tell me that he's changed and that he wants to be a part of the girls' lives. He wants to help financially, too, and he said he'll help me out until I can find a job. And a lot of the change in him was due to Anita. She was determined to help him regain his faith, and he's trying to get his life right. He wants to help support the babies and be a part of their lives."

David felt like an idiot. If he'd only asked, this is what she'd have told him. "Aw, man. I thought that you wanted him again."

Her smile crept up a little higher, and she blinked through the tears. "I have one more question," she said, her thumb moving in tender circles across the top of his hand as she spoke.

"Anything," he said. "I promise I'll answer."

"You said you wanted me to love you." Her eyes locked with his, and the compassion David saw almost moved him to tears, as well. "Why?"

He didn't have to think about his answer. He gave her the truth. "Because of how much I love you."

She eased forward in the bed, moved her face toward his and said, "I do love you, David. I love you so much that it killed me to think about leaving you. I don't want to leave Claremont. I don't want to leave you. Ever."

Their last kiss had been timid, tender and sweet. But this one held the intensity of the emotion passing between them, the promise of a future together, the eagerness of beginning their life together and loving each other forever.

"Now that's more like it," Marjorie said, entering

the room with a smile stretching into both cheeks and with Shea Farmer following in her wake.

"Well, I take a couple of days off, and you go and get the whole hospital excited about the beautiful twins on the fourth floor." Shea held up a small paper red sack. "I did want to come up and see you and the babies, but I also needed to bring this. I'm not sure when it was left at the nurses' station, but apparently, I've turned into something of an honorary elf for Secret Santa. He left this with a note asking me to deliver this to you."

"Deliver what?" Marjorie asked.

"A candy cane for David and Laura, but you aren't supposed to open it until you leave the hospital," Shea said. "Wait…" She pulled a note out of her scrubs pocket and read it. "He said you're supposed to read it after you leave the hospital but before you go home."

"O-kay," David said.

"I've got to get back down to the children's floor," Shea continued. "I'm glad I got to see all of you, and I'm very happy about the girls."

"Us, too," Laura said.

Shea had been gone only a few minutes when a different nurse came in. "Laura, your little ladies will be ready to go in about five minutes. We're sending for a wheelchair for you now."

"Wonderful." She waited for the nurse to leave. "I wish I could have had a little more time to get the apartment ready. Mandy said she still had the cradles from when she and Mia were babies and would let me borrow them, but I haven't even put them in my room yet. They're still in one of her storage areas." She looked at David. "I am staying here, aren't I?"

"If you can forgive me for being a horse's behind,"

he said, which earned a tiny snort of a laugh from Marjorie.

"I think I can," she said.

"And if you can live with the fact that I'm currently unemployed with no prospects whatsoever of a job."

Marjorie emitted another laugh, but Laura reached for his hand. "We'll sell the bookstore together, and we'll find something for us to do together. I want to stay here, David. I want to be with you."

Ten minutes later, all of Laura's and the babies' things were in the trunk, Grace and Joy were buckled into their infant carriers in the backseat and David helped Laura into the passenger's seat. While everyone hovered around the car oohing and aahing over the scene and snapping photos right and left, David hovered over Laura to buckle her in and to steal a tender kiss.

She loved him, and she wanted to stay in Claremont. It'd be the perfect opportunity for him to give her the ring he still carried in his pocket…but he still didn't know how he'd support a wife. And he couldn't ask her to marry him without being able to take care of her. So he said a silent thank-you to God for giving him a beginning to the life he wanted, and he said another prayer for God to help them complete the story.

Then he circled the car, got in and prepared to drive her home. But Laura pointed to the candy cane sticking out of David's shirt pocket. "Ready to read it?"

He nodded and withdrew it while the rest of their families headed to their cars so they could apparently get to the apartment before them and make sure the place was ready for the new arrivals.

"Go on, I can hardly wait," she said, placing her

hands together at her mouth as David peeled back the paper around the stem and silently read the note.

"I don't get it."

"What does it say?" She leaned over to see. "We're supposed to go to that address?"

He nodded, dumbfounded. "I guess so."

"Do you know where that is?"

"I know exactly where it is, and I…really don't understand."

Chapter Twenty-One

It took fifteen minutes for David to drive to the address Secret Santa provided. He turned down the familiar gravel pathway that he'd traveled often growing up but hadn't seen in several months.

"Are those peach trees lining the road?" Laura asked.

"This is actually a driveway," he said, "and yes, they are. The peaches are some of the best you'll ever taste, too. I used to eat so many when I was little that my folks were afraid I'd get sick."

"You've been here before?"

David pulled past the last trees lining the drive and then viewed the open fields that bordered the white farmhouse and red barn. "I own it," he said, blinking to make sure his eyes weren't playing tricks on him. But they weren't. The barn had a fresh coat of paint, as did the white fencing. But the barn and the fencing had nothing on the house. "That's my grandmother's house. My house now," he said. "But the last time I saw it, the windows were boarded, and the house needed painting badly."

"That's your house? David, it's beautiful! It looks like something out of a magazine."

He'd dreamed of seeing the house look like this again. "I don't understand how…" He stopped as a man exited the front door—the new red front door—and waved.

"Isn't that Savannah's daddy?" Laura asked.

David pulled the car up to park beneath the big oak in front of the house. "Yes, it is." He got out as Titus Jameson walked to meet them.

"Hey," he said. "That's perfect timing. I just finished." He looked into the backseat. "Oh, wow, they're as pretty as I heard. Congratulations."

"Thank you," Laura said, also exiting the car but slowly.

David glanced her way. "Honey, you okay?"

She nodded. "Yes, I'm fine. That wheelchair was hospital policy, so I put up with it, but they've been having me walk for the past two days. I'm good to go."

David smiled at her determination. He loved that about her, loved everything about her, in fact. "Okay," he said, and then turned to the guy standing by the car. "Titus, what—well, what are you doing here?" he asked, opening the door to the backseat and unhooking Grace's infant carrier so he could carry her inside.

Laura opened the other door for Joy, but Titus intervened. "Here, that'll be heavy for you to get with the seat and all," he said, and then he proceeded to unhook Joy's carrier.

"I figured you already knew why I was here," Titus said as they walked toward the house. "But I really wasn't sure how he did it all—Secret Santa, I mean. Remember when I came in the bookstore not knowing what I was going to do about work and Christmas for Savannah? Well, the next day I got an envelope of cash and a credit at the building supply store with instructions to fix this place up for you. So that's what I've been doing," Titus said with a grin. "He's left me notes every now and then about things he wanted done, and when I got a note—on a candy cane, of course— I did what it said."

"Seems like everybody does," Laura said, crossing the porch and putting her hand on the door. "Can we go in?"

"Of course," Titus said.

Laura opened the door and then held it wide so Titus and David could carry the babies in. They placed the carriers on the hardwood floor near the stairs, while David stood in awe. The walls had all been painted the original shade of creamy yellow, and the furniture that had previously been covered with sheets had been recovered with new fabrics in shades of rust and gold that gave the place a homey, farm appeal.

"I could so live here," Laura whispered.

Titus winked at David. "Listen, Daniel and Mandy are watching Savannah for me, and I want to spend some time with her today, so I'm going to head on out. Everything is done here. This morning was the last finishing touches. I'm going to leave so you can have some privacy to see your new home."

David nodded as Titus saw himself out, and then he simply moved through the place to appreciate the beauty of the restored home. "It's exactly like I dreamed," he said. Then he heard Laura's gasp and turned to see what had her attention.

She faced the fireplace in the living room and stood

with her mouth open as she focused on the photograph above the mantel.

"I never saw the photo," David said, staring at the picture, "but I remember when Mandy took it."

Laura blinked several times as she took in the image of herself, reading to the children's book club, Savannah leaning against her and peering at the book and Kaden peeking at the page. Several other children faced her and leaned forward to hear every word. "That touches my heart," she said.

"Mine, too."

The front door opened, and David turned, expecting to see that Titus had forgotten something, but instead Zeb walked in.

He'd started moving slower lately, and today was no exception. "Okay if I come on in?"

"Of course," David said, walking to welcome their guest. "How did you know we were here?"

"Titus," he said, smiling as he moved to the stairs, held the rail and then sat down beside the carriers. "They're so beautiful."

"Thank you," Laura said.

"I…" Zeb began, then reached out to touch Grace's tiny hand. "I have something to tell both of you, before the others arrive."

"Others?" Laura asked. She walked over and sat on a cushioned chair near the stairs. David moved to sit beside her and held her hand.

Zeb nodded. "I believe a few folks are in on this little secret, or they will be soon."

"Because of Titus?" she asked.

"Because of Secret Santa." Zeb looked up at them

and smiled. "All of those years that you've been giving me those books for free," he said to David, "I kept up."

"You kept up with what?" David asked, confused.

"With what I owed. I kept up with my debt," Zeb said. "I had a debt to repay. That's the thing about helping others, about giving to others. God gives you back so much more. All these years I've been visiting the hospitals and the shut-ins and the nursing homes, I've gotten close to a lot of folks, lots of times during their last years, their last days." He sighed, apparently reflecting on some of the people he'd helped over the years. "I give them my time." He shrugged. "I give them God's love."

David concentrated on listening to everything Zeb had to say.

"And when it comes their time to meet their Lord," Zeb continued, "they leave the stuff that doesn't matter up there to me, 'cause they know I'll give it to the ones who need it, and I do. To the best of my ability, I do."

"Oh, Zeb." Laura reached for his hand.

"It's you, isn't it? You're Secret Santa," David said. Zeb nodded. "I am."

"I can't thank you enough," David said.

"I'm just doing what's right." Zeb looked at the sleeping babies. "This place was meant for the four of you."

"Oh, Zeb, we aren't—I mean, David hasn't asked me," Laura stammered, but David merely grinned at the older man.

"No, I haven't, but I've learned something over the past few days. When you've got something to say, or in this case, something to ask, then you certainly shouldn't waste time."

Zeb grinned, and Laura's mouth dropped open.

"David?" she asked as he moved in front of her and lowered to one knee.

"Laura, I've loved you for longer than I was willing to admit, but I'll never make that mistake again. If I'm thinking that I love you, I'll say it. If I want to hold your hand, I'll hold it. If I want to kiss you and love you and cherish you for the rest of my life—and I do—I promise I'll do it." He slid his hand into his pocket and withdrew the ring that'd been keeping him company for the past five days.

Laura gasped as he opened the box. "That's—that's my ring!"

"If you'll say yes, it is," David agreed.

"Yes, yes, oh, yes!" she said as David slid the ring on her finger and marveled at the beauty of the three sparkling stones, even prettier on the hand of the woman he loved.

"For our past, our present and our future," he said.

"Maybe you can have a Valentine's Day wedding," Zeb said, "so I can be there to see it?"

David didn't like the way that sounded, at all, and from the way Laura tensed, she heard the same thing. "Zeb, what are you saying?" David asked.

The older man took another glance at Grace and Joy then wiped a couple of tears away. "I've been waiting a long time to be with my Dolly again. And now, according to the doctors, I don't have to wait much longer. Three months at the most, they say." He turned his attention from the babies to Laura and David. "That's why Valentine's Day might work."

Laura's tears were flowing now, and she took Zeb's

hand in hers. "Valentine's Day would be perfect, especially if we have you there."

David nodded, unable to speak for the emotion squeezing his heart.

"I want you two to run the bookstore the way you have, taking care of the children in town and also those special ones at the hospitals and the nursing homes. And, Laura, I know you wanted to teach at a school, but what you do at the bookstore, that's important teaching, too. And at the hospital. I truly believe you were meant for those things."

David believed so, too, and he wanted the bookstore to stay open and for her to be able to continue working with children there, but even with a place to live, he wasn't sure...

"David," Zeb continued, breaking into David's thoughts.

"Yes?"

"Your bookstore is going to be fine now."

David was floored. What was Zeb saying? "Going to be fine now?" he asked.

Zeb nodded. "The line of credit on the farmhouse is taken care of, and as of this morning, you're debt-free."

"Zeb!" Laura exclaimed, and David shook his head. "It's—gone? Paid for? All of it?"

"All of it," Zeb said with a nod.

"I— Zeb, I don't know what to say."

"You should tell your fiancée about her Christmas present, the one from you, since she'll be able to use it now," Zeb said.

David hadn't even mentioned the gift to Laura, since he had thought they wouldn't get to use it, but he swallowed, cleared his throat and said, "The work that my dad and I did over Thanksgiving upstairs, and that I've been pecking away at ever since…"

"Yes?" Laura asked.

"We finished a room for the girls, a place for them to stay when we're at the bookstore. Thanks to my dad's help, it turned out very nice. I think you'll like it."

"I've seen it," Zeb said. "It's beautiful."

"Oh, David, thank you." She hugged him tightly and held on. "And, Zeb, thank you so much for giving us this gift!"

"Zeb," David said, "I don't know how we can ever repay you."

Zeb's mouth slid into a smile. "I do. Say you two will take over, when I'm gone on to see my Lord and be with my Dolly."

"Take over," David repeated.

"You need a new Secret Santa," Laura said, obviously putting the puzzle together quicker than David.

"I believe I need two, if you get right down to it," Zeb said. "It's been a lot for one person to handle, but I've been watching you over the past months, the love you have for children, for the community and for each other. That's what I was looking for, what I prayed for, and God gave it to me…with you." He reached in his back pocket and pulled out a tiny black bank book. "This here will tell you what I have in the account for your giving. Actually, what you have, since I've already added your names to the account. And this is how it works. The more you give, the more you'll have in the account. I know it doesn't make sense, but that's the way God does things." He smiled. "Trust me."

David took the book. "We do, Zeb. We do."

The sound of crunching gravel alerted them that someone else had arrived.

"That will be all of your family and friends," Zeb said.

"How did they know to come here?" Laura asked.

"That's easy. Candy canes."

Epilogue

Laura hadn't even realized her father was interested in changing schools until he announced he'd taken the eighth-grade teaching position vacated by Mr. Nance at Claremont Middle School. He transferred in January, so he and Marjorie were already settled into a house not far from the town square by the time Thomas had the blessed opportunity to walk his daughter down the aisle on Valentine's Day.

"Are you ready, honey?" he asked, patting Laura's hand.

Laura looked to the front of the church, where Brother Henry held his Bible and waited to perform the ceremony, and David stood waiting to make her his wife, to love, honor and cherish her as long as they both shall live.

Thank You, God, for this day, and for the man that I love. Thank You for our baby girls and for making my family whole again.

Grace began whimpering from her spot in Marjorie's arms, but Joy, as usual, slept away in the arms of her Papa Zeb.

Laura concentrated on every word of the ceremony, on every beautiful emotion pulsing through her being as she said her vows. And then David surprised her when he asked for Marjorie to bring Grace and Zeb to bring Joy and stand beside them.

Then Brother Henry continued, "David, repeat after me. With this ring, I thee wed."

David took Laura's hand and gently slid the ring on her finger. "With this ring, I thee wed."

In the rehearsal, this was the part where David kissed her, but instead of that happening now, Brother Henry spoke again.

"Because this marriage is so much more than the joining of two hearts but is instead the blending of four lives, David asked to also give a token of his love and devotion to their daughters."

While Laura watched in awe, David withdrew two small gold rings from his pocket and lovingly slid one on each girl's tiny finger. "I love you," David said, then looked to Laura. "All of you. You are my life, you are my love."

Brother Henry nodded. "And you may kiss your bride."

David took the woman he loved in his arms and replied, "Gladly."

* * * * *

Dear Reader,

Growing up, I remember my Paw-Paw picking turnip greens and leaving them in sacks on the porches of those who he knew loved the leafy veggie. He would deliver them early in the morning before they woke and never told anyone of his gift. One woman reciprocated by bringing Paw-Paw cakes and leaving them with my grandmother at the house when he was out in the field working. Neither said anything about the gifts. Over the years, I've heard other stories of secret givers, but it's the Secret Santa stories, the ones that happen in the season where we're thinking about God's gift of His Son, that touch my heart the most.

I enjoy mixing facts and fiction in my novels, and you'll learn about some of the truths hidden within the story on my website, www.reneeandrews.com. While you're there, you can also enter contests for cool prizes. If you have prayer requests, there's a place to let me know on my site. I'll lift your request up to the Lord in prayer. I love to hear from readers, so please write to me at renee@reneeandrews.com. Find me on Facebook at www.Facebook.com/AuthorReneeAndrews. And follow me on Twitter at www.Twitter.com/ReneeAndrews.

Blessings in Christ,
Renee Andrews

Rainbow Girl stepped into his field of vision from the kitchen area. *"Hallo."*

Eli's insides did funny things at the sight of her.

"Did you need something?"

He cleared his throat. "I came for a drink of water."

"Come on in." She pulled a glass out of the cupboard, filled it at the sink and handed it to him.

"Danki."

She gifted him with a smile. *"Bitte.* How's it going out there?"

He smiled back. "Fine." He gulped half the glass, then slowed down to sips. No sense rushing.

After a minute, she folded her arms. "Go ahead. Ask your question."

"What?"

"You obviously want to ask me something. What is it? Why do I color my hair all different colors? Why do I dress like this? Why did I leave? What is it?"

She posed all *gut* questions, but not the one he needed an answer to. A question that was no business of his to ask.

"Go ahead. Ask. I don't mind." Very un-Amish, but she'd offered. *Ne,* insisted.

He cleared his throat. "Are you going to stay?"

She stared for a moment, then looked away. Obviously not the question she'd expected, nor one she wanted to answer.

LIEXP1218

He'd made her uncomfortable. He never should have asked. What if she said *ne*? Did he want her to say *ja*? "You don't have to tell me." He didn't want to know anymore.

She pinned him with her steady brown gaze. "I don't know. I don't want to, but I'm sort of in a bind at the moment."

Maybe for the reason she'd been so sad the other day, which had made him feel sympathy for her.

He appreciated her honesty. "Then why does our bishop think you are?"

"He's hoping I do."

His heart tightened. "Why are you giving him false hope?" Why was she giving Eli false hope?

"I'm not. I've told him this is temporary. He won't listen. Maybe you could convince him to stop this foolishness—" she waved her hand toward where the building activity was going on "—before it's too late."

He chuckled. "You don't tell the bishop what to do. *He* tells you."

He really should head back outside to help the others. Instead, he filled his glass again and leaned against the counter. He studied her over the rim of his glass. Did he want Rainbow Girl to stay? She'd certainly turned things upside down around here. Turned him upside down. Instead of working in his forge—where he most enjoyed spending time—he was here, and gladly so. He preferred working with iron rather than wood, but today, carpentry strangely held more appeal.

Time to get back to work. He guzzled the rest of his water and set the glass in the sink. *"Danki."* As he turned to leave, something on the table caught his attention. The door knocker he'd made years ago for Dorcas—Rainbow Girl—ne, Dorcas, but now Rainbow Girl had it. They were the same person, but not the same. He crossed to the table and picked up his handiwork. "You kept this?"

She came up next to him. *"Ja.* I liked having a reminder of…"

"Of what?" Dare he hope him?

She stared at him. "Of…my life growing up here."

That was probably a better answer. He didn't need to be thinking of her as anything more than a lost *Englisher*.

Don't miss Courting Her Prodigal Heart *by Mary Davis, available January 2019 wherever* Love Inspired® *books and ebooks are sold.*

www.LoveInspired.com

Save $1.00

on the purchase of any
Love Inspired® or Love Inspired®
Suspense book.

Available wherever books are sold,
including most bookstores, supermarkets,
drugstores and discount stores.

Save $1.00

on the purchase of any Love Inspired® or
Love Inspired® Suspense book.

Coupon valid until April 30, 2019. Redeemable at participating retail outlets in the
U.S. and Canada only. Limit one coupon per customer.

52616033

5 65373 00076 2 (8100)0 12391